GOD'S LAST SHOT...

Charleston, SC
www.PalmettoPublishing.com

God's Last Shot...
Copyright © 2022 by Dwight Fox

Paperback ISBN: 978-1-68515-547-6
eBook ISBN: 978-1-68515-548-3
Registration: TXu-2-119-397

GOD'S
LAST SHOT...

BY DWIGHT FOX

PROLOGUE

God was frustrated. Earth had gone bad again, as usual. The Conservative Angels argued that Bush, Cheney, and the rest of them were poor acolytes without the vision to mold a lasting peace in places like Afghanistan and Iraq. The Liberal Angels read the New Testament and argued that Islam was a substantial attempt to find God, but the adversarial pursuit of oil gummed up the works.

The Conservative Angels were frustrated; they were Old Testament acolytes who thought the strict governance of rules, laws, and free enterprise would make everything fall in line. The trouble was too many gray areas with the humans made any effort to manage them futile.

The Devil laughed at all of them, God and Angels. He sided, of course, with chaos, or perhaps anarchy. He even considered unregulated capitalism somewhat close to the eye-for-an-eye feeling of the Old Testament Conservative Angels. Hell, creation was just going to go bad anyway. Humans were merely victims of their whims. Who could wait for a questionable afterlife when pleasure could be had *now*?

So, God was frustrated again. This time he thought he could make it happen. Humans seeing His divine plan for them, loving Him, and hopefully understanding how to love each other.

But this time God would make things a little spicier. Let the Devil have his due. Two new worlds would exist. One medieval in nature, prone to prophecy and superstition. A place where danger and chaos were common, and the restraining influence of secular humanism and laws offered no hope of relief for humanity.

The other growing quickly more sympathetic to science and laws. But even the modern world with its developing systems of industry and acquisition could be a very cruel place. Each would give the Devil and God playgrounds to test their influence on humanity.

As usual, the egocentric nature of the plan made some of the New Testament Angels a bit nervous. But He was God, after all.

The Devil grinned; God always needed his influence to use adversity to shore up God's own relationship with the humans. The Devil often wondered about his role. Did he exist to bring Hell anywhere a contrast was needed? After all, he and God were just different sides of the same square. The Devil loved chaos and suffering. God was the answer to the chaos and suffering.

So God created a new world with subtle differences in biological life and in the humans. Terra was like Earth in many ways and remained very close to what God had created before.

TABLE OF CONTENTS

1.
NEW WORLD HERO

"Joe Brown!" the announcer shouted. Joe was wearing number twenty-two, dressed in the aerodynamic purple and silver uniform of the Stormer pro football team. "Game on the line," the announcer boomed.

God had liked Earth, but things just were not panning out. Some of the Liberal Angels took pity on the humans. The humans were so beleaguered by their own desires and conflicts with each other that they failed to see God as He defined Himself.

Many Angels became upset when God launched this new scheme. God would create the two planets that could sustain humanoid life.

Each of the two new planets would be prone to the nightmarish creation of the Devil as well. But now the Angels would be allowed to influence outcomes and outperform God in His folly. God so often wanted to prove to the Angels that he knew best. The more modern planet would be called Terra. The medieval-styled world would be called Hellrun.

Arleosa, the Jewel of Heaven, Angel of Angels, feared the worst. In council and in private, her thoughts were voiced thusly: "How much more suffering will be seen before God's vanity is fulfilled?" Arleosa felt great sympathy for the humans. She vaguely remembered the rush of emotions a person might feel. As an Angel she both pitied them and envied them. Long ago, God had forbidden Angels to contact humans, and yet this new scheme with two planets gave the Angels a temporal chance to call out to the humans and support them.

The new world creations offered an opportunity to magnify the Devil's ability to influence humans. On Terra, God would choose a consciousness among the lower Angels to go in human form, spread the good word about redemption, likely die horribly, and leave a legacy humans might use to motivate themselves toward angelic and ultimately godly understanding. Hopefully on the new medieval world, a human might be found who could develop a godly consciousness and lead the people to God. Standard operating procedure—a little stale but innovative, with two planets in one solar system and open air, not space, between them. The physics could be worked out later. After all, God had poetic license to be truly creative.

"Joe Brown," the announcer bellowed in a heavy bass voice that shook the PA system and got everyone's attention.

Joe took the pitch from the quarterback, going left, swinging wide to the outside. Suddenly a crack of daylight shone in his peripheral vision to the right. Effortlessly, like a water bug in a still pool, he swerved right and flowed into the opening. He accelerated furiously into the middle of the field. Fifty yards later he was in the end zone, securing a championship win for the Stormers. God and the Angels loved a good football game. So did the Devil. That new planet Terra was entertaining.

At the press conference, Joe Brown, third-year pro, seemed embarrassed by this success. He had never been injured, but the question from the hometown reporter made him turn brick brown-red. "Joe, how are you getting faster, coming into the league a 4.2 sprinter, now still going strong at 4.07? That is unusual. Your last forty yards was run in 4.0 seconds flat. That's otherworldly."

Samantha Jameson questioned him. Joe knew her. He nodded to get a better look at her firm and shapely hips and legs. *Whoops,* he thought to himself, *straighten up and look professional. My female fans won't appreciate me being so fascinated with Samantha.* He smiled to himself. "Well, Samantha, I've been 'blessed,' you know…just hard training, solid rest."

Arleosa laughed, entertained. She told some Angels nearby God must be feeling good this guy is "blessed." Joe Brown muttered to himself as he left the podium. No one could hear him, but his words were, "No attachments—live for the moment."

Things had progressed well on Terra, but none of the lower Angels felt like sacrificing themselves to be the "Son of God." That was a brand that no one wanted to own, the implications being too grave: high acclaim but a painful and violent death. Jesus, everyone knew, was not the same since He returned from Earth. His faith in God had been shaken, but He continued to pursue His need for validation from the humans.

God paced in an agitated state, seemingly uncertain of His next move. No Messiah would present him- or herself.

Many of the Angels were fresh from reincarnating from life to Heaven and were reticent to leave their new home for a mortal and often painful existence. It wasn't like Heaven was one big cocktail party, but it was security without pain.

Without a Messiah, rudderless humanity tried to find its own path.

Consciousness groups evolved on Terra claiming that life in the moment—living now—was the best course, deeming unnecessary attachments like cars, jewelry, and such as superfluous, even anathema, to a happy life.

No Messiah stepped forward from the lower Angels; no one was willing to go back to the corporal world and feel pain again. For what? God mused over the dilemma, but by then it was 2030 on Terra, AD 2030. AD was the end of man's belief that death was permanent. Somehow, between the consciousness movement and hopefulness from the humans, a religious tradition evolved. A few Angels tampered with the humans quietly, not wanting God to be jealous. Soon there were doctrines and rules in place formulating a spiritual path. The movement became a household term: *Compassion Now.* Belief in reincarnation sprang as if it were a weed.

Joe Brown's season ended, and as usual, he found himself in a school, speaking to the high school students. "The future begins with a choice in the moment now! Only with those first good choices can a good life be built. Care for those around you—family, teachers, and parents—for they are the foundation upon which we all can stand. Without God, there would be no moment of choice to own, play, and be cognizant of His presence in your life."

God kind of liked this Joe Brown. Not only was he a great footballer but he had an inkling of the spiritual growth and a willingness to share his message.

Joe had grown up in the modern-day projects of New Haven, a city in the Northeast. He had run with a tough crowd, moved drugs all the way into high school. Then he found religion wrapped in a football. He was a walking stereotype: single mom raising him, no father in his life. He and his mom went to church regularly. Joe had one thing the streets didn't teach: he had insight.

"Joe, you could do something special," Father John, the pastor, liked to say, "But understand this: life can leave you dead before you even get started." Joe could feel the concern Father John reflected and listened. Father John was respected in both the church and the Black community. He was a square-built man of vague beginnings. He connected well with people because he had suffered and had his faith tested by war, unemployment, and personal loss. His life had gone from anger to faith as he learned to help others channel their frustrations. He genuinely appreciated helping others improve their spiritual and emotional lives.

Joe had seen his mother's friends cry when bad things happened to their Black sons and daughters. The day came when Joe felt like he needed to make choices that lifted him above moments of extreme risk. He would tell the story of his redemption to teachers, students—anyone who would listen.

Of course, like all men, he had weaknesses. These mostly resided in the form of female sportscasters. He liked being fawned over, and subconsciously the attention reminded him of his mother. Good journalists applauded his achievements on screen in professional but glowing terms. In private, Samantha shared his bed repeatedly. Joe couldn't resist her round, high butt and shapely legs, fully blossomed in every way. In secret, their lustful explosions could last all night.

Often Arleosa would linger in the shadows, wonderingly envious and wanting to taste what she no longer could. Thinking of her past material life, Arleosa wistfully remembered the sweet embrace of erotic flesh that faded from reach when she attained angelic stature.

Time passed, and Joe felt he should be moving on after fifteen years in the harrowing world of pro football. Most pros were lucky to last eight. He had run the ball like no other. Blasting past the line with raw overpowering force, belying his six-foot, 230-pound frame. He was sometimes called "Power Burst" for his seemingly magical explosion, pushing past bigger players and gathering himself to run sixty yards or more to score.

He was invariably offered commentator jobs, such as play-by-play announcing, but they never lasted. Joe, easily bored, set off in many directions at once.

In the end, he joined a private military firm. He was a spokesman for the firm and, no stranger to risk, trained and functioned as a private soldier. In one situation, he led a small force into the Afraili continent to rescue a group of five oil-survey workers who had trespassed on foreign land to survey oil in an unmapped tribal region. This mission required engaging with a small paramilitary squad and breaking into a prison compound after gliding in with jet wings. He and two men blasted into the compound, freeing the oil workers who had illegally entered the region. Joe was essentially a mercenary, and though his conscience bothered him, he needed and even yearned for the action, excitement, and risk.

In one particularly bloody operation, Joe volunteered to use jet wings and fly into a base camp of Molaki warlords. The warlords had captured the equipment and sensing devices used to find oil. The oil workers had been executed, but the equipment needed to be destroyed. The oil was there, and the corporation did not want the warlords appropriating it. This was a time much like the American Gold Rush of 1849 but more organized. Corporate representatives, often poorly prepared, would land on the Afraili continent seeking to set up camps, hold off the local populace, fly out the oil on jet tankers, make several trips, and then pack up when the warlords mustered the manpower and resources to force them out.

In one foray, Joe and a team of two others prepared to find missing oil surveying and drilling equipment. A beacon had sent out a signal indicating the oil equipment locations. Coordinates were determined, and Joe's team, overhead in a jet tanker equipped for military operations, waited for the call to action.

At 0600 hours the coordinates of the beacons reached the jet tanker. Joe and his team waited as the jet tanker drew close. Joe barked out directions: "Search for and destroy the equipment. Blast our way to the extraction point. There's a tree line close by. Once there, we get to a clearing a mile and a half away. We should be clear for transport from a hover jet. We stick together where our firepower will help us cut through to the tree line. Expect heavy resistance."

Joe and his crew hoped to slip in unseen, but this was unlikely once the beacon had emitted its signal. Warlord crews would search the sky, waiting for the predictable return of the oil companies for their equipment. When companies tried to get their equipment back, they faced extreme risk no matter the level of mercenary support they employed. Sometimes the warlords would ransom the equipment back to the corporations.

There was a cycle at play. Ransomed equipment meant the warlords got more arms with the money they received. More arms meant they could control the profits from oil on their land. Eventually the corporations would have to pay more for the oil when they could no longer just take it.

Joe was packing one .50-caliber sniper rifle, an assault rifle, and a 10 mm long-barrel automatic pistol. Everybody on Joe's team carried charges for destroying the oil-detection equipment. They also carried grenades and claymores to help cover their retreat.

Once over the target, the team made the jump, and personal jet wings carried them from the air tanker. Five hundred meters down, they would make a controlled descent, banking horizontally, followed by quick dives as they found their target and monitored the ground.

Today would be characterized by heavier-than-expected resistance. Clusters of concussive small-arms fire spilled upward from the ground. Joe's communications went dead for a minute. He could smell burning fumes, and smoke blurred his vision and stung his nostrils. His armor felt hot in places. While in a descent, he swung horizontal, banking into a hard left turn. Communications were working again. "Best go in straight—second phase landing away from target," Joe warned the team. He was about five hundred meters up and started diving toward the tree line, one hundred and fifty meters away from the aerial point directly above the target. The irony was not lost on Joe that this was a target surrounded by gun-toting tribal liberators and warlords attempting to free their land and oil from corporate greed.

It was these times that made Joe think, while five hundred meters above death, *what am I doing? Trespassing, blowing up stuff that doesn't even belong there—on somebody else's homeland. I'm on the wrong team, aren't I?*

Four hundred meters down, such queries were ridiculous. He could feel heat again and hear the pop of gunfire. His team was now diving toward the tree line.

Three hundred meters. Fast descent and below the gunfire again.

Two hundred meters. The bullets and heat found him again.

One hundred meters. Trees started to rush up. Joe angled between the trees, as did the others, finding relative safety, cover, and concealment.

Just under one hundred meters, the jet wings started to break the speed of the descent, and the landing phase began. The landing phase ended as they touched down.

In the clearing of the target, 101 liberators raged forward on foot, ready to surge into the jungle trees and kill the oppressors.

Landing, Joe and his team hit their radar scanners, which lit up the positions of the oncoming enemy horde in red. It also lit up the team members in a green glare. It was like having a halo where everyone's position was clear whether they could be seen with the naked eye or not, cover and concealment notwithstanding.

Almost as one, Joe and his team dropped their mobile claymores, which, when activated, skittered and ran like army ants through the foliage and trees toward the onslaught of the red-haloed horde. About six inches long and three inches wide, the mobile claymores would reach a position right before the tree line, wait for more red halos to gather, and *boom!* explode in a concussive wave of shrapnel and explosive fire. Joe's team worked in concert so three bombs went off almost as one. Fire lit the edge of the jungle. Trees and flesh burned. Smoke billowed all around, blinding and confusing the enemy as they, unable to stop, staggered into the mangled, burned bodies of their tribesmen.

Joe signaled, and the two moved forward as one. They converged on the enemy, bringing themselves right in the middle of the enemy force.

Joe loved this part best. Close quarters, like football. Muscling and shouldering enemies between bursts of his pistol, always using cover to close on any red halos while his team moved closer to the tree line's edge. Then finally, almost as one, Joe and another teammate reached to their waists and drew their Vibro-Blades. The weapons were a recent addition to their combat gear. The Vibro-Blade, Viper-Blade, or VB, as it was called, extended three feet from the hilt, issuing a round, three-inch-diameter energy field. Used for hacking, it rarely made an entry wound. Instead, a hacking outcome resulted in a big mass of red flesh, appearing much at first like a bruise. Internally, under that bruise were fractured bones, bleeding organs, collapsed lungs, hearts too busted to beat, and knees too broken to stand on. The VB made a sizzling sound, smelled like ozone, and crackled when it hit—pay dirt. Flesh. It could also be used to rupture lock and security seals. A dynamic breaching agent.

Complementing the VB was the lightweight armor used effectively for close-range fighting as well as long-range protection.

The tribesmen could smell the scorched bodies of their kinsmen, and fear had already cast grave shadows upon them. That fear would grow. Darting between cover and concealment, Joe worked his way parallel to the tree line. Ducking under small trees, then wielding the VB, first to hack a hamstring here, then a pelvis there, leaving a trail of shocked, immobile tribesmen in his wake. If shock did not encumber them, then a hack to the skull finished them. Likewise, his two teammates worked parallel to Joe along the tree line but deeper in the forest. Darting behind trees, aiming and firing pistol shots at short range, and then flanking enemies, only to pop up and hack a knee, neck, or exposed shoulder, creating a shockwave of disabling pain, causing an enemy to crash down in a heap.

When the enemies had been dispatched, no more entered the woods. The rest stood back, shaking their rifles, shouting angrily, but no one else would venture into the woods.

Now Joe and his team disappeared into the tree line like phantoms, but first they sent another set of mobile claymores skittering toward the remaining tribesman, identified by the mass of red halos from the scanners.

As the first mobile claymore found targets, the blasts sent red halos into dissolution. The targets, having been destroyed, emitted no signal to be scanned. Tribesmen fired wildly at the tree line. Joe and his team sat or lay behind cover unseen. Their armor adapted to the foliage around them and slowly changed color and pattern to mirror the environment.

"Sniper positions, all go," Joe whispered. Registered signals popped up on his face screen, indicating where his team was positioned. The team was spread out fifty meters apart, facing the general location of the equipment.

The tribesmen wanted to secure the equipment for themselves so that they could get the oil from their own land. They could produce their own oil as opposed to making high-risk trades and disadvantageous deals, which had hurt them in the past. The tribesmen knew they could sell the oil rights. But with the technology to make the process work, they'd be in charge. It was important for them to use violence to control their land. No one would risk exploration in hostile territory without knowing for sure that the oil was there. The tribesmen knew from experience that letting company men do exploration, even under contract, set themselves up for a legacy of imperialism. Once a company was present in the land, they could interfere with the tribal leadership and undermine it. Companies would do anything to gain influence by pitting the tribal leaders against each other, manipulating them to come up with better deals to outdo each other and ultimately benefit the oil company.

Joe connected the silencer, lined up his first target, took a slow breath, exhaled, and shot.

A short sound erupted from the muffled shot. The tribesman was hit. Blood exploded from the back of his head as the bullet entered his forehead, exiting in a mass of gray and red splatter, showering several of the other tribesmen.

A tribesman whose posture indicated leadership started to give orders, and the tribesmen fell back into defensive positions. Tribesmen fired shots toward Joe and the team's position. None of the shots found a target. *Pit, phitooh!*

Joe and his team moved like silent, unseen shadows. They were deploying silenced weapons that were decimating the opposition one by one.

Finally, Joe did a scan count and noticed the opposition was fewer. He set out the last mobile claymores. *Kaboom!*

A cacophony of blood, smoke, and shrapnel set off another wave of fear and destruction among the tribesmen. This was part of Joe's combat strategy—to emotionally and physically cripple the opposition. Some of the tribesmen ran off. Gunshots rang out from the leader's weapon as he warned the rest to stand firm.

Joe signaled his team that this was finally endgame. Joe started running toward the target, and in three steps he was at full speed. His armor transformed, becoming light and flat against his body. Jets near the heels of his boots fired, allowing him to jump twenty meters at a bound.

As had been planned at this phase of the operation, Joe's team triangulated their fire to cut down the opposition so Joe could reach the targeted oil machinery in a clearing behind the tree line. Joe continued to move forward, dropping behind any cover he found, firing a few pistol shots, and then bounding forward again toward the target.

Suddenly, Joe's team stopped firing from the tree line. Joe was flanked by enemies to his left and leaped among them, Vibro-Blade crackling and sizzling as he hammered the tribesmen surrounding him. His armor rose and became reinforced in scaly bumps.

The tribesmen's rifle butts were now crashing toward Joe. A glancing blow struck him. Joe spun away, slashing the VB murderously in a horizontal arc.

After Joe eliminated the tribesmen who flanked him, his team started moving toward Joe. The team moved as Joe had, firing, dropping to cover, blasting the enemy. Their VB, hissing and crackling, left bodies in the wake of the three combatants.

Enemies started to flounder, not knowing whether to fight or run. Most ran. The rest were cut down by Joe and his crew darting among them, their VB cracking bones and rupturing organs until no tribesmen remained.

Joe would not need extraction. He would order a pickup for the equipment. He and his team would get a bonus. Joe radioed transport, and they picked up the equipment. Joe and his crew would stay in cover and wait.

Joe's crew included Sam Thames, an ex-soldier and ex-police, and Tim Jacks, another long-term mercenary. As a team they had made this trip a half dozen times, more than any others. Some men died in the fighting; some refused to return to fight again. Joe remained for the love of the money and the excitement. But deep in his psyche, he always wondered how it would ever end. Would the tribesmen ever truly own their own land?

Joe benefited from the imperialism, but he questioned how long it could go on.

✝ ✝ ✝

It seemed to happen overnight. But Joe knew the precipitating thoughts had obviously started years ago. Joe knew he had been part of it—a mercenary who fought to rob the Molaki Afraili tribesmen of their oil.

Over time, the tribesmen would come to understand their plight. They would strike. Terrorism would be the tool.

It was a warm summer day. Corporate tankers were populating eastern cities of Molaki Afraili as they often did.

Joe lived in New Castle, the largest eastern city of a nation much like America on Earth. New Castle was a large center for trade and financial acquisition where corporate people made deals for oil and other resources.

Joe was trying to rejoin society. He could see the result of his mercenary work all around him. The oil corporations had benefited from his work.

He withdrew from public view. Always a big attraction for political and corporate activities, Joe had promoted corporate life and football activities—specifically those of his old team, the Stormers.

He drifted in and out of church attendance. He had served well, advancing economic interests that benefited his country's economy. But increasingly, it was hard to process all the killing he had done with the pride he once felt in his faith. He was sick of himself; his conscience ate his innards. It was time for him to leave the life of a mercenary. It had taken a while, but finally he saw himself as an instrument of greed and needless destruction.

He had changed his life in high school, not wanting to get sucked into the conundrum of drugs and immorality. He could change again.

Joe recognized he had succumbed to poor values after all. The values were legal and brought money and acceptance. However, he was stealing from the Afraili tribesmen. Though his society rewarded him, it was still wrong.

Might as well have stayed a drug dealer, he thought.

† † †

God marveled sadly that it would happen again in his second creation. The date would be the same. How ironic. September 11. It would be September 11, 2020, on Terra, but September 11, nonetheless. In God's second creation, the dynamics of exploitation would result in mass destruction again.

† † †

Back in his high-rise in New Castle, Joe sat and watched the game that had made him great. He sat alone. Samantha let herself in and sat next to him without speaking. She watched him. He was only forty-two but had deep lines and furrows in his face like a man much older. Samantha had dreamed of being part of Joe's life, but now she felt hopeless and could no longer touch him emotionally. Marriage? He'd never propose. Therapy? He wouldn't go. Samantha lingered in his life, loving him yet not having that love returned.

They drank and partied. They had sex, but to Samantha's disappointment, it was never lovemaking. Joe was always distant, and Samantha never felt complete with him. He had kept a few sports gigs and started to withdraw from even those. He drank more heavily, and the nightmares never left him. He remembered a descent into a combat zone where one of his friends was killed and the warlords had desecrated the body. A grotesque mass of disfigurement was where a face had once smiled and offered friendship.

His small band had fought violently to retrieve the body, seeking confrontation with the enemy. They intended to punish the enemy in the name of their fallen comrade. He remembered the funeral.

"Satyra," Joe spoke softly to David's wife, "I am so sorry."

Satyra, for her part, found it difficult to look at Joe. She associated David's death with Joe. David made a good living, given all the money that mercenaries make. Despite the money, it was hard even before his death. There were often on-and-off grumbles about the battle being waged and the moral dilemma of violently stealing oil from a people who owned it. Satyra knew this benefited her family.

"Satyra." Joe looked at her, but she looked through him. Her raven hair shone. Her face perfect. She wondered why Joe was unable to keep David safe.

She teared up. Joe tried to comfort her, putting his arm around her shoulder. She wept, then suddenly moved away. Joe rushed out of the home, crestfallen. He had hoped to comfort Satyra, had once almost thought she should be his life mate. David and Satyra bonded while he played football and wooed others, like Samantha. Others who nibbled at the breadcrumbs of affection he spread. But the resulting emotional meal was always too small to feed even a sparrow.

He got into his sports car and sped off. He made it home, but he couldn't remember the drive. He hadn't drunk anything, but he felt numb.

Sadness woke him the next morning. Numb and sad, he didn't feel like he could get out of bed. He popped the remote, and the television came on. Smoke, debris, and fire were being shown in an Afraili port. Tankers in the port were burning. Oil tankers, partially sunk, belched flame and smoke. Explosions came intermittently as sirens wailed.

Joe couldn't move. He just gazed at the screen, absorbing the tumultuous destruction that dominated it. This was live, as the bottom letters reminded the viewers.

There was more, but Joe turned off the TV. He left his apartment, started running down the street, and ran for an hour. He went to the nearby park and sat on a bench, eyes brimming with tears.

He started walking to church. He had slept in a sweat suit, which was now soaked with perspiration. His conscience was aflame. Guilt clung to him like the cold sweat on his skin.

13

✝ ✝ ✝

Deity vanity!

God sighed. This second try was like the first: disappointing. No Messiah was present on Terra. The modern era had commenced. God was getting angry, but there were contingencies in place.

The Devil laughed robustly and sent signals to God, proclaiming the fallacious vanity of His efforts. He communicated from Hell via images of chaos occurring on Earth and Terra. Telepathic messages flowed through Heaven routinely. God would not allow Satan to visit Heaven, even though he was once a renowned Angel. No peace treaty existed between God and the Devil.

Satan continued to saturate Heaven with the gruesome images. The images scared the lower Angels. There was big pressure to go down and take on the Messiah role. Nobody wanted to do it.

God created Hellrun along with Terra. Humans could live there and did. They were still in a medieval state and were offered a chance for a primitive Messiah to capture the imagination of the population and their world. But no lower or higher Angel would join in the grand plan. God fumed; the Devil laughed.

Arleosa fretted and wondered about the state of God's plan. The Devil seemed to be running the show, mocking God, urging a finality on Terra, and attempting to influence the medieval world, Hellrun, as well.

Terra was quickly falling from God's path. Man's greed for oil would trigger a jihad of great magnitude—but not just yet.

On Hellrun, the Devil's own dominion could be seen merrily on display. Demons ran amok, fighting various human tribes and enslaving anyone who attempted to create an ordered society.

On Hellrun, the second planet designed for human life, things were chaotic, but mankind made halting advances, creating steel and developing agriculture. The Devil's influence had suppressed humanity's ability to advance beyond feudalism. No Angel came forth to do the Lord's work on Hellrun. Arleosa knew that Hellrun was a key to bringing humans together. If they could somehow unite in the Devil's backyard to defeat him, what a redemption that would be. She knew this would abate God's frustration.

Somewhere in the ethereal world of the Angels, the Angels watched God fume and ducked out into the vast reaches of their universe. Always at harmony with the divine plan, they needed naught and were easily drawn away from the plight of humans.

Some Angels hovered, absorbing the plight of humans. God caught them and asked them to be part of man's salvation. Man, who at his best was like God and the Angels—loving, caring, bringing a consciousness of divine inclusion and support. At his worst, man was like a devil with no conscience—killing, excluding, creating as much Hell as the Devil himself.

Which half of man's nature would come forth, God or Devil? God needed a win to somehow know validation and vindication. Good would win out over evil.

Arleosa asked, "Is it really so simple? If your glory is the forthcoming testimonial to your omnipotent plan, then why does no Angel venture to be your Messiah?"

God expanded his radiance, blinding Arleosa, who, quite radiant herself, was only an Angel. But she remembered a life she no longer could feel. Human suffering, always a tug of war between what's right and the need to survive. Abstract principles of goodness versus the material demands of survival in the flesh, which was known to be weak.

☦ ☦ ☦

Joe wandered about, barely maintaining a semblance of dignity. He drank daily and tested drugs he would never have tried. He was trying to forget. Nightmares lined his every sleeping moment. He needed pills for everything: to sleep, to keep going, to keep commitments. Samantha loved him, but now she functioned like a handler, getting Joe to appointments. Often chauffeuring him to his medical doctor and imploring him to come with her to therapy.

Remarkably, Joe's doctor found him healthy in spite of the drinking and poor sleep. Joe kept working out a few days a week.

The doctor warned him, "Joe, get some therapy. You can't keep going like this."

Samantha functioned like a common-law wife, attending medical appointments with him and filling in the parts Joe purposefully left out. She could see the guilt painfully eat at Joe. When the Afraili ports blew, he started a steep descent. Good friends died in increasing numbers as the corporations tried to gain back a toehold on Afraili oil.

✝ ✝ ✝

One fine, warm summer day was the final straw, heavy as a hammer swung mightily at the camel's back.

Seven Afraili men engineered the capture of an oil transporter. The men were well educated and versed in technology. They knew the systems of the Transoil corporation, and it appeared as if they were peacefully bringing in the oil transporter to the air docks above New Castle—the air docks floated miles above the New Castle port docks on the ocean's edge at the northeast coast. But the Afraili men dipped mightily at the last second, missing the docks and plummeting toward the middle of the city. There would be only seconds to track the air tanker as it plummeted toward the middle of New Castle itself.

Gorged with oil, bloated, rigged with bombs and dripping fuel, it descended faster and faster, falling away from the altitude of the air docks, miles above the city. Alarms started to go off below the air docks. Seconds remained before impact as the descent continued in a diagonal line to the heart of New Castle.

The explosion went off with a fire wind aftermath as destruction emanated from both flames and impact force.

2.

THE TWILIGHT
OF SINNING

It was a Sunday. Joe sat in church the day after September 11. The minister's voice boomed: "Chickens coming home to roost, perhaps."

Joe cringed. He knew those chickens, armed roosters; he had been one of them.

"Justice is not of Terra, this planet, but God's alone to decry," the minister continued.

Samantha sat in the congregation as well, a few pews over. She knew Joe would be uncomfortable. She wept silently. She desired to be close to Joe, both physically and emotionally. They had been close at one time, but he would fade away, staying just out of touch and emotionally distant. During this time of guilt and complicity for the tragedy that occurred yesterday, September 11, he seemed to be miles away.

"Joe, how you holdin' up?" The minister, Dr. Prolovion, approached him.

Joe felt his firm hand on his shoulder. A hand surely three times as big as any normal hand.

"How is your conscience, brother? Are you good with God?"

"No," Joe answered. "I am bad with God, and God wants no part of me; I guess I don't give a good Goddamn."

✝ ✝ ✝

Weeks later, Joe wandered the crater that had been a booming section of New Castle, miles from his home. He was drunk and staggered through the crater. He had learned where the checkpoints were, and he slipped between them. The authorities' evidence search had been largely completed. Only a gaping hole needing to be watched remained. Even a drunken Joe could evade sight and wander into the pit. Four hundred meters and change, it was a true symbol of an aggressive society brought to a standstill—at least for now. Thousands had died, including men, women, and children. The flames had engulfed the city, and there were still hot spots within the pit. The pit became a desolate reminder of vulnerability.

Joe's vulnerability grew as the pit sat smoldering. He had slept in the pit from time to time, too drunk to go home. His life was falling away from public view. He mourned his actions that made him responsible for creating the forces that ultimately allowed the pit to exist. He knew how this came to pass. He felt a sense of guilt that bound his emotions to a depressive sadness. He longed for the freedom he felt when he'd played football. He lost contact with Samantha, and even when she tried, she could not find him.

His guilt grew like a living thing, crawling into every crevasse of his consciousness, only temporarily abated by hard liquor, weed, or opiates. His home stood empty. He didn't pay bills much anymore. He was losing his grip on emotional connections and everything else that made for a once-orderly, well-constructed life.

Before truly falling away from public life, he had been interviewed by police and print and television news media. He was asked the question "Were Afraili tribesmen really capable of striking New Castle?" too many times. This only made Joe sink lower into the abyss surrounding him, much like the pit sunk low in the middle of New Castle.

☦ ☦ ☦

Angels sought contact with God, who seemed to withdraw from His world, much like Joe had withdrawn from his.

Arleosa pulled toward God. "What plan now?" she asked.

Humans had once again fallen into a bitter dispute. No Messiah could undo the damage now. Terra was becoming more disappointing. There would be more war and chaos despite the intervention of science and modern politics. Despite God's use of the modern world, Terra seemed to be plummeting toward failure like a burning air tanker.

"Why not a more direct and less hazardous approach?" Arleosa held council with God and a few of His most trusted older Angels. "None of us wants to live again in the pain of flesh." Her voice sounded like a song. "But in times of old, we would descend and talk to men to help them understand the meaning their lives held. The need for material gain lies rooted deeply in a will to survive. When we Angels walked and visited among men, we gave them hope and a vision for more. We were responsible for them. And yes, it was not perfect. Satan burned and fueled avaricious passions in men who always want more. But we had a toehold on their consciousness. Urging them to do a little more. Noah's ark, Joan of Arc. We were with them when they needed us most. But we did not need to die on the cross to have the needed influences."

Other Angels started to chime in, agreeing with Arleosa. Her conscious presence, in many ways—though none would say it—rivaled that of even God.

"I wanted them to use their own internal might," said God. "I desired one of my Angels to return to Earth and show the humans that they were made in my likeness."

"They need help," Arleosa implored. "They have always shown signs of divinity. But they cannot taste what we know living on that muddy rock."

"*Help?*" God boomed. "A Messiah would help. But none of you will go!"

Arleosa rose up. "Let me use the old ways differently, God; you still have your Earth with its failures and successes and Heaven as well. Let me cast an angelic presence into your new worlds to see what successes can occur."

Joe staggered on the outskirts of the pit. He had taken to sleeping in a metal storage container. His guilt ached and burned his consciousness.

He stepped out of the container and looked around. He still held a bottle filled one-fifth with liquor in his hand. Three thugs confronted him, gathering closer in the darkness of the starless night.

"Give us what you got, and we will go easy on you," one of the thugs taunted Joe.

Joe was disheveled, wearing an old spandex workout shirt and tights. Even then he looked impressive. His debaucheries had not withered the physique that had enabled his greatness on the football field.

The thugs circled Joe, who smiled thinly through thick lips.

The thug on his left had a blackjack and moved to flank Joe in order to strike him. Joe wheeled away from the arc of the blackjack, sidestepping the thug and slamming the bottle of liquor heavily on top of the thug's head. Slipping behind the middle thug, Joe rammed his training boot into his lower back. The third thug, reacting to the trouble of his comrades, lurched forward to hit Joe in the head with a makeshift club. Joe grabbed his wrist, causing him to drop the club. He squeezed hard, and the thug's fingers went numb. As the thug staggered, Joe pulled on his wrist, bringing him to his knees. Then, in a final move, he slammed his knee into the thug's head. Joe stood alone over the three thugs lying silently on the concrete.

✝ ✝ ✝

Arleosa stayed after God. "We won't get what we want unless we take measures. Measures that justify the end."

God shot Arleosa a withering look. Somewhere above Terra lightning cracked and thunder boomed.

✝ ✝ ✝

The Devil laughed at the sound of thunder.

"More theater," he surmised. "God is always getting angry with the humans, making things a little easier for me and mine."

✝ ✝ ✝

"You have done this yourself many times. The ark, what about that? A means that led to a reasonable end, if you survived." Arleosa faced the withering look. Lesser Angels gasped and withdrew, fearful of God's wrath. "The crucifixion of Jesus was a way to find an end to a messy situation, give humans a salvation to...well...pray for."

God looked weary, a kind of infinite fatigue only God could carry. A weariness born of creative and infinite hope, laced with unresolved expectations. God radiated energy, compelling and infinite even in fatigue.

"What is your plan, Arleosa?" God asked.

A hush filled the firmament.

"I will find a savior from among the humans. A joining can occur that offers less outright risk to an Angel but still empowers your children—humans. Let me, as in the old days, offer influence. Join the human world, find your Messiah, defeat the manifestation of Satan."

"Do what you will." God gasped in relief at relinquishing some responsibility to Arleosa.

✝ ✝ ✝

Joe looked down at the three thugs lying in the street. He frowned, then smiled gleefully. He threw down the broken glass bottle still gripped in his fist and started running. He ran past his apartment home and away from the carnage of New Castle. He ran to the realization of his life: he had contributed to the devastation of New Castle by his actions. Suddenly, as if the sky opened, truth rained down on Joe Brown: *A mercenary in pursuit of profit. A Black man taking the wealth of Brown men. All his life locked into the seduction of money.*

It began to rain, wiping the scorched smell still lingering two months later.

He looked around, stopped running, and decided to go home.

✝ ✝ ✝

Arleosa prepared to leave Heaven. Her form would reach a baser material energy manifestation. But the risk would be small.

✝ ✝ ✝

It was Sunday. Joe went to church. He picked up a few clothes from Samantha's, where he had left them. He accessed his account and paid off his home, which was almost locked in foreclosure. He wore a brown suit, double breasted and shimmering with a gold hue. He did not go unnoticed. There was a whisper surrounding him that threatened to turn into a roar.

Samantha had come to church with Joe, even though she was no longer his lover.

Dr. Prolovion addressed the congregation. "Redemption can be found if you are looking for it. Desire—it is in your heart." He did not mention Joe by name but spoke directly to him. Redemption and self-forgiveness were the themes. He also talked about loyalty and truth. Joe understood exactly what Dr. Prolovion meant. For years the congregation had supported Joe. They cheered for him on the football field. But once he became a mercenary, they questioned his pursuits. At one time, Dr. Prolovion had refused Joe's contribution, wanting no part of Joe's "blood money."

3.

HELL IS FOR HEROES

On God's other planet, Hellrun, mankind struggled in a medieval state. Castles dotted the landscape to the east. Peasants tilled the land, and knights and lords sought to bring order to a primitive, chaotic world. God had developed Hellrun to give a more primitive human population a chance to reach a state of faith. Perhaps this could be more easily accomplished without the intervening forces of modern sophistication.

Demons forayed out of the ancient hills and attacked the men. City-states joined in force to repel the ancient evil. God hoped the more evident threat would lead humans to faith.

Often peasants were forced to leave the crops to become pikemen. They had to hold off the Demons and other nightmare visions that would appear from the deeper reaches of the forest. The Demons spilled out to the plains where men made their homes, lived, planted, hunted, and died, sometimes horribly.

The horse had been a game changer for the lords and knights. They rode out with their swords, lances, and bows, propelled by the speed and leverage of the great destriers they rode.

The western plains stretched on seemingly forever. The horse became the key to connecting the outposts of men across the plains. Unity was needed in these times of danger to repel the Demon hordes from the outposts of humanity.

Often, the Wildriders would help the men by suddenly appearing at the back of the flanking Demons. The Wildriders used their short bows and quarter horses to nimbly strike rear flanks and wheel away at great speed, only to strike again minutes later. The Wildriders appeared and then quickly disappeared as if they had mystical abilities.

† † †

Regardless Kotutan, king of Westaway, the furthest western outpost, had outstripped his northern and southern sister outposts in progress.

Kotutan's outpost was the tip of a triangular strategy between the southern and northern outposts. The territory in the center of the triangle was patrolled to create a safe area for each of the three outposts and held enough land to graze cattle and grow crops.

When Demons appeared, it was often Kotutan's scouts who found them foraying out of their western caves to assault the world of men.

Deep in their caverns, the Demons forged steel and armor. Armor and weapons were the only industry Demons developed. As a result, their armor was fine and weapons sharp. Their blood-red skin, pointy ears, snoutlike noses, and large, sharp canine teeth in their elongated jaws were a fearsome sight on the frontier. No animal could stand them long enough to be domesticated for their use.

Between the Wildriders and Plainsmen, the Demon threat would result in many battles. But still they came, always scavenging from the men, stealing cattle and committing raids.

Attacks continued. King Kotutan sent out more scouts to locate and decimate the Demon hordes venturing into the triangle area held by the frontier outpost.

Wildriders slipped in and out of the region, providing welcome support to the Plainsmen. They made vicious light horse attacks on the Demons, who knew no boundary between the lands of Wildriders or the Plainsmen.

The Wildriders were nomads rotating between high western mesa strongholds. Due to the high elevation of the mesas, the Wildriders could not be easily located, so their best defense was their invisibility. The Wildriders were the greatest horsemen of the western plains. They wore scant bone armor and leather harnesses that covered their torsos. The harnesses held throwing knives, axes, and leather waterskins. Only about five feet in height, they could duck to the side of their horses at full gallop, no longer visible targets. They were unusually strong. Their short swords and weapons were made from strange materials that no Plainsman had ever found. Their steel was strangely flexible and seemingly unbreakable. When it seemed the Wildriders were mortally wounded in battle, they would return a week later, fighting vigorously from horseback. Their brownish-green skin created a natural camouflage that they used to their advantage.

The Plainsmen grew crops, built forts, and moved further west. Conflicts with the Manwolves and primitive packs of Giants who used clubs and other crude weapons had marked their advances. Trade and alliances for common defense were quickly developed between the Plainsmen and the Wildriders as they had common enemies in the Giants and Demons.

Both the Plainsmen and the Wildriders began to search the western mountains for Demon caverns, seeking to end the threat at its source.

These searches were often short lived. The Plainsmen needed to secure their holdings. An offensive against the Demons made them vulnerable. Crops needed to be grown, animals tended to, and fortress walls manned.

Patrols went out daily. On horseback the Plainsmen rode out with full leather-reinforced scale armor bows, lances, and swords. They had very little in the way of provisions. They hoped to strike any Demons they came upon and quickly return to the safety of the fortress. The great destriers they rode were weapons themselves, able to trample an opponent or crash in his skull with their forehooves. The knights of the Plainsmen could strike with heavy force and break a Demon band.

Battle with the Demons came at a cost. Every knight knew being struck by Demon steel and falling in battle evoked a savage hunger. Demons were known to feast on human flesh without reservation.

The Demon hordes increased their attacks. As the cattle grew and crops within the Plainsmen's triangle increased, the Demons were more attracted to the area. They scavenged and killed, as was their way.

The smell of human flesh could waft through the air of the outposts at any time, a demoralizing reminder that the Demon presence was becoming more constant.

The Wildriders also increased their support of the Plainsmen. The Wildriders knew if their hidden spots became known, they would face the Demons at home as well.

Bladeswift, a chief of the Wildriders, was forward thinking. He and his people all worshipped nature and lived in concert with it. They considered the Demons outside of nature and a force of unknown evil.

The Plainsmen worshiped the God of Industry. They believed growing crops, raising cattle, and advancing their numbers and land were the ultimate achievements. They were a population always in search of fertile land. The Wildriders had dubbed them Long-Striders for their constant search of land to build settlements upon. The Demon threat was in direct opposition to what they wanted to achieve, literally and figuratively.

The Demons never built more than a hut but made fine weapons to aid their attacks. They scavenged from anyone unlucky enough to be in their path. The Demons, by nature, were the foe of every species.

The Plainsmen often prayed for a king who would refine the path of industry and thus protect and enhance their life. Prophecies indicated this might happen in a time of great need.

Kotutan, king of the westernmost fortress, dreamed he would be that prophet. His western fortress had spearheaded the holdings of the Plainsmen. He had ensured the safety of a growing population that was in the thousands. His fortress city was a hub of trading for the various small bands of families that traded for supplies and farming implements. Increasingly, these supplies included crossbows, longbows, swords, and spears, which were needed for protection.

The Demons had started attacking the trade routes between the forts and settlements. Their red skin, pointed ears, and spear-tipped tails created great fear. Men and women exposed on the trade routes were more vulnerable and easier to kill and rob of goods. The Demons would ambush and savagely attack the mounted knights who were on patrol.

Trade between the three fortresses was starting to slow.

The great trade route from the East, which cut through the middle of the Plainsmen's holdings, was also being attacked. Further, the Demons assailed all the settlements that supported the eastern trade route. This was a vital link for the Plainsmen. The East, with its established city-states and industry, was a mainstay of support for the Plainsmen. The city-states of the East has organized militias that included pikemen, cavalry, and supporting forces to repel invaders as needed. Kotutan sent more forces east to support the trade route. Six hundred riders would go out and erase the Demon presence from the eastern roads. His city would be thin, but he believed the ramparts and walls would hold against any direct attack.

Little did Kotutan realize, the Demons had a strategy that was purposeful and directed. The attacks on the eastern trade route were a ploy. The Demons doubled back from the eastern route and marched toward Westaway. The Demons sought to take a stronghold, grip the world of men in fear, and dominate them.

An envoy of Wildriders appeared at the western fortress in advance of the Demon convoy. They sought out King Kotutan and were entertained in the fortress meeting room.

The Wildrider who was the speaker for this venture explained the threat.

He introduced himself, saying, "I, Bladeswift, will show you where the Demons are. They are coming swiftly, with siege engines being dragged by huge Giants. We must not wait! We must get to them before they near the city walls."

Bladeswift indicated the probable route the Demons would travel to the fortress on a map.

Kotutan thanked them. "You have always been our friends, even as we sought to share this land and its sustenance."

"We are waiting," Bladeswift spoke, "to come with you in the field. We will not defend a fort. It is not our way to fight inside walls. But if you can muster forces, we will help in the foray to break the Demon convoy."

✝ ✝ ✝

Joe Brown spent forty days and nights getting his life in order. By the end he had made peace with Samantha. He had prayed for forgiveness for being a part of the forces that triggered the destruction of New Castle.

He had come to grips with his recent past of being a greedy Black man trying to exploit the resources of Brown men in Afraili.

He started using his military skills to clean up the city. He joined the brigade at the local police station. For a while he went on patrol in the city. Vandalism and robbery were high; a frontier-type atmosphere permeated the city.

People did band together, but the city's outcasts, the criminal elements, took this as a time to go on the offensive. The people on the fence who were unemployed and bitter no longer felt they needed to restrain themselves. After the destruction wrought in the city, they started to commit criminal offenses, mainly theft.

Martial law was being considered by the mayor, Rebecca Townsend, the first woman mayor of New Castle. *What a bitter pill to swallow*, she thought.

Then things started to really unravel.

A body, probably of a homeless man, was found in the pit. It was partially eaten and drained of blood. His leg was missing at midthigh. Joe and his brigade team searched for evidence of the killer. They found no obvious clues that would bring them to the culprit.

An autopsy revealed strange claw like marks and bites that left the impression of fangs.

A few more partially eaten bodies started to show up. A big-time gangster named Black Swanson and half his crew were found one night near an armored car. Black Swanson had attacked the armored car about six blocks from the pit. A jewelry store, Clarion's, still functioned amid the dust and grime with a cracked foundation. A power generator had been employed to keep the electricity going. Shoppers were few, but business was picking up.

It had been near closing. Black Swanson led a brief shootout with the armored car personnel as they left Clarion's. While investigating the shootout and deaths, investigators discovered the partially eaten bodies.

The pit now seemed to dominate New Castle. Its mangled debris created an ominous and cavernous wasteland of metal concrete and ruined machinery.

Joe, along with the other police personnel, was working more hours in an effort to stop crime in the city. Joe felt he was partly to blame for the attack on New Castle. If he could help solve some of the city's crime problem, he would feel a lot better about himself. Joe was eager to get back in his community's good graces. Church had started to welcome him. Society at large began to ask his opinion again. Sometimes he was embarrassed, even shamed by his mercenary work and references made to his city's destruction. He had to accept blame in part for the enemies mobilized against his nation. His transgressions led directly to their attack on New Castle. Joe's firsthand knowledge of mercenary work for oil ironically made his opinion important.

Strange things continued happening in the city, seemingly emanating from the pit. Unusual animal trails leading from the pit into the less ruined part of the city were noted. Upon inspection, the trials had odd patterns of soot and dust and footprints with four toes.

One day Joe Brown led a team of two others, whom he knew and felt confident about. It was a bright day. The acrid smell of the explosion that lingered in the pit was evident. Another smell commingled with that one: a deeper, more pungent odor of fire and gunpowder.

4.

THE DEVILS BELOW

The morning was bright, the sun shone through the clouds, and bright sparkles lingered.

"The evidence leads this way," Joe briefed his team members. "We've never seen anything like this before, but at least there is a trail. There are some obvious footprints in the dust on the trail. The apparent feet only have four toes. There seems to be something behind, brushing the footprints; that could be a tail."

On they went, descending into the pit. Rubbish cinder blocks and mangled steel girders led them down the path. There was plenty of room for three men to walk abreast. As far as they could see, there was a large gaping hole, two hundred meters in diameter, of darkness and destruction.

"Joe, we need better lights," said Sam. "This ain't gonna work. How we gonna see?"

Soon a helicopter loomed above them, shining a floodlight on their intended path.

"No problem," Joe countered. "We have light."

Tim Jacks held a handkerchief to his face. The acrid burned-out smell was overpowering.

Blood splatter lay ahead of them. Drops, then large splatters half a foot in diameter. The light showed a path that wound deeper into the pit. It wound down deeper but followed a pattern of circular decent. No corners, just gently winding circles going down. The path started to narrow fifty meters down. Joe controlled the pace, with Tim and Sam taking flanking positions a few feet behind him.

Tim Jacks was like Joe: a veteran of Foreign Corporate Mercenary Service. He was White, went to a military academy, even played college ball like Joe. He never moved on to pro but served his country briefly in the only sanctioned war on the Afraili continent. The one to avenge New Castle when the pit was blown. But within a few weeks, he was sent home due to war crimes he was perceived to have committed. Nothing was proven, so he took his leave from the military but came back to assist in regulating the chaos that continued to haunt New Castle. He did not have the feelings of guilt, nor could he have understood Joe's feelings about his fellow men of color in Afraili.

Sam Thames was not your average policeman in New Castle. He had been in small gunfights against armed criminals. He had two months of special weapons and tactics training and held his scoped weapon with confidence. He was a good shot, athletic like the other two, and he stood six feet and weighed close to two hundred pounds. Both Sam and Tim were reunited in the brigade with Joe to protect New Castle.

Suddenly the light from above was darkened by a shadow. A very large flying shadow. Joe could still see bits and pieces of bodies, but the shadow obscured his vision momentarily. The three men looked up to track the shadow, but as quickly as it appeared, it was gone. There was a scratching against rocks and a swishing sound. There were heads, hands, legs, and feet littered on the ground. Joe and his team observed blood in various stages from dry to shiny, wet drops. As they wound their way down, the light from above was useless. Joe gave the instruction, "Lights, men!"

Lights, attached to assault rifles, lit the descending way down the dark path, which narrowed to twenty meters across.

A large, winged figure arose from the darkness below, flying toward Joe who was looking to his left. The flying creature came up slightly to Joe's right, briefly appearing in his peripheral vision.

Tim fired first, followed by Joe and Sam. Several quick, controlled bursts. A scream echoed throughout the area. The creature rammed into Joe before it fell. Joe stumbled back as some sort of talon raked across his body armor, scratching it but not touching him underneath. He scrambled to his feet quickly, and all three men shot rounds as two more flying beasts came upon them from the bottom of the pit. Tim pushed forward recklessly. Both beasts rammed into him. Tim fired and both beasts took hits. He moved forward, firing, allowing himself to be vulnerable. Both creatures raked his helmet and torso, and one still scrambled toward him. Tim fell to the ground but continued to shoot. Joe, in a flash, released his rifle to hang by its strap on his shoulder. He grabbed and activated his Vibro-Blade, and the familiar ozone smell filled the air. Joe swung quickly with a backhanded downward arcing blow, crashing down on the creature's neck and back. It lay in a heap.

Its head was like a man's but with tiny horns emanating from the top of its forehead. It had pointy ears and clawed feet, which had four toes. The wings looked like a bat's but spanned eight feet. At the end of each wing were talons attached to a four-fingered "hand." Its wings were attached to each arm and shoulder. A tail protruded from just above the creature's butt.

Sam Thames exclaimed, "Holy fucking Bible stories, this thing there is the Devil!"

Indeed, thought Joe. Tim got to his feet, VB in hand. Sam had never owned a VB as the price was too steep. He pulled a steel machete from a sheath on his left hip.

"Pistols and swords!" Joe's voice boomed.

Five Demons like the first few came running toward them quickly— not flying, just running, carrying metal spears and shields.

"Close in together!" Joe gave the command as he leveled his six-shot hand cannon toward the five.

Kaboom!

The shot hit the first Demon's shield, temporarily stunning it and knocking it back into two of the others.

They were in a phalanx, Joe noted. He tried to get another shot off as Sam's big 10 mm pistol caught one Demon square in the face. Tim Jacks was already on Joe's left and began to arc his sword straight down toward the Demon's head. As he did, the Demon lifted his shield to block the blow. The Demon's response was too late, and the shield bounced to the ground followed closely by the Demon's pointy-eared, horned head.

Joe slid forward, slapping one Demon's shield away with his sword and then arcing it back to crash into the Demon's torso.

Once the remaining Demons fell, all three men were struck by the Demons' shiny brick-red skin, the like of which they had only seen in apocalyptic religious works. All three shared an inward dread that darkened their hearts even as it increased their resolve.

"Assault weapons!" Joe's voice cut the amazed, hushed silence and brought them back to the now—to the sound of clawing feet and flapping wings.

Shadows, in which the team's flashlights could not determine any forms, held the promise of more Demons moving quickly up the path.

"Wait for the light to shine on them," Joe ordered. "Stay disciplined."

Sam, Joe, and Tim shot in concert. They shot in short bursts and then rotated their fire to overlap each other. More Demons surged from above and below. Luckily, the space above Joe and the team was still small as they descended the tunnel. They braced together, firing at any space that held a Demon.

"Don't let them get close," Joe warned. "I need space and time to get on the radio to describe what we found here."

Joe never carried extra gear that distracted from the environment. Now he needed a radio and was under stress to communicate the direness of his team's situation. He needed his commanders to understand the threat they faced. He was concerned for his team but also feared for the city as a whole. Now he needed to get that radio in his hand, but he couldn't. Groups of spike-tailed Demons swarmed the air from the open tunnel space below. The clatter of claws came up the tunnel floor. Joe needed time. Time to act, time to contact help.

Joe was silent now, no time to speak. He had his Vibro-Blade in one hand and his pistol in the other. Tim had his Vibro-blade out as well. Sam fired into the onslaught of approaching Demons.

All three men were taking small hits as the Demons lunged forward with pikes and crude swords. Some of the Demons stopped to fire their primitive short bows. Demons from above fired arrows and threw spears downward as Joe and his team ducked and swerved, dodging the projectiles.

Joe, Sam, and Tim constantly shifted position to avoid the barrage from above. There was an unnerving feeling that no matter what happened, the team couldn't escape. Their position was fixed: a shifting target trying to parry a horde of blades. They tried to ease back the way they had come, but they couldn't—losing one beat would mean the swarm would run over them. Sam, an excellent shot, stood to the rear between Joe and Tim. Using his assault rifle, he held the Demons at bay. Joe checked his ammo. He was running low. He signaled Sam and tossed his revolver to him. Sam caught the revolver, a fission gun made with a revolving chamber that released a high-velocity energy burst when its hammer struck. When the burst hit a target, the edges of the blast exploded, and the middle accelerated. It could easily produce a gaping hole and did so as Sam expertly fired into the oncoming horde. Despite Sam's excellent shots, fear gripped Tim, Joe, and Sam.

Kapow!

The fission pistol took a Demon's chest out and still managed to kill the one behind it.

Tim and Joe hammered their swords from every angle. The Demons hung back to avoid being shot. From their positions they fired arrows, often striking Joe, Sam, and Tim. The arrows slashed their armor and penetrated their flesh with small but damaging injuries that slowed their responses.

"Move back," Joe coughed out hoarsely. But it was already too hard to move. Sam's fission revolver was finally out of energy, and having expended all of his other ammo, he reached for the machete at his belt. He brandished the machete, only to drop it as his hand was pierced by a Demon's arrow. He staggered as another arrow struck his shoulder. He felt faint but resisted falling as gravity pulled him toward the ground. He swung his rifle butt viciously into the jaw of an approaching Demon, who sagged back, slowing the progress of the Demons behind it.

Joe stepped into the gap between them as Sam withered, staggered, and finally slumped to the ground. Tim recklessly dove forward with his Vibro-Blade, slamming great horizontal arcs into the Demons approaching his position. He bled from about five wounds. Arrows had slammed into his armor, damaging it and allowing other arrows to penetrate his body. He was losing blood and speed.

Joe pulled Sam between them and, like Tim, swung his Vibro-Blade with great fury. As a result, lances broke in the Demons' claws, and their shields buckled. The Demons relented, and their onslaught slowed. Discouraged, the Demons held back and fired arrows.

Joe and Tim renewed their attack. Joe, deflecting the flying shafts with small, quick arcs of his blade, as Grand Master Quiker had taught him at the academy. Tim attempted the same, executed three deflections, then staggered as a fourth arrow shaft hammered into his chest. He dropped to his knees. Joe, seeing Tim's plight, heaved up a Demon's body, grunting as he pulled it toward his torso to use as shield. He grabbed a brick from the ground and hurled it twenty meters toward the Demon archers preparing to fire at them.

✟ ✟ ✟

Arleosa could wait no longer. The carnage and stench were imposing. She touched Joe. *Was he dead?*

The presence of her aura in the pit frightened the Demons, and they froze momentarily. She heard a voice she knew well.

Satan whispered—a loud sound with a hissing resonance that filled the chamber. "This is my time. You cannot have a victor here, my sister. All is mine—the humans are coming back to roost in familiar blood and fire, as always."

Arleosa breathed her essence into Joe, and to a lesser degree, Sam, and Tim. All three lingered between life and death.

"Joe," Arleosa spoke.

Joe heard a voice in his head. He felt like this was death. He stood in a material vacuum, distantly aware of Tim and Sam sharing this time with him. He could feel a presence but saw only a golden light permeating everything around him. He was unaware of his wounds. He felt a sense of well-being, and it resonated with him. This was beyond the intensity of feelings he had as a toddler being nestled in his mother's arms. *What is this?* He felt tears crowd into his eyes, a great joy overwhelming him. Then, nothing.

† † †

Satan fumed.

† † †

King Kotutan was furious. His trade routes were being overrun by Demon raiders. These Demon raiders consumed everything, including the lives of his subjects and the goods and food they produced.

The Wildriders rallied toward the fortress of Westaway. According to King Kotutan's information, the Demons were preparing a siege as they moved closer to the fortress walls.

Knights had been drawn away from the outpost to protect the trade routes to the East, leaving the outpost without a force to ride out and break the oncoming Demons.

Giants pushed siege engines, and they, along with the Demons, marched inexorably toward Westaway. King Kotutan's scouts marked their progress.

While riding hard to Westaway, the Wildriders spotted dust rising from the trail of the Giants and Demons heading toward Westaway. The Wildriders flanked either side of the massive column of Demons. The Demons were dressed in chain mail, carrying shields, swords, and spears. Some in the rear carried bows. They looked to be a thousand strong, no doubt fed from the bounty of the trade routes. They marched, slavering and yammering, encouraged when they saw the spires of Westaway in the distance.

King Kotutan was dressed in armor that molded to his body. The armor appeared like the scales of a dragon. Great plates of leather and hide bolstered his body as though he was born to wear it. He must go out and aid his own defense.

Wildriders continued to flank the Demon convoy. Bladeswift, the great Wildrider warrior, assessed the convoy, trying to determine his best next move.

✝ ✝ ✝

Joe could not move. He was aware of Tim and Sam near him, knowing they were barely alive. He looked up but saw nothing. His mind seemed to feel he was alive, but he could not sense his body as he had throughout his life. He drifted about easily, rudderless. Yet he felt life. His wounds seemed to disappear; his pain faded. He felt a light, warm, and comforting feeling flowing through his body. In his consciousness, which seemed to be slowly growing, he felt as if he was suckling at his mother's breast. But he had no memory of that even before. Now he did. Like an infant secure with his mother, he felt a deep satisfaction. He felt a belonging he had never felt since. He was more than at home; he was all that life had, yet completely detached. He felt love.

Joe's mother had been a prostitute who had loved a "john." She had fought hard to love and keep Joe. She had worked the trade until some john killed her. He had been five years old, barely in school. Joe remembered his mother had loved him. Relatives stepped in to help. He always felt loved, but he was saddened by the loss of his mother.

Joe's dreams ended. He was in the pit again. He was alone. Arleosa appeared like a beacon of bright golden light. She spoke like the tone of an organ. She spoke words that felt like thoughts bridging a gap between her and Joe. She felt his mind touched his thoughts, and the process reversed itself.

5.
AWAKENING

Joe looked up; his vision returned. He felt his limbs, stood up, and started to walk. Sam and Tim limped behind him, having sustained many wounds. Joe moved well, and he did not seem to suffer as Tim and Sam painfully lumbered up the tunnel.

Joe could use his radio now. Communications were up. He moved further away from a heap of brick-red Demon bodies in the tunnel. The Demons' bodies had been ripped and crushed by many rounds of ammo and the bludgeoning blows of Vibro-Blade.

Armed men rushed down to greet them.

Joe pushed forward. "I'm okay," he said. He looked back, gesturing toward Tim and Sam.

Captain Johnson appeared at the lip of the tunnel. "What happened, Joe?"

"We were swarmed by some sort of Demon. Take some men, send a mobile tracking camera down first, and look!"

"Okay," Johnson said. Johnson was a seasoned veteran of the New Castle PD. He had hunted murderers and fought gang members in fire-fights throughout the city.

"I know the answer," Joe said. "I need to get somewhere. You need to close this pit as soon as you bring the camera up. I'll figure out what to do. This needs to happen now!" Joe staggered from what seemed to be a hundred blows and cuts that had penetrated his armor. Then, as if a hand had taken firm hold of his whole body, he straightened, stood firmly, and smiled.

Captain Johnson started radioing urgently. He got a camera feed of the tunnel up and running. The camera displayed the carnage of Joe's battle. Demons lay strewed about: mangled, dead, and dying. In the place where Joe's team had made their stand, there was a fading light slowly darkening against the path of the tunnel. Men scurried down to pick up Demon corpse samples to bring back to Captain Johnson. Captain Johnson got the confirmation he needed. Soon trucks started to roll in and converge near the tunnel. SWAT members arrived carrying explosives. Several cement trucks arrived as well.

Captain Johnson went to see Joe and his team in a nearby makeshift infirmary. Several ambulances were positioned beside a portable, tentlike plastic structure shaped like an igloo that provided shelter for Sam and Tim. They lay resting on cots while the medical personnel examined them. Tim grinned as a shapely blonde hovered over him, trying to undo his gear and armor. Sam too seemed in good spirits, though not as joyful as a wiry male nurse quickly examined him.

"Where's Joe?" Captain Johnson bellowed. A bit of spittle was starting to form on the crease of his lips. He was obviously frustrated.

"Gone, Captain," Tim explained. "Said he had to get moving, that there is more at risk he needed to see about."

Captain Johnson didn't understand. "How's he seeing about things with those wounds he has, you guys? Besides, I need to understand what those things were. You guys look torn up, but you're talking, smiling..."

Tim grinned. "We'll give you a full report, but we need treatment." He smiled longingly at the blonde.

Captain Johnson turned on his heel, talking loudly into the radio. "Locate Joe Brown. He's needed for a debriefing! I need him now!"

☩ ☩ ☩

Joe was at his apartment, peeling off the battle armor. Dried blood was caked on it, his blood mingled with that of his adversaries. Some of the dried blood smelled of brimstone; he scraped some into a paper bag. He put several plastic garbage bags on the floor. He peeled off his gear and dumped it into the open bags. He appeared to be alone. But he was comforted, and his wounds seemed less grievous by the minute, where minutes before he was groggy and having difficulty thinking. *Blood loss*, he thought. Now he was moving quickly, preparing; his thoughts were racing, but he felt no sense of panic. He felt as though he was being helped and supported to make sense of what had happened. His spirits lifted from a swirl of PTSD symptoms.

Joe walked down to the underground parking garage and dumped his equipment in a garbage bin. He got in his car and drove up the ramp and into the city.

Joe had made several calls and left messages for Captain Johnson, Reverend Prolovion, and of course, Samantha.

He headed for the air docks miles above the city. The air docks had been developed long after flight was mechanized. After planes came space-ships and then came air tankers that could hover and fly at great speed. Once the military started using air transport heavily, the antigravity advances were quick to follow. Tankers and warships could be moved through the air like ancient ships had moved through oceans and seas. Oxygen was rich, even in the upper strata of Terra's atmosphere. For many, flight was a haven, easily making the sky a refuge as floating structures buoyed by antigravity technology supported widespread development of airspace organizations.

Joe awoke feeling a sense of purpose that heralded a beginning. It came from his near death in the pit.

Or had he died?

He seemed to think he had died. His wounds were devastating. He had lost a great deal of blood. Yet he remembered the feeling of completeness he had felt.

Somehow, he was now wedded to purpose. He felt a presence guiding his actions. In church, he had never felt this sense of completeness. But now, spiritually he felt, well, as if God was on his side. As if he had a guardian Angel. He was alive! The golden glow had saved him as well as Tim and Sam. This he knew. If this was a chance for redemption, he was going to follow it.

Joe knew Captain Johnson had been trying to reach him since yesterday. Joe waited in the parking lot of the New Castle Police Department Strategies Unit. He decided he'd rather not face Captain Johnson at this time. He sent a short digital message to Captain Johnson's email. It sounded like a command: **Collect evidence as seen close to pit. Need to research something before report is completed. Will contact soon.**

Johnson cursed and got angry when he received the message, but he already had enough to work on. Several of the Demon corpses had been hauled out of the pit. A photographer from the *New Castle Searcher* had gotten a picture of a Demon into circulation. The city potentially faced panic.

Joe reached the outside edge of Eastern New Castle. The airports were one-half mile above, accessed via sky elevator. Joe took a moment to glance into the ocean. The sun was rising in the east. He had not stopped to watch a sunrise for quite a while. Colors of hazy red and yellow merged as clouds seemed to part quickly with the emergence of the sun. Seabirds, gulls, and a few eagles glided across the ocean sky.

Joe sent a final digital message to Samantha: **All my love—sorry I can't be here. Know you don't deserve this, but I have to do something. I know you have a life. I wish I could stay, but things got bad in the pit. News is leaking out. You'll understand soon. I love you.**

His emotions swirled. He realized how much he cared for Samantha, but he'd never allowed their relationship to be fulfilled. Somehow, he'd return—if she still loved him. He'd fix things, but now he had to go.

"Access allowed," the monotone metallic computer voice hummed. "Joe Brown identified," it added. "See Captain Johnson ASAP."

"Acknowledged, will do," Joe announced.

He had arrived at the New Castle airports and police training installation. It was early, but training was underway. Cadets scurried through the facility, buckling belts, sliding pistols into holsters, and moving quickly to the range and exercise facilities connected to the port.

Joe knew where he wanted to go: Advanced Training Techniques Investigation Technical Undertaking Development Enhancement. The ATTITUDE wings. There were six enclosed hallways—all part of the police facility floating above the city. Three halls to the west and three to the east. Each hall led to a large, assembly-style workroom area. The halls on the west side adjoined the three halls on the east side via a main spine hallway. The three on the east were dedicated to current police training. On the west side, the first hall to Joe's left contained the Innovation Chamber. Each hall was joined to the main hall at right angles. It looked like a large dragonfly with six wings. No other facilities were near it, for security reasons.

Joe stood at the portal of the main hall just after exiting the sky elevator. Further to the east, he could see air docks for police air vehicles and industrial air tankers.

Joe eyed the west side of the hall, where the Innovation Chamber lay, and an Air Command Vehicle was docked between it and the sky elevator. He didn't have access to go any further but wanted to give it a try.

Finally, he saw a sign: "No entry—ATTITUDE installation. If you can't get in, you don't have clearance."

Smart-ass thought Joe. The ATTITUDE installation held the most recent developments in combat and policing. Joe felt there might be something there that might help him.

Then he understood. The whole installation floated on antigravity buoys, but ATTITUDE sat outside the middle western hall. It was separated by about twenty meters. Joe looked around. He couldn't risk the twenty-meter jump. But he could find another way into the ATTITUDE installation.

Joe was starting to feel a little worried. He had thoughts of urgency and didn't understand why he was about to break into the ATTITUDE installation. He was going to risk everything—his career, the trust people had put in him. He knew he had to do this though.

All along he felt a presence waking within him. He felt a sense of belonging. To what, he wasn't sure. But it felt right somehow. He went to the communication station and signaled Captain Johnson.

"Johnson here."

"Joe Brown reporting, sir"

"Joe, where...You're up at the floating ports!" Johnson fumed. "Why haven't you finished your report?"

"Look, sir, I need your support. I'll complete the report in transit. I need to get into the Air Command Vehicle," Joe pleaded. "I can get to the bottom of this—"

Johnson cut into a rant, "You don't have the clearance for that, and what the hell will you do in there or use it for?"

Joe started to speak in a way he had never before. "Captain Johnson, you'll find the DNA of these creatures is nontraceable to anything our science has seen. They have been building right under our noses, but their DNA indicates they can't be from here. I think I know how to find an origin for them."

Joe paused, and Johnson broke in. "How and why, son? I'm trying to seal that hole tight, let the fear die down, and get the city back to normal."

Joe was startled by Johnson's response. *Bureaucratic bastard*, Joe thought to himself. "Look, Captain Johnson, close that hole—good, great idea. But they might come through another hole that was opened by the terror attack. Who knows what else can happen? More holes could be popping out at any time. There seemed to be hundreds of those things down there, breeding and getting ready to attack again." Joe stopped, giving Johnson time to think. "I will get some DNA results back showing that the creatures don't match anything seen on this world ever before. Let me use the ACV and check out traces left from the pit where more of those Demon things might be. I know what to look for; I've got samples I can have processed at ATTITUDE, and I can make sure the city doesn't have any obvious hot spots. I'm here now; I can get this done quietly, and then there'll be a measure of security. We'll all win or get closer to winning, anyway."

"Okay," Captain Johnson relented. "You're up there already, and the sooner you get going, well, something will be known at least."

Ah, thought Joe, *it's beginning to sound like Johnson's very own idea. Great, now I can get this game up and running.*

Joe was able to call a self-driving shuttle once he was cleared by Johnson. Joe needed to make sure he was prepared. He briefly saw something in the combat innovation room that caught his eye. He checked out a brand-new armored battle suit, olive green in color and with camouflage capacity. The suit had visual binocular and scanning ability. It could also be compressed into a belt buckle worn around the waist. The ABS, or armored battle suit, offered substantial protective support. It could be used to climb sheer walls with its Magni Grip adhesion in the feet and hands. The suit could also enhance the physical strength and speed of the wearer.

Joe picked up a sniper rifle, semiauto carbines with and without scopes, and several high-caliber pistols. There were explosives, including grenades and his personal favorite, mobile claymores. A new Vibro-Blade was available too. He packed all of this into the ACV, a jet-propelled saucer-type vehicle that was intuitive to handle and very mobile. It was made for city flying, as it was able to zip and hover between buildings. It also contained one medical pod that served as a flying ambulance in emergencies.

On a trophy wall that overlooked the ATTITUDE facility rested an old single-shot ball and cap rifle. Below the rifle, a single-shot ball and cap handgun, much like a flintlock, was mounted. Joe picked up a few sacks of gunpowder and threw it all into the ACV.

Joe got in, powered up the ACV, and left, hovering. He then ported just outside the ATTITUDE facility. He started feeding samples from the pit into the ACV computer. The samples were scanned speedily due to the computer uplink in the ATTITUDE facility.

Easy as pie. Joe felt some pleasure in outmaneuvering Captain Johnson. The ACV was packed with enough food and water to last Joe for weeks. It had two floors. On the top floor was its cockpit and data computer.

Joe prepared to scan the city. He sent out tracers—radar programmed to pick up specific characteristics—and grinned. *Okay, Johnson, here's your scan*, he thought. *Nothing will be found, but I'll be long gone.* Joe started typing his report, feeding it through the ACV's communication system right to Captain Johnson's office.

Joe punched coordinates into the ship's auto flight control. He went downstairs to sleep as the ACV left Terra's atmosphere. He dreamed of fighting in the pit, dying, and coming back to life. He saw an Angel in his dream. He felt warm and then nothing.

Joe awoke and climbed up to the cockpit where he found the sun shining through to greet him. The ACV was moving away from Joe's world, past its sun by a wide turn and then quickly accelerating, placing Terra's sun between his ship and Terra.

Joe put the ship in hyperdrive. He started heading for a green and blue planet. He could see the planet with the ship's telescopic system when angled through a looming wormhole.

Joe was hungry and went to the ship's stores downstairs to fix a pop-up meal. He undressed and showered after setting the meal in the microwave oven. Joe looked over his body and noticed the cuts and wounds were healing very well and were almost gone.

Joe got up and ate his meal, got in the cockpit, and watched as the wormhole approached. Suddenly there was no light on either side of the ship. Some light glimmered and flickered ahead, presumably coming from the other end of the wormhole.

He looked at the ACV's fuel consumption instrument panel. It indicated fuel consumption had been suspended while the vehicle was in the wormhole. As the ACV emerged from the wormhole, Joe could easily locate the green and blue planet.

How did I know this? he thought. But he knew—or did he? An icy chill gripped him as he realized what he was doing. *I don't know exactly where I'm going, but I feel that this leads me somewhere I need to be.*

Joe got back in bed, but before sleeping, he heard a chirping sound from the communication panel. It was Captain Johnson, "Joe, these things don't match anything in our historical data DNA—nothing. Where are you? We can't locate your signal. Please advise."

Joe knew it was too late; nobody would reach him from Terra now. It was all on him. He drifted off to sleep. He felt as though he was being caressed gently, lovingly. It was as though a blanket of security warmed him. Then nothing.

Joe awoke in a panic. He sensed he was close to his objective, but he was worried. How did he even know to be worried? He'd made a decision; *I chose this* he said to himself. *I don't know all the answers, but this is my path.* The panic slowly subsided as he started to control his breathing, feeling the blanket of security that had covered him through the night. A sense of love filled him.

He slid down below to check his gear. Autopilot was on course for the green and blue planet that was his unknown destiny.

"Joe." He heard a voice in his head, melodic and soft but easily understood. He glanced around, expecting a person. A radiance filled the ship close to where he stood. He remembered the pit. Had he seen the same thing there—a radiant light? Warmed and feeling uplifted, Joe continued checking his gear. He looked upon the armored battle suit. It looked golden where before it had seemed to be olive green. He picked up the almost-ancient musket, fingered it, and tested its mechanism. He did the same with the flintlock pistol. He was getting close to, for lack of a better term, Terra 2. He scanned the planet as he drew closer. He set the parameters of the scan to locate outposts of civilization in a frontier setting.

6.
MODERN HERO FOR AN ANCIENT WORLD

At the heart of his scan lay three settlements. One furthest west and one each on the north and south. The settlements were spread over a triangular area that had holdings aligned with them.

In the far west, he could see a column moving toward the settlement. He scanned the area. It revealed the same creatures he'd fought in the pit were marching on this other planet. A quick telescopic link from the scan confirmed the creatures to be those seen in the pit—within a 95 percent certainty. *Perhaps this is their home,* Joe thought. *Maybe this is their point of origin, and that's the reason I'm being directed here.*

Joe had an odd feeling: warmth mixed with what he knew from the recent past—deep dread. He thought about his mother and the love for her he could never really have. He thought about Samantha and how he could not give her his true love or what she deserved.

He picked up the sniper rifle semiauto .50 caliber. He'd seen siege engines in the columns. Joe tried on the armored battle suit. He felt like a knight going for an important joust. He flicked the Vibro-Blade. It sizzled and hummed. He holstered two high-caliber pistols and moved the ship northwest of the settlement. Time for a surprise. Time to get busy.

Joe performed several scans from above, noting short, muscular riders flanking the Demons' columns on each side. Some rode large horses and carried bows and long swords. Others, carrying lances, cantered on magnificent destriers with shields mounted on the horses' flanks. Each horse wore a simple harness; a loop around the horse's chest and back provided rigging for shields and other equipment. The riders on the destriers were outfitted as a heavy cavalry force. They wore formfitting turtle shells that covered their torsos. Plumed helmets of the same material adorned the riders.

He noted a settlement. Bowmen, wearing chain mail and full helmets, looked from the walls toward the columns. Joe set the ship for a landing.

Joe started to form a plan as he donned the ABS. The plan would be simple. Joe would land behind the columns and move west on foot. He would position himself between both columns and work his way toward the western gate of the settlement.

He could see the riders flanking each side of the column and could tell their attack was imminent. He hoped it would be clear he was an ally when he fired his first shots. He had to land the ship on a hill to the south of the looming conflict amid trees and brush, then hasten back to the columns. So much rested upon his becoming an ally of the primitive men in the settlement. He also sensed that he would need the support of the cavalrymen flanking the columns of Demons he saw.

There was more.

In the columns, he noted creatures he'd only seen in nightmarish movies. The scan had been inconclusive. The creatures had never been introduced to the database. The Demons, he was familiar with; but these strange, manlike, giant creatures in the column were new to him. They pushed siege engines and wore heavy armor. Some carried oversized clubs and crossbows.

Joe quickly fitted the ABS, giving it time to sync with his body. Bands of armored material, flexible yet protective, covered him. The ABS was a tight-fitting armored battle suit that could change colors to fit the environment. It had a helmet that featured protruding globes that covered his eyes. The eye globes were opaque and increased his peripheral vision. They also had a telescopic enhancement that gave Joe binocular sight range. The edges of the ABS were smooth and contoured to him. The equipment harness clung snugly against the suit's surface and pulled everything in close to Joe's body. He looked like a futuristic knight or a man-sized bug in an exoskeleton.

He got equipped with the .50-caliber sniper rifle, the Vibro-Blade, and two semiautomatic pistols. He landed the ship on autopilot and sealed it from the outside. He moved to the edge of the hill and scoped the moving columns. They were four hundred meters west of him and about a metric mile from the western settlement gate.

✝ ✝ ✝

King Kotutan waited upon the ramparts of the settlement. The Wildriders informed him of the Demon column advancing upon his fortress settlement. He knew this inevitable confrontation fit a prophecy of doom elevated in dogma by his religious counselors. He had seen and fought the Demons recently. But now other strange creatures had joined the fray.

Nightmare visions from some children's fable designed to keep them inside at night now become real, thought Kotutan. *But how? No need to become undone now.* He would be strong.

Some settlers herded cattle inside the fortress for protection. Others dispersed their charges to the grasslands within the triangular area controlled by the three Long-Strider outposts. The cattle could be retrieved after the culmination of the looming skirmish.

Joe geared up the ABS, telescoped the columns, and located the siege engines he'd seen earlier. The siege engines looked to be catapults and large crossbows with hooked quarrels. The hooked quarrels could be used to latch onto the fortress walls and pull them down.

Looking from the hill, Joe set up the .50-caliber sniper rifle. Zooming in on the left column through the scope, he observed a Giant and several Demons pushing and pulling a catapult. The Giant resembled a man, with his hulking muscularity and lurching gait. His body was as hairy as an ape's. He was naked, save for a leather belt attached to a loincloth covering his privates. A large club was strapped to the back of his belt. Joe aimed carefully. He was three-quarters of a metric mile away. The hill gave him the advantage of firing down at the large target that was moving slowly and predictably.

Before firing, Joe assessed the column on the right. He noted another Giant pushing a catapult. Joe formulated a battle strategy to kill a Giant in both columns and thereby slow each column's progress.

Joe brought his attention back to the original target, waited, exhaled, and fired.

Kapow!

The Giant fell forward, heavily jarring the catapult. He slumped to his knees and then fell on his side. There was a halt to the left column as the creatures nearby looked fearfully for an assailant they would never guess was three-fourths of a metric mile away. Upon hearing the crack of gunfire, the Giant pushing the catapult in the right column looked left and saw his tribesman fall dead. He looked stunned and walked toward the fallen Giant. As he walked, Joe fired again.

Kapow!

The second shot dipped low, catching the Giant in the base of his neck. The Giant spun and fell midway between the columns. Blood gushed from the Giant's neck. He panicked and writhed as icy fear gripped his mind. He went into shock and finally died.

Seemingly out of nowhere, a crowd of Demons drew up and around the two dead Giants. Joe strung the .50-caliber sniper rifle on his back and started running.

From the outpost, King Kotutan heard loud cracking noises. He watched in stunned amazement as both columns stalled. The ensuing confusion jolted him into thinking the Wildriders had started their attack. King Kotutan witnessed Bladeswift, the Wildrider chieftain, rein away and break off his flanking movement to veer away from the right column he'd been shadowing.

Joe was running hard. He covered a quarter mile in thirty seconds, according to the electronic log feed in the ABS.

He stopped and shifted left toward the left column. There were Giants in the front of the column Joe hadn't seen before. Joe squatted on one knee.

Kaboom!

The blast from the sniper rifle echoed in the wind. A Giant staggered and fell dead, a large hole gaping in his back. Joe felt some apprehension. He wondered how long it would take for his victims to wheel around and become his assailants.

Joe ran diagonally to shadow the right column. Through the brush, he could vaguely make out the group of light cavalry he'd noticed from the ACV. Joe sought to move into position to strike the head of the right column as he had the left column. He smelled the horses of the light cavalry near him.

The Wildriders watched Joe, seeking to discern his motive. They veered away from his position.

Joe moved behind a clump of brush. He fired once again.

Boom!

The .50-caliber sniper rifle blasted a Demon and then struck a Giant in the thigh. The Giant collapsed in a heap. Joe never knew he could be that good of a shot. Somehow, he was better than ever, calculating the attack on two assailants with one shot.

Joe shouldered the sniper rifle and unholstered his pistols. The right column was turning on his position. They could see him. He saw several Demons coming directly at him. Quickly he moved forward, springing within a few yards of the nearest Demon. He was momentarily hidden from sight. He started firing the pistols point-blank. The first Demon fell back, revealing a second Demon leveling a crossbow at Joe. He dove sideways and fired quickly while still in the air.

Crack! Crack! Crack!

Three Demons fell back and recoiled from Joe's attack; the rest milled about in confusion.

Joe suddenly heard the thump of arrows hit several Demons. Joe looked right and saw the light horsemen had decided to help him.

Joe rolled and came up, firing both pistols. The pistols spit out sharp, penetrating hits, clearing a path to the Demons at the front of the columns who were now headed his way.

The light horsemen dipped toward the columns, getting close, letting their arrows fly in waves. Their horses intuitively put their riders in perfect proximity to their targets. Then like ghosts, they disappeared from the column, leaving dead Demons in their wake.

As the horsemen dashed away, they leaned on the flank of their horses away from the Demons' returning fire of crossbows and thrown lances. A few of their mounts were struck down. Their riders rolled to the ground, sprang up, and ran into the brush. Joe felt like things were moving in slow motion. The light horsemen had given him the time he needed to load his magazines.

Joe rolled into the brush just as a quarrel shot past his head. He could see the left column was moving toward his position. He could feel and sense the anger and the outrage emanating from both Demons and Giants alike. There were also fur-covered manlike creatures of squat stature carrying swords, shields, and lances. They had fangs. Joe stood up in the brush, fired two shots, and sprinted left.

He flanked the column, now from the low brush; the ABS blended into the foliage nearby. He fired several rounds and circled around the column again. The light horsemen returned and darted in on the column closest to Joe, shooting their curved bows causing rapid destruction. Demons, Giants, and smaller beast-like men gnashed their teeth and cried out in rough growls of anguish.

Joe could feel his consciousness reaching out beyond him to grasp the chaos around him. He had support and knew he had to go beyond the two columns and place the fortress at his back. He curved around the right column after making a diagonal sprint. The left column had become disorganized. Beast-like men, Giants, and Demons alike fired crossbows and threw lances, sometimes hitting their own crew.

Joe grinned and kept moving, firing the pistols as he dashed for cover. *It felt like football again*, Joe thought. *Running for glory.*

A Giant's club butt flashed toward his face. Joe was already near the siege engines that the Giant had been pulling. The Giant stood eight feet tall, burly and muscular, with an arrow protruding from the left thigh. Still he lurched forward, barely able to hammer down on Joe's head with the club butt. Joe fell back and tucked his chin to allow the club butt to glance his forehead. Joe pivoted left and looked up, firing the high-caliber pistol up at the Giant's head. As he pivoted, his right foot bumped into one of the dead Giants he had shot earlier with his sniper rifle. The shot glanced off the Giant's forehead.

"*Argh,*" the Giant bellowed, blood streaming down his face into the eye closest to Joe.

The Giant gripped the club with two hands and turned toward Joe, who was regaining his footing. The club arced down toward Joe, who was a bit shaken. Unknown to Joe, two light horsemen were near him, shadowing his position.

Thump, thump.

Two arrows suddenly protruded from the Giant's lower back. He staggered midswing. Joe braced and jumped backward, away from the downward-arcing club. As he jumped back, he twisted and fired a shot that hammered into the Giant's upper chest.

Joe had two thoughts: *How'd I get away?* and *Man, this is serious.*

Joe rolled upright and faced two Giants bounding toward him. Both wore armor, and instead of clubs, they carried heavy lances as long as the Giants were tall.

Joe was out of ammo in each pistol—no time to reload. He holstered both effortlessly as the ABS enveloped both pistols.

He reached for the Vibro-Blade. He was late as the first Giant aimed his lance at Joe's heart and started to thrust. Joe crouched low, ducked under the lance, and rammed his right shoulder into the Giant's lower gut. The Giant staggered and fell back. As Joe moved away from the staggered Giant, the second Giant lunged and drove his lance toward Joe's torso.

King Kotutan watched from the fortress ramparts. The strange knight with the thunder and lightning rods had turned the Demon columns away from the fortress. The Wildriders had helped, of course, *but who was this strange knight?*

"Now!" Kotutan bellowed. "Open the gates; help our new savior!"

From out of the gates poured seventy riders in heavy dragon-scale armor, carrying lances with swords and shields strapped to their waists and saddles, respectively. They rode big stallions whose legs and chests were protected by leather bindings and rhino hide. At the front of the column rode a knight, larger than the rest, on a huge mount. He wore a silver helmet, and at its top flowed a jet-black plume. He headed toward Joe, slashing on either side of him, cleaving the backbones and necks of Demons and other nightmarish creatures blocking his path to Joe.

✝ ✝ ✝

Sir Ataka rode with urgency, the black plume on his helmet dancing in the wind. He rode to the front of a *V*-shaped formation of heavy cavalry. Switching quickly from sword to lance, Ataka drew his massive arm back and let his lance fly thirty meters—a marvelous feat, especially on horseback. The lance protruded from a Giant's chest as he lurched toward Joe. The Giant dropped to his knees, dead. The shaft of Ataka's lance hung like a skewer in the Giant's back.

Joe righted himself and drew his Vibro-Blade. He started down the right-side Demon column, which had fragmented. They started to regroup to mount an attack against Joe. A fanged beast-like man slashed at Joe with a short sword. Joe stepped inside the arc of the swing. He caught the blade with a shattering blow of the Vibro-Blade. The Beastman's sword broke, and Joe thrust the Vibro-Blade into his neck.

Ataka lunged forward toward Joe. The Demons, Beastmen, and Giants started to fall back, scattering into the woods. They ran down the trail they had come from, with Ataka and his heavy cavalry giving chase. The Wildriders harried the retreating force.

Joe was not sure what to do.

Follow the fight, he thought, and he started running toward the hill where he'd originally landed.

At the base of the hill, Ataka and his cavalry were circling a shield wall formed by a few remaining Giants, Demons, and Beastmen. They fired arrows into the mass but had little success.

Joe surveyed the scene, started reloading his pistols, and packed them in their holsters before unleashing his Vibro-Blade. He ran straight at the shield wall. Demons fired arrows. Some struck, making small wounds he felt acutely at first and then less as he ran; other arrows cascaded off of his armor.

He stopped in front of the biggest Giant and slammed his Vibro-Blade into the Giant's shield, creating a hole in the shield wall. The Giant staggered back. Joe jumped left quickly, moving slightly behind another Giant, and he slammed downward on the crouching Giant's back with the Vibro-Blade. He collapsed, fell forward, and lay still.

No more Giants remained, and the cavalry swarmed the disorganized shield wall, hacking with broadswords, viciously piercing the bodies of their enemies.

Joe, sweating furiously under his armor, spun and darted, raining down blow after blow on the enemies. They were ferocious but eventually lost the will to continue.

The death of the last Giant and the shield wall's destruction ended the fight for the Demon horde. The heavy cavalry hacked down the last of the remaining creatures that had not fled.

Several knights were slain, but the largest knight, Ataka, peered down from his stallion at Joe with appreciation.

"We are in your debt, great warrior," Ataka said.

The words rang in Joe's ears. They sounded foreign, but Joe understood them. It felt like the time he made rookie of the year. He had been lauded by the whole sports world.

Ataka continued, "Our king must meet you."

"Yes." Joe heard himself mouth the strangely accented words as though he was acting in a play on a stage from ancient times. He explained that he had equipment to pick up on the hill.

Several cavalrymen went with him to the ACV. Joe entered his ship, and the cavalrymen looked strangely at it. Joe opened the ship and picked up more ammo and two primitive flintlock firearms. He grabbed the sack of gunpowder and sealed the ACV. The cavalrymen offered Joe a horse. He packed the supplies into his suit. Ammo and gunpowder easily fitted into its various straps and pockets. He tied the primitive firearms to the horse's saddle straps, which seemed to be made for cargo. Joe rode to the fortress flanked by the cavalry and Ataka, who was at least a head taller than all the rest and had arms twice as large as the others.

Shortly, Joe could see the fortress banners and men cheering from the ramparts. The gates opened, and in they went. Joe looked around the vast expanse that was the fortress. There were small patches of plants growing in raised-bed gardens. He felt oddly at home.

In the middle of the fortress was a large brick building with huge open doors. There were several flights of stairs that led up to the doors. King Kotutan waited in shining dragon-scale armor. The armor was thick, like the scales of a giant snake. Two rows of men in chain mail and helmets were on either side of the steps.

Ataka escorted Joe up the steps to meet the king. All along the procession were children and women, staring and speaking in hushed tones. As Joe reached the top, he noticed wizened men in hooded cloaks through the door, gesturing and making symbolic gestures.

Joe bowed upon reaching the top stair near the wide-open doors.

Ataka spoke, "Here is our king, Kotutan. King Kotutan, here is the knight who turned the Demon horde from our gates."

"Please," Kotutan urged, "come sit at my great table. We will prepare a feast, but first, please, and with deference to you, uh, lord, tell us—how did you find us?"

Joe knew they had questions. They all sat at the table, King Kotutan at its head, and waited politely.

"Uh, it's just Joe. I am not a lord. I'm a simple warrior. I do not understand everything enough to tell you a lot. But I know I was meant to be here."

☦ ☦ ☦

Arleosa smiled at God. "I have produced your Messiah, and indeed he has a world to save. Has he not, oh Lord?"

God frowned. "He is no Messiah—just an inspiring warrior. He does not even know what he's doing. I was looking for more." God seemed to pout and withdraw emotionally.

Arleosa seized the initiative. "He has yet to realize his full significance. Look at the influence and how it has been realized. He went through a wormhole on a local cruiser not even meant for space travel and saved a fortress all based on faith. Oh, my Lord God, we have our Messiah!"

God seemed flummoxed. "Indeed, Arleosa, your influence is great, but a Messiah?"

"Yes, my Lord," Arleosa spoke on, "he barely recognizes my influence but quickly does what must be done. He has a divine spirituality connecting him to us all. Thy will be done, oh Lord. The quickening of his spirit will be a process. So much is yet to be done, but we have come so far so fast. Joe Brown seeks redemption, a purpose, something we want for him."

"True," God said. "Time is still with us."

God paused for a moment. "Have we heard from Satan?"

"No!" Arleosa exclaimed.

"Well," God answered, "hmm, he is on the move, and now the stage is set. I must continue; already the hour grows late. Okay, Arleosa my Angel, let us see this Messiah work. I have no choice now unless I start over—all over again."

That was the problem, thought Arleosa, *starting over again. The pain it caused for the helpless minions caught in the grip of God's plan and the process of Satan proving who was right. Neither of them is right.*

"It has to end—and in this time of the Messiah Joe Brown," Arleosa said. "He would have never gotten to the wormhole if you'd not made space breathable with free-flowing currents and streams. This allowed a craft meant for short travel to find a whole constellation not found by the people of his home world. Brilliant, my Lord!"

"Flattery, Arleosa!" God beamed. "The game is yours to join. Hell will tremble; Satan will join us again and give up his folly."

Arleosa laughed inwardly. If only they could be all together again. But she knew in her heart Joe Brown, in his own way, was even more exciting than Jesus.

✝ ✝ ✝

The king and Joe sat together. Joe undid his helmet and let his face show. His woolly hair billowed out from under the helmet. The cords of muscle stood out on his bull neck. The people around him were a stark contrast to him. They had light brown to white skin. All had straight hair. Ataka was taller than most, with broad enormous shoulders. He and Kotutan were well over six feet tall, where most were only half a foot taller than five feet. Kotutan was muscular and tall with a trim waist. However, his movements were at times heavy and not fluid. Ataka looked to be a natural athlete, fluid and supple with extraordinary muscular bearing.

Joe looked around. Serving girls came into the room and the smell of charred meat wafted in.

A hooded, cloaked figure approached King Kotutan. He dropped his hood and whispered to the king. Joe watched quietly and waited. Joe was distracted by the approach of a nearby serving girl. Her gossamer dress revealed her to be physically attractive and fit. A welcoming smile adorned her round face.

As the throng of people surrounding the king grew, one of the cloaked figures was introduced as a priest. Osala the priest spoke eloquently after conferring with the king. His head was shaved, and he was as tall as the king but much thinner.

"We have seen your coming, great one. Are you not he who was written about in our holy books?"

"How would I know?" Joe looked incredulous. "I just got here!"

The man looked flustered. The king waved him away. "Enough! Whether a prophecy or just good luck, we have a powerful ally and heeded one in our midst. Tell us, though, how have you found us, and what is your purpose here? What guides it?"

The room, or great hall, fell silent. Joe stopped thinking about the serving girls. "I don't understand." He dipped his hand into his plate and chewed a piece of bread. "I have come very far to help your civilization in facing its most dire threat, a threat that will end your reign if it is not vanquished. I have the answers to how you can get that done. I will prove that I can help you." He pointed to the priest in a kind manner. "I am here to help—that is all. Prophecies may or may not be relevant."

The priest looked frustrated but bowed graciously and with the king's leave left the hall.

The king spoke with great urgency. "For years now we have pushed west. We encountered the riders who supported you, the small tribesmen. We call them the Wildriders. We have made an alliance with them. They too are threatened by this forceful host that seeks to crush our growth, our life."

"Do you know where these creatures came from?" Joe inquired when the king paused.

"No one has seen their encampment and lived to tell the story. In truth, we would rather fight and hope we face our final enemy. The wisemen speak of prophecies. Well, if you represent one side of a prophecy, those creatures represent the other. Any way we see it, tough times are ahead."

The king and the hall grew quiet.

"Let us eat for at least today," said the king. "There is a cause for joy. We lost few men, and the Wildriders again came to our aid. We are not short on allies; we have a new one whose presence is like fifty on a battle-field. Eat! Drink! Live!"

A serving girl poured wine into Joe's cup. He smiled solicitously at her, hopeful and optimistic. She blushed but returned his smile. After all, he was their savior for now.

There were barbecued beef ribs smelling strongly of hickory and mesquite wood. Joe ate ravenously. Small, flat loaves of bread had been lathered in butter by the King's cooks. Mounds of greens were also served by the cook's assistants. Joe, not much of a wine drinker, appreciated the vintage he consumed with gusto.

"Whenever you are ready, we have a large room prepared for you," said the king. "Guards will be nearby and servants as well. On the morrow we will seek an audience with you. Show us then why you have come."

Joe continued to enjoy the festivities until finally fatigue overtook him.

Getting up, Joe put his helmet visor back on. It covered his head completely, giving him the appearance of a masked superhero. He took it off immediately, recognizing the hush of the people and not wishing to be rude.

"Sorry. I am with allies now," said Joe. "Old habits die slowly." He chuckled.

With that, there was a laugh, and King Kotutan grinned easily.

"Now if I might, I will take my leave, King Kotutan."

"So be it. At first light, we will await you," King Kotutan responded.

Knights, still in full battle armor, saluted Joe as he passed. There were other men and women in elaborate clothes Joe guessed to be either merchants or lords of some sort. He was let out of the hall into a room with a large bed. *Spartan, he* thought. Rugs lay on a wood floor. There were a few furs on the bed and a washbasin on a bench in a corner of the room.

"Good night, Joe," said the host, a short man who had appeared to orchestrate the feast earlier.

Joe heard the door close behind him. He collapsed on the bed and dozed off. He awakened, not sure whether to take off the armor. As comfortable as the ABS was, he did not want to sleep in it. But he did. Once again, he went to a place of dreams. Soft, caring dreams—his mother holding him as he suckled her breast. A feeling of contentment, almost on a level of making love to Samantha.

A voice called to him, lovingly and soft. Arleosa was present, and he began to know her as the golden light that had rescued him from death. He should have felt traumatized and fearful as he had no sense of what had happened to him. It had been only a brief time since he emerged from the pit. Beat down, ragged—he should have been dead. *He had been dead.*

Suddenly he awoke from his sound sleep, startled, and panicked—then calm again. He drank from a cup. *Water. Soothing.*

He felt a golden light pervade his consciousness. Quickly, like a man possessed, he took off the ABS. He dug into the mattress and covered himself in the coarse sheets and furs of these primitive medieval people. He dreamed again of the golden light, of being loved and directed to a place he now found himself. He knew that he had to be here. He was secure. He chose redemption and knew this was it. His sleep was deeper than he'd ever known. The golden light...

✝ ✝ ✝

There was a knock.

Two knocks, more urgent.

He awoke, donned the ABS in seconds, and opened the door. King Kotutan stood there with three heavily armored men who appeared to be medieval knights.

"Come," he said, "let us show you our life. Know you and you know us."

"Yes, yes, for sure, I'd like that," Joe found himself saying.

Kotutan, in chain mail with a bow, a quiver of arrows, and a great sword, bowed. Joe bowed in return. Down the steps, they went.

Joe had already attached his weapons to the ABS, which had special compartments allowing for seamless storage with a minimum of bulk. Today, this seemed especially true. Joe walked with a light stride and felt weightless. The golden bands of armor seemed to shimmer and radiate light.

But how could that be? Joe thought.

In the yard by the king's quarters, he saw workers bustling about. Knights in dragon-scale-plated armor rode full speed on armored horses, bashing blunt lances at each other. If one fell, the other, still on horseback, would charge and hack down upon his foe with a practice sword made of a blunt piece of dull metal.

King Kotutan motioned to Joe. "Do you ride, and would you honor us with a show of your prowess?"

"Yes," Joe heard himself say cockily and with some measure of eagerness. He had not ridden a horse in years.

A large black stallion was brought out by a squire. Its mane was kinky, like Joe's, and the tail a bush of kinky, puffed hair. Its legs were long in proportion to its body compared to the other horses' legs.

"One of our finest." The King gestured toward the stallion.

All around, knights stopped talking and watched in rapt attention as Joe mounted the stallion. King Kotutan handed Joe a blunt lance. The squire normally sent to do this gasped, then stumbled out of the way.

The jousting area was a fifty-meter oval with room to maneuver left and right. It favored a hard charge. Joe had observed some of the action upon reaching the area.

Joe jumped on the horse, which reared and pranced good naturedly as Joe maneuvered it around, hefting the lance. He waited to see who he would compete against.

Suddenly from behind a fenced area came Ataka in black and gray dragon-scale armor. He dipped his lance toward Joe in salute. Joe did the same, and they paced away from each other, wheeled their mounts, and charged. Ataka built up speed on his white charger—the beast of a horse moved in three bounds up to full speed. Ataka threw his lance. Before Joe could think, he heard a swoop in the air and looked up to see the lance heading toward his chest. With no time to move the horse, he brought his own lance up, flipping its point diagonally toward Ataka, pivoting his elbow, and deflecting the thrown lance. Ataka's actions seemed to be in slow motion to Joe. Ataka was upon him, blunt sword drawn, ready to hack a man he expected to be unhorsed. Joe reached back to his chest with the lance, locked his elbow, and extended his lance toward Ataka's ribs, which were exposed. Like lighting, the shaft of the lance struck Ataka in the ribs.

Ataka buckled in the saddle, rode out some distance, lurched over, and uttered in a painful gasp, "Yield—I yield."

Ataka was helped from his horse by nearby squires. There was a small grandstand filled with squires, craftsmen, and shopkeepers taking a break from work.

Ataka rose from the ground. Joe wheeled his horse around. Ataka stood and looked up at Joe.

"Good show," Ataka mused.

"Excellent skills," said King Kotutan, seizing the moment, not wishing any more risks to be taken ended the contest. The king recognized Joe's superior armament—in his full ABS attire, Joe looked like an alien super-knight to these people: the insect eye shades, fitted helmet, bands of armor clinging to his body, formfitting and symmetrical on his muscled frame.

The hooded figures from the previous night's feast appeared, gesturing and yammering to each other. King Kotutan knew there was great speculation as to who Joe was.

"Let us see the country," King Kotutan spoke, and a retinue of soldiers and knights appeared on horseback. "We will breakfast in the field. Our force can escort us out to the pastures where our people graze their cattle. After yesterday's attack, we must be ever vigilant."

☦ ☦ ☦

Before long, the gates were opened by the fortress guards, and livestock were moving behind King Kotutan and Joe. Joe rode easily on horseback and was becoming accustomed to the large stallion minute by minute.

The people had earlier brought their dead into the fortress and quickly but ceremoniously buried them in a graveyard near a back wall.

Outside the fortress, Demons were being stacked by laborers, and a great blaze was set. The siege engines and dead Demons, Giants, and Beastmen were burned in a pile, even some of the knights and squires assisted the laborers.

King Kotutan motioned Joe onward. "Every year we look to expand our holdings, but we are locked in a never-ending battle with these creatures. Look at the country—full of promise but full of death for our people as well. Let us head out. There in a stream just south of our fortress. We must get there ahead of the cattle to protect them while they are watered. Do you hunt, Joe?"

"No, I have never been so lucky, but I'd give it a try."

Ataka, Kotutan, and Joe sped south. They left their horses to graze in a verdant clearing. A few guards with crossbows followed to watch the horses. Down a slope they crept. Joe, making no noise in the ABS, followed Kotutan and Ataka.

By the stream stood a large buck, fifty yards away. The king brought a large bow up, and Joe heard a sizzle in the air. The buck dropped in its tracks by the stream it had been drinking from. Two guards hurried forward to pick up the buck and pack it on the back of a mule.

"We must head back to check on the grazing cattle," said Kotutan. "We must be ever vigilant, so we are not surprised by another attack." Kotutan eyed Joe appraisingly. "Joe, the wise prophets say you are a special being sent to deliver us by the sword from these Demons. To lift us up and help us gain dominion over this land. To help our people prosper and live rich, full lives."

"I believe that is true, King Kotutan." Joe looked quizzically at King Kotutan under his shades and helmet. "But I am not sure of how and why. We faced a momentary threat from these same creatures at my home."

"Where is that?" Kotutan implored, wishing to grasp this strange warrior and his purpose.

"There, beyond your sun. I have a means to travel you've never seen but will one day master, I am sure."

The king mounted his horse, and Joe followed him back to where the cattle grazed.

"Do you rotate the pasturing?" Joe asked.

"Of course, but not often enough; as you see we are fearful of Demon attacks," Kotutan responded.

Kotutan again began to query Joe about his origin. Joe answered as best he could without sounding too bizarre so the king might understand.

"All will be told later, Your Majesty, but believe me, our homes have a common cause," Joe said to the king.

The countryside was beautiful. Bees hummed and buzzed around while birds chirped noisily in large trees. There were fields beyond the canopy of trees on either side of the path. They traveled north back to the cattle pasture. Joe sighed wistfully as he took in the natural beauty around him.

King Kotutan paused briefly, surveying the surroundings. "Joe," he said, "Who are you? What is your purpose here with us? We are grateful but know you not."

The sun sparkled on Joe's shades and glimmered off the ABS. Lacking words that might soothe the king, Joe said, "I have come to lift your humanity and give you what you already own."

There was a murmur from the nearby guards. Everyone paused for a minute. Joe wondered what he had said. He thought it was something to ease the king's mind. Hell, he didn't know why he was here, truth be told. He knew intuitively but not in a material sense. Joe was just beginning to grasp his purpose.

Arleosa beamed in Heaven in front of God.

Joe felt his body lighten.

"This is our land, Joe," the king began. "But we cannot own it, because the threat to our people is so great. You have seen it and fought to protect us. What more must we do? Is there something special? Your weapons, the lightning rod you always carry. I dared not ask at first. Do you have an answer?" King Kotutan grimaced.

"King Kotutan, I must travel to my ship and bring you a mighty set of tools." Joe spoke in a serious low tone. "I must have you assemble, if it pleases you, King Kotutan, your best metalworkers and crafters of weapons. Your blacksmiths and metallurgists."

"When do you travel, Joe?" Kotutan responded. "Name the time."

"Tomorrow at first light, with a small escort and a few pack animals, if it pleases you, King Kotutan."

The sun dipped lower, and the cattle were driven to the fort by mounted laborers. Evening would be upon them soon and with it a meal in the king's great hall. The priests would join them, King Kotutan informed Joe.

Joe took some time before the meal to go to his quarters. He took off the ABS and took a bath prepared at his request by the king's servants. He dozed briefly in the tub. Again, feelings of contentment flooded his consciousness. He dreamed of a golden light. He could vaguely see a woman's figure in the middle of the light. He could see the symmetrical lines of her body. Joe felt vaguely aroused and comforted.

A knock on his door. "King Kotutan awaits you, Lord Joe." A guard's voice startled him.

"On my way soon!" Joe jumped up and went to pick up the ABS. It seemed to shine brighter now, very luminescent. The buckle that could hold and compress the whole suit crackled with energy. Joe grasped it hesitantly. He dared not be in this strange world without the suit and therefore unprotected. There were two places in his mind now. One, the sense of peace and the golden light enveloping his consciousness. The comforting figure of a woman within the light he associated with everything supportive in his life. He could not help but think of Samantha and all she had meant to him. Two, his mortal fear, the death he had seen and wrought. The terrible danger he faced and would continue to face. His mind raced. How did he get to this? He started to perspire. *Will this be my redemption? I hope so.*

The suit—get it on, he thought, configuring the buckle around his waist. The suit expanded around the buckle and enveloped Joe's body. Boots, holsters, Vibro-Blade, sheath—all in place. Joe sighed in relief as his confidence and motivation flooded back into his consciousness.

He stepped out into the corridor and with his escort marched resolutely to the great hall. He let his helmet and shaded sunglass visor recede back into the ABS so the people could see his face.

In the great hall, he was directed to a large chair close to the king. Across from him sat three hooded figures. Gaunt men in robes. *Priests,* Joe thought.

There was a wild boar sizzling over an open firepit below a chimney. A metal cover could be rotated over the firepit. Joe was hungry, but he could see in the barbecue pit the technology of these people at work. He felt hopeful. Beautiful women came out and started pouring wine into metal cups. The three hooded figures did not drink but allowed their cups to be filled nonetheless.

Suddenly, Joe was alerted to a drumbeat, melancholy in its pace but steady. Joe sipped some of the wine. Women wore gossamer robes over tight-fitting undergarments.

King Kotutan whispered, "Look at them, Joe. If there is a God, this is what I thank him for!"

Joe smiled appreciatively and sipped some more wine. Indeed, the people within the fortress were built athletically, a testimony to the exertions required in their primitive life. Their hygiene also appeared to be up to modern standards. White shiny smiles graced their mouths, and pleasant fragrances surrounded them.

The drums sped up, and after disappearing for a few moments, the women reappeared. One woman carried a sword and shield while another a bow with arrows. The drumbeat quickened again, and another woman appeared holding a stick shaped like a rifle. Suddenly, the three voluptuous women were surrounded by men dressed like Demons and Giants.

These men were painted red and had horns as well. There were Giants appearing to be two men balanced upon one another with a large costume that hid them.

The three voluptuous women athletes quickly vanquished the Demons and Giants. The small stage was cleared. The women strutted and pranced to the applause of everyone in the hall. The drum slowed to a melancholy beat.

King Kotutan whispered, "Joe, the priests say you are a prophecy fulfilled. But watch, listen, and let me know what you think." Kotutan winked and eased back into his chair.

The three hooded figures appeared. Hoods suddenly were swept back simultaneously in one movement by all three figures.

Joe felt a sense of anticipation. A tingle rose up through his spine and lifted the hairs at the base of his skull.

The taller of the three figures began a rhythm intonation. *"Ohh, maa."*

The guy had quite a voice, Joe thought, *and he could carry a note for quite some time.*

Then there was silence. No drum. No nothing.

One of three priests came forward. He spoke in clear bass tones. "God brought us to this world and challenged our belief in him by our right and will to survive. Our survival is to be equal only to our faith. But one is meant to help us measure that faith. One will help us assemble our faith in a path to ultimate survival. A gift will be given by one to all of us and our progeny." The priest paused, and his gaze bore into Joe.

"Joe," the priest intoned, "Who are you?"

For effect, Joe donned his helmet, stood up, and explained, "I do have gifts, and I will make you prosper and have dominion over the Demons, over the hell they bring. On the morrow we must travel to my ship. I will show you the work that must be done to secure for yourselves what God commands to your keeping. But I caution all—even though I bring a path, it will not be easy. You speak of faith. Faith will be tested. The path we take now will fortify you and yours, but the act of such fortification will draw out the very devils we seek to be free of. There will be a mighty and catastrophic war, but in the end, well, we should win." Under his visor he winked in Kotutan's direction, knowing the gesture was obviously unseen.

✝ ✝ ✝

The next morning, Ataka led an escort of forty cavalry and several wagons pulled by mules out of the fortress gates. Riding in front, next to Ataka, Joe checked the ABS's GPS and picked up the location of the ACV. They were soon joined by a contingent of twenty Wildriders.

The party reached the ACV without difficulty.

Already he could see them staring at the ship, questions forming in their minds. When Ataka asked how it got here, Joe shrugged. "It flies but not very far. Usually I'm trying to conserve its fuel supply."

"Fuel?" Ataka questioned him.

"Yes," Joe said. "Like a horse needs hay and water."

Joe ended the conversation, worked the ABS controls, and linked it to the ship. The door flew open. Joe gave directions, and soon piles of his own ammo and the musket and flintlock pistol were loaded up along with powder and cap.

In the cockpit, Joe ran a scan. No Demons had been seen since his arrival and the ensuing conflict. The trade routes of the three outposts had been left alone. Still, Joe somehow felt the presence of something as he had felt it in the pit.

The ABS link was something Joe hadn't paid much attention to. He could have brought the ship to the outpost remotely, but he thought it would be too much for these primitive medieval people to see right now. Besides, he wanted them to be hungry for the knowledge he would bring them, not overconfident. Joe excused himself to secure the ship, and they left with the supplies. King Kotutan sent more knights out to meet them halfway from the ship. They arrived back at the fort without incident. Entering the gates, Joe saw everything he asked for ready and waiting. Craftsmen waited in the yard of the fortress outpost. Blacksmiths, carpenters, and scientists. Engineers were also available. All of the people who built the mechanical devices of this society were present at Joe's whim.

He took out the musket, loaded it, and fired it at a nearby target.

Dead-on!

He watched as the target splintered. It had been a large post for sword practice. Now it was cracked and splayed apart. There was a hush among those assembled.

"Joe," King Kotutan said, "give us your particulars, and my people will make these weapons. But it will take time."

"There will be time," Joe said. "But not a lot of it."

✝ ✝ ✝

The evening meal was sparse—no more feasts. Just meat, bread, and green vegetables. Wine was brought out by the kitchen staff and serving girls.

"King Kotutan, What of your practices with cattle?" Joe asked. "I believe we can make these more efficient. Much in the way we will modernize your weapons."

"*Modernize*: What is this word, Joe?" the king asked.

"It is a word that reflects how to face the future, make things better. In this case, rotating your herd through more pastures will allow better feeding of the cattle while not exhausting any single pasture. That will allow the grass to grow back more quickly in all the pastures. More yield over time, more cattle."

"I see," King Kotutan said. "A wonder we had not thought of it."

Joe discussed the growth pattern of the grass with some of the herders that King Kotutan invited to the meal at Joe's request.

Everything was shaping up. Joe thought he would be ready.

Envoys needed to be sent north and south to the other two cities once the weapons were made.

No settlement could be left vulnerable, Joe mused.

Back in his room, he prepared for sleep, assembled his belongings and ammo, and checked the ABS. He linked to the ship, using its cameras to scan. All was quiet. He dozed after a while.

Several serving women appeared and asked if he'd join King Kotutan in the bath chamber.

He did not like being out of the ABS. He felt comfortable, but still, he had doubts.

Who knew when an attack would come? he thought.

He knew their people would need time to make the weapons. And besides, they welcomed him now; their priests thought him some prophet of sorts. But Joe understood religion and how it could be turned on its head.

One bad move, he thought, *and I will be a black devil from the very same pit as those Demons.*

"Just a minute!" Joe yelled toward the door.

He busily went about compartmentalizing the ABS into a large-belted band around his waist that he could wear under his bathrobe.

He was escorted by the serving girls, three voluptuous women. They touched and caressed his shoulders and waist as he walked. They were clad in sleeveless dresses that reached midthigh—barely.

When he arrived at the bath chamber, he greeted King Kotutan and slipped off the robe. Three girls dressed like the three who had escorted him were in the bath with Kotutan, caressing and stroking him with cloths and brushes. One hovered above him out of the water while two caressed Kotutan from within the bath. The bath was a circular structure ten feet in diameter.

About the size of an institutional hot tub at an athletic club, Joe thought.

"Is there a queen?" Joe asked, impertinently given the circumstances, but oh well, he was a prophet.

"Yes," Kotutan replied, "but she chooses seclusion. She knows you are here. She prays daily that you are our salvation. Me, I need the freedom to act and secure things." His hand caressed the very round bottom of a nearby serving girl. He winked at Joe. "Your belt, Joe. Do you not wish to have more comfort?"

"This belt is my lifeline. It contains my armor. It is the conduit to my ship and my technology. You will soon see why it is so important. The battle I fought, the battles we will have to fight..."

The belt had a golden glow momentarily. Kotutan looked transfixed and then just as quickly resumed fondling the serving girl. "This technology you speak of—Is it related to the task you have assigned my craftsmen?"

"Yes, that is it," Joe answered. "The weapons they are making are a link to the advancements you need to defeat the enemy. The weapons are a start that will tip the balance. But in many ways, equal to that is the rotation of your pasturelands and the rotation of your crops as well. I will instruct you on crop rotation later. To defeat the Demons, your whole civilization must prosper. You're reaching out to the, ah, Wildriders is a part of the same strategy. Especially important." Joe paused.

King Kotutan continued following Joe's vein of thought. "Alliances," Kotutan spoke.

"Yes," Joe answered.

Kotutan mentioned how the Wildriders and his own people were the veil that protected humankind from the onslaught of unrelenting Demons. This was prophesied in our books of "Faith," just as Joe's coming.

Joe eased back into the water. He thought of his life as a mercenary on Terra. He thought of Samantha, and remembrance of her brought him a new level of security. He felt anchored in a feeling of love and warmth that had no logical explanation.

Arleosa brought the golden glow into Joe's belt. The emotions Joe felt were from a void as eternal as Heaven itself. Arleosa's feelings were reciprocated. Arleosa felt the longing in Joe for security and love. She enjoyed that as he enjoyed the security she transmitted to him.

Joe propped his head on a ledge in the pool. He let his head fall back, and the soft hands of a serving girl placed a bathing sponge under his head. He dozed off.

He awoke suddenly. The pool was empty. No serving girls present, Joe said he would be fine alone to meditate. The king had left. He looked around. No one. Then suddenly time slowed, and in walked a single woman.

"I am Kotutan's queen, or he is my king." She spoke in a melody so harmonious that Joe thought she must be singing. But she was not singing—just talking. Her face was a perfect oval of beauty. She wore a veil but was otherwise naked. She leaned down to get in the pool. She cast the veil aside. Her lips full and round, her chin strong, but her body—Joe thought she was a perfect hourglass with fully round calves and firm, ample breasts. Soft brown hair framed her face. She was all at once pretty, cute, and beautiful.

Joe raised his head with a startled expression. She slid into the pool directly across from him. Joe felt groggy, his head fuzzy from dozing off.

"My name is Saluiana, queen of this westernmost settlement. You, then, are our Messiah?" Then, smiling calmly, comfortable in her nudity, she rested her head back on a bath sponge, closing her eyes, awaiting Joe's response.

"Ah, uh," Joe found himself slow to respond. Normally, he would have answered quickly and resolutely. He paused, composing his thoughts. He found his voice finally. "I am here to help. If a helper is a Messiah, yes, but in my mind, he is just helping. If the help is useful, does it lift another into a state of security? Well…yes. Then if a whole group of people is lifted to a state of security, then perhaps a prophet has come. What would you have of me? I can help. I am a helper. I have come to raise your civilization against the attacks that will come. I have come to bring gifts already in creation. A prophet, perhaps—not. The things I bring have been known already here. You share it with each other and the Wildriders as well."

"Joe, what would that be?" Saluiana asked.

"A life shared in alliance with others," Joe heard himself say.

The belt glowed. Joe's feelings of satisfaction disappeared, and he felt a strong yearning to prove his benefit to Saluiana. She rose from the pool and put on her robe. Joe glanced at the perfect roundness of her ass, her thin waist, and her athletic legs that were so perfectly proportioned. His nature rose intensely, and he sighed and let his head fall back on the sponge. Then in an instant, Saluiana was gone.

† † †

The next morning, Joe reviewed the progress of the craftsmen and discussed how they could make rifle barrels shoot farther. He needed the blacksmith to reverse engineer the musket and create the necessary grooves in the barrel.

Joe showed the blacksmith the grooves on his own musket. The blacksmith was able to measure the grooves in Joe's barrel and make a determination on how they could be produced.

"Very important for distance accuracy!" Joe said.

He talked to several blacksmiths and made sure they conferred with each other. It was hard to get a group of people who did not do mass production to do everything the same.

Joe left them to it with a grim reminder: "Demons dead from a long distance are better for a life to be long lived."

It didn't sound too catchy, but everyone got the point.

King Kotutan urged his craftsmen on.

At Joe's instruction, they implemented the pasture and crop rotation procedures.

Things were starting to come around, but Joe was still uneasy. No Demons had been seen since his arrival.

Had he been that successful?

He almost wished for an attack to bring urgency to the rifle production.

But he had to be patient. Their people had never undertaken rifle making before. Simultaneously, he had another group of craftsmen working on a handgun.

Joe had a system of combat in mind. Rifles for long-range battle and handguns for up-close fighting. Both the rifle and handguns were to have long barrels for accuracy and range.

He thought about the queen and wondered if she realized his intentions. He wondered how she played into all of this but knew the queen was reputed to be a potential ally.

He continued to motivate and persuade Kotutan's subjects that his measures were needed.

The next day, King Kotutan was present at the breakfast table in the great hall. There were new faces at the table and also men from the crews of engineers and the agriculturist Joe had met days before.

"Joe," said the king, "these are my advisors: some you have met, others unknown to you. They have questions about the urgency of your requests. For example, the rotation of crops and pastureland changes the way we do business."

"How so and why, if I might, King Kotutan?" Joe asked, bowing in deference to the king.

A short, muscular man in the robes of a noble asked to speak. "You see, our sharing of the land changes the taxation, which means less tax paid to the king, but it also means we grow less and graze less, potentially lowering the ceiling on our growth and those monetary gains. There have been no attacks since you came."

Joe stood up, placing his helmet and visor on. Then on second thought, he yanked them off, not wanting to appear too aggressive. "I know you want a thriving economy, and now my requests seem unnecessary—no attacks currently, true. But the attacks will come again. For now, I ask that you share your resources for the common good. One with another until such time as your lands can safely be expanded once the threat is ended. But I caution you. The agricultural schemes I offer will help your growth rate as well. The weapons I have instructed you to make will give you a long-range advantage that you will need."

Joe sat down and lounged back in his chair. Just then the queen appeared with the three hooded priests. She sat beside Kotutan, and the priests stood behind her at a respectful distance.

It occurred to Joe he should get back to the ship and run some scans. Even if the people were complacent about the Demon threat, Joe would at least know the Demons' locations.

The threat was out there; he could feel it. At night, the presence that seemed to comfort him also issued a warning. Joe knew he needed to continue to act by fortifying the practices of these medieval people in a medieval world bedeviled by Demons.

† † †

Days passed. Rifled barrels were fitted to rifle stocks, and pastures were prepared for rotation. The preparations for the spring planting had begun.

At times, Joe would grow frustrated and tired of the arguments Kotutan's subjects advanced. Mostly their greed seemed to play with their minds. They wanted their individual rights so they could grow crops and raise cattle at a prosperous level. *Sell and grow prosperous* was the motto of the nobles.

Back east, there were profitable markets for their crops and cattle in the wide pastures of the frontier. King Kotutan's nobles longed to sell their crops and cattle in the East, where their profits could be magnified in the markets there.

However, now under duress and threat, Joe was asking them to share the land and integrate their crops for the common good. Joe's plan was twofold: develop better crop and cattle growth while consolidating their development in a more manageable, confined area that required all the stakeholders to unite and maintain safety.

Days turned into weeks. The pastured herds grew fatter. The spring planting showed promise. Whenever the nobles found something to contest with Joe about, the queen would appear, the three hooded priests always slightly behind her. The arguments would subside, but the subjects continued to challenge.

"Who is this, Joe Brown?" the nobles would ask. "With his dark-brown skin, challenging our way of life." The queen implicated an answer by her presence. When Joe saw the queen, he felt she was there to support him. But she also communicated to him on a level that solidified the presence growing stronger within him. At night, it urged and comforted him. The queen reassured him without speaking, making him sense his purpose was right and good despite the self-focused chattering of the nobles.

Joe ran a limited scan from his ABS and confirmed there were no nearby threats, Demons or otherwise.

King Kotutan was nervous—worried about his kingdom, worried about the productivity of the nobles who questioned him. One thing was certain: western expansion, by Long-Striders was temporarily halted.

The Wildriders came to trade and discuss the concerns they had in common with the men at the fortress. The Wildriders wore their light armor, their muscularity pressing against it. Their muddy olive-colored skin obscured some of their facial details. Never had Joe seen a tribe of men so homogeneously muscular and overly fit. They were known to have reflexes and speed that defied normality.

Even the Wildriders, with their preternatural physicality, were concerned about the Demons. The Demons had begun to creep up toward their mountain strongholds to block the Wildriders' passing.

The Wildriders had taken casualties after several great charges down narrow mountain passes to break through the Demon resistance.

Joe's scans did not reveal the conflict the Wildriders faced. The Wildriders agreed to escort Joe to his ship if he could provide aid to their encampment. Joe would help them and in turn gain their support. They had invaluable familiarity with the surrounding area. Joe slept on everything and said he'd be ready to go at first light. Joe rested peacefully. He thought of his mother, then Samantha. He felt a sense of security he had never known in the past before the pit.

In the morning, the Wildriders waited in the yard. The queen mysteriously came to bid Joe support, appearing in his room in a threadbare dress hemmed above the knee. If Samantha had been wearing it, she would have called it a minidress. The queen had his attention, in any event.

"Be careful, Joe," she whispered.

The day was gray, and the clouds hung low in the western sky. Joe was up sipping his coffee. *Stimulating*, Joe thought as he felt the invigorating rush of the coffee quicken within him.

Joe did a mental review. Never one for checklists, he made mental notes with the system within the ABS. *But was it that or something else?* Joe did remember the ABS having some memory-supporting feature, but he had not tapped into it, had he? He did not think he had. No, he had not.

"Joe!" King Kotutan announced from outside his door.

The king had come every morning since Joe's arrival to greet him and start the mighty savior on his day.

Today the queen arrived with him as well. Joe noted the queen was dressed more regally in long, flowing gowns. She must have slipped in to see him earlier only to reappear now with the king.

Out on the parade drill grounds, the craftsmen waited. The soldiers guarding the gates had rifles as well as bows. Many of them looked down the sights of their rifles, assessing their aim.

The Wildriders were present as well. Joe recognized some from the battle when he had first arrived. There were twenty Wildriders on muscular horses. Joe could see dried blood from wounds suffered by the men and horses. Most of the blood had been washed off, but faint, telltale red smears were still visible. The Wildriders wore leather harnesses and shields; some warriors had leather helmets adorned with feathers. They carried bow and lances attached to their saddle harnesses.

Ataka stood on the parade drill grounds as well, ready to mount. He wore leather armor and carried a long carbine and pistol in a holster at his belt. Joe smiled approvingly. Already the culture of the gun was making itself known.

Joe spoke up. "Is that the way you carry your short gun?"

"Yes," Ataka replied, understanding Joe's intent. "In a holster or sheath, just like my sword."

Ah, they catch on fast, Joe thought. He donned his helmet and waited for the king to grace their pending journey.

✝ ✝ ✝

God seemed frustrated, but Arleosa was not the least bit perturbed.

"Already they all have guns!" he boomed.

"Not all, Your Eminence," Arleosa chimed in. "They have what their Messiah has brought to share with them. Sharing being so important to the consciousness and spiritual growth of the humans."

God looked cross. "I had hoped these primitive medieval people still had a chance, but instead you bring this assassin to their world, and now they can become more aggressive!" God looked accusingly at Arleosa.

"It is good, my Lord. Before they can realize their true kinship, they must struggle and unite. It is happening already. Joe Brown gathers them to pool their resources to create a unified defense against the Devil's minions." As a reminder she added, "*Our* Devil, the onetime Angel, Satan."

God fumed. His aura became a hot red, and Arleosa chose to withdraw from him.

"Indeed, some things have been accomplished. The humans join together in greater cooperation to support each other," God acquiesced. "But the carnage—How will it make them understand?"

Arleosa broke in. "Because, oh Great Almighty, they will understand and know, as will Satan, the carnage is too great. The carnage will be so great even Satan will abandon his revenge."

"But that should have happened before, and it didn't," God challenged.

"Joe Brown was not your instrument before, my Lord," Arleosa countered. "I am with him; he will understand what no human has ever understood, save Christ."

"That being?" God asked.

Arleosa responded, "War is hell, making both man and Angel pray for Heaven. Even Satan will save his pride and be with us." Arleosa sighed. "I will have Satan enveloped in such a quandary he will realize his vanity is folly."

Bladeswift was among the twenty Wildriders who joined Joe at the gate that morning.

Joe observed Bladeswift and his mount. He noted his scarred face and leather armor with multiple slash marks in it. Bladeswift's arms bulged with muscle. He wore a leather helmet adorned with several large raptor plumes. He wore kneepads and leather plates guarding the insteps of both feet. Joe guessed he stood about five foot two. This made his mount seem larger. His mount was a gray destrier with a saddle harness and a shield attached to the left front of its chest. The horse, too, was scarred, and its tail was bobbed short. It had a feral look, and its gray color contrasted with the muddy olive-green color of Bladeswift.

This fearsome warrior also carried a bow, arrows, and a lance. Joe thought, *this man is a lot like me.*

Ataka joined the men at the gate with twenty more riders of King Kotutan's host. The knights wore full armor of chain mail, heavy shields, and lances. Ataka carried a long rifle and pistol to try out in actual combat. Forty men plus Joe ready for battle, a formidable crew.

Joe raised his visor, and before he left, he rode quickly to King Kotutan. Joe handed a parchment to Kotutan.

"I almost forgot this; it is especially important. It details a large gun called a cannon. It is like the rifles you made. It fires a long-range charge that will blow up and kill enemies. If the men start on it, I will oversee its completion when I return."

"Done!" King Kotutan responded.

The gates opened, and Joe, Ataka, and Bladeswift led the group out. Saluiana waved from the ramparts with a white handkerchief, smiling languidly, looking at Joe.

Strategy. Where was that voice, that presence, to guide him? Joe thought it had momentarily left him, but now he sensed a plan forming. More to the point, he felt the gaps in his understanding being filled by Arleosa. He had not felt this enlightened since he left the pit. He must get to the ACV to pick up gear before riding up to the mountain passes.

Bladeswift spoke, reminding Joe of the urgency of their situation. "My village is poorly defended. The women and children are vulnerable. My wives and my own children are there. We need your support in protecting our village."

Joe told the men it was important to first go to the ACV. He explained he would collect ammunition and explosives and that he needed to scan the area for enemies.

King Kotutan said the Giants dwelled far to the northwest and Joe should be wary of them joining the Demons in the battle.

The Demons had been slowly growing in the area and had increased their attacks on trade routes.

While riding to the ACV, Joe counseled with Ataka and Bladeswift, trying to glean as much from their perspectives as possible.

The party of about forty arrived at the ACV without incident. They made camp and formed a perimeter around the ACV. Though the ACV was covered by brush and other vegetation, it still operated well. When Joe opened it, he grabbed munitions and explosives.

Joe ran a scan from the ship that detected quiet in the general area. The scan revealed wildlife, including predators and deer and other herbivores in the area. He pressed the scan further, looked out, called to Ataka and Bladeswift to enter the ACV ship, and explained what he was doing. He arced the scan toward the plateau of Bladeswift's village. There massed all around it were red specks. He explained to them that the red specks surrounding the plateau could only be Demons.

"See here," Joe said, "massing all around the plateau. I've set my instruments to pick up their heat signatures. Always hot. They are very distinctive. Our time is short."

Bladeswift was worried. "My people can hold for a while. Riding hard, we can make the village by afternoon tomorrow."

"Yes," Joe agreed, "we cannot have them waiting much longer."

Joe asked them which path would be best for reaching the village and attacking the Demons. Bladeswift outlined several routes.

After discussion, it was decided Ataka and his heavily armed knights would blast a hole behind the Demons and surge up the plateau through their resistance. Joe would ride support through the passes, dismount, and move up through brush and trees to provide direct aid to the villagers.

Joe looked around the ACV to see what else would be helpful. He picked up surgical supplies to heal puncture wounds and to stimulate consciousness in fallen comrades. Joe added foil blankets to his battle pack.

Joe went out of the ACV, followed by Bladeswift and Ataka. He would sleep under the stars with these men he intended to fight with and for. He listened to the small talk as he began to doze off. Bladeswift worried about his wives and children, who were hidden in mountain passes above the plateau. He talked of having a more peaceful life: less war, more hunting and lovemaking. Ataka too longed for less fighting and a chance to have a normal routine, to have a wife and family. The risks were innumerable, Ataka said. And he felt his life was stuck in the conflicts, erupting with Demons, Giants, and other nightmare creatures. He wanted to settle down. Many of the men had similar aspirations and wished they would return alive.

Finally, Joe fell asleep. His consciousness was seized, by Arleosa as soon as deep sleep enveloped it. The soft feminine voice he heard before, this presence, was with Joe again. This time stronger than ever before. He sat up momentarily then rolled over and went to sleep. The ACV's sentry scans would alert them to intruders. Joe doubted the other men would trust the sentry scans, but he did, and he fell back asleep again.

He heard a voice calling out to him. It was the essence of a mother calling to comfort a child. A golden radiance radiated toward Joe who could feel it bathing him in golden light. The certainty of purpose he usually felt enveloped him once again. He was on the trail of Demons. Here in the forest, he was exposed but felt as secure as if he were in his bed at home. Nothing would touch him save the golden light.

A voice whispered, "Be well, help them, no need to worry, Joe. I'm always with you. I will guide your actions. As you have chosen a path of redemption."

Joe's apprehension melted away. Shouldn't he be afraid? There was a small corner of his humanity that shivered in recognition of the enormity of all that had happened to him. He stood on another world. Sure, interplanetary travel was common. But the ACV had never been used as a tool in that capacity.

How would I even know I could do this?

Now he was ready to arm a force of men in a global frontier conflict and forever change their culture through science and engineering.

Joe awoke with a start. It was as though he had never been sleeping. But he was rested and ready, a sense of purpose and resolute confidence flowing in him. It was like an injection.

Bladeswift, who had been worried and doubtful about his village's safety, was uplifted and ready to go. Ataka, who was war weary, straightened and wore his armor proudly.

Joe jumped into the ACV to quickly gulp down a couple of cups of coffee. He had set a timer to make the coffee the night before. A twenty-five-mile ride to the base of the plateau where the village sat awaited them. Joe sealed the ACV, strapped on his extra munitions, and was ready. They rode in a beat, a rhythm flowing from the hooves of the horses pounding the ground below them. Joe had never seen horses like these, big destriers, riding long and hard. The Wildriders, moving ahead, scouted at a great speed while still reading the trail ahead. No signs of Demons yet.

Suddenly the trail opened to a long, flat plain, and each of the forty riders urged their horse to greater speed.

Joe looked like a great futuristic knight from a space-age chess game. His visor set and the great .50-caliber sniper rifle rested across his back. He also carried a high-powered semiauto pistol and an assault rifle. The Vibro-Blade was attached to his waist. Soon they were at forty miles an hour. Joe could see the top of the plateau after riding for thirty minutes. At forty-five minutes, he could see the whole plateau, base to top, which was several miles above.

A battle plan continued forming in Joe's head.

As he neared the plateau base, he could see Demons and Giants parking siege engines. Much of the brush and trees above the base of the plateau were on fire. The Demons intended to burn down the growth around the perimeter of the village. Bladeswift could see the flames moving gradually higher. Inevitably they would reach his village, creating fear and chaos throughout. Then eventually, the Wildrider villagers would be exposed to attack. Bladeswift looked despairing and sad.

Joe's plan leaped forward in his mind like a whisper from somewhere in the depths of his consciousness.

"Bladeswift, take your twenty," Joe yelled. "Can you find a way to the village? If you can, we will make a heavy attack up the main trail, distract the Demons and Giants, and take down the siege engines that are burning down everything."

In a minute, the Wildriders were flanking the Demons, and Bladeswift powdered his weapon. There was a muzzle flash as he rode at a dead gallop.

Kaboom!

A Giant in midpull of a siege catapult crumpled to his knees. A Demon, who was preparing to put a flaming charge of wood and balled-up straw into the catapult cup, missed and dropped the charge of flaming wood and straw.

There was confusion in the line of Demons and Giants. About thirty started to move away from the flaming embers. In a split second, Bladeswift and his Wildriders moved into single file, quickly filling the gap and firing arrows, securing a path and ripping it wide by the upward trail. Several Giants and Demons began to move from the plateau base perimeter, attempting to fill the gap ripped open by Bladeswift.

There was a thunderous clap as Joe shot a Giant trying to set up another flaming catapult charge.

A wave of Demons quickly followed behind Bladeswift and his riders. They were on foot, but some began to flutter upward on leatherlike wings. Joe quickly hammered a few shots, felling the airborne Demons.

"Follow the Wildriders!" Joe bellowed.

Ataka and his knights charged up the narrow trail behind the Demons and Giants. The Giants and Demons heard the clamoring and clanging of leather and armor coming up from their rear. Thr Giants turned toward the noise and were met by knights who hacked and stabbed with their broadswords. In the meantime, Wildriders had spread through the woods, darting uphill through old deer paths and unseen horse trails. Their horses, nimble as unicorns, disappeared into the paths rising toward the village.

Joe could see partly through the trees and up toward the plateau top, several hundred meters above. Joe slung the great .50-caliber sniper rifle and pulled his Vibro-Blade. It hummed, and the familiar chemical smell of ozone filled the air. Joe swung behind a line of Giants running up the narrow trail. Joe felt as though he was reaching into the mind of his horse; it followed his needs so closely. Maneuvering up the trail diagonally to give him an angle, he slammed the Vibro-Blade heavily across the back of the nearest Giant. Falling heavily, the Giant swayed off the trail, leaving Joe's path clear. Joe could see from his peripheral vision the Giant writhing in pain. Joe sped forward and sweat flicked off his horse's flanks and chest. Now he, like the Wildriders, swung into the woods, moving toward the top of the plateau. He was hoping to cut off the upward surge of the Giants and Demons from reaching Bladeswift's village.

Joe couldn't see any one of his comrades. Ataka was long gone, and Bladeswift must have been close to his village. On the trail above Joe, there was a line of Giants, Demons, and a few dead bodies from each species. In a moment, every Demon and Giant turned their head collectively to face Joe.

"Shit," Joe muttered to himself. He stowed the Vibro-Blade and pulled out two high-powered pistols.

"By the numbers, you bastards!" Joe yelled. "I've got ninety-nine problems, but this trail ain't one!"

A Giant with matted fur and a row of bones protecting its torso lumbered toward Joe, who spurred his horse forward. He had no spurs, but he squeezed his heels back on the horse's flanks. His horse felt and sensed Joe's intent. Pointing both barrels forward, Joe started firing.

Boom!

A heavy shot tore and sheared away part of the bone vest. It fragmented as the shot slammed into the Giant's chest. The Giant staggered back, then lurched forward, his fetid breath within smelling range of Joe's nose.

Joe recoiled and slammed the butt of his pistol into the Giant's nose. Blood dripped profusely as the Giant staggered backward. Joe aimed and blasted the Giant right above the bloody nose. He fell backward and off the trail. Joe galloped forward, both pistols ready. His horse was synced to his intent. He dropped the reins and used his feet and knees to direct the big destrier up the hill.

Joe yelled out, "Where you at?" hoping to give the illusion of numbers and let any allies in the area know his location. A Demon glided between the trees down toward the trail, almost on top of Joe. Joe felt his shadow falling as much as saw it. Reaching up to guard himself, he felt talons rake across his forearm and head, grazing through the surface of the ABS. Joe looked to the sky and found himself lying on his back. The Demon floated down seeking to rip at Joe's torso with the claws on his feet. Joe rolled off the trail, still holding the pistols.

Kapow, kapow!

The Demon fell back, the left side of his chest a bloody ruin. Joe looked back for his horse. The large destrier was rearing and kicked a Giant in the chest, sending him toppling backward down the trail.

Joe jumped and spun toward his horse, remounted, and galloped up the hill again. There was enemies ahead and behind.

He screamed, "Come on!"

He heard a reply: "I am here."

It was his own mind. Or was it? Even with a plan he was now alone, but the voice assured him he was not. With a pause in the action, he had time to doubt the outcome; he had time to feel his vulnerability.

"I am here," he heard again, and he started to redouble his efforts. He started to feel a little relieved, though he did not understand why, as his situation was not resolved.

The Giants were all that was left between Joe and the top of the plateau. They had similar builds and walked ponderously, grunting, and sweating in the heat of the day.

Joe kept riding and then abruptly hopped off his horse. He unslung the Vibro-Blade and crept along. The horse understood his intent. It lingered not far below him on the trail, following him. Joe silently crept forward until he had reached the nearest Giant. The Giant's own noise in trampling up the trail masked Joe's approach. Joe slammed the Vibro-Blade viciously against the Giant, causing him to fall in a heap; dead, Joe sensed.

He slid to the side behind a tree, then quickly remounted. Pushing up the hill, he expected opposition. He fired several times from the handguns, putting well-placed shots in two Giants one hundred meters above him on the trail. In spite of the wound, one Giant turned and swung an axe at Joe, who used the armored forearm of the ABS to fend it off with a quick block followed by another shot to the Giant's body. The Giant fell and spasmed on the ground before becoming still. Its matted furs and various clubs strung to its harness now covered with leaking blood.

Joe looked up and saw Bladeswift's village. There were sounds of combat ahead: metal clanging and arrows slamming into armored bodies. A ring of knights surrounded the village. Ataka sat on his horse in view of the Demons, who ringed the circle of knights. Ataka would charge out of the circle of knights and slam his broadsword down on the head of a Demon, then swing back into the circle. Once the knights reloaded their carbines, they would fire a volley, sending a Giant or Demon reeling backward, writhing in pain or stilling in death. There were only a few Demons and Giants left, forty circling the village. Bladeswift was nowhere to be seen.

Ataka could not see Joe coming, but he needed no help as his battle plan unfolded. Ataka fired a shot into the line of the Demon attack. Then with three knights, he rode out and charged the Demon line that circled the village. The knights, heavily armored, used their swords to make a hole in the lines of the Demons circling the village. The village itself offered little cover. The knights crouched behind boulders and a makeshift corral the Wildriders used to contain their horses.

The knights held the line. The village was empty as far as Joe could see. Then he understood. Bladeswift had emptied his village, taking the women and children away. Running hard, Joe was only able to use the ABS for a partial scan of the village. There seemed to be a few dead near the huts. Joe ran faster to join the conflict, which remained a few hundred meters away. He could see several bodies as he approached—seven women and three children. There were warriors, knights, and Wildriders among the dead as well.

Joe felt the familiar glow within him: comfort during chaos. The golden warmth enveloped him. He picked up the pace, covering the remaining distance in miraculous speed thanks to the ABS and the golden warmth that seemed to empower him.

He thought he heard a whisper, "Joe." It sounded like Samantha, but she was not there.

Joe turned away from the village as soon as he reached the outer ring of defenders regrouping, loading their rifles. He pivoted on a crisp cut and ran toward a burly Giant rushing toward Ataka, who bravely sat reloading on horseback. The Giant was running hard. Sweat dripped from his brow, his matted fur stank, and Joe could see dark shadows under his arms as he hefted a spiked club overhead in preparation to stamp it on Ataka's head. As Joe approached, he witnessed Ataka slide his horse to the side. Ataka prepared to use the rifle. Joe, running with both pistols, slid to the ground, letting his momentum carry him almost under the Giant, who now attempted to adjust his momentum and slam the club down on Joe.

Bam! Bam!

Two shots slammed into the groin and lower abdomen of the Giant, who writhed in pain. Joe rolled forward under the staggering legs of the Giant to see his comrades, four Demons and three more Giants, rushing toward him. As he raised his two pistols, gunfire cracked. The Giants and Demons fell back, bleeding and stumbling. Two fell silent; two Demons and a Giant were wounded but seemed to have had enough. They lumbered back to a line of trees across from the village. Joe holstered the pistols and brought out the Vibro-Blade. He whistled, and his mount came up behind him. Mounting, he pursued the remaining enemies.

Joe quickly cornered the remaining enemies beyond the tree line. While Ataka and the knights held the village, Joe functioned as a knight on a chessboard, taking the right angles needed to seek and destroy the enemy. From horseback, Joe swept around the enemy with great speed, slamming the Vibro-Blade down on the breastbone and head of several remaining Demons. He swung back to the village after riding down all the Demons or Giants he could find.

Once back in the village, he asked about the preceding events.

Ataka explained. "When we arrived, a few of the Wildriders were covering the trail of their women and children, firing arrows and charging from horseback. A battle took place here just as Bladeswift arrived. The village was surrounded, by Demons when we got the call for aid. Twelve of the village women and children were killed in the early hours of the attack. Finally, Bladeswift was able to get the rest out. But now he mourns his dead, and the security they knew is gone. He declared this great evil must be silenced forever!"

Joe felt overwhelmed. *How is that going to work?* he thought. *This is going to be hard. Do I even know how to conclude this? But they are right!*

"Yes," Joe responded, "the end must come, and we must inform King Kotutan that the plan must be executed as I have enumerated it. We will arm everyone and move forward to wipe the Giants and Demons out where they live."

He thought to himself, *I don't quite know how.* Joe made a silent prayer, hoping the presence that hovered so close would have an answer.

"Where has Bladeswift gone?" Joe asked.

Ataka replied, "They have gone to the next plateau. They will unite with their tribesmen and meet us on the open plains west of here, hoping to locate the civilization that produces the Demons. The Giants are further in the wilderness. But they are only the teeth of the jaw. 'Break the jaw, and the teeth will have no place to lodge,' Bladeswift has said."

Joe said, "Then we resupply here. How do we let King Kotutan know our plans?"

Ataka was not sure, "I don't know, Joe. But we have to fight our way down to the plains." He paused. "Do you have a way to get word back to the king?"

Me? Joe thought. *This is beginning to be a lot of responsibility.*

"We don't have to know right now, but we will need to leave in the morning," Ataka said. "We will bury Bladeswift's people and our own, then post guards, gather provisions, and ride to the western plains if you are in agreement, Joe."

"Yes," Joe responded.

The sun set, and Joe took off his helmet and sat by the fire. He had helped bury some of Bladeswift's tribesmen and a few knights. Ataka and his men also sat by the fire. Joe knew battle, but now he was the focal point of the storm. He felt pressure he had never known before. Sitting by the village with the others seemed to help.

The village fireplace accommodated a large, assembled group. Fur skins for bedding were placed all around the fireplace in an uneven circle.

Joe rolled back on the skins and imagined the life of the villagers before the Demons arrived to attack the land. He fell asleep and dreamed. Joe slept deeply and despite the potential danger that lay all around them. Arleosa spoke directly to Joe as she never had, infusing his dreams with the purpose she hoped for him. She enumerated what role his allies would play. Arleosa influenced and urged Joe to think of the queen as an ally, because she would help the king understand what must be done. Arleosa showed Joe her human form, comely and magnificent, gaining his full attention. She knew Joe would need to be galvanized.

Joe dreamed of his past; throughout his life, in play and then again in conflict, Joe was someone people could depend on. Joe woke up suddenly. He could hear the horses being tethered, men gathering armor and provisions. He donned his helmet and stretched briefly. Checking his gear, he went to mount his horse.

"Ataka?" he asked.

Ataka, already mounted, rode over to where Joe stood.

Joe walked out from the village sleeping area where the fire began to burn out.

Ataka said, "Joe, we have a decision to make. The enemy could be ready to raze our fortress. Bladeswift's people are scattered around the base of this plateau, hiding and waiting. How can we take care of both needs?"

Joe swung into the saddle and paused briefly. "Where exactly will Bladeswift be, Ataka?"

"Hiding with his people. They will be somewhere close." The answer had the ring of certainty.

"Yes, we do have a decision to make. You go to King Kotutan and get me started on the tracking of Bladeswift's people."

"I will send you with the remaining villager. She can show you the way." Ataka pointed to the burial ground fifty meters away. There stood the last villager, somehow alive and seemingly unhurt. She was burying those of her relatives who did not survive the attack.

She stood five feet, one inch tall and was wrapped in furs from head to toe.

"That is Sika," Ataka announced. "She will show you the way to find the villagers and Bladeswift, hopefully."

"Yes, good," Joe said, in his mind questioning how this would work.

Sika came toward them, buckling a sword to her waist. She picked up an armored leather vest and strapped it on over her furs. From a harness above her ample backside, she pulled out a feathered leather helmet of dragon scale and placed it on her head. The helmet had a purple plume. Next, she grabbed a shield that had rested against the shovel used to bury the fallen villagers and knights. Her mud-green skin was barely visible under the helmet. She walked lightly and appeared to be aware of everything around her, eyes darting here and there to the tree line where danger might present itself.

Joe had been wondering how this would work, but now he thought perhaps he knew.

Ataka announced as Sika approached, "Sika is a shield-carrier sister to all warriors, a princess of the Wildriders."

Joe nodded respectfully, and Sika offered her hand in acknowledgment. Joe shook it firmly, one simple downward motion and no more.

"Well met," he managed to say.

"Hatanai," she yelled, and a large golden-brown quarter horse appeared.

The horse had a leather harness with a bow and quiver of arrows attached to it. A quick flicker of movement, and Joe saw her on the horse as if she had teleported. Joe noticed the tone of her muscles when her skin peeked out from under the furs. Triceps, biceps, and shoulders hinted at Sika's strength. Her thighs and calves showed the muscular symmetry of a sprinter.

Joe called to his horse and, not wanting to be outdone, leaped and straddled the saddle like a high jumper. He caught his leg in the mane of his horse, landing in the saddle, nonetheless.

Sika laughed, as did Ataka. A moment later, all who were watching joined in the laughter, Joe included.

Ataka said, "We will ride straight down the way we came. They will not expect that. We will kill as many Demons as bar our path and then drive hard for the fortress. Sika will track and take you wherever you need. Take care of her, and believe me, you will be taken care of." With that, Ataka and the rest rode full gallop down the trail.

Joe saw five Demons coming up the hill onto the plateau, shiny horns glinting in the light of the fast-rising eastern sun.

Kablam!

Ataka fired, and a set of shiny horns fell out of sight.

"Follow me," Sika commanded.

Joe could see a single braid falling below her helmet. They took off west at great speed, the village disappearing behind them as they sped down from the edge of the plateau.

"Where will they go?" Joe asked breathlessly as the wind rushed against his helmet. Leaves and dust kicked up by Sika's horse cascaded around Joe's visor.

No harm, Joe thought. *I am protected physically and spiritually.*

They rode down a winding path between giant oak trees and mesquite scrub brush. Sika knocked an arrow so fast Joe could barely discern her intent.

Fwitt!

Joe needed the clarity of the visor to follow the arrow's path. The armored battle suit allowed him to track anything he locked onto.

"Bwaahh." The Giant cried out and reeled backward with an arrow in his forehead but not before launching an axe toward Sika.

As the axe reached her, she tucked the bow down and leaned, brushing her right forearm into the side of the axe blade, knocking it away.

"Trust me. I will show you the way," Sika said

Joe could see Sika's forearms were covered in scaly dragon-skin gauntlets. Sika's horse charged at breakneck speed down the hill as though possessed.

Joe followed as closely as he could. Sika's horse had long, nimble legs that allowed it to move, while his destrier was laboring under Joe's weight.

Sika sensed Joe's plight, slowed, and brought her horse to a bouncy trot. Sika took off from the trail and began to circle laterally, picking up a sign, moving up the plateau and then down again.

Joe tuned his ABS's sensory system to his awareness of the tracks, which were barely visible amid the roots and trampled shrubs. Scrub brush obscured the trail of both horse and human footprints in the ground.

Sika saw the ground with an eye so quick that even on horseback going at high speed she knew how to follow the trail.

Joe followed as best he could, adjusting the armored body suit to scan for enemies who might be present.

Sika and Joe were close to the bottom of the plateau. Joe changed magazines in his pistols. He reloaded the sniper rifle. He checked his helmet. He was ready for anything.

Finally, Joe and Sika doubled back around the bottom third of the plateau. There was a small clearing of mostly grass and green patches of scrub brush. Joe could see the remainder of a herd of horses just above the clearing.

Bladeswift rose out of a scrub-covered hole in the ground. He was so well camouflaged that Joe did not immediately see him. He was bloody from half a dozen cuts; Joe mused some of the blood probably belonged to other creatures.

Sika motioned Joe to dismount as she patted her horse's rump. It joined the herd above the clearing. Joe did the same, and his horse followed suit.

Joe and Sika greeted Bladeswift happily. Bladeswift hugged both in turn. A great wave of relief passed over his face.

"I have sent about fifty warriors to clear the path below," he stated. "They will wait in ambush until the force that pursues us gets moving up the plateau. Then they will strike!"

Joe looked at the clearing, which was about the size of half a football field but oval in shape. There were women and children rising from camouflage holes in the ground. Their olive, mud-green skin and clothing blending into the environment. Joe had trouble tracking them.

What manner of camouflage is this? he mused.

Bladeswift continued, "When the battle starts, as surely it will, my plan is to slip our women and children past the conflict and let the warriors use stealth as much as possible. But a distraction will be needed to draw away any Demons and Giants who pursue the women and children, who will be heavily guarded but still vulnerable. Many of my men will have to fight on foot using stealth. Not our choice but we must get all the children and women out on all the horses we have!" Sadness gripped his face once again.

Joe offered, "I can create a distraction of such fury all your enemies will want to kill me!"

"No, Joe. I need you and Sika to help bring the women and children to safety. However, my plan does call for you to first spring the ambush and then head back here to protect my tribesmen. Is that asking too much?"

"No," Joe countered, "let me slam the jaw down hard on the ambush and be back here quickly."

Sika stated, "We have fought the Giants and Demons for years off and on. They always sought to claim our mountain homes. They cannot bear to hold back. They envy what we have. They will come lumbering up the trail when hunger and impatience get the best of them. The herd of horses represent food to them."

Joe asked, "How did all this come to be? Where I am from, we encountered the Demons but not Giants. The Demons were born from a great cataclysm on my home. Prior to the incident, they were only a figment of myth, religion, and evil stories."

Bladeswift said, "Joe, the Giants have always been here. An ancient race made in a halfhearted effort to ruin the world of men. Always seeking to have what men have but too brutish to sustain a society that can thrive. It is almost as though God played a cruel trick on them, letting them prosper, but at some point, their savagery brought their society down from within."

Sika continued the story. "The Demons came out of the earth. They have been here longer than the Giants. They are aimless, always ravaging humankind, sometimes fighting each other, but they were never a consistent threat—until now. It is almost as though God was angry at the Giants and sent the Demons to punish them and us."

"How did you come upon this understanding?" Joe asked.

"Our seers can sometimes get a glimpse of the heavens, Joe." Sika responded.

Abruptly, Bladeswift asked for silence. Running up the plateau toward them was a Wildrider. He wore naught but a loincloth and carried a sword as long as he was tall. As he ran, he swung the sword into the sheath on his back.

"One of the scouts has come," Bladeswift eagerly announced. "This must be our chance."

The scout picked up speed. He was about five feet two, the average height of a Wildrider, but Joe was not used to seeing them on foot. The scout was a blur. His ankle-high moccasins seemed to barely touch the ground. He looked to have perfect symmetry of physique and the balanced muscularity of a modern sprinter. His hands free of the sword, arms pumping fluidly and picking up speed, he reached them quickly. He addressed Bladeswift, who waited expectantly for him.

"The Giants and Demons push up the hill, my chief. They have a few winged Demons who may have seen the horse herd. They will be focused on the horses. They are coming!"

Bladeswift whistled. Out of the scrub brush and high grass came scores of women and children dressed in buckskin. They carried sacks slung on their backs that Joe guessed carried provisions. Some had bows, quivers of arrows, and short swords.

They are a beautiful people, Joe thought. *So reminiscent of the Aboriginal Plains people, warriors of antiquity I know of.*

"Joe," Bladeswift said urgently now, "our plan is to hit the Giants and Demons while the women and our children all ride out and escape, but we must charge down the hill and hit them fast and hard. You and Sika alone will have horses. We will follow as fast as we can to bring support. As soon as we are past them, we will bear hard left and head to the next plateau, where we will meet with the women and children. From there we can ride double. You and Sika will be hammer and shield. Strike quickly and have no remorse!" Joe checked his pistols and mounted his black destrier. Sika reined up next to him, nocking an arrow in her bow and then lightly touching her sword.

She turned to Joe. "We have lost many brave people to this enemy: women, children, and warriors. Make every shot count, Joe."

Joe had the pistols ready. He would mount a charge that would make the Demons cringe and Giants turn back, or so he hoped. "Got it," he uttered. "Let's do it."

"One more thing, Joe," Bladeswift said. "I have men in the trees. Don't look for them, but when you hear my whistle, bear left through the gorge near the bottom of the plateau. We will all rendezvous with the women and children."

The trees are thickest at the plateau's base, Joe thought. *What did Bladeswift mean?*

Joe and Sika raced down the hill at breakneck speed. As the trail opened, the Wildriders ran on foot behind Joe and Sika. Bladeswift led them. He carried a great sword almost as long as he was tall.

Joe saw the first Demon carrying a shield and pitchfork.

Like some image from an ancient religious book, he thought, *meant to scare children into conformity.*

He leaned forward.

Kapow!

Joe planted a shot between the horns on the Demon's head. He reeled backward down the trail.

More Demons appeared on the trail, blocking Joe and Sika's path.

Sika sent two arrows out quickly, catching one Demon in the thigh and another in the neck. One Demon perished on the spot. The second struggled to stand. After drawing her sword, Sika slashed down heavily on the struggling Demon. Joe witnessed his head roll down the trail.

Demons and Giants, Joe thought, *oh my!*

The Giants were coming up the trail, eight feet of misbegotten height and bulky corresponding mass. They were slow, dumb, and dangerous, with murderous intent. According to Sika, they readily ate human flesh.

Two Giants charged at Sika, carrying spiked clubs. Sika guided her horse to the edge of the narrow trail, barely allowing her room to avoid the descending club of one of the Giants. She made a backhand slash of her blade, catching the Giant in the neck, carving a deep gash that spurted purplish blood.

Joe sped forward and shot the second Giant in the heart at close range as he lurched toward Sika. The Giant's face was transfixed in death as he tripped and slammed backward onto the trail.

Joe and Sika galloped down to the heavily forested tree line. The resistance of Giants and Demons thickened. Bladeswift and his runners reached the tree line just as Joe and Sika blended into the forest.

Bladeswift and his warriors used the trees and shrubs for cover, darting out onto the trail just long enough to shoot an arrow at a Demon or slash a Giant's hamstring before retreating.

Bladeswift whistled a warning.

"Sika!" Joe yelled out.

Her horse stumbled momentarily. She reined the horse to the left as two Demons rushed to hack her down. Her arms worked furiously as she hefted the sword in a two-fisted blow. Her forearms and triceps bulged against the buckskin she wore.

Joe quickly placed a shot into one Demon's torso, and he sagged away from Sika.

Bladeswift moved forward and off the trail to his left. Lumbering forward was a Giant in a horned helmet, something Joe had not seen before. He carried a rusty machete. Chain mail covered the torso, and he had leather shin guards and thick leather kneecaps. He sought to spring toward Sika, who was still building forward momentum as her horse stepped over the bodies of the two Giants she and Joe had killed.

Joe spurred his horse forward to aid Sika. Bladeswift stepped onto the trail again, directly at a Giant's side. Mercilessly, he swung a two-handed blow with his sword.

Joe moved forward to give aid. The thought of a home run hit entered his mind.

Bladeswift's sword cut deep into the side of the Giant's right knee, nearly severing the lower leg. The Giant stumbled forward. Another Giant approached before Bladeswift could kill the first.

Joe reeled off two shots in an attempt to finish Bladeswift's handiwork, killing the Giant with the nearly severed leg. The second Giant stumbled momentarily, bleeding from his shoulder, but continued forward, trying to reach Sika.

Sika gained the time she needed. Suddenly, as if by magic, her bow was in her hand, and an arrow was nocked, drawn back, and released in one motion.

Phwwp!

The arrow stuck the Giant in the upper chest. But the Giant kept coming. Joe was charging down the trail, the Vibro-Blade in his hand. He rammed his sizzling blade into the head of the Giant. Bladeswift leaped out from the trail, slamming his shoulder into the Giant's chest. He landed, stepped back, and drove his blade up into the Giant's abdomen before he could right himself.

Suddenly, out of the forest flew balls of flame slamming and bursting into explosions of fire on the trail. The remaining Giants fell back lest they get burned. One of Bladeswift's men was burned. He muffled a scream and jumped out of the burning bushes and onto the trail. Sika offered her hand, and he leaped onto the back of her horse.

Bladeswift commanded, "Abandon the charge, back the other way!"

"Follow me!" Sika yelled out to Joe.

Joe and Sika rode into the brush. The horses slowed but still moved quickly. Joe followed Sika, who picked her way to a barely hidden path that ran parallel to the base of the plateau.

The Demons were giving chase on the edge of the trail behind Joe and Sika. Ten Wildriders descended from the trees. They shot arrows at the Demons as they jumped downward limb to limb. Accurate arrows protruded from the necks, chests, and heads of several Demons.

The Demons had given chase, but the tree descending Wildriders flanked them as Joe and Sika took the path. The Wildriders sent a storm of arrows blocking the approaching Demons and killing or wounding many of them. After their assault, they quickly ran down the path behind Joe and Sika.

Suddenly Sika took a sharp downward turn.

"Now!" she yelled. "Fast, very fast!"

Joe spurred his horse. The brush was yielding to the grasses of the plains. They were nearing the bottom of the plateau and flat ground. Behind them came Bladeswift and the Wildrider warriors. The ground gradually flattened but looming 150 meters away was a horde of Demons and several Giants mounting catapults with flaming balls of tar and wood. Sika dropped her rider so he could join the other Wildriders. Joe eased his horse's gallop. He unslung the .50-caliber sniper rifle and sighted the pulley used to release the fireball. A Giant with prongs was fitting the already-burning tar ball onto the catapult.

Joe reined his horse to a walk. He whispered, "Sika."

"What, Joe?" she said.

Kaboom.

His shot hit the Giant in the head. The Giant tumbled, dropping the tongs and causing the fireball to fall on top of him as it slipped from the edge of the catapult's mounting container.

"Left," Joe yelled.

They veered to the side where Joe had disrupted the catapult shot. He knew the other Giants would not be a threat if he swung left very quickly. They swung to the right again, closing the distance like the wind. Only Bladeswift and his warriors were left behind.

Sika and Joe flew like mounted shadows. Joe unleashed his pistols as he approached the horde of Demons and Giants clanging their shields and pikes together. Joe reeled off several shots before he veered away from the horde.

He waved Sika on, and she fired several arrows. In the middle of the Giants and Demons was a huge metal container carrying fiery tar and chunks of burning material.

Jumping from his horse, he swept in among the Demons. Three leaped to bar his path.

Kapow, kapow, pow!

Joe worked their line from his left. The Vibro-Blade was in his hand. He moved forward torturously, slamming his blade into the kneecaps, groins, and chests of the Giants guarding the firepot. He darted backward to avoid the clumsy swings of the Giants' clubs or the Demons' pikes. He continued to slam his blade into them as his armored battle suit absorbed glancing blows. Inexorably he moved closer to the firepot. Sika was still at a distance, firing her arrows and reducing the resistance Joe faced.

Bladeswift and his Wildriders did the same. Arrows protruded from the exposed thighs and shoulders of the Demons and Giants. Giants had little armor, and some staggered like horrified pincushions on legs, arrows stuck in every conceivable body part.

Joe reached the firepot. He sheathed his Vibro-Blade and hefted the firepot up and forward, tipping the contents onto a nearby siege engine, causing it to burn. He slammed his sword into the two remaining siege engines, separating the wheels from the apparatus. Finally, he took some burning embers he had scooped up on the shield of a fallen Demon. He poured the embers onto the remaining siege engines, causing them to burn.

He looked up. Bladeswift cheered. All the Wildriders lifted their blades in exultation for Joe. For a moment, he was back on the gridiron, playing again. A golden hue seemed to emanate from the armored battle suit.

"Now to the next plateau!" Bladeswift roared.

Joe mounted his destrier and galloped easily behind Sika. He could see the high crest of the next plateau in the distance. Fires were glowing at its base. He calibrated the ABS visual system. Yes, there was a host of Demons and Giants by those fires.

As they rode, the wind-blown grasses undulated in a hypnotic rhythm.

✝ ✝ ✝

"Sika? Why do the Demons and Giants kill and scavenge your people?" Joe asked after a while.

"They seem envious, begrudging us our way of life, our flexibility. Many years ago, when the Long-Striders came and built forts, we could have gone to war against them. We found that we could live together.

This infuriated the Giants who had always lived here in the wilderness expanse of mountains and forestlands. The Giants took umbrage against the Long-Striders, attacking and raiding their early settlements. We helped as best we could. We also knew the Long-Striders might help us drive out the Giants when the time grew desperate."

"What of these Demons?" Joe probed.

"They came much later as the Giants shrank in numbers. They seemed to have grown out of the very earth itself, with their reddish-brown clay-colored skin as testament. They are intelligent, having forged weapons. But they are depraved like the Giants, eating the rotting flesh of their own brothers. Some say they have the worst qualities of any being on two legs. It's as if an angry God made them to punish us all."

The sun was setting off to the west. Bladeswift broke in, "We will camp until daylight. Demons don't see as well in the daylight, but at night they are more sure sighted. We attack at dawn. The sun will be in the Demons' eyes. The Giants will be in support but in the open at the base of the plateau. They will be easy to hit."

Bladeswift gave the call to set sentries and sleep in shifts. Joe fixed the binocular function of the armored battle suit and scanned toward the Giant and Demon encampment. There were perhaps one hundred Demons and about twenty Giants. They were about a mile away, and their campfires burned brightly. Joe could hear a drumbeat.

"Only the Giants beat drums. They, like men, use the beat for motivation and draw courage from its rhythm," Sika said as she stepped toward Joe, handing him dried meat, a jerky of some kind.

Joe took his helmet off and bit into the jerky. He was hungry. He had not eaten for quite a while.

Sika offered him water from her waterskin. "Our savior." She looked into Joe's eyes intently, then embarrassed, looked down as if studying his armored battle suit, its creases and grooves molded to Joe's physique. His wooly hair sparkled slightly with moisture from his sweat. The Afro lifted as Joe pushed his fingers through the bushy hair, and it resumed its natural shape.

Joe sat down with the others.

"Thank you for helping earlier," Sika said. "You kept them off me when my horse stumbled." Sika looked intently at Joe.

"You have helped me equally, and—I thank you as well." Joe had a hard time figuring out what he wanted to say.

"There would be no fire," Bladeswift said. "The Giants and Demons may know we are here, but at best let them guess our numbers. Soon others will join us by dawn at least."

† † †

Arleosa was quiet.

God radiated ambivalence: low-level frustration interlaced with a small level of satisfaction. "So, Arleosa, this is my Messiah? Ha! He kills like a trained assassin."

"But," Arleosa broke in, "he's united a civilization in sharing and protecting itself from your most terrific adversary, and he does it the way it has always needed to be done! After all the proselytizing, it has been our way to die for the humans. Be it prophets or terrorists bent on mass destruction, once the boundaries are set, it is always a war!"

God relaxed. A sense of calm enveloped him.

Arleosa relaxed as well. "You see as do I that the humans have no control—once we lose them into whatever world of your choosing, neither do we. The influence that motivates them is survival. And now Satan rallies Demon and Giant alike to manifest his cause. He was cast out and now plots the ruin of all you have striven to create."

God wavered, considering Arleosa's words for a moment more. "What is the nemesis of hope, Arleosa? Is it just Satan and all he represents?"

"No! It is not Satan but the thought that striving, creating, and loving is useless to help the people with their lives." Arleosa paused. "Joe Brown is a creator for these people and an answer on which to build their lives and create a society that supports them. He gives them a chance to understand what you want for them."

"Satan wants their pain and suffering to ameliorate his ousting from Heaven. But pain and suffering were never his alone to command. If Joe

Brown can smite the very entrance to Hell's gate and let Satan know he, too, can weary of suffering, then, Arleosa, Joe Brown will indeed be a warrior Messiah!" God concluded his speech and suddenly appeared in another part of Heaven, cavorting with Angels and hoping in Joe Brown.

† † †

The sun was rising. Joe awoke with Sika's head resting on his shoulder. They had talked long into the night. He had vague remembrances of dreams. Arleosa radiated golden rays into his consciousness. Joe intuitively understood more about what he was doing. He had been sent—but at the same time decided to come. He had been influenced, but he chose this for himself.

Sika awoke with a smile. She touched Joe's helmet and arose. She was soon chewing a mouthful of jerky. Nothing sexual had happened between them in the night, but Joe still felt a profound sense of love and caring for her. They had talked about God and why humans must struggle so much.

Joe checked his pistols and completed a new scan. The sun rose and obscured his vision to the east. Turning west, he scanned the tall shapes and shorter crouching ones, Demons. He checked the .50-caliber sniper rifle. He was geared up, ready. Finally, he unsheathed the Vibro-Blade with its humming monotone sound and smell of ozone. He swung it in a quick downward arc and just as quickly sheathed it. The sparkling hum ceased, and crackling energy evaporated, leaving only an equally balanced handle. He stuck the handle in his harness with a downward swipe.

Sika lifted her bow, tested its string, then quickly stored it on her harness, and drew her sword. She picked a few throwing knives from sheaths in her boot.

Joe mounted his great black destrier, Sika her quarter horse.

The sun began to slowly climb. Bladeswift checked its angle, looking to see if it would be shining in the eyes of the Demons and Giants. There were more Giants and Demons than the evening before. Their throng seemed to be disorganized. Their attention was transfixed on something above them on the side of the plateau.

Bladeswift had been looking to the west for some time. Finally, Joe could see why. A herd of Wildrider horses galloped from the plateau past the Demon and Giant camp to rally with Bladeswift. There were enough unmounted horses for every Wildrider and then some. Joe thought some of the bowmen riding toward him had been among the trees the day before.

Joe lifted his pistol in salute to the incoming warriors. Bladeswift mounted his stallion with a leap and one hand for leverage. The warriors arrived in a cloud of dust, and Bladeswift greeted them with his war cry. Joe continued to scan toward the enemies.

Bladeswift rallied the Wildriders who accompanied him. "The trap is set. Our brothers from the next village will defend their homes, and we will attack and break the host. We'll need to ride quickly. They know we are here. They will try to ascend to the next village before we can catch up with them. Now," he roared, "is the time of blood and fire. Rage and terror will be ours to let the enemies know that Demons are not from Hell; we are!"

With that, everyone mounted and rode—Bladeswift in the first wave. Several waves of riders followed behind him.

What is the battle plan? Joe thought. His large destrier, fast and enduring, could not keep pace with the furious strides of the Wildriders' quarter horses.

Sika, seeing Joe's expression of momentary hesitance, said, "Flank, Joe. Use the element of your long death instruments." With that she moved into the second wave of Wildriders.

Joe moved wide to the right flank, losing more ground. The Giants were using catapults to fire burning payloads into the woods of the plateau above them. Bladeswift and a few of his warriors had the single-shot muskets. Bladeswift fired a shot as they closed upon the line of Giants. One of the Giants clutched his lower back and stumbled, falling forward into the catapult he had just fired.

Above the Giants and Demons, the woods were on fire. The flames grew to twenty meters in diameter and continued spreading. Joe could see trails by which the Demons started to ascend. Even then he noted Wildriders on foot pop out from behind trees and shoot an arrow or sling an axe. The Wildriders almost always hit something they aimed for. They cared about saving the villagers more than the risks they were facing. They just wanted to stop the assault on their people.

Joe continued to swing wide, looking carefully for Sika, wanting her to be safe. Unslinging the great sniper rifle, he pulled to within fifty meters of the Giants. They were busy loading their catapults, but a few had turned to hold off Bladeswift's closing wave of Wildriders.

Suddenly Bladeswift reared left, followed by those behind him. Another prominent Wildrider chieftain moved right, followed by half the wave. They angled in a moving semicircle, none blocking the sight line of the others. A hailstorm of arrows pinned the Giants and Demons as they formed a line in an attempt to arm the catapults.

Joe observed the first wave move out. Sika joined the second wave. Joe's horse stood still. He pointed his rifle at the Giant nearest his position, who was hefting a club to ward off the second Wildrider wave. Abandoning patience, the Giant charged from his spot in the line in a vain effort to break the chain of oncoming riders.

Joe didn't breathe.

Bam!

Joe's shot slammed into the torso of the Giant, and blood spewed as the shot exited the other side of the Giant's body. The Giant kept running as though he had not even been hit. Suddenly he pitched forward, lips moving, yammering some incoherent sounds.

He must have been some kind of chief, Joe thought.

The Giants abandoned their line, some running wildly forward, others up into the trees after Wildriders. The Demons formed a tight ring and held position, laughing at the obvious lack of Giant discipline.

Joe laughed to himself and found a Demon who was chuckling particularly hard at the Giants' lack of discipline. The Demon was well equipped with a pike, bow, and shield. He looked to be a Demon captain.

Kwamm!

The Demon's head nearly exploded. His body flew a few feet and slammed to the ground.

They are not chuckling now, Joe thought.

With that, his pistols were out, and he galloped toward the ring of Demons.

Joe lost sight of Sika, but he was ending a threat. He felt angry about all that was happening. The Wildrider village being attacked by Demons and a second Wildrider village in peril. He did not know Demons and Giants, but he knew he cared for Sika and the Wildriders.

Bladeswift is a good warrior, Joe thought. *He fights to preserve his way of life. The Long-Striders sucking up land was only a natural path to the inevitable. But they had been at peace with the Wildriders. That was good. So much different than Aboriginal people and colonizers where I come from. A different world—more hopeful.*

Joe closed in like a hammer on nails; each pop of his pistols nailed a Demon, each crashing in a pile of bones and entrails. Blood oozed from a half dozen Demons' wounds. Joe rode out of the ring of Demons—now a ring of deceased Demons.

Sika fired arrow after arrow as the Wildriders climbed the plateau, anxious to reach the second village. She rode faster, catching up to the first Wildrider wave. She had unsheathed her sword, swinging from either side of her mount, slamming it downward on the breastbones and heads of the Demons as she quickly pushed forward. The Wildriders clung mostly to the trail, but they spread out, seeking to find a path up through the wooded brush. Ascending the plateau, the Wildrider waves broke into small skirmishes and pockets of violence as they fought the Giants and Demons.

Suddenly Joe saw what he feared the most. A Demon lurched forward and stabbed into the breast of Sika's horse with a pike. The horse stumbled, kicking out with its forelegs. The horse's hooves punched into the Demon's head, killing him. The horse fell forward as Sika slipped off behind it. Sika held her broadsword, and the Demons quickly flew to her position, their teeth gnashing, and their pikes aimed at her. Sika, sensing the pressure, rolled backward, descending the hill by two meters. Pikes slammed together where she had been standing a moment before. She raised her sword to guard against the next attack.

She barely saw the arrow the Demon farther up the incline had loosed. It bore down on her. Her sword deflected it and caused it to sink into the armor just about Sika's waist.

Joe had made his way up the plateau. He careened his horse in front of Sika, blocking the Demons from her.

The fight continued as Joe reeled off round after round. Sika, regaining her balance, moved to flank the Demons charging at Joe. She was moving very quickly, slipping behind trees, ducking behind boulders, then hacking with her sword after her arrows were expended.

Joe realized how deeply he feared for Sika. He worried about the village up ahead as well. Joe did not have time to reload. The Vibro-Blade was in his hand as he moved up the hill slashing from side to side, attracting the Demons to his position.

Why do they continue? Joe thought. *I am death to them as they are death to human life on this world.*

Joe thought he heard a whisper urging him forward. He wondered, *where is this going, and how will it end?*

Sika urgently hacked at a Demon's thigh, causing him to slam to the ground. As she walked over him, she punctured his throat with her dagger.

They were almost at the village. Joe could see Bladeswift moving to the top of the plateau. Joe reined his destrier up the hill.

He froze in horror as he witnessed Sika take an arrow in the throat. She dropped to one knee, her eyes lifeless and her body in a stupor. Joe rushed to her side. Underneath the visor, his eyes welled up with tears. He knew Sika was gone. He kneeled behind her and slammed clips into his pistols.

Pow! Pow! Pow!

Joe was coldly accurate. The Demons would not desecrate the vessel of Sika's soul, inside a now-lifeless body.

A few Giants came charging down at him. He dropped to one knee and continued to fire at them. His pistols knocked back the advances of the Giants. Joe could smell the stench of burning flesh. Bladeswift and the Wildriders were on the plateau's upper surface. The Demons and Giants started retreating to the far side of the plateau. The village was on fire. Wildrider women and children littered the landscape, frozen in death. Many were missing limbs. Some of the bodies were charred by the fires. There appeared a great desecration throughout the village grounds.

Joe carefully carried Sika's body to the top of the plateau. Bladeswift shuddered. His green-olive complexion turned yellow.

The smell of burning flesh was strong. The village was smoldering. Huts had been in flames, but now only smoke billowed above them. There were bodies of warriors in various positions around the village. Around the perimeter lay ten Giants and about fifty Demons, all dead.

Joe carried Sika's body as if she were an infant. Joe prayed silently. He could feel the presence that followed him since his death, or near death, in the pit. He thought of the miracle that allowed him to survive and thought how good it would be if Sika could receive such a miracle.

✝ ✝ ✝

Arleosa frowned. God looked as grim as ever. "A miracle, my Lord. Give them hope."

"No," God boomed. "Every miracle coddles them and gives them false hope. How will they ever cease their misgivings if we save them from each one? No miracle...they must find their own path."

Arleosa bowed low. "A miracle lets them know the possibilities...but yes, pain is the reminder to help them see the destruction of their actions. But it was not their destructiveness. It was he whom you no longer recognize: our poor Devil, once an Angel, whom we wish to restrain. What example does that set? How can we ask so much of them when we will not forgive him?"

"Stop!" God boomed. "You dare too much, Arleosa...though you have a point. But indeed, the Devil must relent, not because we forgive him, but because his own temerity is his undoing."

✝ ✝ ✝

Joe could see the blood trickling from Sika's neck. He stopped for a moment. He laid Sika down. Looking closely at the wound, he used his visor in the ABS medical mode. Sika was not bleeding heavily. She was in shock. Quickly, he used the life-support cable in the ABS and gave Sika's body a synthetic adrenal injection. She quivered. Joe quickly worked to move the arrow from her neck and cauterize the wound. Sika's eyes opened briefly before she passed out.

Joe looked up. Bladeswift was standing beside him. The village still stood. Wildriders were coming out of the holes in the ground and from under huts. Many were wounded, but they had stayed and held off a major assault on their village.

Fiery catapults had caused many of the casualties, Joe surmised. *But the Wildriders had held the village.*

✝ ✝ ✝

"There are no miracles, Arleosa," God declared. "Only the greatest love can bring life where there is none!"

Arleosa eased back. She hated the preaching. Repeatedly the same lesson. What is left to prove? Suddenly God was gone. Arleosa befuddled, looked, felt, and listened. Nothing.

✝ ✝ ✝

A defensive perimeter was being reinforced by Bladeswift and his people. Rations of nuts and jerky were distributed. Logs were placed to bolster areas between boulders.

"This is not our way, Joe, to set up stayed defenses," said Bladeswift, "but it will be good for now. Soon the horses will be here to take women and children to the open plains. In the south, they will find security from the Demons—for a while anyway. Next, we must end the threat for all time. How, I do not know. You are a key in all this. We must find the Demon pit and close it for good!"

Joe rested near Sika, attending to her needs.

What next? He thought.

Sika's eyes fluttered. "We know where they are, Joe. Their pit, their home." She leaned back; her eyes closed.

What do I do now? he thought. He lay down next to Sika after making sure she was resting quietly. In the morning he would call for the ACV. He wanted the resources of the ACV nearby. He'd wear his helmet to bed and use the area radar alarms of the ABS. He'd program it for the general description of Giants and Demons. That night he slept dreaming of Sika being by his side in battle. He also felt the presence he knew and associated with the golden comfort he felt in his dreams. Somehow Sika was a part of that. Sika and the presence were awfully close, he felt. Simply different frequencies of the same light.

He awoke and felt torn. *What now?* He thought. Then sleep came again, and he knew *somehow* there would be a way.

When he awoke, he found Sika resting in her bedding, chewing a mouthful of jerky slowly and deliberately. At times she would use her other hand to caress her neck and secure the bandage wrapped around it. Her eyes fluttered, and she seemed to doze off, still chewing.

Joe looked over at her and took off his helmet and smiled as her smile met his.

She laughed lightly and closed her eyes but kept chewing. Her words echoed in Joe's mind: "We know where they are, Joe." She had said. Again, Joe's insecurities grated upon him. *So now...*

Joe donned his helmet and started working on the program to bring the ACV nearby. Bladeswift approached Joe and waited for his response.

Joe made preparations and a signal was coming into his helmet. The ACV would be there in hours. It could shelter Sika and very possibly restore her to full health.

Bladeswift spoke as Joe turned his attention to the Wildriders. "The runners will come soon, and I will assess how my people have fared during this tragedy. The Demons always come back in more numbers. There must come an end to all this."

Joe looked at him. "How can this be ended? How? Tell me." His voice became more distraught. The weight of all the fighting was hitting him.

He had almost lost Sika. In fact, he believed he *had* lost her. *Why was she so important anyway?* he thought.

"Joe," Bladeswift spoke quietly, "the natural rhythm of the universe favors you. Not your weapons, but you. The people will follow you. When we go back to the Long-Striders, you will see if the lessons you gave them still hold."

Joe thought about the things he had instilled in them. Were they in place? The crops being rotated, guns being made. The people still cooperating with each other.

As if on cue, the ACV appeared low in the sky. Joe started working on bringing it down to the ground. Bladeswift and the other Wildriders looked in awe. The craft slowly descended, and Joe opened the hatch. He quickly gathered Sika in his arms.

"Bladeswift, please come." He laid Sika in the health-bay incubator. It was made up of a sterile plastic bed with a soft mattress made of synthetic fibers. "Now watch, Bladeswift."

Lights started flowing on a console next to the incubator. Joe was reading a console message and following its instructions. A probing tendril touched Sika's neck.

Bladeswift startled. "What?" he exclaimed.

Joe said, "Be patient, no harm will come to her." He had never used this, but information was streaming to him from its console, and the ABS reinforced that information

Joe followed the instructions. The probe expanded at its tip, and the round expansion covered the wound on both sides of Sika's neck. She had been sleeping when Joe placed her into the health-bay incubator. Her eyes fluttered. She smiled and fell back asleep.

Bladeswift looked curiously at Sika as she rested in the health-bay incubator. "Many have died, Joe. I cannot find my wife. Perhaps she has escaped to another village."

Joe reached out and patted Bladeswift's shoulder. Bladeswift nodded in acknowledgment.

Joe offered, "We will end it and rid your people of this menace. I will help find your wife and child. You have my support without reservation,

Bladeswift." Joe remembered his home. It had been months since his arrival. He wondered about Samantha and about New Castle and how the city fared.

Joe was brought back to the now as Bladeswift hollered toward the door of the ACV. Joe grabbed some explosives and more ammo. Joe could see that there was lot of activity beyond the ACV door. Bladeswift was out the door. He looked surprised and mildly relieved to find Ataka on horseback with a host of riders. Bladeswift's relief turned into urgency as he saw a new wave of Demons and Giants about to assault the village.

Several Giants were firing slingshots as they emerged from the woods. Joe saw Ataka, who had been swinging around to protect the village, fire his musket toward one of the Giants—but not before a rock glanced off the ACV. Ataka's shot seemed to fire in slow motion. Joe watched the smoke frothing out of the barrel and watched the ball cut a swath through the air, leaving a wind trail. Joe thought, *like a surfboard cutting a swath through water.* He could see every ripple in the air. He heard the impact as the metal ball ripped into the Giant's ribs and blood spewed out of the wound right after impact. Joe watched as the Giant lurched and stumbled to one knee. All this in the blink of an eye. Joe felt the pain of the Giant as if it were his own.

Joe looked around. Their position was untenable. The Giants rushed in, firing slingshots, and swinging their clubs at anyone in their path. Ataka loaded one more ball, fired it, and watched as a Giant lumbered forward, falling face down. As another Giant closed in on Ataka, he quickly slung the rifle into his saddle harness and fired his pistol at the Giant. Ataka was riding just beyond the perimeter of the village, sword in hand, as the Giant, though badly wounded, tried to slam his club down on him. Ataka drew his sword and thrust it into the Giant's chest while his horse lunged forward. A large gash appeared in the Giant's upper chest. The force of the blow, with Ataka's warhorse lunging, slammed the Giant backward onto the ground. It looked to Joe like a slow-motion film reel when in fact the blow took less than a few seconds.

Joe reeled off a few shots, stemming the tide of Giants and Demons lurching toward the village. Bladeswift was moving quickly from cover to cover as he loaded and discharged his musket.

The onslaught continued. Joe kept firing unhurriedly, though the conflict raged around him. He had closed the ACV, so he did not have to worry about Sika.

He knew the village could soon be overrun by Demons. He fired repeatedly. Now a new problem emerged: flying Demons overhead. Exposed as Joe and his companions were, the Demons could just dip down and slash at them from above. They held daggers and short swords in their hands. Their wings were attached to their bodies between their wrists and waist. Joe realized they couldn't truly fly but were able to glide from surrounding trees and down into the village, unable to ascend again.

It's like a dance, Joe thought. He moved to the rhythm of the assault. Where forces flowed to the village, he countered, now hammering forward with the Vibro-Blade and quick vicious strokes, breaking Giant kneecaps and cracking bone-reinforced leather vests. He surged back and forth, avoiding a heavy club blow to shoot his high-caliber pistol into the mass of Giant and Demon flesh. Joe could feel his movements and reactions flowing at a pitch he had never experienced. But in a sense, he hoped the killing would end soon.

How long must I continue? he thought, even as his sword blows came faster. His pistol shots punctuated the decimation of the Giant and Demon onslaught.

Bladeswift was moving quickly, flanking the Giants from the edge of the village, firing arrows and running for cover.

Joe was tired. *When would this end?*

Bladeswift called out, and suddenly from the opposite side of the village, thirty Wildrider horsemen appeared with long lances and shields moving on warhorses at great speed, slamming their spears into the main thrust of the Giant attack.

Joe, Ataka, and Bladeswift withdrew into the center of the village and started skirmishing the remaining Demons, who descended from the air. Landing, they attempted to cause panic by attacking the rear flanks of the Wildrider defense. In a heartbeat, the three warriors hacked down the previously airborne Demons.

It was all over. No enemies remained standing.

There were sounds of wounded Demons and Giants lying in pools of blood. Demons writhed and growled. Tens of Wildriders lay dead or wounded as well. But the attack had been stopped the allied forces of Joe the Wildriders and knights.

As in the previous village, Wildrider women and children sprung out of the earth and moved to assist the wounded. They wailed in sorrow for loved ones lost on the battlefield. Quickly they sought to bind wounds, apply herbal ointments, and make solicitous prayers to the process of death. Burials were quick.

Bladeswift explained to Joe, "Their souls live forever and are forever with us as well."

Demons and Giants were piled together and burned by the surviving fighters, some while they were still dying. Wildriders were efficient, not just physically but spiritually as well. The dead were buried very quickly. Bladeswift called his riders and began to assemble a travel caravan. Ataka conferred with Bladeswift and Joe. "We must get back to King Kotutan and refit our forces," he said.

"Yes." Bladeswift agreed the home of the Demons must be breached by us, not now but after preparations were made.

Ataka broke in, "There is much to refit, Joe. The people have prospered under your lessons. Many guards carry two guns at the fort, using the long rifles to snipe Demons attempting to scout from a distance. You have done well by us. The king praises your lessons, and Queen Saluiana says you are a prophet."

Joe looked around and pulled off his helmet. It appears they had left the fortress months ago. But no, it had only been weeks. *What did Ataka mean?* he thought. *One thing is for sure: the Demon pit must be found and breached.* Joe shuddered, remembering the journey he, Thames, and Jacks had taken. Almost killing them—indeed killing them. Joe could not say for sure, but they were alive now.

The Wildrider caravan was quickly assembled. Outriders guarded the flank of the caravan. Horses hauled everything the Wildriders needed.

Joe planned to take the ACV with Sika and return to the fortress. There he would meet Bladeswift when the caravan arrived.

While at the fortress, he would evaluate the things he had put in place. The civilization he now understood to be reaching full bloom.

Sika had two handmaidens who would accompany her and Joe in the ACV.

"Have you ever flown?" Joe asked them.

"No," they answered in unison. The two young women, Atunia and Musana, were in training with Sika to be warriors and trackers. One day they would learn the spiritual values of the "warrior way" from Sika.

"Joe," Sika called out.

They were in the ship, waiting to take off. Joe worried about the caravan and started a scan looking for the opposition as well as his allies.

"Sika," Joe asked. "How are you?"

"Good," she responded.

"I'll resume my duties." Joe said. "But now you can rest. We'll be flying to Kotutan's fortress."

"Flying?" she asked.

"Yes, flying."

"Are you an Angel, Joe?" Sika asked. "When I fell in battle, you scooped me up, and I veered into the world of death. I looked up, and you were not just Joe but someone else *and* still Joe. Someone more. I thought I would surely die; then you picked me up, and I knew I would live. How, Joe?"

"I, too, have known the feel of death, Sika," Joe began. "I was in a Demon pit in my world. I was with two others. We should have died. We fought to the bitter end. I lost consciousness and awoke. We were cared for later, but somehow, we all three survived. We had suffered a score of wounds, and death was imminent. I awoke knowing I had survived something catastrophic. But I had no idea how. My wounds bled, but I mysteriously recovered quickly. Look, your neck looks better already."

"You want to change the subject, Joe. Do not. We must recognize what happened. What has joined us together, Joe." Sika implored him.

"You are right, Sika. I am joined with you by this bond, but I don't know where this is all going. I hate to stop this but let me get the ship going. We need to get to the king."

Sika eased back and closed her eyes. "Don't forget—this conversation must continue, Joe." With that, she began to sleep soundly.

Joe calibrated the control on the Bioregenesis Incubation Chamber, BRIC for short. Joe knew Sika would sleep through the whole flight. He went up to the cockpit and started to work on the flight plan. The ACV could fly to a designated location by itself.

Soon a scan showed the signs of life Joe was looking for. It was the people in the western outpost. The Long-Striders as Bladeswift and the Wildriders called them. Kotutan should be waiting for them, along with Saluiana and her religious followers.

Joe ran a scan to determine the development of the outpost. In just a few weeks, things looked better. There was fresh grass growing in all the pastures. The pasture rotation was working. The new crops were rotated, by fortress settlers and already responding with good early growth. Joe scanned for armament. That, too, was in evidence.

The Wildrider caravan was miles from approaching the walls of the outpost. Things had started to get better already. Joe thought about where he should land. The ACV might scare the Long-Striders unnecessarily. But at the same time, he had to consider Sika's recovery and his need to have his resources close by.

One of the nearby pastures might be best for landing the ACV. He would leave Sika comfortably resting. Still, the Long-Striders would see his approach. The sun shone brightly now at his back. *Oh well, land I must*, he thought. The ship glided down into the pasture. Sentries patrolling the area took cover. Joe quickly opened the door to show himself.

"It's Joe. Don't worry; don't worry." He walked out without his helmet. He saw two sentries hiding in the brush. When they saw him, they lost all fear and cheered, shaking their weapons in the air excitedly. Joe noted they carried both rifles and pistols.

† † †

"Satan grows restless, my Lord, and he wishes to show his might," said Arleosa. "He sees your gains as a provocation. And yet he is happy with the carnage it presents because it shows his path and his ideas. All our goodness is subject to the will to be mighty but not benevolent. Violence is a way of life and always sustained." Arleosa contained herself, ending her monologue.

"Yes," God said, "so then what? Are all good things won by overcoming violence only meant to end in more violence? In my first world, Earth, the Germans were vanquished after World War I, then as a result of the Versailles Treaty's restrictions, World War II erupted. They lost again. It doesn't matter who's right. No one gets the right message nor gets along in the end."

Arleosa was wounded by God's cynical outlook. She knew the violence would end. First, though, the Demons must be vanquished. It was essential that Satan understand the futility of his incursion upon humanity.

God said, "I have him on Hellrun where he seems in control, but this will expose his vulnerability as well."

"God," Arleosa began. "Satan was vanished out of vanity. He could not be subservient to the will of God. Of you, my Lord."

"What now?" God asked. "Arleosa, should we welcome Satan back into the life of Heaven to once again doubt his own worth and betray all that Heaven stands for? Huh? Let him once again see his own folly?"

"Perhaps, my Lord," Arleosa answered. "It is only to help him understand that his ways will lead him to be overwhelmed. But no one really wants that. The defeated often crave revenge and never forget the wounds they have suffered."

† † †

Satan sat in his tunnel. He produced more Demons, conjured from whatever source he could find. The Demon women gave birth at twice the rate of humans. Breeding like rabbits, they created more soldiers for their army. At times Satan himself would copulate with the Demon women. No horns graced their heads. Red eyes and comely hips greeted him at such times. His orgasms were long and tempestuous. *If God could see me now*, he thought to himself, laughing. In no time, his seed would reproduce a Demon ready to fight for his king.

☥ ☥ ☥

"Bring about such a glorious conflagration that Satan himself will feel his head seared as if by a thousand suns," Arleosa elaborated. "Let Satan himself see how faulty this chemistry of war is. In the end, even he will want peace!"

☥ ☥ ☥

Joe sat down as a guest of the king and queen. Joe was introduced to the others at the table, the religious Sages were present. They started with wine.

Joe removed his helmet. He sipped the wine casually, complimenting the king and queen on its bouquet and, of course, taste. "Hmm, exceptionally good, King Kotutan. This vintage complements Your Majesty's hearth." The wine was dark and tasted of oak barrels with hints of cherry, tobacco, and robust, dense grapes.

King Kotutan rose to speak. "We have begun to see great changes with the help of our prophet, Joe Brown."

Nobles were seated all around, as were knights. Ataka had was seated as well. Bladeswift and Sika sat together with a contingent of Wildrider chieftains.

"We have greater protection now and greater armament that is able to strike from a far range," the king said. "We have benefited from the changes in the way we orchestrate the growing of our crops and the grazing of our cattle. All can be seen to move in a positive direction. Thanks to Joe Brown!"

Cheers from within the dining hall rose. "Joe Brown! Joe Brown! Honor him! Honor him! Honor him!"

Joe rose to his feet. He thought of denying the title of prophet, then decided against it. These people could benefit from his being a prophet. It might prove helpful later.

"The things I do, I do to help all my brothers here," Joe said. "The great evil we stand against will need all our best efforts. I thank you all. King Kotutan, Bladeswift, Sika, Ataka the great knight, and of course Queen Saluiana. Thank you for seeing me so kindly as a part of something that Sages see as a prophecy. I will do my utmost to fulfill the faith of your prophecies." To himself, he thought, *Me, a prophet. How could this be?*

As if in reassurance, Saluiana licked her lips after sipping some wine and glanced longingly at Joe, who caught her gaze, though Kotutan did not notice the chemistry between them.

At night after the dinner festivities, Joe retired to his room, just off the main dining hall area. He had not been out of the armored battle suit in weeks. A bath had been drawn for him, and wine was poured from a pitcher by the tub. He got in the hot water and continued to sip the wine lazily. He had not had sex in quite a while. *Well*, he thought, *that will have to wait. I have a battle plan to make. Sika can help me find the Demon pit, she said. How can I raise an army? Many will die. Now what?* He thought some more and dozed off in the tub.

He awoke suddenly after vaguely remembering a dream. The golden glow had surrounded him; a voice had whispered into his ear its most fervent hopes. There would be adversity, but it would be well worth the trouble. Life always meant death. But death was just a signature of life's story. To suffer and know joy—that was a good life. Suffering is meant to be temporary, like life. But suffering teaches us the most and gives us the knowledge of that which must be avoided. *Such riddles*, Joe thought.

Then he saw her. Sika stood there. She was radiant in a flowing gown. No leather armor. Her small but pert breasts pressed against the outline of her clothing. Her hips were beautifully round and athletic and feminine as well. Sika's smile, radiant and loving, was directed toward Joe. Joe flushed briefly. Then it came to him. It was not what must be avoided but what must be cherished above all things.

Sika reminded Joe of Samantha. Sika was just as beautiful. However, she was shorter, with the forearms and shoulders of a warrior and the strong legs of a Wildrider. She slipped onto Joe's bed. Joe rose from the tub. Sika handed him a blanket as he got up, then sat back on the bed. Joe donned the belt he used to carry the compressed ABS. He could then slip some ordinary pants and a shirt over it. *Like a superhero*, he thought, grinning to himself.

Sika stood up, pressed herself against him and hugged him tightly. Joe felt himself rapidly becoming aroused. Sika, feeling this, clung to him silently. She lovingly caressed his neck and buried her head against his chest. Joe had always been sexually attracted to beautiful women, and he wanted Sika. But he also adored her in a way that was incomprehensible to him. They stood there holding each other for a while. Both seeking to understand what this moment meant, they drew away from each other and sat on Joe's bed. Sika's two hands wrapped around Joe's right hand.

"Sika." Joe began. "I have to go to the Demon cave, and you've said you know where it is."

"Yes, Joe. We scouted to within a mile of it from a high plateau. I could see them coming out. We were looking for new lands but felt the plateau was too close to them. We had to sneak our way back, killing by stealth as needed. The land was teeming with them. At times we assassinated their captains to stave off attacks we guessed they were preparing for."

Joe stopped her momentarily. "How far was the cave? How well guarded?"

Sika went on. "Joe, they don't have sentries posted. The Demons were freely moving in and out. They scoured the land for any chance to launch assaults against us and the Long-Striders, who've continued their westward expansion."

Joe sat back; he thanked Sika with a warm, overly generous hug. She pressed tightly into him. Then again, they sat down, holding hands.

"I don't want you to feel pressured, Joe. I am indebted to you for my life, and I have great love for you. I know you have a purpose here. A purpose for all of us, and I know you will need my help."

"Thank you, Sika," Joe said slowly. His emotions were tempered by the care he felt for her. "Stay and sleep the night here, if that is okay—if it won't damage your reputation."

"Don't worry, Joe. I am a seer meeting with a prophet of the people."

Joe dreamed again as he did almost every night. But the dreams were intensified. Sika rested by his side, tremendously feminine and beautiful and with all the athleticism of a world-class athlete. Joe awoke briefly and looked at Sika. Her perfectly oval face, even the green-brown olive skin, was something he had to get used to. Still, it was radiant. Again, he fell asleep. The feelings of security intensified. Suddenly he felt as if he was in a battle, fighting in slow motion yet still faster than the Demons and Giants.

7.
A MURDER TO RESOLVE

The next morning, he awoke. Sika was up, wearing her battle clothing: leather gauntlets, tunic, and leggings. Joe smiled approvingly. They hugged intensely for a moment.

The great hall was set for breakfast. "There has been a murder," King Kotutan announced loudly when they sat down, before even a crumb was served.

Joe had the armored battle suit on a belt. He had a simple tunic, short pants, and float-fast sneakers he had retrieved from the ACV. He hit a few buttons on the belt.

Thwipp, and the armored battle suit was on, helmet and all.

He sensed the alarm in King Kotutan's voice. Queen Saluiana started to weep. She grasped a cloth handkerchief and then straightened in her chair. Joe looked for the three wisemen and saw only two. Within the armored battle suit, his nape hairs started to tingle.

Kotutan continued. "He who was one of our wise spiritual guides: Twolaga, the seer, the greatest of our wisemen. His throat was clawed or bit. His head nearly severed."

There was a collective gasp in the throng. Nobles, serving girls, servers, cooks—all looked stunned.

Many suspicious thoughts arose in Joe's mind. A golden glow seemed to encompass his thoughts. He was alert and ready to control the situation. He knew he'd be involved.

"Take me to the scene, my lord. I will help find the answer," Joe suggested, "to locate this perpetrator."

The remaining two wisemen chanted together in unison:
The blow was dealt,
The fire burnt.
No peace be found
On the palace ground.
The Devil lurks in
Secret, sure, waiting
For the day to turn.
Darkness folds the night,
Enfolds, the Devils waits
To undermine and chase
The victorious into a fright.
Darker grows the death night,
The holy have no place to hide, in silent
Steps, the Devil will glide.
What could have happened? Joe wondered.

Kotutan took a bite of the eggs, swallowed some coffee, and beckoned Joe to follow him. Rising quickly, Ataka moved to follow the king. Saluiana remained behind, sitting with her head down.

The king headed to the temple. It was a separate, cone-shaped two-story building. They went through the door and up the stairs. Surrounded by guards lay Twolaga, the senior priest wiseman Sage, spiritual leader of the Long-Striders. Joe began to scan the body. He noticed immediately that Twolaga's throat had been ripped out. A large bite mark enveloped the wiseman's neck. Twolaga's throat lay partially severed, and his neck's vertebrae were visible. From the look of horror in Twolaga's dead eyes, he'd undoubtedly faced his attacker.

Joe watched everyone's reaction. The good news—no gunshot had killed the priest. He needed the population to be armed against Demons, not each other.

Joe started scanning with the armored battle suit, identifying any biological material. Joe fed the information back to the ACV so the computer on board could process the scanned information. Joe was doing something he had learned—police work—and the Armored Battle Suit was designed to aid him. He quickly did a breakdown of the crime scene as he continued to scan. The guards, and even King Kotutan, deferred to their Messiah.

The priest wore his hair long, and some of it had been torn away by the bite. Twolaga had struggled as he faced his attacker. Under Twolaga's nails, Joe scanned some hair, dried skin, and dander. A different type of hair was discernible as well. Joe transmitted everything back to the ship. The men in the room watched curiously as the pale-red beam emanated from Joe's visual portal. The portal was represented by a live screen that bulged out symmetrically like an orb, oval in shape. Joe couldn't help but wonder how he was being seen by these people.

Joe asked to be shown out to the building from the second floor. He saw a slight footprint residue on the floor. Scanning, he was moved to walk out onto a balcony. In the sunlight, the residue disappeared. The sun and warm daylight air had evaporated the footprint residue.

The other two wisemen, Osala and Boswan, entered from the stairs below. They were quietly disconsolate but reasonably composed. A series of thick vines clung to the building, ascending and entwined with the metal railing of the balcony.

He looked over the railing and scanned. There were damaged vines where an assailant might have climbed up or down the vines. *Perhaps this was the way the assailant came up*, Joe thought. "These must be cut after I'm done here!" Joe commanded, speaking about the vines.

Off in the near distance, Joe could see the ten-foot fortress wall and ramparts. He scanned and saw some faint prints in the packed dirt that led up to the wall. *A heavy person or creature*, Joe thought. The scan indicated that as well. There was also a faint dander residue in the dust by the wall and rampart. The trail of residue and prints led north into a surrounding forest that bordered the plains.

"Ataka, put your men on alert. We're going for a hike." Joe was getting a limited feed from the ACV, but it was telling information. Wolf dander. *Hmm*, Joe thought.

"Do wolves attack people on this world, Ataka?"

"Not usually, but there are predators who will. Not many though," Ataka responded.

Joe followed the limited trail. In the forest, the softer ground left more prints due to the moisture and shade.

Joe continued to scan. He could see the woods thickening and darkening ahead.

"We need to push ahead. The trail is still worth following." Joe realized he only had a pistol handy. A big .10 caliber but nothing else except his Vibro-Blade.

Ataka was wearing his pistol and a broadsword. He wore leather armor with dragon-scale reinforcement.

"Be ready, Ataka. There's more to this than meets the eye."

He moved forward, and the trail disappeared in the underbrush of the deep forest. It occurred to Joe that if anyone could pick up the trail again, it would be Sika. Why did he move so quickly without her? Then he understood. In the back of his mind, he knew he sought to protect Sika. Now he knew she would be a part of the answer.

"Ataka, go back and have Sika join us. I'll post here. Quickly now, and say I requested her; she will come. Escort her here."

Ataka turned on his heel and started to jog back to the fortress.

Joe studied the ground and trees ahead. He scanned into the underbrush, but nothing was clear. The trail ended. He inched forward, searching and scanning. Nothing was visible.

He reviewed the scan information from the ship. "Wolf dander. Interesting." He reported to those nearby.

The forest shrunk into a narrow valley surrounded by trees close to the fortress. It was so dark, almost impenetrable, in the morning sun. *It must be about 9:00 a.m.*, thought Joe. The armored battle suit confirmed 0901 hours. No light shone through the canopy of trees—there was only darkness. *How can this be?* Joe asked himself. *Is the sky suddenly dark? Where is the sun? This can't be good. Impenetrable darkness sounds like some more weird science fiction shit!*

There were more trail particles for his suit to scan. However, he couldn't be sure the particles were not from small animals in the area, and the scan could not discriminate. He had seen all manner of wildlife since he arrived.

Soon Ataka arrived with Sika by his side. She was dressed in her leather warrior outfit and carried a pistol. Her bow was slung over her back with a quiver of arrows. A long sword was also sheathed at her back. Joe greeted them warmly. Two guards accompanied them.

Sika investigated the darkness. Joe explained his progress so far. He did not want Sika around for this, he thought. He wanted her safe, but this was the mission. The mission was to save this world from Demons and such. For that he needed Sika.

Sika's nose crinkled. She led them farther into the brush. As they went farther, Sika grew more intent. The sun peeked through briefly. She looked around and walked into a clearing.

More prints.

Joe scanned—they were the same ones he'd seen before.

Moving further through the canopy of trees, they came to a clearing. Sika mused, looking around.

"They came from there," she said, pointing north toward the plains. The sun was heading toward the noon hour. The rest of the forest continued to be dark, but where Sika pointed was bright and clear. Sika pointed again toward a half-eaten buffalo lying on the ground about eighty meters north. Sika approached it as Joe scanned. More prints. Slash marks had pierced the buffalo's neck. The marks looked like claws, not teeth.

The group of five moved beyond the dead buffalo, with Sika leading Joe, Ataka, and the two guards. There were faint prints in the prairie dust. Sika stopped abruptly. A cave opening appeared fifty meters away.

"There," she said. "Everything leads there!"

Joe scanned toward the cave opening. "We have to get closer. I'm not getting anything. Sika?" he asked.

"No, don't get closer," she warned. "There's no reason to get closer."

"Okay then, back to the fortress."

Joe responded to the urgency in Sika's voice. The sky was clear, but no birds could be seen. They headed back, looking over their shoulders. Suddenly, a vulture landed on the half-eaten buffalo. Back in the wooded canopy, light shone through. Birds could be heard chirping. Joe felt a

burden lift from his shoulders. "What now, Sika? The cave opening...
what is it? Where does it lead?"

"Shhh, Joe," she whispered. "Don't speak more until we are in private.
No need to get these people upset."

The guards and Ataka were out of earshot of Sika's low whispers to Joe.

Sika looked worried. "Joe, we must seek an audience, a formal audience with King Kotutan, the two remaining priests, Bladeswift, Ataka,
and lastly, Queen Saluiana."

"Oh shit, Sika. This sounds like serious...uh, shit."

"Yes, Joe. It is perhaps the reason you are here!"

That afternoon Ataka posted extra guards on the ramparts. The temple
was also secured and more guards added to the watch there.

Joe and Sika spoke to King Kotutan briefly but discussed nothing
specific. Joe knew he would need things from the ship: explosives and
more ammo. He thought about teaching Sika to use a semiautomatic pistol.

Once at the ship, he gathered C-4, grenades, and mobile claymores. He
didn't have a lot, but he had enough to turn the tide in his favor against
anything he'd seen so far on this planet. *But still*, he wondered, *what could
it be? How deep could a cave be, and what could it hold?*

8.
THE AUDIENCE

In a sparsely decorated room in the back of the fortress behind the main hall, Sika, Bladeswift, Ataka, and King Kotutan met. Last came Queen Saluiana dressed in form-fitting robes more regal than Joe had seen anyone wearing thus far. *After all, she is the queen*, he thought.

"We cast them aside long ago!" King Kotutan's voice boomed throughout the room.

Sika gave a glimpse of what she knew to be present in the cave. None were happy to hear it. Joe sensed the Long-Striders would just as soon deny or forget the validity of Sika's words. Joe had little to go on except the feeling of integrity he placed in Sika.

Bladeswift commanded a towering presence, even at five feet, two inches tall. He was swathed in leather dragon-scale armor and spoke even more profoundly than King Kotutan but with much less volume.

"We know that upon your ascension, Long-Striders displaced the creatures of the forest. Some were dangerous to all our existence, some not. The Manwolf clans were the most dangerous—only second to the Demons who assail us now. You fought and won. We helped secure the peace by fighting with you! But this day had to come. We did not defeat all of them but only drove them away. Now they return, perhaps driven back to us by our very own enemies, the Demons and the Giants!" Bladeswift was impressive, his voice melodic, the shiny scales of the dragon armor shimmered in the light. Candles and lanterns flickered.

Evening was here, and Bladeswift's words impacted the throng. They were uneasy. King Kotutan looked angry and confused. But then Saluiana spoke. She rose, majestic in her ornamental gowns. They clung closely to her body, accentuating her comely shape. The slit in Saluiana's gown revealed a well-toned calf and thigh. Her hips swelled into a clinging enclosure above the slit. Joe felt his nature rising even in this tense and difficult meeting.

"We have betrayed the nature of God," she said. Joe turned his attention from Saluiana's body, voluptuous as it was, to the commanding tone of her message. "We could have found a way to bring the Manwolves into our fold. Yes, they are different—so different from us—too different to overlook as we overlooked the differences between us and the Wildriders. Men of smaller stature versus men of wolf's fur, fangs, and claws make too big a difference to overlook. So! Here we are. A new enemy who was an old enemy. What can we learn from this?"

"But they are devils, my dear, too willing to kill and slaughter," Kotutan pleaded with his wife, the queen.

"We have driven them to it, in part," she countered.

Joe could see the enmity he thought existed between King Kotutan and the queen. No wonder she visited alone and seemed always aligned with the priests. But now a priest was dead. How would that affect the policies of this kingdom? Joe strived to understand what his role might be and whether these Manwolves were a threat, as everyone perceived them to be.

"How do we even know the Manwolves are responsible for the death of Twolaga?" Sika asked. "How can we be sure until we confront the evidence by going to the cave mouth? I sensed great danger when we were close to the cave. I have a great fear about what is happening so close to your territory. I feel it must be confronted before long."

Joe sat quietly and put his helmet back on. He checked his pistols. He leaned back wondering, *What now?*

☦ ☦ ☦

Arleosa bowed in the presence of God. "The field grows crowded, my Lord—Satan seeks to confuse and divide. But our Messiah, Joe Brown, will find the answers. Even now his allies help him to understand the true nature of things."

There was a long pause. "Too much of the guns, Arleosa, too much killing. The Devil laughs in my face!"

"He won't laugh forever!" Arleosa countered. "A conflagration and a battle so great will occur that even the Devil will shrink from evil. It will be a monumental struggle. In the end it will strike a spiritual tone. That can happen yet!"

† † †

Joe got up from the table. "Let me confront the danger and understand it for what it is. Perhaps a measure of understanding can be achieved without violence!"

"Yes, Joe," Saluiana said in agreement. "Without violence, possibly."

That night Queen Saluiana visited Joe. She slipped through the fortress unseen, appearing at her leisure. She wore a clinging gossamer gown. Joe could see every curve of her voluptuous body. Joe was barefoot, with the armored battle suit belt secured to his waist. A T-shirt and shorts were his only clothing. He had been tinkering with his guns and checking a kit filled with explosives, just in case.

The queen sat down as Joe beckoned her to do so. He secured his weapons in the portable force shield that he had placed in the corner. It was a simple metal canister that, if Joe wanted to, could be secured from his armored battle suit control panel, which was a part of his belt.

The queen looked questioningly at Joe as he bolstered a large semiauto pistol onto his belt. He faced the queen, who sat on his bed. He felt the normal level of arousal he always did in her presence. He tried to focus his mind on why she was here with him in his room.

"I want to go hunting," she announced. "You, me, and Sika. Perhaps Bladeswift and Ataka can join us as well."

"All seasoned people, Queen Saluiana, and trusted people who can hold steady in a crisis," Joe said.

"I want to hunt in the direction of the Manwolf cave. To scout—perhaps to even feast with the Manwolves if our hunt is successful."

"We will be successful with such a hunting party, I would think. But how do you know the Manwolves would want to feast with us?" Joe asked.

"If we offer, and I am present, I believe they will want to share whatever the hunt brings."

"What of the king? Even in so formidable a party as ours, won't he be worried about you?" Joe asked.

"Of course. But he knows I know about the Manwolves. If the murder is their doing, I will know that too. We need allies and clear answers, Joe. If there are more enemies nearby, we need to know that too! At an hour before first light, I will be ready, and the rest will join us. I'll see to it."

She stood and bent close to him, pressing her hip into his shoulder, and kissed his forehead and hair. Joe felt his nature pulsing, but he just sat there. The queen was gone in an instant.

That night Joe dreamed of Samantha. He floated into sleep remembering their lovemaking: the long, deep kisses, and his long member being so welcome as they undulated in a wave of passion. Samantha's hips, thick and engaging, molding to Joe as he thrust and as he grasped her ample buttocks. Both he and Samantha moaning in orgasmic exhilaration.

And then he dreamed again. Arleosa joined him in his dreams. The warmth and security of his mother filled him with joy. He saw Arleosa, radiant and filled with light, only for a moment then he knew—vaguely he detected another presence greater than Arleosa filled with light. Too much light.

He was up before first light. The armored battle suit was secured on his person and the sniper rifle slung over his shoulder.

"No horses," Ataka said. "Even well-trained mounts might spook if they encounter a Manwolf." They breakfasted quickly on coffee, sweet buns, and bacon.

After eating, they marched out of the gate, quickly onto the plains beyond the wooded area where Joe could see the cave mouth. There were deer darting in and out of the woods, browsing for leaves and shrubs. Buffalo could be seen on the plains at either side of the cave mouth. Joe steadied the great .50-caliber sniper rifle. The shot hummed out of the barrel and, almost like magic, a buffalo dropped dead. Then from one hundred meters a deer. Joe was accurate and on target.

Sika moved forward with Ataka and Queen Saluiana, who was dressed in leather garments and dragon-scale armor. Bladeswift flanked to the left, sniffing the air for any signs of Manwolves or Demons. The five joined at the spot where the buffalo had fallen. Ataka and Bladeswift made quick work of butchering and skinning the buffalo and building a large fire. The meat was hoisted on skewers, and herbs were applied. In an hour, the fragrance of wood-roasted meat filled the air.

Queen Saluiana closed her eyes and sniffed the air. "Soon they will come," she said.

Soon the hairy Manwolves, with clubs, spears, and slings, came out of the cave mouth. Saluiana beckoned to them. Several Manwolves came and squatted by the fire.

Ataka and Bladeswift offered them meat. The Manwolves let their weapons rest at their sides. They sucked the meat from the rib bones and chewed tendons and ligaments with relish. There were now seven of them. Bladeswift had finished skinning the deer and cooked it on fires. A comely Manwolf woman cut the deer in segments.

Joe was struck by the beauty of the open plains near the cave entrance. He marveled at the blue sky as noon approached. He reflected on his life in New Castle and thought of Samantha as he observed Saluiana talking to the Manwolves.

The Manwolves spoke in low, guttural tones—grunts that, when heard under the right conditions, formed words that were understandable.

Saluiana addressed the Manwolf hetman: "There has been a murder in our temple. It was one of our most senior priests. The signs and marks lead to this direction. Can you help us to understand what has happened?"

"There is a grimness here now," the hetman spoke. "We have heard of the death and knew it would find its way back to us. But it is not of us. Death stalks the land. We are being killed because we will not yield. Come see for yourself in the cave. There is no trap for you, Queen Saluiana, but open warfare awaits all our people."

Saluiana bowed low in acquiescence to the perceived truth of the hetman.

"Our pack leader would speak to you, Your Majesty," the hetman concluded.

"Yes." Saluiana again bowed low to accept the offer. There was silence. More of the Manwolves came from the cave, including women and even small children. They were a very attractive people in spite of their hairy bodies and pronounced canine teeth. The men wore naught but loincloths, and the women, some quite well endowed, wore no torso covers. Some of the men, women, and children wore nothing, and their privates were exposed except for the fur that provided a natural covering.

Sika had been gone briefly. She returned with a deer slung over her shoulders, moving effortlessly as if she were a large man carrying a rabbit. Soon the deer was skinned and thrown on a small metal grate over the fire. Joe looked around. He took in the surroundings where the plains met the woods. He took his helmet off and absorbed everything around him. The smell of the wood, the cooking meat. He looked up at the blue sky, so wonderful to look upon. He reminisced about the days he played football and went to big summer barbecues before training camp started.

Later in the day, Bladeswift was more relaxed than Joe had ever seen him. Sika smiled lovingly at Joe from time to time. Saluiana waited, appraising all around her. Even Ataka ate some of the barbecued meat.

Then the quiet was broken by the beat of drums. Joe put his helmet on. The peaceful reverie was ended by the sudden commotion.

The Manwolves started chanting, "Ohtokan, Ohtokan, Ohtokan." The drumbeat continued.

Suddenly Joe saw what the fanfare was about. He stood about six feet, six inches tall, this Manwolf with jet-black fur and inch-long fangs protruding from his mouth. He wore a loincloth that bulged with virility in Joe's appraisal: *well, hung* would have been the term. He carried a large club that Joe thought must have been the thigh bone of a buffalo. He wore no shoes but padded lightly on the ground. His eyes were red in color and burned with intensity. Joe immediately scanned this Ohtokan to see if indeed he was the murderer they pursued.

Queen Saluiana, filled with guilt, acquiesced to this Manwolf chief. She beckoned him to sit and eat from the hunt. She offered him buffalo, venison, and wild boar.

Joe's attention wavered from the barbecue and focused on Ohtokan.

Ohtokan bowed and sat down. Taking their cues from Saluiana, members of his tribe immediately retrieved pieces of meat from the fire and handed it to him. Ohtokan eyed Joe curiously. Joe was in full scan mode, running a feed from his helmet to the ACV. There were some organic similarities between Ohtokan and the murderer, but he didn't seem to be the one.

Saluiana began her supplications to Ohtokan, "Oh great Ohtokan, we are happy to provide this offering to you and your tribe."

"Yes, yes, and we have been quite hungry of late. Thank you."

His language was more like a guttural groan but somehow barely discernable. "Our people did not kill the priest, but we know, I know, who did," Ohtokan said. He seemed bereft of ego and just kept eating.

Must have been a long time since his last meal, Joe thought. He ate ravenously like, well, a wolf. Joe sensed no subterfuge would come from this creature.

"Please, great Ohtokan, tell us what happened," Saluiana said.

"I was there," he began, "tracking the killer through the plains and woods. I know of him; he has slain many of our tribe. He has come to our cave home, attacking us as we slept."

Hmm, Joe thought. *Perhaps that explains where the trail led.*

Ohtokan began describing in painful detail his effort to track and slay this killer, only to find the killer was making his way back to his own home.

Saluiana implored him, "Why did you not come to me for aid?"

Though there had been peace recently, the Long-Strider expansion campaign had mauled and beat the Manwolves from a prominent presence in the area. Sometimes the removal had been through force, at other times just by claiming land for pasture and farmland. Saluiana, Joe surmised, had been an unsuccessful advocate for them.

"I cannot come to the Long-Striders for aid, lest I be accused of the priest's murder. If I could have stopped the murder out of respect for

Queen Saluiana, I would have. But I was too late." Ohtokan reached for a pouch secured to a thick rope tied around his waist. He reached inside and produced a large scale about three inches in diameter. It had some strands of hair on its edges and some blood on its underside.

Joe started scanning and sending the feed to the ACV. He sat quietly waiting. The scan came back as a hybrid. The hairs were lupine. The skin was Demon.

Joe took his helmet off. Saluiana introduced Joe to Ohtokan.

"I am Joe," Joe said. "I want to know where the creature who was attached to this scale can be found. Can you help me?"

Sika looked startled at Joe's words. Then she composed herself.

Ohtokan looked at Joe, appraising him. "We have heard of your coming...you are the great Demon Killer, the Thunder Death who comes in no time! Thunder Death who comes in an instant! We have followed your coming. But can you kill the one that is a master among Demons? He hides in shadows, falls upon all of us with death. We call him the Demonogre—even Demons fear it!"

Joe leaned back, away from the fire. Sika nervously touched her sword and the single-shot pistol she had received from Joe. Saluiana looked nervously at Ohtokan. Ataka shifted and rose from his seat by the fire, put on his helmet, and moved his lips in what seemed to be a silent prayer.

Bladeswift, quiet until now, spoke resolutely but conservatively. "The day has come when the picture of our demise can be drawn. We know the threat has been coming for quite a while. A determining blow must be struck to show we can prevail. Ohtokan will show us the way to that path. Joe is the blow we need to consecrate victory."

Ohtokan rose abruptly, still chewing venison. He said, "Then tomorrow we will find him. I know a path through our caves from whence he comes to attack Long-Striders, Wildriders, and any who stand in his path."

Saluiana stood and interjected as only a queen might. "Long have you suffered by our people, Ohtokan. How now is it that you bring yourselves to our aid?"

Ataka looked toward the queen. It was hard to discern the expression on his face, as he had donned his shiny black helmet.

Ohtokan, in a series of grunts and strangled words, uttered, "We live less now that Long-Striders have come, but with Demons attacking, we live not at all."

Joe could see the pride this creature had, and intuitively he knew it took a lot for him to utter those words—and not just due to his problems with enunciation.

There was silence for a while as the eating resumed and more Manwolf women and children came out to share in the feast. Soon a throng of Manwolf warriors joined as well. Some wore dragon-scale armor. Joe made a note in the ABS computer, *Dragon-scale armor,* and another note about improving the weaponry of Manwolves.

Evening came, and before the party concluded, the Manwolves shared some of their strong stout beer. Joe had again removed his helmet and enjoyed the smell of wood and cooking meat. He drank the cool beer and smiled to himself, his thoughts going back to his former life. Barbeques with extended family members as a child and then as a man with friends and, of course, Samantha. Joe couldn't help but compare any attractive woman to Samantha. Sika and Saluiana were good comparisons—Joe thought each self-reliant and capable in their own way.

The evening came, and darkness began to fall. The little party of Ataka, Saluiana, Joe, Bladeswift, and Sika would be returning to the fortress.

Ohtokan himself grasped a torch, and with several of the pack warriors, escorted the party back through the plains and forest to reach the ramparts.

There was a great sound of distress from the ramparts when the Manwolves came into view. Ataka and Queen Saluiana hailed the fort to reassure the guards. Ohtokan bid them farewell until tomorrow, when an undecided small force would join him to find the shadow Demon who lurked mysteriously in the caves where his pack had taken refuge. As he bid them farewell, Ohtokan and his pack warriors took off running through the woods.

Magnificent athletes, Joe thought. He would be hard pressed to surpass their speed even using the ABS, which augmented his own movements.

That night he received separate visits from both Sika and Saluiana. They both offered healing herbs and restorative mushrooms they insisted he eat in the morning. Sika offered a nighttime remedy she said would help restore him from the effects of drinking the harsh stout beer offered by the Manwolves.

Joe sat on his bed, resting comfortably in a moisture-wicking T-shirt and shorts he had brought from the ACV.

Saluiana had come and gone, but now Sika sat with him, explaining the use the herbs and mushrooms. She described how more could be found in the caves of the Manwolves, as well as throughout the forest, if he needed more of them.

Joe donned his pistols and the .50-caliber sniper rifle despite Sika assuring him they would not be helpful in the caves.

He knew. But he loved striking from a great distance as a tactic and a way of creating fear in the enemy.

"I have heard of this creature we stalk, Joe," Sika spoke in hesitant tones. "He is the Demon who creates the most chaos. He often, but not always, travels alone. Bladeswift once wounded him but was almost killed as a result. He is intelligent and rageful at the same time. Where is your sword, Joe?"

As almost an afterthought, Joe picked up the Vibro-Blade. He turned it on and checked it. It was charged and ready from ambient energy as well as proximity to the ABS. Joe sought one last thing: the feed from the evidence collected from the murder scene. There was a mixture of Manwolf and Demon particles. Perhaps Ohtokan had tried to prevent the murder but had not been successful. Perhaps he feared to show how vulnerable he'd become, now marginalized by the Long-Striders, and facing extinction via the Demons. Joe knew the Manwolves were facing a species-ending fate.

Saluiana believed something was afoot. She had shared her guilty misgiving due to the long-standing oppression of the Manwolves by King Kotutan. The Manwolves had always been hunters, gatherers, and raiders. The raiding included anything they could take, and cattle was often on their short list.

The Long-Striders had hunted and warred against the Manwolves and had beaten them into a sort of submission. No Manwolf would threaten the Long-Striders. Saluiana worried the Manwolves wished to draw the Long-Striders into more conflict with the Demons to bolster their own security in some way.

Joe pondered the politics of his situation. Manwolves, Long-Striders, and Demons, all wanted something they did not have dominance and control, the age-old precursors to calamity. The night was growing late. Joe turned the Vibro-Blade over in his hand. Sika nodded approvingly. He took a small chip from the ABS and inserted it into the hilt of the Vibro-Blade.

"This will help me know how best to hit," he said, looking intently into Sika's eyes, wondering if she knew what he meant.

"Um." She looked quizzically at Joe for a moment, then said, "A blessing or charm from an Angel?"

"Exactly," Joe answered. "Indeed, just like that!"

Sika bid Joe goodbye until the morning. She kissed him on the cheeks and forehead, hugged him to a point of intensity that overwhelmed him. He felt the familiar attraction. Catching his breath, he returned her hug in the most tender way he could. With that, Sika was gone.

Joe slept restfully from the moment he put his head down on the feather pillow. As it usually did, a golden glow streamed through his consciousness. He saw himself in a great battle with one opponent. He recognized it as a large Demon. But this Demon wore heavy armor. Dragon-scale armor. His eyes gleamed with intelligence. He swung a great sword and an axe. The great sword was wielded by one hand. It would be impossible for a mere man to use such a sword with one hand. The axe was employed to block and counterstrike. This creature stood seven feet tall and was thickly muscled. He looked to be a half ton in weight. Arleosa pushed the light of hope into Joe. He was momentarily fearful but slept soundly the rest of the night.

Arleosa looked at God. "It's not our fault if Satan pushes his agenda. There will be suffering like so many times before, but in the end, suffering brings them all back to you, does it not?"

God seemed troubled. He withdrew to the higher celestial towers and said not another word. Arleosa was left wondering.

✝ ✝ ✝

Satan sat alone in Hell. He was very angry about the recent events. *God never played fair*, he thought. *Now, some new Messiah, God's house negro from another planet, sought to upstage what surely would be my crowning moment. I will shred the faith of the Long-Striders, enslave everyone, and prove that, well, aggressive devilishness runs amok in all cases. But, no, this new Messiah—I must have his head. My newly concocted Demon, Deathmet, will do the trick.*

He sat quietly, fondling a beautiful devil woman. He caressed her buttocks, allowing his hands to follow the line and curve of her voluptuous hips. The devil people were Satan's augmentation. They looked human but were a higher form of Demon. Their skin had the reddish hue of all Demons, but they were a beautiful version designed to keep Satan company.

Now, he thought as he caressed her further, *Deathmet will get the job done.*

"You are beautiful, my lord. Do I please you?" she asked. Satan was indeed impressive—a red glow emanated from his body. He had no horns but sharp red eyes. The Devil could never reach the transcendental spirit energy of God and true Angels. He must always toil in the world of matter until, well, a violent death found him. Such was the course he chose when he refuted God. No access to Heaven was apparent. By all appearances, he was a handsome, muscular man. Brick red in color, but perfect in every way. The devil woman he fondled was the same. Beautiful, voluptuous.

Once Satan seduced humanity, he had only to plant his seed into the often quite-willing human women. Then he spawned children and minions. The Demons had come from a concoction of synthetic life the

Devil honed into both human and Demon form. His female voluptuaries seduced human men. He molded genetic material into Manwolves, Demons, and devil people. Eventually they had no humanity left to speak of. They were all the seed of Hell.

☦ ☦ ☦

When the morning came, Joe awoke as well rested as ever. He had dreamed of an eternal life where he was secure and wanted for nothing. He had experienced the golden glow once again. It nurtured him, comforted him, and strengthened him.

Arleosa beamed. She would slowly become closer and more apparent to Joe. A bond was connecting the two of them. It was reinforced by the new connections he was making with Sika and Saluiana, who were increasingly becoming more important to him, in ways no woman had ever before.

As usual, everyone gathered in the great hall for breakfast. Sika, Bladeswift, Ataka, and even Queen Saluiana would venture forth. The queen would act as a liaison; her relationship with the Manwolves was needed.

Queen Saluiana spoke of concerns about the murder of the wiseman and what it might mean.

Joe secured and checked his pistols. The Vibro-Blade was charged and ready. He had secured one more weapon that had stood the test of time: the fission revolver. It was a huge pistol in a holster located on the small of his back. He also carried a few explosive devices just in case.

Sika stood proudly sipping her coffee and eating the seed bread the Long-Striders baked. She wore leather boots and forearm guards, a skin-tight tunic laced with dragon scales, and baggy leather pants. She carried Joe's gift, a one-shot rifle-barreled pistol, and a quiver of arrows. Her bow was strung over her shoulders. She also had her long sword and a machete.

Ataka, too, was set for business. He wore black armor with scales from a large, mature dragon. His great sword was sheathed on his back. He also carried a rifle-barreled pistol, a long bow, and a quiver of arrows.

The queen appeared. She carried two short swords, a pistol, and a large, curved bow.

Bladeswift was equipped with a great sword, a bow, arrows, and a rifle-barreled pistol.

"Where are your shields?" Joe asked, almost embarrassed by his urgent question.

Ataka spoke in response. "This is a hunt, Joe, not a war raid. We must find the murderer and slay him!"

Joe knew they would be on foot through the caves and deep down into and the Manwolves' dens.

King Kotutan was late to this early breakfast. He looked uncomfortable and distressed.

Why is the king visibly shaken? Joe thought as he drank coffee and chewed on nuts and beef jerky.

King Kotutan directed his queries to Joe and Sika. "Have you concluded your findings?"

Sika spoke quickly, "Yes, Great King. The thing we are looking for is not a Manwolf. It was something else. We will have to go deeper into the Manwolves' caves to track it."

The king still looked distraught.

Joe responded, "I factored in everything. My analysis results were about the same as Sika's. A Manwolf was present, but something else was in the area as well. Something that was a cross between Demons and Manwolves but was more closely aligned to the Demons."

"I will trust you can protect the queen," said the king. "She must accompany you as she can soothe the animals. I—I—" the king stammered, "have not been a friend to them." There was a hush in the hall. "I am in part the reason we now fear or suspect them. I drove them into their caverns because they were a threat to our progress. I went too far."

The two remaining priests, Osala and Boswan, joined the group in the hall. They were dressed in their robes and hoods.

The king stood, staring. Stammering, he managed, "I was warned by the priest and my queen, Saluiana. But I would not heed. Now I have opened access to our rear guard. Perhaps all this is due to my oppression of the Manwolves." With that, the king wished them well and left with the priests, who consoled him.

The group proceeded to the stables, mounted, and rode out the gate. They rode into the fading darkness until the Manwolves' cave mouths dimly came into view. They dismounted, and Bladeswift's well-trained horse led the other mounts back across the plain to the fortress.

Out of the darkness stepped Ohtokan. His belt carried his bone club. Joe stepped forward and acknowledged him. Bladeswift, Ataka, and Sika all bowed to him.

Ohtokan rallied them. "We go quick. The smell of the beast is upon us in the caves."

Beast thought Joe. *How ironic.*

The descent into the caves was dark. Joe grabbed a flashlight from the ABS. The rest lit torches. Ohtokan and a warrior led the group.

"Keep light down—we will spot for you." The guttural tongue of Ohtokan sounded odd in a whisper.

There were long, dark tunnels leading to the Manwolves' shelters.

Must be terrible to sleep right by your enemies, Joe thought, *never knowing when they might come up to raid and kill you.*

No wonder Saluiana felt bad, and the king was expressing guilt. The Manwolves were pushed to a point of no return. If something weren't done, they'd be just another extinct group. It reminded Joe of his country's early history. How the new world was overrun with Long-Striders and the native people were reduced to a way of life on reservations where they were impoverished. The Manwolves had a fighting chance with a little help. No wonder they wanted to help find the priest's killer. They wanted help.

Joe scanned ahead with the ABS's night-vision mode. The cave wound down left and then right again, based on Joe's GPS. They were about two hundred meters below the surface and still descending.

The two Manwolves, Ohtokan and his designated tracker, started to move more slowly. Joe got one of his pistols ready. He had three guns, including the fission pistol. The Vibro-Blade would provide close-quarter support.

Joe noticed the Manwolves crouching lower. Sika nocked an arrow, Bladeswift unlimbered his great broadsword. The queen drew her twin swords. Ataka pulled his long bow, nocking an arrow.

9.

THE CULPRIT

Ahead Joe could see the body of a partially eaten and burned Manwolf. His thigh and ribs had been roasted over a fire. There were still a few burning embers. Joe could smell the burnt flesh and charred wood.

Farther down, past the embers and Manwolf remains, the tunnel took a ninety-degree turn, as if it had been excavated. Joe scanned ahead using night vision and the scanning device of the ABS. There was nothing in view. The cave tunnel expanded and extended another hundred meters or so.

Ohtokan grimaced but kept going. He crouched on one knee, shifted his club, and resumed a low-posture movement.

Joe continued to scan forward, but he was limited without the ship's assistance and power.

More dead corpses of Manwolves littered the cave tunnel as they descended. The corpses were partially torn apart, sometimes missing arms or legs or even having ribs torn out. There was a stench that started building as they went farther. Joe knew the smell of death, but this was just a little more intense.

They were startled to see dead Demons as well. Several of the Demon corpses had smashed heads. Ohtokan grinned in satisfaction.

Sika and Saluiana crinkled their noses almost in unison. Joe, observing them, grinned to himself. *Vive la différence*, he thought.

Weapons lay littering the tunnel. Spears, axes, bows, and quivers of arrows attached to the bodies of Demons.

Ohtokan hissed, "Wait, be ready!"

Joe moved closer to Ohtokan and his pack mate. Joe estimated they were five hundred meters underground. The ABS GPS indicated the same. Joe picked up his pace, staying close to Ohtokan. He took his pistol out, checked the hand-cannon fission revolver holstered at the small of his back.

Ohtokan stopped suddenly and grunted, "There!"

Joe couldn't see anything, but a few seconds later, he saw what Ohtokan was pointing at.

Flanked by several armored Demons, Joe saw what appeared to be a giant Demon at first glance. He stood at least seven feet tall, with huge shoulders and thickly muscled legs. He was covered in dragon scales from head to toe. He wore a helmet with large devil-like horns. Behind the faceguard of the helmet, Joe could see the familiar brick-red complexion. The huge creature had no shield but carried an axe in one hand and long sword in the other. The axe had a spike above the blade and one at the back end of its handle. The whole thing seemed to be made of welded steel.

These dragon scales thought Joe. *Not too many creatures had them. Sika said you had to be involved in killing a dragon to get them. Enough of this thinking.*

Suddenly Joe's attention was riveted on Ohtokan, who threw a spear he'd picked up en route. It seemed to whistle in the air as it abruptly struck one of the Demons guarding the creature's flanks.

"I am Deathmet!" the large Demon bellowed.

Joe marveled at the plausible appropriateness of the name. *Laughable,* he thought.

Ohtokan's pack mate hurled a second spear. It, too, found its mark, knocking down a second Demon directly beside Deathmet. The humor drained from Joe as he realized this challenge would be his.

Ohtokan turn on his heel. "We go now, because if you lose, we must move our tribe or face Deathmet!"

Out and away, they bounded gracefully and quickly, leaving the scene after taking down two Demons. Sika and Bladeswift made quick work of the remaining Demons guarding Deathmet. Joe advanced, firing his two semiautomatic pistols.

Deathmet staggered but appeared unhurt. Advancing, Deathmet was upon Joe, swinging the long sword in a horizontal arc right at Joe's torso. Joe ducked, but the sword was followed by a by jab from the spike on Deathmet's axe handle. Joe pushed the axe aside with the armored wrist guard of the ABS, making sharp contact. Jabbing upward, he slammed the butt of his pistol into Deathmet's jaw.

Reeling backward, with little time to swing the long sword, Deathmet brought the handle butt down hard. Joe, seeing the blow coming, started to roll but not before taking a hard glancing blow to the head, which emitted a cracking sound. Standing, Joe felt slightly dazed. In the background he could see Ataka, Bladeswift, Sika, and Saluiana firing arrows. They were holding off a score of Demons seeking to reach and aid Deathmet.

Time seemed to slow; Joe reeled off several rounds past Deathmet to bring down the supporting Demons coming against the group. Ataka had dropped his bow and was slamming his broadsword in an arc into the neck of a Demon.

Saluiana, the queen, had Joe worried. *A queen coming to fight.*

Saluiana wielded her two swords expertly. Her athletic body and full hips thrusting the sword with great leverage, sticking the knee and stomach of one Demon in a whirlwind of spinning cuts. Joe had timed his shots well. He had taken down a few Demons as they closed in on his companions.

Sika fired arrows from a distance at Deathmet. Bladeswift set up on the opposite side of the cave but had little room to make the crossfire of arrows he and Sika intended to inflict. Little damage was done to Deathmet from the arrows. However, the arrows helped even the odds by killing many of the Demons. Deathmet lurched forward as Joe produced his Vibro-Blade. Joe dodged sideways, avoiding the downward arc of Deathmet's broadsword. Deathmet swung his axe. Joe moved quickly, sidestepping the axe and simultaneously pinning Deathmet's arm down with a palm thrust. Gripping his Vibro-Blade with both hands, Joe slammed it into Deathmet's hamstring and butt area. Deathmet staggered, but as he did, he spun and jabbed Joe with the spike in front of his axe blade. Joe felt the blow cut into the ABS and rolled backward.

Before rising, visibly stunned, he heard Sika gasp. She fired several arrows that glanced off of Deathmet's helmet. Deathmet had fallen on one knee and now struggled to rise and regain his balance. Joe sheathed the Vibro-Blade and pulled his fission revolver, the hand cannon. Joe stepped forward, shaken, but aimed right at Deathmet's torso.

Blam! Blam!

Two shots hit Deathmet in the chest, slamming him back. Before Joe could get off another shot, another Demon entered the melee and threw a spear at Joe's gun hand. Joe almost lost the fission revolver.

Deathmet was on his feet, charging at Joe. Joe dropped under the sword strike and rushed forward, slamming his shoulder into Deathmet's gut. Joe wrapped his arms fully around Deathmet, heaving him into the air and slamming him backward on his head. Ataka and Bladeswift moved forward, hacking Deathmet with their swords. Joe moved forward as more Demons entered the melee. He fired his pistols, cutting them down. Sika and Saluiana fired their arrows at the massing force coming up from around the bend of the tunnel.

Joe emptied his pistols and went back to locate Deathmet.

Ataka and Bladeswift engaged Deathmet for only a few moments. He shook them off like a rhino knocking back a pack of wild dogs with its horn. Deathmet's sword and axe blows were devastating, driving back Ataka and Bladeswift. Both seemed stunned by the fury of Deathmet's attack. Joe fired into Deathmet with the remaining shots of the fission hand cannon. Deathmet turned away from Ataka and Bladeswift, who were in retreat. He spun around, and before Joe realized what was happening, Deathmet kicked him forcefully in the head. Joe sprawled on the ground, barely conscious. He rolled back as Ataka and Bladeswift renewed their attack, charging in with blows that finally began to cut away some of Deathmet's dragon scales. Distracted by Joe, Deathmet had little time to defend against Ataka and Bladeswift. Bladeswift and Ataka knew the advantage would not last long.

"Back around the corner," Bladeswift yelled as he reached to help Joe stand up.

"Go," Joe whispered, producing the Vibro-Blade.

Deathmet charged as they moved to round the corner away from the massing Demons. Joe pushed forward, this time deflecting the broadsword cut he knew was coming. It was followed by a knee thrust, which he blocked with his forearm. Deathmet's axe slammed into Joe's shoulder. Joe reeled back and slumped to one knee.

Ataka and Bladeswift protected Joe's flanks, making side-slicing cuts at Deathmet, holding back any Demon wishing to aid Deathmet's struggle. Joe got up. Again, he darted low and deflected Deathmet's broadsword. As the axe fell, he blocked that as well, his Vibro-Blade dancing like a pixie in the moonlight. Finally slamming forward, Joe caught Deathmet in the gut with a punch. He gripped the Vibro-Blade with both hands and slammed it into the ribs of Deathmet, who staggered with an audible groan.

Joe's shoulder burned with pain. Demons started to fill the tunnel. In one final defiant act, Joe slapped Deathmet in the face with his palm. He grabbed Deathmet's helmet, yanked it off and backhanded Deathmet with another slap before the helmet could hit the ground.

The Demons rushing in were stunned by what they saw, gesturing wildly, seeming to laugh.

Joe watched, left shoulder burning, as Deathmet was unable to respond. Finally, Joe slammed his right fist into Deathmet's stomach. Deathmet fell backward.

Joe turned toward Ataka and Bladeswift. "Run!" he bellowed.

Saluiana and Sika remained, firing arrows. Several of the oncoming Demons, transfixed by Deathmet's apparent defeat, were caught unaware, and Saluiana and Sika's arrows hit them in their throats and stomachs where their armor was thin.

Ataka and Bladeswift reached Sika and Saluiana. As they did, Joe was surrounded by Demons. All four of them let fly a volley of arrows. Joe faced Deathmet, who just sat on his ass momentarily before attempting to rise. By the time he had reached a knee, Joe was cracking the Vibro-Blade into the ribs, knees, and shoulders of several Demons. Upon being struck with the blows, they lost interest in Deathmet's plight as they succumbed to their own.

Joe faced a standing Deathmet. He stepped away, spun back, and slammed a kick into Deathmet's face. Without losing a step, he ran toward his four companions. Looking over his shoulder, Joe saw Deathmet sprawled flat on his back. Joe fired a burst of rounds at the pursuing Demons, then he and the rest sprinted back the way they had come. Joe reached into his harness and found two grenades. Pulling the pins, he threw one back around the corner. As he continued to run, he made sure his comrades were clear then threw the final grenade against a tunnel wall near the turn he'd just made.

That grenade bounced and angled toward the still-pursuing Demons. *Boom! Boom!*

Joe scanned back for pursuing Demons, but none were there. He set a trip wire with an explosive just around the next corner. He felt this would close down pursuit and might even shut down the tunnel opening.

Once they reached the surface, Ohtokan joined them. Joe warned him of the explosive trip wire with some interpretive help from Saluiana.

Joe's shoulder was burning as the five headed back to the fortress. Sika looked around and picked some flowers and other herbs. Joe wondered at the timing of this.

Back at the fortress gates, King Kotutan greeted them.

Joe was in obvious pain. He noticed Sika bite off a few pieces of the herbs, chew them, and then spit into a pouch. Just inside the fortress, Joe stumbled to one knee, as Deathmet had, but no kick came to greet his weakness. Both Sika and Saluiana, who were fresh from the king's embrace, flew to lift him to his feet as though he were their firstborn child.

In Joe's room, the two women pulled and tussled with the ABS to no avail. Finally, Joe triggered the releases, and they were able to get it off. Sika poured the contents of the pouch she'd been spitting into and stirred it into water. She was a little dazed. She offered Joe the water.

Saluiana lifted the glass to his lips, urging him. "Drink, Joe."

Joe drank the bittersweet brew. He soon understood why Sika had looked dazed.

He leaned back on the bed. The ABS was on his belt. Saluiana sought to undo the ABS.

Joe touched her hand. "No, dear queen, it should stay. The belt must remain."

Sika nodded approvingly. "A true warrior. Never far from his armor."

Sika grinned, and using a mortar and pestle, she ground away the herbs collected earlier, producing more of the powder, which she poured into water for Joe to drink.

Joe leaned back again and slept. When he awoke, he saw Sika and Saluiana sleeping on cots by his side. The pain in his shoulder had decreased from a sharp pain to a dull ache.

Joe could see the light from a hallway under his door. "What time is it?" he asked.

"It's 6:00 a.m.," Sika offered.

Joe stirred, and both women sought to caress him into restfulness.

"Don't try to move too much," Saluiana said. "Your shoulder was badly pummeled, but no surgeon looks to be needed."

Joe closed his eyes. "Coffee! How 'bout some coffee? I need to confer with King Kotutan. There is grave danger. I dreamed of the Devil marching on this fortress. Deathmet is his messenger. Believe me, it's later than it seems." With that, Joe fell back on his bed and slept until the afternoon.

It was one in the afternoon when Joe awoke. The dull ache in his shoulder had subsided to a light pulsing throb.

Saluiana had left the room. Sika remained, staring adoringly into Joe's eyes, lovingly offering him coffee. He started to stand. He fell back on the bed, gently guided down by Sika the last few feet. He would not meet the king today. Sika got into the bed beside Joe. They slept.

Joe saw a vision of Demons marauding and attacking Long-Strider settlements across the western frontier. It dawned on Joe: Why he did care? Weren't these Long-Striders just like the people who had enslaved his ancestors centuries ago? As a final affront, he had fought to secure oil for them. How could all this be? The Demons were a threat to both worlds. Even the Long-Striders had made peace with the Wildriders. But Demons would wipe out all humanity; even though humanity was often at odds with each other, the Demons were a wake-up call that everyone should become united.

Joe realized he'd wanted acceptance all along. Football and mercenary work offered both, but the mercenary work shamed him, because he had committed violence to get oil. To make money for himself and others.

A descendent of slaves, he had become an instrument of the very values that once enslaved his people. Colonialism.

The Long-Striders were colonialists too. But they had accepted him and allied with the Wildriders. The Manwolves had not been so lucky. They had been too different: both in looks and their nature.

The Demons were a fine contrast. There would be no empathy for them; they wanted to devour humanity. No enemy would have such a unifying effect on society. The Long-Striders overlooked Joe's Blackness because they needed his help. Because they were in a time of need and crisis, they accepted Joe—he would help them survive by altering the values of their society. They would become greater allies of the Wildriders. Sharing wealth would occur more readily between the nobles and settlers to defeat the Demons.

Joe was well beyond acceptance; he was their Messiah. Ending pain and suffering were great motivators for unity. He wanted to keep the world intact, raise humanity to a higher standard, and let them see that a Black man was doing it. This could be a redemption for him. A way to absolve himself of some of the suffering his mercenary work had caused.

☩ ☩ ☩

Arleosa looked up at God, who was musing over the current events that had befallen His Messiah, Joe Brown. Grudgingly, He started to accept Joe. He admired the way Joe appreciated the responsiveness of Saluiana and Sika: two women who clearly loved him but who he would not take advantage of because he loved them too. Satan had sent the better of his concoctions to meet Joe, who though hurt, got the best of the fight psychologically, defeating Deathmet without having to kill him. *A ploy,* God thought, *but a useful one.*

Arleosa knew God was pleased and yet worried how all this would end. Arleosa knew she needed more from Joe Brown, much more, but what would God want from him?

Secretly Arleosa wished Joe would become more intimate with one of the women. Sika was the safer choice. Arleosa thought a fulfilling love connection might serve Joe well, though the obvious drawbacks would come to light. She longed to live through Joe and his love life to vicariously experience the lust of the flesh to feel and be a part of his orgasmic pleasure. She knew God was right. Stay on the task—let Joe reach his full capacity as the Messiah she needed him to be.

✝ ✝ ✝

Joe slept until the next morning.

When he awoke, Sika sat making herbal concoctions and pouring them into vials. As Joe opened his eyes, Sika proffered a cup of green liquid.

"Drink this, Joe. It will help you heal," she said.

Joe's shoulder still throbbed. He thought he needed to get to his ship and into the ACV's healing pod. Joe stood up and started to use his left arm. He swung the Vibro-Blade weakly. However, he felt loose. His shoulder seemed to be coming around. He drank more of the green beverage. It tasted of cinnamon and nutmeg. But there was a strong presence of wheatgrass Joe knew from his own world. The more he drank, the better he felt.

"Enough, Joe" Sika warned. "Wait and go to the sauna. There you can stimulate further healing with the heat."

Sika was clad in a plain short dress and sandals. Her athletic legs and shapely hips, as well as her butt falling out the back of the dress, caught Joe's attention immediately. He was feeling better already.

Joe sat in the sauna. Sika removed her dress, revealing what seemed a cross between underwear and a bikini. They sat there together. Joe dozed off. He dreamed that Sika and he were lovers. They were engaging in foreplay, kissing, and fondling one another. The dream ended with Joe and Sika having wild sex.

Joe awoke, sitting there shirtless in his athletic shorts with the belt of the ABS on his waist. Joe fell asleep again and dreamed. He dreamed of being in battle. There were Demons, and he was alone. He was fighting and slaying an army of Demons, then Deathmet arrived, and Joe was beat within an inch of his life. The sky parted, and golden light shone everywhere. He felt the presence of love and motherhood he had grown accustomed to. In the dream he was given directions to go somewhere. But he had never heard of this place before. It was called the land of the Hivers.

The next day Joe awoke, and he was handed a cup of coffee. He drank greedily at the edge of his bed. Sika poured more coffee into his cup from a clay pitcher. She was dressed in leather and dragon-scale armor. Joe, taking the cue, activated his ABS. The helmet was on, and he started flexing his wounded shoulder.

Sika led him to the parade ground to the east of the king's quarters.

Sika pointed to what looked to be an oval track. "Let's run a few turns," she suggested.

It was close to 6:00 a.m., and Joe was feeling hungry, but he knew he wanted to test his readiness. They were off, and Sika set a blistering pace. According to the info in the ABS, they completed the first quarter mile in sixty seconds. Then they slowed and plodded along at a jog.

Sika started heading for the main gate. Joe pushed after her, the ABS vents starting to cool his now-perspiring body. Sika ran to the gate, launched herself, and grabbed the ten-foot rampart where the guards stood. In an instant she was over and on the other side.

Joe wondered, *what's this going to be about?* Feeling competitive, he launched himself up on the rampart in one bound. He landed next to one of the guards, who was startled by his presence. In an instant, he was over the wall, running right behind Sika.

Sika kept pushing hard, with Joe suddenly falling farther behind. His shoulder started to ache; several days in bed had weakened his stamina. He was laboring now.

Sika looked over her shoulder as if to say, *Come on, Joe, Where you at?*

Joe slowed even more. "Okay, I get it. Now how about breakfast? Not ready for this. Not ready for the battlefield either."

"One more speed up, Joe. All out. Try it." Joe started accelerating. Sika had started sprinting, but he was next to her in no time. He passed her after forty meters. Sprinting sixty more meters, Joe pushed hard, then settled to a jog.

"Breakfast waits," Sika chided.

They jogged back to the fortress. Mercifully, the gates were opened. No more heroics. Joe was happy to just jog on through side by side with Sika. Once in the main hall, Joe drank coffee while he sat in front of King Kotutan and Queen Saluiana.

Sika sat by Joe, wearing her armor, ready for anything. Joe diminished the ABS to his belt.

"No, Joe," Sika warned. "Everything must be worn except the helmet. You must prepare!"

Joe knew Sika was right. He enveloped himself in the ABS and continued drinking coffee.

Joe was served eggs and bacon, which he ate ravenously. Hotcakes were also brought by the serving girls. Joe beckoned one.

"No, Joe." Sika's voice was sharp. "First you must get back your strength. Once you're in full form, there will be enough time for hotcakes and honey as well!"

Joe looked startled. "Okay, right!" Joe's look of dismay caused Queen Saluiana to blush.

Joe tried to gain his emotional equilibrium. The presence he so often felt seemed to whisper to him.

"My king," Joe said humbly. "What of these Hivers, indigenous to the south that live, like, well, an insect hive?"

A hush fell over the hall.

"*The Hivers?*" King Kotutan responded, almost choking on his last bite of bacon. "How did you come to even know of them, Joe?"

Joe was eager to respond. "I found reference to them in a dream. They seemed to have the numbers needed to turn the tide, to make the Demons turn back—perhaps rout them."

"Know this, Joe. The insect men, or Hivers, hate us. They are not our allies. They would invade here themselves if there were a need. They hate our ponderous incursions in this land, but their needs have never brought them here. They only go where they need to."

"Your Lordship, Demons bring Hell wherever they can." Joe said. "Are not the Demons a threat to the Hivers as well?"

"How we could ever get them to help us is beyond my thinking," The king snapped.

"Joe, why this idea, and how would you proceed aside from this dream you had?" Saluiana interjected.

Joe mused for a moment. "Perhaps in a quieter setting, I could go into more detail," Joe remarked. Sika looked horrified but said nothing.

Joe's shoulder had improved daily. The sauna and herbs were restoring his strength and vitality, allowing him to condition more effectively day after day.

Joe was out on the parade ground with Sika soon after breakfast. He practiced swordsmanship with blunt weapons. This was followed by conditioning: wind sprint intervals and pushing weighted carts. After the conditioning, there was an herbal massage.

"Why the Hivers, Joe?" Sika asked. The day had grown into late afternoon, and they were back in Joe's room. "They are the most formidable and exclusionary society in our world. We fear what could happen if they stirred from their part of the world. But they prefer the lush southern jungles, bounding with tremendous animal life. Vicious animal life that only the Hivers can contend with."

"Have you ever been among them?" Joe asked Sika.

"No. No, but we've seen them from a distance. During our explorations to the south. We concluded long ago, as did the Long-Striders, no further southern explorations were warranted."

"Tell me more," Joe asked.

"Let's wait until after dinner," Sika implored. "Do not speak of it at the meal. It will upset those around us."

After dinner, Joe and Sika returned to his room and sipped wine.

Sike returned to the conversation about the Hivers. "The Hivers are, well, like a hive of insects. They have a king and a queen. They are small but well built. In fact, they are born with armor attached to their bodies.

Their weapons are simple: swords and spears. No bows and arrows that we know of. No shields either. They wear no additional armor. They communicate in an unseen manner. The warriors swarm enemies with sheer numbers.

"Once the Long-Striders considered settling there. In fact, a young Kotutan led an expedition of a hundred. Only a few returned, maybe seven. They were decimated by a swarm of Hivers. The Long-Striders pierced the Hivers who came close with bows and crossbows. Many Hivers kept charging, even as arrows pierced their armor but did not kill them. Crossbows worked best at close range, but they take time to load.

"The southern lands are treacherous. Even though the Demons seem to be everywhere, they also hesitate to encroach too far into the southern lands. The South has so many varied forms of life. The Greenflyers are said to wage a guerrilla war from their fetid swamps. They attack any living creature who ventures near them. They crave flesh and consume any creature they can take down to feed their young. The maturation of their young is determined by how much they're fed. They fly like hornets and descend from the trees and cloudy skies to hit and kill. They drag away what they can or come back for it later. Often, they attack, kill, and wait for men to bury their victim, only to come back, disrupt those funerals, and kill more. As terrible as the Greenflyers are, when they encroach into Hiver territory, they are beaten back by the Hivers."

Sika grew sullener as she explained the southern lands and their life.

Joe was eager to hear as much as possible.

"Joe!" Sika protested, "The South is impenetrable!"

"Good," Joe responded, "because so is Hell!"

Sika's eyes narrowed. "What does that mean, Joe?"

"It means Hivers are needed to defeat the Demons and conquer Hell! The Hivers!"

Sika became more forceful in her tone. "The South is its own special Hell. It's teeming with life, and death is all around. The few humans who survive there live in trees—scavengers more than hunters. They live off the refuse of others."

"How do you know so much, Sika?" Joe asked.

"Because I was the young Kotutan's scout."

"But you are young yourself," Joe countered. "How could that be so?"

"I'm older than I look," Sika said, laughing. "Seen many things, felt the anguish of the southern world. I've seen huge tiger wolves and elephants. Ohtokan came from there before he found the shelter of the caves. Only the Manwolves could survive in the way humans might, because of their strength and feral senses. The humans of the South are craven scavengers who will probably be extinct one day, if they aren't already. Even Ohtokan found life in the South too difficult.

"You must rest, Joe. That shoulder is better; your fitness is good. If the South is in your plans, rest and sleep. Tomorrow we'll talk more."

It was late, Joe realized. Sika kissed him on the cheek, a comforting gesture he welcomed and looked forward to. He embraced her fully and felt a strong tinge of sexuality climbing into his loins and heart.

Sika, feeling his growing passion, froze but then embraced him eagerly.

"Joe," she said, "we both know we have work to do together—real work!"

Slipping from his embrace, she moved easily out of the room.

That night Joe fell asleep like a man with no worries.

Arleosa came to him and reassured him he was moving in a good direction.

God commands Angels; Angels support humanity, she thought.

Joe was back in shape, and with Arleosa's blessing, he gained strength and resilience. Joe felt the energy residing within his body. A certain feeling, vibratory in nature, that he had experienced previously. It made the world seem slower and less threatening, even the South.

Arleosa breathed dreams into Joe. He saw the South and its life. A fearsome place of large mammals, prey and predators, but dominated by the presence of the Hivers. Not a civilization as people would see it but a force organized to survive with collective principles and organic connections, acting as an entity for the good of the Hive.

The swamp dwelling Greenflyers were the closest thing in the South to Demons, slicing to death whatever bore flesh in their vicinity. They stood four feet tall, with an internal cartilaginous skeleton and an armored exoskeleton, much like the Hivers. They were hard to kill and flew with fly-like wings at great speed using aerial ambush. Two long, razor-sharp prongs emanated from each forearm and over their wrists. With these, they would fly down and rip through the armor of warriors. They later retrieved the bodies for food.

Joe awoke to see Saluiana, the queen, by his side. She looked lovingly into his eyes. She handed Joe a hot cup of coffee. He was barely awake, and he looked up and smiled.

"Why the South, Joe?" Saluiana asked. Joe snapped his mind away from Saluiana's gossamer nightgown, her nipples pressing against the fabric. Joe saw the shadow of her private area underneath the gown. Her round hips and shapely thighs and calves made Joe's nature rise.

"It came to me in a dream," Joe began. "The Hivers are the key to winning. They are selfless before the interest of their Hive."

"What?" Saluiana interjected. "How can you know so much? You are an outlander. We have barely been to the South. Our king, my husband, once led an expedition there. The Hivers and Greenflyers were such a threat that few came back. Kotutan was almost killed! Sika shared your thoughts. I hope this is not an intrusion. But when I heard of your plan based on a dream, I could not believe it. I don't think the Greenflyers will be much help. They're too chaotic. But you need to be aware of them. They present an element of danger in the South that might be manipulated with the right opportunity. But Hivers are not chaotic and present a force unparalleled by any, except the Demons."

"When I came here, it took everything to get your nobles to make sacrifices for the common good," said Joe. "The Hivers all know their Hive is the common good. The Demons have threatened the South, barely, but that will do. Sika knows how the Hivers are interconnected; she with her extraordinary senses can understand how they function. Sika and I can make the Hivers understand!"

"Have you asked her to go?" Saluiana demanded.

"Not yet. Still thinking on that. I could go with Sika or by myself. Just not with an expedition. An expedition attracts unwanted attention, we'll see!"

"Joe. This plan. Sika…" Saluiana paused. "We could lose both of you in a heartbeat." Saluiana looked terrified and frustrated, unable to say more.

"Look, my queen." Joe was getting formal to keep a layer of calm.

"Don't *queen* me, Joe. Between you, Sika, and me, it is just us. Respect that, because we see what few can."

Joe heard himself saying, "Okay, Okay."

Before either one of them could think about putting on the brakes, they were enfolded in each other's arms.

Joe had been doing the best he could to keep within the boundary. Before he knew it, Saluiana was on top of him, her gown opened, and she straddled him in one fell stroke.

Suddenly, the queen had an emotional reflection and stopped short of her intentions. She rolled from Joe and closed her gown. Without waiting a moment, she mumbled, "I am sorry, Joe. I must remain loyal to the king and our people!"

Joe stared at her. She gently touched his erect member, smiled regretfully, and left the room as quickly as a ghost might. Joe fell back on the bed. He was going to have a good breakfast, at least.

In the great hall, Queen Saluiana sat next to the king as she always did. Sika came later. Joe had more coffee and a plate of eggs and sausage.

Sika waved away a server bringing Joe hotcakes and syrup. "Joe," she said, "training will wait until after we talk about the South!"

The two priests, Osala and Boswan, entered the hall and sat down to the left of the king and queen.

Bladeswift, Ataka, and several knights and nobles filed into the hall. Ohtokan was escorted by several knights who looked uncomfortable in his presence. Some of the nobles could be seen to scowl and be heard to mutter curses.

Joe took it in; the hatred for Ohtokan was still present. The two priests seemed to regard him in a neutral manner.

Saluiana the queen greeted him with honor. "Great Ohtokan, welcome, and thanks for granting our request to be here!"

King Kotutan, on cue, stood very kingly, welcoming Ohtokan, the priests, and everyone to this meeting about the South.

Joe was still formulating a strategy while listening to Kotutan's welcome. He was directed to the South in a dream by the presence that guided him. Sika understood the power of the Hivers, but she doubted the success Joe could have in recruiting them.

There were stories about the dangers of the South and its insect men: the Hivers and Greenflyers. There were even conversations about strategy against the Demons, whose numbers were suspected to be great. Finally, the conversation came around to Joe's plan. Everyone was edgy. The story of Deathmet had been told over and over. He'd allegedly been seen again, leading raids in the settlements beyond Kotutan's walls. "Why any settlers would remain so vulnerable is a mystery," Kotutan wondered out loud.

Joe's firearms technology had spread, though limited to single-shot capacity. The guns gave hope. Many of the guns were made for cartridges instead of muzzleloaders. Shotguns were being produced too. On the frontier these were anxiously sought. Frontiersmen traded gold, diamonds, and furs to possess these valuable weapons.

Joe had set the future of this world on a path to sophisticated arms more quickly than would have ordinarily happened. The people had materials conducive to making guns that they quickly employed. They were also able to rig explosives to ambush Demon raiders.

Things were taking off quite nicely, Joe thought.

There were materials available including mineral deposits that could be used to resupply Joe's formulas.

The Long-Striders and the Demon incursion were locked in a stalemate.

The Long-Striders could hold off the Demons and even ravage their lines.

The Demons had grown more ferocious over time, somehow adapting to the firepower of the Long-Striders. They were bigger, like Deathmet, but they still wielded swords, spears, bows, and crossbows. A double-barrel shotgun could make a small settlement safe enough for the Long-Striders to plunder minerals, metals, and other resources before Demon pressure sent them on the move again—back to the safety of the fortress and Joe's cannons.

Kotutan preached patience. No new lands could be established as large settlements. The Demons held progress in check. Joe's cannons protected the fortress, but expansion was the heart and soul of Long-Strider economic policy.

Kotutan seemed kinglier than ever. "Tell us of your plan, Joe!"

Joe rose to his full height of six feet. He dwarfed most of the Long-Striders by several inches, and his impressive muscularity was part of that overshadowing. Even without the ABS, he was a notable figure. The Long-Striders were hardly sedentary people. The knights themselves barely rivaled Joe's chiseled musculature. Joe was wearing silk clothing with the ABS belt on, ready to cover him in armor.

"It came to me in a dream. The Hivers and their forces make the South impenetrable, along with the Greenflyers and other animal life. Otherwise, you would have settlements there as well. Where you go, the Demons follow, raiding, looting, killing! There are no Demons holding sway in the South. They may foray here and there, but no large force penetrates that realm to disrupt the life of the Hivers!"

Sika sat quietly, wondering how Joe knew all this. She had shared her limited knowledge of the South with him, but he seemed to speak about it as if he'd been there.

"Even now the Demons seek to heighten their power," Joe continued. "They are mounting beasts to aid in their attacks and becoming more organized. The Demons will want the South as they want this fortress. We need allies. I will go to the South and rally the Hivers. They are not your friends, but they can understand a growing threat!"

Jaws dropped.

Sika stared at him, having a hard time accepting his words.

Joe outlined his plan, which was still in progress. He had explained what must happen. He hoped to have Long-Strider arms production increase while he was gone.

His feelings for Sika made him want to keep her safe, but he knew she would be useful on a trek to the South. The South was a vast jungle where Hivers rode giant bees into battle in their intermittent war against the Greenflyers.

The dangers would be great, Joe thought. *I'm afraid, but I should go to the ACV and send my power of attorney to Samantha.*

When the presentation was over, Joe asked to speak to Ohtokan and Sika. His mind was made up. He knew what needed to happen.

That afternoon he trained with Sika using a steel sword developed from alloy formulas he had brought from the ACV. These were the same alloys used in the gun barrels of the Long-Striders, with some modifications. It was a resilient blade—strong, with just the right amount of flexibility.

His shoulder felt strong, and his stamina was good. Speed was not an issue. Joe looked forward to another fight with Deathmet. The next time, he'd finish the fight with his sword, not his hands.

Joe could make things slow down as he had in a previous battle. Not all the time, but at times he could move much faster than those around him and strike a succession of tremendous blows or shoot accurately to take down many targets.

† † †

At the evening meal, Sika huddled near Joe. The great hall was filled with nobles and other investors who were literally banking on the fortress's expansion and continued existence. They were anxious to get things moving; the Demons were slowing progress.

King Kotutan was to speak briefly before the meal started. He also wanted to hear about the frontier.

Several frontiersmen discussed their losses and recognized that progress, once slowed, had gotten much worse.

"My lord, King Kotutan," one muscular frontiersman began. He wore a holster that could have carried a double-barrel shotgun. Joe could see loops in his belt that must have carried shotgun cartridges.

"I am Magnor, the miner and sometimes hunter. I led a group of eleven other men into the northwestern mountain ranges to collect iron for weapons and silver and gold to make us rich!"

When Magnor said *rich*, a roar of laughter chorused up from the assembled throng of nobles, frontiersmen, and settlers.

"We started on horseback. Mules carried a good deal of supplies. We were able to reach our objective and started extracting metals within weeks. We had been there before and gotten out with little Demon contact. This time, when we were leaving, after camping and working for several weeks, we were ambushed by a force of mounted Demons. They must have waited until they saw us ready to leave, or they may have stumbled upon us. All of us had guns and swords. We blasted with our shotguns, but they rode in on us so fast we were overcome." His voice broke with emotion, and he hung his head low.

He continued, "I had my trusty shotgun and quickly dispatched two mounted Hellions. These Demons were different: no horns, just the brick-red skin and pointed ears. They came in waves, lances raking us and cutting us down. When it was over, only a few of us remained. We rode like hell out of there. We had never seen them riding horses before. These weren't regular horses either. They were big, black stallions like the one Ataka the famed knight rides. Oddly, they snort smoky fumes and have leathery, almost-armored skin, with no fur save for the manes and tails. They have no hooves. Paws would best describe their feet. As we gathered ourselves to ride off, we were reduced to using bows and crossbows. I was afraid to load my shotgun even though I had cartridges. My bow was quick, and I needed it, surely. We rode and circled behind some boulders, then I loaded my shotgun. A few of my mates had only cap and powder weapons. I ordered them to use their bows, not crossbows either. Too long to load."

Joe noted Magnor's concern. Joe had gone the simple route at first, but now it was time for sophistication if the Long-Striders were going to survive.

Magnor exhaled and continued. "Anyway, we fired some rounds and arrows. I wanted to gather up some more minerals—iron, gold, and silver—but the Demons found our position and came at us again. We were down five men already. I loaded and shot, too afraid to ride off and turn my back but also too afraid to advance. Finally, they came upon us as we circled together. I had my men wait until they were upon us. Then we fired everything we had at once. Demons and their mounts fell. I collected myself. We gathered our mounts and checked to see if the path was clear.

No other Demons were around. A few lay dying, and we dispatched them by sword. We gathered our supplies, packed our horses, and took off. Most of the mules had been killed, but we had two left and packed our gains from mining and rode off."

Joe came forward in full ABS suit, save for the helmet. He faced Magnor and acknowledged his bravery and contribution.

King Kotutan came forward, and Joe stepped to the side. Joe noted Magnor wore leather armor and knee guards. His boots were well built, and there were worn-down grooves in his leather breastwork. The apparent result of fast battles. His leather gauntlets were supple but reinforced at the back of his hands. He had sharp brown eyes and weathered skin. His wide shoulders were topped with a large bull neck. His legs were well muscled, and his square butt reminded Joe of a powerlifter. He wore a leather helmet, which to Joe's eyes looked like a WWI fighter pilot's helmet. He looked more muscular than most though. Joe understood these were not a passive people. Joe recognized that Magnor was the heart of what it meant to be a Plainsman or Long-strider as the Wildriders called them.

A few more settlers and frontiersmen came forward to speak. Many had lost family members—wives and children—to the Demons, who roasted and ate their victims.

Finally, all the testimonials ended. Kotutan King was satisfied. There was much to get done.

Joe said he needed some time and trekked out to the ACV. He pulled up diagrams of weapons using the ACV computer. He simplified them and printed them out. The specifications were dumbed down for people who still hadn't reached fourteenth-century technology.

It was starting to rain, and Joe could hear the drops as they pitter-pattered against the hull of the ACV. Joe checked the ACV's communication system. There weren't many messages. Joe figured the distance was too great. But over the months, some messages had arrived. Samantha had sent a message imploring him to stay safe and return as soon as possible.

Joe sat back and felt his eyes welling up with tears. Joe read the other messages that had come in. Captain Johnson, of course, implored him to return the ACV, implying the obvious transgression of taking it and hoping he was safe.

Joe decided he'd better send that power of attorney to Samantha. He started recording and left his voice signature on the message with a thumbprint that would be sent along with it, identifying the message as Joe's. It would take a long time to get there, he imagined: back to Samantha in New Castle.

Joe checked the computer in the ACV, doubled his searches, and determined what would be necessary to help the Long-Striders manufacture the more modern weapons that they needed.

Joe heard a knock on the outside of the ACV. He quickly opened the hull without thinking.

He climbed out of the cockpit and down to the ground. He sensed Sika's presence and heard her whisper.

"Joe! Joe!"

Then he saw him. *Deathmet.* He was striding forward on a giant destrier. The animal had leathery, hairless skin with large paws. Gray steam flowed through the nostrils. Its color was a mottled gray with black spots.

Joe was armed with his Vibro-Blade, steel sword, and fission revolver, which was tucked in the small of his back.

Joe jumped from the ship, landing ten meters in front of the mounted Deathmet. As he landed, Deathmet spurred the mount forward, his sword drawn. He sought to slash down Joe. Joe spun to the side, drawing the fission revolver. Deathmet's blade crashed down into thin air. Joe shot one blast, striking the mount in the chest. He aimed for Deathmet's left shoulder as Deathmet carried his axe in his left hand. Joe shot again. Deathmet fell back toward the rump of the Demon destrier, dropping the axe. He rolled to the side of his mount and stood up faster than Joe would have imagined. Blood dripped down Deathmet's left shoulder. He came hurtling toward Joe with his sword arcing down, but suddenly the arc went wide. Joe saw Sika firing an arrow, then another as Deathmet stumbled.

Joe unsheathed the steel blade and moved forward, making a mad slash at Deathmet's head, literally knocking him senseless and sending his helmet rolling to the ground. Sika kept firing as Deathmet sought to regain his equilibrium. He staggered and lurched toward Joe.

Time slowed for Joe, but in Deathmet's mind everything sped up.

Deathmet came to assassinate Joe. He was driven by pride and embarrassment. He sought revenge because Joe had slapped him. Deathmet was so driven by revenge he brought no support to aid him.

Now in a cascade of emotions, Deathmet recognized his folly. Joe had backup; he did not. Deathmet looked around and eyed Sika, who was still hitting him with arrows. Suddenly he wanted to deal a blow—if not to Joe, then to this huntress who seemed intent on killing him. He changed his direction midstride and moved to slash Sika, who quickly ran behind a tree.

Joe was enraged. He drew the fission revolver and fired.

Bang! Bang! Bang!

The shots shattered Deathmet's dragon-scale armor and slammed into his back. Joe ran forward and with all his might drove the steel sword into Deathmet's torso before the Demon could fully turn. The blade rammed through Deathmet's spinal column and out through his solar plexus. He collapsed face down in the dirt.

Back in Hell, Satan winced.

Sika turned to face the carnage; arrow nocked. She saw Joe standing over the corpse of Deathmet the Archdemon. It was a good day.

Joe could hear an old rap song in his head: "It Was a Good Day."

Sika moved toward Joe and the two embraced. Ataka arrived shortly, having heard the shots from Joe's fission revolver. Bladeswift, the nobles, and even Magnor the miner arrived on the scene. They expressed joy over Joe's victory and great relief that he and Sika were unscathed. Queen Saluiana arrived with the two priests, Osala and Boswan.

The rain stopped. The two priests lit candles, as did Queen Saluiana.

King Kotutan emerged. "This is a great day for us. A great victory has been achieved."

Osala and Boswan sang in unison, "Let us pray."

And what a prayer it was. The two priests, deftly playing off each other's comments, thanked the nobles for their economic sacrifice and in keeping their efforts focused on collective survival. They thanked the king and queen and knights. Ataka was mentioned by name, and the Wildriders were noted for being staunch allies. Before long, the courage of all those in the fortress had been acknowledged.

Lastly, Joe Brown's presence was noted as "a gift from God Almighty and a means to survive the Demon hordes and enrich the life of every Long-Strider."

"We have yet to feast," King Kotutan announced.

The throng started to file back to the fortress.

"What of the body?" Sika asked Joe. "We must burn it. Not let the Demons find or retrieve it."

Osala came forward, "Yes, Joe. This should be done."

Kotutan was beckoning them to follow him into the fortress.

"Can we do it later?" Joe asked, not fully understanding the importance of the task.

"No," Boswan broke in. "Now!" He sounded desperate and unpriestly.

Ataka came forward. "I have some squires here who can get the job done," he reported, presenting two youths. They wore the uniform of warriors in training, consisting of leather harnesses and loose-fitting pants with sturdy boots.

Sika threw a torch on Deathmet's body after beckoning the squires to throw sticks and twigs on him. A small fire started.

Suddenly from the fort came several riders, gesturing wildly. "Back to the fort!" one of them yelled. "Demons are coming."

Joe heard a cannon go off from the fortress. Looking for the object of the cannon fire, Joe turned and was shocked to see a mass of mounted Demons. Rain started to fall, putting out the torch that was thrown over Deathmet's body.

Joe prepared to fight the Demons who were heading his way. Ataka and several knights escorted the king and queen back toward the fortress.

Joe advanced. There were a few rounds left in the fission revolver, which Joe fired into the now-charging mass of mounted Demons until he was out of ammo.

Several cannon shots were fired from the fortress, dispersing some of the charging Demons.

Soon the rest of Demons would be upon them, too close for cannon fire from the fortress to be used.

"Run for the fort!" Joe boomed.

Sika fired arrows at the Demons, who were now fifty meters away. The king and queen were almost to the fortress walls. Bladeswift surged out of the fort leading a group of twelve Wildriders, firing pistols, arrows, and rifles at the Demons.

Joe urged Sika into the ACV. He closed the hull and grabbed several weapons before emerging. He opened the hull, carrying an assault weapon. He fired several shots. The Demons stopped their charge and surrounded Deathmet's body with a shield wall. Deathmet's body was hauled onto a large Demon destrier, and off they rode.

"Stop them, Joe," Sika yelled, loosing arrows into the backs of Demons.

Joe fired his weapon, but the Demons rode into a copse of trees, taking Deathmet's body with them.

Sika was distraught. "This is bad, Joe. The Demons come back to life sometimes if they are not completely destroyed."

Sika, in a show of great speed and stamina, ran toward the fort. "Aim there," she yelled, looking over her shoulder and pointing to the trees. She could see where the Demons hid.

The cannons belched flame and exploded in the trees where Sika had pointed. There were sounds of pain and groans echoing from the trees.

"Again," Sika yelled.

Joe was roughly one hundred meters from the fort and started scanning the wooded area. He couldn't make out much, even with the ABS's binocular capacity.

Joe ran toward the trees. The king and queen and priests, along with the nobles, had fled to the fort at the first sight of the Demons.

Joe was running hard.

Sika yelled, "tell them to stop firing. Joe's out there now."

Reloading the fission revolver wasn't an option. Joe was sprinting. He had the steel sword and his Vibro-Blade. He armed the Vibro-Blade, which sizzled with energy.

Several mounted Demons confronted Joe. Joe launched himself at the closest Demon, spinning in the air and cutting into the Demon's waist, bringing him down. The Demon's mount reared up in fear. As he landed, Joe rolled under the mount of another Demon, ramming the Vibro-Blade into its rib cage. The mount collapsed, but not before Joe could roll from under it. He ran toward the Demon who sat with Deathmet's body lying across his destrier. Several other mounted Demons milled around, fearful of leaving the trees due to the cannon fire, but now that had ceased. They rode, leaving the trees and rapidly moving away from Joe.

In one last effort, Joe launched himself up onto a ten-foot-high tree branch.

Something told Joe he might have one good shot in the fission revolver. Time slowed and he aimed.

The Demon carrying Deathmet's body on his horse was thirty meters out.

Bam!

Joe fired and watched as the Demon's head exploded. He fell off his mount, whose reins were taken by another Demon rider. Then they were gone.

Sika came running up to Joe, but not before firing an arrow that struck a Demon. There was a groan in the darkness, and the sound of Demon paws striking the earth receded.

✝ ✝ ✝

Finally, everyone—the king, queen, priests, and nobles—gathered in the great hall.

The meal was somber. Certainly, the threat of the Demons was affirmed as constant, but they could be defeated as well. Joe was consoled by Sika. He was frustrated about not stopping Deathmet's body being spirited away.

"I should have told you earlier, Joe. It's okay—we'll get them next time," Sika said.

Joe eased back and with Sika's reassurance decided to enjoy the evening meal.

Sounds like what coach used to say after a tough loss, Joe thought.

The priests gave their thanks. Osala spoke of "all things that come to pass exist as life and the struggle to extend it!"

Osala looked to Queen Saluiana. "My queen. There has always been talk of the South. You have championed the cause of understanding."

He looked at Ohtokan. He had been invited to remain for dinner, despite protest from others, who still held resentment against the Manwolf tribe.

Boswan, too, took up the issue. "The Hivers have never been allies, but they hold the key to the South. If they see a threat from the Demons, they may align with us, but they are not like other people. If anything can be done to gain their respect, Joe is the one to do it!"

Big-game pressure thought Joe. Easing back, he sipped some wine and bit ravenously into pork spareribs. He thought of the sum of his life so far.

What had brought him to this point—on a far planet bringing firearms to a medieval people?

He thought about the risks. The existence of Demons in this world and his own marked a universal threat that could not be ignored. Joe had seen bad things before his own mercenary raids in Afraili for oil. He was ashamed of his part in that. But now fighting Demons was liberating: no shame involved. It was time to do everything possible to win. This was indeed redemption.

Joe took some time to really enjoy the company of Sika, who looked to him like a...he wasn't sure, to be sincere. But it was good. He admired her as well.

Bladeswift and Ataka were there eating and drinking as well. Even Ohtokan seemed relaxed as he, too, participated in the festive meal.

Saluiana kept looking at Joe. She tried to catch his eye but demurred due to the king's presence and the very public meal.

After the meal, Joe said he would be leaving for the South inside ten days. He entrusted the weapon diagrams to the blacksmiths turned weapon manufacturers.

He and Sika retired to their rooms. Joe had sent private messages to those he wanted to join him so they wouldn't be embarrassed by a refusal to participate in so momentous a venture.

As usual, Sika sought to join Joe in his room to talk and confer. They often fell asleep together, relaxed by each other's presence.

The dreams came as they slept together. They knew they were together in the presence of the Archangel Arleosa. They felt the presence of a magnificent force they could not grasp.

☦ ☦ ☦

Arleosa spoke to God. "You see, my Lord, Joe Brown is a unifier: a fighting Messiah who atones for past wrongs with action. He brings advances in agriculture, ranching, and weaponry that are moving the Long-Striders forward. Bless them, my Lord! Give them the power to fulfill your will."

☦ ☦ ☦

Joe awoke to see Queen Saluiana observing him quietly. Sika was still asleep.

Joe was in shorts, and Saluiana was wearing a robe over her gossamer gown.

Whew, Joe thought, *don't need to be tempted again, but I am.*

"When you meet the Hivers, carry no guns, or you will be tempted to use them. They will overwhelm you if you shoot. Any great show of force will cause an attack. They will consult with you if you are not a threat. When Kotutan marched into the South with an expeditionary force of one hundred, the Hivers saw them as a threat. They responded by slaughtering the expeditionary force to protect their Hives.

"The Greenflyers will be in the South as well. They are relentless, and guns would be the best option to kill them. But the Hivers are a priority.

Be as swift as possible with the Greenflyers. Turn them away quickly and leave them to feed on each other's corpses."

"Okay," Joe agreed.

This is going to be dangerous, he thought.

"Who should come with me? Or do I go alone, Queen Saluiana?" Joe asked.

"You will be under great pressure no matter what. If Sika goes, can you assure her safety? Ohtokan can track the Hivers as well and probably won't attract much attention. Your humming sword will be good. But be careful not to use it on the Hivers. Take another sword in case a confrontation with the Greenflyers occurs."

10.

INTO THE SOUTH!

Joe was scaling furiously now. He used the Magni Grip of the ABS to climb up a sheer cliff. He needed a vantage point. His steel sword was sheathed across his back. His Vibro-Blade was strapped to a belt on the ABS.

At the top Joe could see the Hive in the distance. The patrols of the Hivers dotted the canyon floor. Joe saw flying creatures that looked like dragons. He noted the height of the canyon walls. Using the binocular option of the ABS, Joe could see some of the bees had Hivers riding them. Both above the canyon floor and in the surrounding areas outside of the canyon, giant vines climbed the canyon walls on all sides. They had blossoms of all colors attached to them. Giant bees sucked nectar from the blossoms, and Hiver patrols foraged for their Hive.

Joe lay flat, resting on top of the canyon wall. He could see the natural position of the Hive. From all four directions, the Hivers had access to the jungle. The Hiver lookouts were stationed on the Hive mound. If they were approached by an enemy from the canyon floor, the lookouts would see the enemy long before the Hive could be caught unaware.

Below him and beyond the canyon walls, Joe tracked the Hive scout patrols. He watched their patterns and tendencies. He scanned with the ABS for signs of life and worn trails.

Something in Joe's scan to the west alarmed him. He searched and scanned more intently. The ground had worn and heavily used trails.

The jungle was so thick Joe had trouble understanding the signs his scans yielded. He'd have to get down into the jungle and find out what was there. Joe crawled over the rock outcropping where he had been resting. Slowly and carefully, he started to climb down several hundred feet to the western edge of the jungle. Finally, he reached the bottom. The jungle was thick, and concealment was provided by the vines, their blossoms, and the trees. Joe heard the buzzing of giant bees. He hunkered down into a crouching position and worked westward. Joe reached the area he had been scanning and found large paw prints on a rutted trail. Joe wasn't sure from what. Periodically, he could hear the clicking sounds of the Hivers walking. He was low off the ground and sometimes crawled. At four feet tall, the Hivers wouldn't miss his over-six-foot frame if he stood toe to toe with them. If he heard Hivers, he slowly went prone to avoid drawing their attention.

Joe had no guns but kind of wished he did. He was hungry too. He hadn't eaten in over twelve hours. He reached into a small pack and ate some buffalo jerky he'd brought for the trip. It was about six in the morning, and the life of the jungle was heating up.

Joe worked his way west, trying to find the paw prints again. He could pick up an acrid burnt smell.

Demons! They are here!

He heard Hivers in his vicinity. They were alarmed, apparently having picked up the paw prints themselves. Joe kept low and studied them. Their alarm turned into anger. Immediately, a runner was sent back toward the Hive. In that instant Joe heard a rustling in the jungle. Forty Demon cavalry emerged, bearing down on the small scout force of five Hivers. The five turned as one and set up a wall of spears. They charged toward the Demons, then separated. Hivers at the widest flank ran forward, throwing spears while drawing swords. No Demon could get around them. They weaved and ducked under the lances of the Demons, then immediately jabbed at the Demon mounts.

Joe could barely see through the foliage, but clearly the Hivers were giving their runner a chance to reach the Hive. Their sacrifice would be great.

The Demons bore down on the Hivers, who after scattering and flanking, had little defense for the mounted charge. Regrouping, the Hivers struck out reflexively to give the runner more time to reach the Hive.

Joe scanned the distance of the runner to the Hive. He watched the runner as his Hive mates confronted the Demons. They leaped up on the mounted Demons, slashing them with their swords.

The Hivers surprisingly blocked the Demons momentarily and prevented the Demons from pursuing their runner.

The remaining Hivers rammed into the middle of the Demon force. The plan to block the middle didn't work, and they were cut down by the overwhelming number of mounted Demons. Amazingly, they disrupted the Demon charge momentarily. Once the Demons cut the Hivers down, the runner had no protection. The Demons were fast closing in behind him.

Joe started running. This was everything he'd trained for and then some. The runner was speeding toward the Hive. Joe ran, barely able to maintain the runner's location on his scanner. Joe picked up speed. The trees were so tall on the jungle floor that little was able to grow beneath them. Joe accelerated, swerving around trees, sprinting and jumping over dead Demons and boulders.

Finally, Joe could see a mounted Demon bearing down on the runner. Joe was gaining on the Demon, and to seemingly help things, the runner turned to face the Demon, somehow sensing the Demon's proximity. In one move, without losing momentum, the runner pivoted toward the Demon and hurled his spear with great force. The spear hit the Demon's mount in the neck and protruded out the other side. The mount reared and fell forward; the Demon pitched forward and landed in the dirt. The Demon scrambled forward and up. He began running toward the Hiver runner, who deftly stepped to the side.

The Hiver runner impressed Joe. He had never seen such a combatant before.

Joe was almost upon them. The runner looked his way as Joe rammed his steel sword through the back of the Demon's spine. Several other Demons were moving toward Joe. Joe looked up and saw a giant honeybee bearing down on the runner. Indeed, it was being ridden by a Hiver. The runner quickly jumped ten meters up, grabbed the extended hand of the rider, and swung up behind him. The rider had rescued him from the pursuing Demons.

Joe was circled by the Demon cavalry, which took passes at him with their lances. But because he was one and they were twenty, they had difficulty staying out of each other's way.

The Hivers, on their bee mounts, circled. The rescue Hiver threw his spear, killing a Demon trying to slash Joe with a sword.

Joe sprang backward, performing an aerial somersault, landing on top of a mounted Demon. Joe's sword point slammed into the top of the Demon's chest and came out at his hip. He reached for the reins with one hand and let the Demon fall as he pulled his sword free with his other hand.

He was exposed to two Demons riding toward him. Suddenly the Hivers flew down from above and rammed the two riders, knocking them off their mounts.

Joe had trouble controlling the Demon mount, which, after feeling the jolt of Joe's weight and seeing its dead master, was panicking. Joe palm-heeled the mount with a quick strike and then pulled its reins hard. Another Demon rode to gather speed. Joe's mount bucked, and Joe could not get it under control.

Slipping off the mount, Joe ducked behind it for cover. With a mighty leap, he crashed into the oncoming Demon mount, causing it to careen to the ground. The Demon's leg was trapped under the mount, and Joe quickly hacked the neck before he could get free.

Joe was losing in the frenzy of combat. The odds were against him. Ten Demons charged toward him.

If only I had a gun. The thought fleetingly passed through Joe's mind.

Joe ran into a thicket of large ferns. He hunkered down, motionless.

The Demons continued their pursuit. They surged into the thicket of ferns. They were barely able to see Joe even as they closed in on him. Joe spun back, pivoting, and slammed his sword into a Demon's gut. As he did, a second Demon spotted him and rushed toward him. Joe counter-charged and sidestepped. He slipped between the mount's front legs and under its chest. He drove up with all the leg force he could muster, lifting the mount into the air. It landed violently; the rider pinned underneath it. Joe skewered the Demon's neck, killing it instantly.

Gotta get out of here, Joe thought.

More Demons were joining the pursuit. Joe ran east, swerving for cover behind trees and ducking into ferns until he reached the southeast canyon wall. Joe quickly ascended the trail, hoping to get clear of the Demons.

The trail was too narrow and difficult for a horse, but the Demon mounts with their paws were having no trouble. They came up single file through the winding trail, unable to see far ahead.

Joe looked over his shoulder and realized the Demon mounts were in single file pursuit. Joe stopped and waited, knowing that the winding cover obscured his location. He used this to his advantage, hopping down on several Demons from above when they were directly under him. He grabbed one Demon's mount and pushed it off the trail down the canyon.

Finally, Joe was able to reach a sheer wall. There were no Demons in sight. Quickly, using the Magni Grip function in the ABS, Joe climbed away from danger. Above him he saw the Bee-Riders riding away as spears and arrows from the Demons below harried them.

Joe reached a spot where he was relatively safe. He laid flat and rested.

So far so good, he thought. *I think there might be common ground with the Hivers. I'm fighting better too. Maybe I'll be able to get this done.*

Joe thought about the last night at the fortress, the dreams and sense of power he awoke with. Ever sense he started this venture, especially from his time in the fortress with Saluiana and Sika, he'd grown stronger.

Even after Deathmet severely wounded him, he grew stronger. Sika and he were kindred spirits. Saluiana was also a kindred spirit, but in a different way.

I will never see women quite the same way, he thought. *The presence that has guided and nurtured me, female for sure, has always been felt.*

Joe's mind and consciousness opened to new channels. The threat of Deathmet was real. He was a leader. Deathmet represented Demon's evolution; they were mounted, and their tactics were evolving.

Joe sensed something stronger than a sinister presence when he met Deathmet. He knew something purposeful and menacing was behind Deathmet.

☩ ☩ ☩

Satan's lust was barely quenched by the several concubines reclining around him.

His passion was ignited by his independence and sovereignty. But he felt he would never see Heaven. He had so much to offer, but he could never get enough of lust, fornication, and chaos.

☩ ☩ ☩

Joe stirred from his intuitive reverie. Down on the jungle floor, he could see a mass of mounted Demons. They were coming from the west straight toward the Hive.

Joe scanned the air above. There was a grouping of the giant bees, each mounted by a Hiver. The Hivers each carried two spears. The mass of Demon-Riders was gaining momentum as they approached the Hive. The Bee-Riders swooped to make a frontal attack. The bees, roughly twelve feet long with wide, muscular bodies, flew down, slamming into the Demons and their mounts. The Hivers hurled their spears, striking the Demons and their mounts.

The second wave of Demons adjusted their tactics and fired arrows. The bees flew up and over the Hive. Joe was critical of their tactics, but then saw the waves of Bee-Riders swing back from the high altitude and crash down on the rear flank of the Demon formation.

Larger Hivers were emerging from top opening of the Hive. They were bigger and more muscular.

Joe watched with the binocular function of the ABS. *Indeed, the Hive was mounting a defense!*

The slope of the Hive was steep, but if the mounted Demons got close, Joe felt they could run up it. Another wave of Bee-Riders descended toward the middle of the Demon formation. Joe's eyes sharpened on the bees shooting penetrating razor projectiles. The projectiles shot out from where a normal bee's stinger existed.

Joe watched the battle. The Demons hit by the projectiles slowed and fell to the ground.

What a battle, Joe thought.

A third of the several hundred Demons were now down. But still, the Demon cavalry surged toward the Hive.

Joe decided. His chance might not come again. He had to make an impression before long. He moved along his perch to gain a better view of the battle. He leaped down, grasping a vine, releasing it, and dropping ten meters onto another vine. He landed in a vine blossom that enveloped him. He spilled out twenty meters below. He reached a series of thick vines and leaped downward from one to the other and finally to the jungle floor.

Once he hit the bottom, Joe started running for the Hive. The Demons had already begun their ascent. Joe ran at a furious pace, perhaps about fifty miles an hour, augmented by the ABS and his own burgeoning development.

The Hivers formed a line of defense near the top of the Hive mound. They had swords as long as their bodies were tall: four feet of steel. In their off hands, they carried short machete-like blades with curved pommel edges perfect for trapping an opponent's blade. The first wave was hacked down by a combination of swordplay and fluid Hiver movement. The Hivers danced among the Demons as if they were wolves bringing down a deer.

Joe entered the melee, hoping for the second time in a day to join the Hiver's cause. Moving northwest, he was on the Hive before the Hivers could react to him.

Once in the fray, he hacked with his steel sword. The sword was effective, but Joe knew the Vibro-Blade would be deadlier because it bounced between blows without penetrating. He quickly sheathed the sword in favor of the Vibro-Blade.

Enough about presentation, Joe thought. *It's not a gun, after all.* Remembering what Saluiana had told him, he feared the technology of the Vibro-Blade would trigger a negative response from the Hivers. Among the Demons, he was hammering his Vibro-Blade indiscriminately. A horde of Demons and their mounts sprang up about him as he spun, leaped, and dashed across the Hive. The Demon formation continued to charge up the Hive. The whacking of the Vibro-Blade crashing into the armored Demons sounded like thunder. Joe was fighting his way up the top of the Hive. He wondered how he'd be received.

The Demons were ascending at a rapid pace on their mounts. They had red eyes, and smoke blew out their nostrils and into the wind. The nostril fumes were a result of an abnormal metabolism fueling the wild rush up the Hive.

The mounted Demons covered the west side of the Hive mound.

Joe reached the first wave as heavily muscled Hivers began to pour out the top of the Hive. Joe looked to the air, hopeful that his association with the Hiver runner earlier would spare him the attack from above that must surely be coming.

Joe attacked the first wave of mounted Demons before they reached the mouth of the mound. Joe wanted to stand out as defending the Hive, not attacking it.

Joe swung the Vibro-Blade hard, dodging between two mounted Demons. He leaped up and slammed the Vibro-Blade down on the shoulder of a Demon, unseating him from his mount. Turning left as he landed, he slammed the Vibro-Blade into the mount's left rear leg, causing it to fall and pinning the rider's leg. Quickly Joe leaped to the struggling Demon and slammed down the Vibro-Blade on his head.

The fight from the air started.

There was a great buzzing sound circling behind the charging Demons. Hivers made a line at the top of their mound, swords and spears at the ready.

Joe ran past the Demons charging in the first wave. Time slowed for him as he weaved away from Demon lances and swords. More Demons charged his way. Whenever possible, he hacked a Demon off a mount. He was also able to take the mounts' legs from under them with blasting slams of the Vibro-Blade.

The air assault arrived in a buzz of chaos attacking the Demon lines, still beyond Joe and closing in on the Hive mouth.

The Hive was ten stories high. Joe saw the bee-riding Hivers skewering Demons from above and from the rear.

Joe worked his way to the south side of the Hive base. Bee-Riders withdrew to the air above as a fast-moving line of Hive defenders ran down the Hive. They assaulted the Demons with crashing swords and spears.

Joe had to take a second look. The air was filled again but not with bees.

Fire catapults, Joe thought.

Joe couldn't see where the fire salvos were coming from, but he watched as they landed on the side of the Hive mound. Explosions ripped the outer shell of the Hive, leaving deep craters in the Hive mound.

Joe was terrified the Demons had turned around and peeled out, heading to the east side of the Hiver mound. Explosions rained down on the west side of the mound with deafening bangs.

Joe looked up in search of the Bee-Riders. None could be seen.

He ran around to the west side of mound, and there he saw three catapults lined up in the jungle. The Demons had quickly cut a swath through the jungle and had set up catapults. The catapults hurled flame-enveloped balls three feet in diameter that exploded upon impact.

Joe looked with horror upon the carnage.

The Hive had crumbled in spots up to ten feet in diameter. The Hiver defenders had never seen such an onslaught. Though they were shaken, a small party of several Hivers ran down the Hive toward the catapults.

At times a Hiver would peek out of a chasm and hold a spear in position to protect the aperture that erupted after the explosion.

Before long Joe could see the Hivers busily filling the gaps in the Hive mound from the explosions with boulders.

Joe knew this was his opportunity to seal the deal with the Hivers. He ran at top speed toward the nearest catapult. The Demons defended the catapult as two Giants loaded and set it.

Joe felt a level of fatigue now. The conditioning with Sika was instrumental, but he had to push harder.

He was nearing the base of the Hive mound, and the Demons regarded him angrily. Joe launched himself toward the Demons protecting the catapult. He surged ten feet into the air and thirty meters forward, landing before the Demons could respond. He landed on the closest Demon, crashing down on his knee and cracking his head with the Vibro-Blade. Down he went, dead.

Joe caught the next Demon across the kidneys on the lower back, sending him slumping to his knees. Joe ducked under a lance from a mounted Demon who came to protect the catapults. Joe surged upward and, using the Vibro-Blade, slammed it into the abdomen of the rider, who fell over with a *thunk* onto the ground.

Moving forward, Joe faced a Giant, who abandoned loading the catapult and picked up a club. Swinging clumsily, he sought to pound the club down on Joe's head. Joe, sensing the danger, lurched forward and made a quick horizontal slice, cracking the Giant's knee and forcing him to fall.

From the west came a buzzing sound. Close to the grounds Bee-Riders descended, riding double. The second riders slipped off their mounts ten feet above the ground.

Joe took it all in even as he fought. A swarm of Hivers hacked and jabbed the remaining Giants into submission, which ultimately meant death.

The smell of blood was in the air. Joe thought he heard more buzzing from the south. But these weren't bees. Four-feet-tall wiry insect humanoids like the Hivers flew in. First just a few, then a horde. A mounted charge from a wave of Demons rushed back toward the catapults, which the Hivers were hacking down.

There was a green blur in the air as insect men landed. They slashed at the bodies of the dead Giants and Demons with the sharp prongs on their forearms. They lifted back into the air, carrying body parts dripping fresh blood. These were the Greenflyers.

The wave of Demons surged forward, but the Greenflyers hovered nearby, hoping to get more flesh. They continued to fly down and hack their forearm prongs into dead Demons'.

Joe started to worry. He sprinted up the Hive mound. The Bee-Riders were flying east toward the Hive, seemingly withdrawing from the battlefield. Joe kept running up the Hive mound. Then as suddenly as they withdrew, the Bee-Riders swung back, pivoting west. Swinging low, they speared the oncoming Demons in masse and withdrew east again toward the Hive.

Greenflyers swung low in their absence, retrieving Demon parts and flying away. Joe was halfway up the Hive mound when he fell into an aperture made by a catapult salvo. He landed inside the Hive mound, tumbling down fifty feet into a chamber of giant mushrooms. Joe shut down the Vibro-Blade. He curled up under a giant mushroom and passed out.

When he awoke, he was surrounded by the Hivers. They looked like upright insect men. They were known to be a human subspecies with humanoid and insect qualities. The Hivers Joe had seen defending the Hive stood with their swords sheathed. They held their six-foot pikes at their sides.

Joe studied them up close for the first time. They stood erect and were sturdily built. Their bodies appeared armored from head to toe. Their heads looked like helmets. Their faces were shaped as though they had articulated shields protecting their cheekbones, chins, and foreheads. Their eyes were big and dark with no visible distinction between the iris and pupil.

The Hive mound felt like a cave. Looking around, Joe saw giant mushrooms growing and billowing out into four-foot caps three feet in height.

Joe did not have his sword, but the Vibro-Blade hung at his belt.

As he touched the Vibro-Blade, he realized the Hivers might not know it's use as a weapon when it wasn't activated.

Before long, he was being prodded forward with the shafts of pikes held by the Hive detainers. He was directed toward some downward steps, and he descended into a large open room.

From below an entourage of Hivers appeared, their heads coming to view. One Hiver was larger than the rest, his head towering above them all. *The king*, Joe thought.

They moved toward Joe. The larger Hiver was muscularly built, and his vitality seemed to burst through his armor exoskeleton. Joe noted for the first-time small orbs on the heads of the Hivers in a place where antennae would be on an insect. From another entrance an armored Hiver woman with great bearing, escorted by a phalanx of Hiver defenders, arrived. The king and his queen stood together. They gestured furiously toward Joe.

Joe's hands were not bound, but he kept them behind his back, trying to be unoffensive. The Hivers were undisturbed, waiting for their king and queen to deliberate.

Joe had a hard time discerning the facial differences in the Hivers. But he noted there were differences in their body types.

A Hiver runner arrived in the chamber and briefly bowed before the king and queen. Joe recognized the runner as the Hiver he had helped during the original confrontation, due to his lean build and thin armor.

Joe discerned a vibe of pulsing mental waves. There was no language spoken, yet a conversation exchange was occurring between the king, queen, and the Hiver runner. The runner gestured toward Joe using an inflection of head bowing and pointing.

Joe "listened" and began to comprehend the meaning of their soundless discourse. He even understood the emotional nuances of their conversation. The Hiver runner was explaining Joe's presence to the king and queen. There were questions as to his being an ally, not an enemy.

Joe realized from the unspoken language that he was going to be released but should not come back among the Hivers.

He panicked.

Wait, wait. He began to communicate his distress. As he did, a show of all the battles with Demons came pouring into his consciousness. He communicated the threat that had been witnessed during the Hivers assault, as well as the history of ongoing efforts the Demons were mounting to attack other races. He continued to communicate the evolution of the Demons, including their mounted status and the fiery and explosive catapult payloads they now employed.

The king paused and considered Joe seriously. The queen looked concerned and communicated her worries for the Hive and her offspring.

The Hiver runner, king, and queen briefly conferred again. Based on his brief intervention on behalf of the Hive, he could stay and share duties with the other Hivers. Primarily, he would scout the Demons with the Hiver patrols. If over time things went well, other considerations would be employed.

Joe surmised the king and queen were still absorbing how much of a threat the Demons were currently. In the past, the Demons had been encountered and repulsed. But now the Demons had adapted to the Hivers' defense. They used explosive catapults and mounted charges. Damage had been done, and that required the Hive workers to seal ruptures in the Hive.

A squad of five Hivers escorted Joe up and out of the Hive through a series of steps that allowed access throughout the Hive levels. They reached the top of the Hive mound. One of them handed Joe his steel sword.

Down the Hive mound they went at a trot. Demons lay dead and dying, remnants of the recent battle. Now and again a Hiver would skewer a wounded Demon with his spear or hack off a head with his sword. As Joe descended, he, too, quickly ranged out of the loose formation of Hivers to hack a wounded Demon to death.

Finally reaching the base of the Hive mound, the Hivers started fires to burn the remains of the catapults. They dragged the bodies of Demons and Giants onto the burning piles.

Greenflyers lay twitching, their wings beating furiously as they struggled to lift themselves into the air. The Hivers rushed past struggling Demons to hack at the Greenflyers murderously.

There was similarity between the Hivers and the Greenflyers. Their bodies were covered in plates of scaled armor. The armor was articulated in a manner to show their muscular bodies and limbs in bold relief. But the Greenflyers had two powerful, insect-like wings. It was clear the Hivers hated the Greenflyers. They hacked off their forearms while the Greenflyers were still alive and threw their razor-edged forearm blades into the fire in one piece.

Once the fires were going strong, Joe "heard" the message to rejoin the Hiver formation and head west into the jungle.

Joe watched intently and listened to know what the plan might be. The Hivers unloosed their swords and started to creep through the ferns, some standing six feet high, obscuring their presence. Joe lowered himself into a crouch and readied the steel sword. He didn't activate the Vibro-Blade as its humming sound might give away his position and that of the Hivers.

A few Hivers took to the trees and used their vantage point to understand what lay ahead. Joe noted the ease with which the Hivers traversed the trees. Joe was wordlessly beckoned to follow them up. Using the ABS's Magni Grip, he climbed to their location nimbly in spite of his larger frame and bulk.

Out beyond the trees and bush lay an open sward. There mounted Demons kept watch. Beyond them, further west, around three hundred Demons were massed, setting up a camp.

Joe longed for his sniper rifle.

The communication was clear to Joe. The Demons must not be allowed to threaten the Hive. The response from Hivers must be a swarm of violence that leaves no doubt about the cost of waging war against them.

A call went out: several neighboring Hives would come to aid this beleaguered Hive. The Demons must be destroyed or thwarted soon. In the meantime, the Hive would mount all available soldiers to go on the offensive. Defenders and workers would remain. If the attack failed, the defenders would fight to the last to preserve the Hive. Even the king would fight in defense of the Hive.

Hive workers labored to bolster the Hive to ensure any ruptures were repaired and sealed.

Joe detected the barely discernable sound of Hiver soldiers massing to leave the Hive.

Joe recognized who the Hiver in command was and followed him down the Hive mound.

A plan was transmitted to Joe's mind from the Hivers. Several Hivers would sneak among the Demons, who were currently busy readying their catapults for movement in preparation for launching another attack.

There were stores of corn and dried meat being unloaded in large buckets by Giants. *The labor caste of the Demons,* Joe surmised. There wasn't a lot of food to sustain such a force. They weren't planning a long siege.

Every now and then, Joe could see a Greenflyer flit among the Demon mounts, kill one, slice his leg off, and fly away.

No wonder the South was off limits, Joe realized. *The risks were great for the Demons as well.*

Once Joe, the commander, and several Hivers descended the mound, they crept into trees that circled the perimeter of the cap. There were small trees and tall ferns that obscured them from the view of the Demons in the camp. The Greenflyers darting in and out created a useful diversion.

On the edge of the Demons' camp perimeter, a Demon guardsman kept careful watch on the mounts nearby. His back was to the trees and ferns as he watched for airborne Greenflyers darting in to kill a mount. The Demon had an arrow nocked, hoping to catch a Greenflyer in the act.

The Hivers were in position. The Demons remained distracted by the Greenflyers. A lithe Hiver slammed his spear through the guardsman's back, armor and all. The spear tip protruded from the Demon's back and through his chest. Before he could fall, a second Hiver pulled him into the tall ferns effortlessly.

Joe moved along with the group of Hivers. A Hiver, who watched in silence, moved forward and cut the pickets the Demon mounts were attached to.

The Hivers are cunning too, Joe acknowledged. Joe was hearing and feeling the plan. He was up next. He worked northeast around the camp perimeter, staying low and activating the camouflage function of the ABS. He matched the color of the green ferns and brown trunks of the small trees. Nearing the next Demon guard, who was looking around nervously and wondering where his comrade was, Joe waited in the brush, drawing himself into as small a space as possible. The Demon looked suspiciously at the unpicketed mounts milling about freely.

Joe calmed himself and time slowed. Joe watched a Demon move past him. Once Joe could see the Demon's back, he leaped forward, slamming his steel sword violently through the Demon. Joe was about to pull the blade out of the Demon, but it was suddenly dragged into the brush by a Hiver. Staying low, Joe followed the downed Demon and the Hiver into the brush. After hastily removing his sword, he headed for the pickets and began cutting them, freeing more Demon mounts. This started to draw more attention, and several Demons approached from across the camp.

The Hivers crept out behind the milling mounts and circled the Demons. They quickly cut down the Demons from behind. Two more Demons approached the area, sensing the activity nearby. Closing in quickly, three Hivers sought to cut down the Demons. A Demon was hacked in the leg and went down. A Hiver moved to his front and thrust a sword point through his chest. A Hiver confronted the remaining Demons. Blows were exchanged, but having dispatched the first Demon, a Hiver dashed sideways, sending his blade crashing against the Demon's lower leg. The Demon went down as a Hiver hacked his head off.

Joe moved in among them, grabbed a Demon's ankle, and pulled him back to the brush. The Demon mounts moved around restlessly within the remaining pickets of the camp.

Joe couldn't be sure if all the Demon bodies had been retrieved, but he saw two Greenflyers overhead. They carried Demon parts, blood dripping from the sky. Joe surmised things would happen soon.

He moved, zigzagging toward the catapults. He got closer to the stored catapult ammo. The catapult ammo sat idle as Giants guarded it. There were three Giants. They muttered to themselves and carried heavy clubs. They were undisturbed by the rustling and stirring in the camp and the milling of the mounts. A Greenflyer hovered above them. They prepared their clubs and waited for him to draw close. But he never did. So, the Giants rested, comfortable in their size and natural dominance.

Joe tried to communicate to the other Hivers that the Demons recognized what was going on. The Demons picked up on the clues left by Joe's and the Hivers' exploits and actions.

Joe hunkered down and lit a small light produced by his ABS suit. Mentally drawing a picture of his plans, he waited for acknowledgment. The Hivers' assent was a nod and a feeling of palpable agreement floating into the consciousness Joe had honed and developed. From behind the

Giants, he flicked a small lighter into the catapult ammo. Two Hivers lit small torches and flicked them into the ammo as well.

The Giants barely noticed the arsonists, but flames billowed out of the metal pallets holding the ammo. They froze, then ran toward the center of the camp.

Joe signaled, and the Hivers ducked low and ran farther north.

Boom! Kaboom! Boom!

The catapult ammo started to explode. An airborne Greenflyer circling above was downed by a shard of shrapnel. The Demon mounts stampeded west at a furious pace, their thundering paws raising dust and causing confusion. Several Demons were felled by the exploding catapult ammo. Further west, the main body of Demons attempted to see what was going on, but they were stilled by indecision due to the explosions.

The Demon mounts were almost out of the camp completely. A few were being ridden by Demons who were having difficulty controlling them.

The smoke and dust began to clear.

Joe scanned with the ABS. The few Giants tending the catapults were either severely wounded or dead. The Demons were confused as they viewed the carnage. Several of their comrades lay dead or dying.

A soft breeze blew the smoke away. Joe could see about one hundred Demons standing with weapons ready, perhaps wondering what could befall them next. The answer came shortly.

A picket line of Hivers, three deep, advanced. Before the Demons could react, a shower of spears hit their ranks, felling their front line. Then from behind a greater line of Demons, who were coming together, came the cry "shield wall!" from a seven-foot Demon Joe knew was Deathmet.

The Demons hastily grouped tightly together, holding their shields. The next onslaught would not find them in disarray. But it wasn't what they expected. Quickly flanking to either side of the Demons, Hivers swept the corners of their formation. Leaping over Demons, at times they landed at the back of the right and left flanks of the Demon formation. They hacked with their swords, cutting down Demons piece by piece: legs, shoulders, knees—anything not covered by a shield. The Hivers' unusual strength ripped through Demon armor, taking solid pieces of flesh from the Demons they hit. Deathmet stood fearlessly, moving with the furious grace that Joe had experienced before. Deathmet's long sword and axe cut down several interlopers flanking behind his line.

Joe felt a signal being given: his small group could strike the Demon line from the rear and rend it asunder.

Joe was flanked by two Hivers on either side of him. He dismissed whatever concerns he had about the attack plan and headed straight for Deathmet. The Hivers seemed unconcerned, perhaps even grateful, that Joe could discern the plan in some cosmic sense. Without hesitation Joe sought to drive the Vibro-Blade straight toward Deathmet's lower back, hopefully crippling him immediately and making him vulnerable to an easy kill and beheading this time. But in the flurry of activity, the battle was not well orchestrated. The Hiver to Joe's left struck a nearby Demon in the hamstring then, leaping up, hacked off its head with a horizontal stroke so fast he barely caught Deathmet's peripheral vision. Lunging hard as Deathmet wheeled and parried, Joe fell back, stumbling momentarily. Deathmet raged forward, slicing toward Joe's head with his axe. Joe shifted position ever so quickly, catching the blow on his shoulder, wincing in pain. *Not again*, he thought. The ABS held, but the burning pain staggered Joe. Deathmet, seeing his chance, sought to land a crippling blow across Joe's legs with his long sword. Joe danced backward, leaping into the air in hopes of avoiding the obvious. Before he could, he saw two Hivers collapse on Deathmet, hacking his legs with their short swords. Joe saw Deathmet stumble and fall. *Behind him*, he thought. *Make it final this time.* The crying lament must have touched the two Hivers. One slashed down on Deathmet's sword arm. The other, using the opening, slammed the tip of his blade into Deathmet's throat. Joe raced forward, seeing Deathmet near death, his gaze fearful. Joe readied his steel sword to help the Hivers hack off the remaining anatomy that secured Deathmet's head to his body. Joe grabbed Deathmet's head and hoisted it above him, letting out a thunderous cry, "Done, you fool!" Demons were assailed from all sides. Many heard Joe's war cry. Those not encumbered looked to gaze upon their leader's head being flaunted like a trophy. Joe pitched the head into the grass whereas many Demons as possible could see it.

Joe could see the end coming. The Demons were disheartened but fought on—not as strongly as before. Joe could see the Hivers were not as many as he thought. But they fought, every one of them, like more than two full-sized warriors. The Demons were down to about fifty fighters, and the Hivers swarmed them, hacking and slashing, using their short stature to plunge under Demon guards, knock them down, and then hack them to death. The Demons squirmed and screamed, bellowing in pain.

Joe felt a command being given to pull back, but first he scooped up Deathmet's head and threw it into the still-crackling flames of the catapults. Joe could hear buzzing insect wings. Above he saw the scout Hiver he had aided mounted on a bee. A horde of bees followed behind him, descending quickly as the ground Hivers scrambled to the perimeter of the battle. Spears flew from the sky as the remaining Demons were brought down. Then the Bee-Riders gained altitude, and the ground Hivers crowded into their vacuum, hacking and slashing. Joe unleashed the Vibro-Blade, best used for stopping foes by cracking and damaging joints and bones. Wherever he swung, a Demon slumped down. Soon many of the Hivers, seeing Joe's effect, dashed into the areas where Demons lay, wincing in pain. The Hivers slew them with powerful cuts and hacks. Joe looked around. There was a growing stillness on the battlefield, all violence almost having ended.

Joe looked above to the jungle vines and blossoms. He saw purple, red, and blue blossoms occasionally being visited by giant bees feeding on nectar. While the ground looked as if it had witnessed a great battle, the jungle itself was beautiful—a living representation of nature at work.

Joe was shaken from his reverie. Greenflyers were zooming in to pick the corpses of the Demons. Joe headed to the Hive, hopeful that this was it for a while. The pace quickened before long. Joe could see the base of the Hive. Its repairs seemed to have been made. Overhead a swarm of bees ridden by Hiver warriors guarded their ascent up the Hive mound to safety.

Joe receded into the Hive with the rest of the Hivers. Openings in the mound seemed to spring up and swallow them. Joe just followed the swarm.

Soon they were in what appeared to be a food chamber. Joe got the feeling he could relax now.

Hivers, obviously female, came out carrying foodstuff that looked like mushrooms from the areas Joe first passed out in. There were chunks in steaming broth. Other things were being served that Joe didn't recognize. The battle was over.

A party was breaking out. Joe's shoulder ached. He wanted out of the ABS to check the damage. Before he could recognize it, the ABS receded into his belt. The female Hivers laughed as their exoskeletons receded, revealing feminine athletic bodies that Joe readily appreciated. Joe was handed a clay vessel and bid to drink as the offerer touched the vessel to her lips and then offered it to Joe, who drank thirstily and felt a rush that both relaxed and revitalized him. The Hiver woman gently pushed him back and started applying a strong-smelling ointment to Joe's wounded shoulder. He munched on the mushrooms from the broth and drank the liquor, which seemed to be some sort of mead, or honey wine. Joe eased back on what seemed to be a bed of feathers. His shoulder felt numb but at least was not painful. Joe munched on something that looked like a large nut of some sort. He drank in the symmetry of the female Hiver who administered to his needs. She compared favorably to any woman he'd ever seen, though her alien features seemed off-putting in a way. Joe looked around. All the warriors who returned were being administered to in some way. *Better than the VA*, he couldn't help but think.

Joe must have dozed off. When he awoke, the Hiver woman was still there, adding more ointment to his wounded shoulder.

It was getting late. Joe woke to find himself in a cocoon-like structure attached to a wall in the Hive mound. The Hiver woman was above him on a ledge, looking at him with what seemed to be a smile. In any event, Joe could feel the positive intonations coming his way from her, so subtle—more mental, like all the Hiver communications seemed to be.

Joe caught the scent of fruit and alcohol—a second round of mead was being served in clay mugs. Joe could smell the rich aroma of berries, flower blossom, and alcohol. The aroma opened a door in his consciousness. He saw the giant honeybees ridden and controlled by the Hivers. They yielded their honey, which he could see was supplemented with ingredients by the Hivers, stored, and allowed to ferment. Every smell had a mental image. *Pheromones*, Joe thought. *I'm being linked to the Hivers by pheromones, and now I understand some of their culture.*

Joe paid attention to the pain in his shoulder and noticed the odor from the ointment applied to it. Pungent and strong, like liniment. Joe could sense the intended well-being coming from the Hiver woman as she put more of the greasy solution on Joe's shoulder. Joe relaxed, feeling not so vulnerable without the ABS covering him. Joe sensed a deep appreciation coming from the Hiver woman, who had left her armor receded and started to look very human. Her forehead had two spots where Joe guessed energy was sent and received in a complex fusion of electromagnetic and telepathic energy. Joe looked at her nose—broad nostrils that could pick up scents just as he did and then evoke a sense of knowing, Joe guessed. *Like my dreams*, he thought. *But no smells are attached to my dreams.*

Before Joe realized, the Hiver woman was caressing the length of his body, massaging every muscle save his wounded shoulder. The pain was fading away. Joe was also feeling the effect of the wine, which was delicious. The cocoon-like bed folded in around him as the Hiver woman dropped down on top of him, asking to be with him. Joe's nature had been rising, and now with his pain receding, he could smell this Hiver woman, who reminded him of cinnamon. Joe took in her body, so well-proportioned yet so small at around four feet tall. Some of the women were taller than others, as were some of the men, but none above five feet. Perhaps the women were bigger for carrying children. Joe touched her exoskeleton armor's edge at the shoulders. He could see similar armor edges at her elbows and knees. Relinquishing the armor made her more human than ever. She had no hair though—what a disappointment. But her physical structures were familiar, and this comforted Joe. Other than the alien-like features, she could have been any woman he knew. His thoughts briefly turned to home. In a sense, the Hiver woman answered him without making a sound. *Home*, he thought. *Thanks for protecting my home.* Somehow, he thought it wouldn't be a good idea to give voice to his pleasure. Yet he answered as their bodies entwined, both erupting in quiet orgasms.

When the lovemaking concluded. Joe sensed *I am connecting with the Hive as a whole, not just to one Hiver; this feels different, and I know them better now.*

The next day, Joe awoke in the cocoon. There was a flurry of activities going on in the chamber. A summons from the king was being given. Joe wished for coffee, but instead his Hiver mistress arrived in full armor with something that smelled like warm chocolate, which he drank greedily. A warm glow filled him, and the rush of stimulation was strong.

Joe was going on a scouting patrol. There was a hasty breakfast of baked mushrooms and potatoes.

Joe was being urged to join a foot patrol at the base of the Hive mound. A side exit hidden from general scrutiny was used. Joe had the Vibro-Blade attached to his waist, and the steel sword hung diagonally on his back.

Hivers generally were four to five feet tall. They were able to move with great speed and agility. Joe was able to keep up, but it took effort. The training with Sika had been important in getting him this far. Joe was with five Hivers carrying spears and swords. They were headed back to the Demon camp. Overhead a squad of Bee-Riders landed, about twenty strong. Joe's patrol rode double with the Bee-Riders.

The Demon camp was all but gone. The charred catapult parts had been burned, and the Demon dead were burned in the fires. *Not much of a camp at all*, Joe thought. He could see some armor and metal weaponry strewed about. The carnage had been complete. Joe was riding a giant Bee that was ten feet in length and sturdy all around.

Next, they headed west to cover the area where the Demons had come from. Dense jungle thinned into meandering meadows. The sensation of flight was nothing new to Joe. As a mercenary for the oil companies, he had flown down to battle wearing personal flight devices. But this was different. Being in the giant swarm of bee cavalry flying over the jungle made him feel like he was part of the Hive. Joe noticed after being with the Hiver woman that he could understand clearer what was being communicated to him. He was closer to the Hivers, more comfortable in their midst.

They flew low to about one hundred meters higher than most plants but near the high cliff-clinging vines. They flew west, looking for signs of the Demons.

From the sky Joe could see how the Hivers riding bees could control the jungle and regions far from the Hive. Joe watched bees flit to giant blossoms on vines, apparently sucking nectar, and then return to flight. Joe got used to the humming of bee wings. He enjoyed the height, always relatively close to the jungle canopy. Joe could feel the positive connection between the bees and the Hivers. Over the jungle, they flew west then south through jungle canopies and over sprawling fields.

During the air patrol, other Hivers would join. None seemed to mind Joe or question his presence. Sure, they looked him over and noted his ABS armor, which some thought was a part of his body.

11.
ALLIES

Joe loved this experience—not just flying on giant bees. Joe could feel the presence of the Hive: the singular purpose, the love they had for each other. There were never wars between Hives. The region was controlled by them. Joe felt that he, too, was a member of the Hive. He could sense and understand the thoughts and smells that kept evoking more meaning about the life of the Hivers.

Joe had not dreamed the comforting dreams of support he had recognized from afar almost every night. He realized he felt support anyway—from the Hive.

As Joe flew over the vine-entangled jungle and its blossoms, he was reminded of gardens he'd known in the past. Samantha had insisted they find obscure gardens to frequent in peace, hoping to maintain the privacy of her and Joe's relationship. An all-world running back was not supposed to date a sportscaster who might be called upon to criticize his play. "Not to worry," he'd say. "I got something special that don't know how to fade." Joe would laugh at his own cockiness. However, now Joe wondered if he been talented and lucky. He was starting to feel he was meant for more. Aside from his dreams, he had never felt so secure as he did in the Hive.

Joe mused, thoughtfully taking time to take it all in. The runner he'd help rescue was on patrol with him too. It felt so good. Even the bee he was riding was, well as far as Joe could feel and sense, *happy*.

No luck on Demons, but their remnants were everywhere.

There were broken-down wheels from catapults and empty barrels that might have carried food or water.

Here and there a Greenflyer tore into a Demon corpse, then upon sensing the Hivers, flew speedily into the jungle. The Greenflyers rarely worked as a team, but if they smelled blood—anyone's blood—they came swooping in on wings that made them the fastest in the jungle over short distances: one hundred meters or less.

Joe wondered if the Greenflyers ever came north; if they did, they'd never be rid of them. The Hivers stayed in their jungle, dominant and responsive to the extreme.

Other Hivers had repulsed Demons as well. Joe could sense the telepathic chatter whenever they crossed paths with other Hiver patrols. There was a sense that the Demons would reveal themselves.

Back in the Hive, Joe was served wine by his consort. As was her way, she ingratiated herself to him completely. Wine and food were served in whatever quantities Joe wanted. Joe plunged into lovemaking with her, and the deeper he plunged, the more a part of the Hive he became. Their joined ecstasy became more illuminating. He was drawn more and more into complete shared memories with the Hivers. He looked affectionately upon his consort, her armor drawn back. The beauty of body increasingly surpassed by the harmony of the Hive she represented. Yet the still-strange face reminded Joe she was in many ways alien to him.

Where is the eternal Hive, Heaven? Joe wondered. The closer he got to them, the more he mixed with them in the Hive, the clearer it all seemed. His consort was loyal to him but only so much as it supported the Hive. Joe was grateful for her support but knew he might lose her to the Hiver ready to impregnate her with fellow Hive mates. The king and queen mated to create top leaders in every caste. This kept the Hivers expanding, even creating new Hives allied to the original Hive. The rest of the creation of Hivers was done through temporary consorts who mated and produced offspring.

The next day would be the same as the last: airborne on giant bees, patrolling for the Demon threat.

Joe wondered at this land, so dangerous and yet so fertile.

The flying was soothing, the hum of bee wings comforting. With the Hivers surrounding him, Joe felt so comfortable. The Hivers circled back to the Hive. Demons were somewhere but not revealing themselves. There was more to this though. Joe sensed that Hivers willingly died for each other and expected to exist somewhere one day in a hive of eternal bounty, the growth of spring and the harvest of autumn eternally supporting their shared life.

Returning to the Hive, Joe was greeted by a new consort, perhaps better proportioned than the first. Were they reading his...pheromones? This was the tallest Hiver woman he'd seen. Over five feet tall, she was an anomaly from what he'd seen. This time he'd try something different. He quickly ran to the honey wine kegs, poured some for both, and offered her a cup before tasting his own. She radiated happiness and kissed him lavishly. *This is very human*, Joe thought. *Very human!* Her face as even more alien, but her body could have competed for best figure with a rap-video dancer. These Hivers read minds. The Hivers connect using their pheromones and start communicating automatically.

That night in his cocoon, he dreamed again. It was as if his revelations stimulated the obvious. He wondered about his ties to Saluiana and Sika. They, too, seemed to know him well beyond words or the obvious attraction he felt to their feminine bodies.

The kaleidoscope of images was more real, more intense than ever. The dream seemed to show Joe in all the most powerful connections of his life: coaches, comrades, lovers, and of course his mother was very prominent, and the presence of Angel Arleosa was revealed again. "Know the Hivers," Arleosa said. "They are bound to each other as we should be bound to God."

Arleosa looked at God. "You see," she said. "He's getting it!"

"Yes, he is!" God boomed. "When I created the Hivers, I knew it was good. But they were just not quite human enough. If they come to help Joe and humanity, that will be the fruition of their creation."

Joe awoke with his new consort nudging her head against his neck. He had rolled the ABS into his belt, which never left him, even during lovemaking. The morning beverage was served. Joe put on his ABS. He sipped thirstily, waking from the night's dreams and wanting more time with his consort. Their lovemaking, even in the morning, was rapturous tuned from the strong mixture of pheromones and electromagnetic telepathy. Joe felt close to this alien, insect-like woman. Her flat nose and oval face had their own beauty. The eyes showing an ebony, shiny, fathomless depth.

Joe eased back, took another sip of the hot beverage, and prepared for the day ahead. Joe learned that today they would fly north to find more indications of Demon activity. They would fly far from the Hive, hoping to catch the Demons in a state of preparation. Perhaps mounting a force for a large foray into the Hiver jungle.

Joe couldn't help but think about Saluiana, Sika, and the Long-Striders. *How were they holding up?* Joe wondered. He knew they had support. Bladeswift would bring his horsemen into the fray as needed. They rotated between the grasslands and high plateaus, ensuring their own needs were met, then striking hard against any sign of Demons and their assaults on the Long-Striders.

Now Joe needed his weapons. It was time to shift his strategy. He needed to show the Hivers how powerful an adversary the Demons could be. But where were they? Were they in hiding, waiting? He could feel something. But not cooperation from the Demons. *Ha, no way*, he mused. *When he needed more from them, they hid—guerrilla warfare? Perhaps.* But if they attacked again, he must continue to show the Hivers he was an ally. He hoped his connection to them would extend to the Long-Striders as allies too. They would be fighting a mutual enemy who was a threat to them as well.

Joe sipped some more of the chocolate beverage. Preparations were being made. His consort brought him the hearty mushroom gruel, a staple for the Hivers, as evident by their mushroom crop in the depths of the Hive.

Hiver warriors were sharpening swords and spears with grindstones. Joe borrowed one from a Hiver warrior and started sharpening his steel sword. The Hiver warriors chided him. They joked that they had never seen such a strange, big Hiver with two swords—one steel and another as mystical as Hiver communications themselves. With that, Joe activated the Vibro-Blade, laughing out loud. The Hivers rarely needed to speak, but now they laughed as well, telling Joe he would be a great Hive mate if he could only keep his swords straight. When Hivers spoke, it wasn't just the words that mattered. Just as with a human's inflection, context feelings wove in and out of the conversation. But for Hivers, inflection and body language were toned with the positive pheromones of expression and a telepathic signal that contained the words. The Hivers liked Joe. His consort came over and hugged him. Joe felt the type of warmth and camaraderie he had known after he had helped his football team win a big game. *Damn!* he thought. *It was like being applauded in a victory where he had gained two hundred yards.*

It was early morning in the Hive, and the day was progressing quickly. The warriors were all moving out of the Hive to the jungle canyon, rapidly climbing the dense vines covering the canyon walls. The bees were gathering nectar from the huge blossoms on the canyon vines. Joe needed the ABS to keep up with them. It occurred to him that he'd never be able to be a part of all this if he couldn't join them successfully in these activities. The bees were descending. As they did, the Hivers mounted them by springing into the air behind the wings. This was a combat mount meant to keep the bees from having to touch ground and become more vulnerable. Joe made the six-foot leap without activating support from the ABS. *Damn, I'm getting stronger. What's going on?*

Joe jumped on an ascending bee with about fifty Hiver Bee-Riders. This was going to be more than patrolling and scouting. The Hivers planned to attack and make their presence felt. Their philosophy was unrelenting. Push the enemy out of their territory violently and permanently. Joe wondered what would happen if the Hivers mounted a large-scale campaign. Joe could help them if they saw the need. Indeed, his plan called for just such an intervention.

The sky was crowded as Joe's squad flew into the air. In the distance Joe could see a canopy of trees. They were headed north. To the east and west were Hives allied to his own. They would search their own areas' holds against any Demon incursion. Joe's Hivers would fly north and deal a blow to the Demons—any Demons they could find.

Joe scanned ahead with the ABS. There were flying creatures up ahead. Why so much activity in the sky here? Then it was clear. There were dragons in the sky. Thirty feet from nose to tail. Joe wondered, *What now?* He needed a gun, but not to worry, the Hivers parted in the middle to avoid the dragons. Joe had wondered about these creatures since seeing certain warriors wearing their scales as armor. Now it appeared that even the Hivers would avoid them. Joe could sense concern but not panic. The Hivers parted to accommodate the two dragons, who flew past without incident. Joe could see the gunmetal-gray scales, red eyes, and large rear talons. Nowhere else were there creatures like these. Two limbs for wings and two large limbs with sharp claws. Joe looked at the mouths—no fire or fumes emitted from its nostrils. *A fairy tale*, Joe thought.

Joe turned his attention to the search for Demons. North and farther north. They flew on. Joe started to recognize this as the way he'd come south. Now he was getting closer to familiar ground. The ACV was within range. He'd taken it to fly south, then landed and hidden it before reaching the southern jungles of the Hivers' land.

Joe could just about drop out of the sky and get to his ship. But it would disrupt everything if he did. His time trying to reach the Hivers had to have continuity. Awash in the pheromones of the Hive, he had to seek a permanent connection. It would be too easy to stop now, get his guns, and do what? The Hivers were the key to the outcome he wanted.

Morning turned to afternoon. The Hivers ate in the air before descending to a series of small ponds below. The bees hovered above as gourds were filled. Then, as if on cue, the bees all separated and returned. They could be seen in the distance feeding from giant blossoms. Now they were on the edge of the jungle. Joe doubted there would be anything like giant flowers from here on. No wonder he never saw giant bees in the North.

Joe sat and continued eating with his Hive mates. He was worried about what to do next. But still the camaraderie was comforting. He sipped still-warm chocolate from a gourd while munching on beef jerky. What a strange journey he was making. How would it end? The Hivers were getting ready to fly now. They urged Joe to join them. *Don't worry; we'll help you…*

12.
PAINFUL MEMORIES

King Kotutan rallied his men along the walls of the western fortress. The boom of canons echoed around him. Long rifles were being fired. The fortress was under full assault. Demon-Riders fired arrows along the wall, trying to break the continuity of firepower holding the Demons at bay. Behind these assaults Giants pushed catapults in place, inching closer to the walls of the fortress. King Kotutan directed his sharpshooters to strike down the Giants pushing the catapults. A few hundred meters more, and his fortress would be taking hits from them. The immediate charge on the fortress made it hard to concentrate on the distant threat of the catapults.

Queen Saluiana sat huddled in the fortress with her wisemen, religions leaders, Osala and Boswan, and the Manwolf Ohtokan. Two of Ohtokan's subchiefs sat in the background, waiting with clubs and axes.

Ataka called out to King Kotutan, "Now is the best time, sire—just before they are close enough to feel victory."

"So now it is…" the king replied. A runner was sent to find Queen Saluiana,

"Wait!" from the ramparts came a female voice. She was loading her rifle, hunkered down in a crouch. It was Sika—she jumped down from the ramparts. "The queen may want my counsel about how to deploy the Manwolves, if it please you, oh king."

"Yes, go hurry. Take this lad Goodswift—he can relay any conclusions back to me!" King Kotutan cared not for wise counsel—just reinforcement. This squire, the runner, a nimble lad of nineteen, was all the way up the fortress steps. The urgency of the situation, signified by the deafening booms of cannons and gunshots, echoed throughout the fortress. A sure proving ground for a young squire. Goodswift was eager to be of service in these dire times and knew the way to the queen. He quickly stepped into the main hall.

"No, No!" Saluiana screamed. Boswan fell, his head caved in on one side by Ohtokan himself.

"We never forget!" said Ohtokan. "We are not your dogs. Men bring disaster everywhere!" With that, he wheeled around, hefting his club to strike Osala next.

Saluiana cowered back, momentarily shocked by the unexpected attack and its savagery. The runner, Goodswift, looked on in horror. He was here to relay the communication of aid. The Manwolves would fight for the Long-Striders and signal the Wildriders using their speed and agility to get clear of the fort. Finally, years of interspecies humanoid strife would end with an alliance against the Demons. But no—Ohtokan sensed Goodswift's presence and urged his subchiefs to attack him. Upon seeing the tableau unfold, Goodswift lowered himself into a crouch then, always a strategist longing for knighthood, sprang forward, aiming past the two Manwolf subchiefs with his single-shot pistol. The subchiefs' attentions were divided between Goodswift and the remaining priest. Ohtokan moved to strike Osala. Goodswift lined up a headshot but realized he could not afford to miss. Time was almost gone. The chiefs turned and closed upon him. There was still a narrow space between them through which the broad, furry back of Ohtokan could be struck. *Blam!* The shot came before Goodswift could even think to fire. The impact hammered into the middle of Ohtokan's back. Ohtokan dropped to his knees, and the subchiefs heard Ohtokan cry out. Ohtokan stumbled while turning to see where the shot was fired from. Goodswift ran around the two Manwolf subchiefs to support his queen, and he tumbled over Ohtokan, who had fallen and lay sprawled on the floor. Sika entered the room right behind him, but she only heard the shot and didn't quite see it hit Ohtokan. She saw Goodswift roll to a standing position between the shocked subchiefs and the remaining priest. Osala, the priest, cowered in fear.

"To me!" Saluiana yelled to Goodswift, and she moved toward Osala, who looked as if he'd seen his death already. Saluiana, having gathered her wits, moved to consolidate the defense against the Manwolf subchiefs and protect Osala as well. She was dressed in leather armor and produced her two short swords. Facing the Manwolf subchief closest to Osala, Goodswift drew his sword and swung it, cutting the knee of the Manwolf subchief. Sika had a loaded rifle but now fired her bow as the fallen subchief gained his feet. *Whack! Whack!* Sika fired her bow—twice to make sure. The subchief fell with two arrows deep in his upper back. The final Manwolf subchief turned in anger and bounded toward Sika. Calmly she moved sideways to make the Manwolf redirect his final lunge, knowing his leaping ability would place him upon her in a heartbeat. As she moved, she calmed her breathing. *Blam!* He took the shot in his shoulder closest to her from ten feet way. He was still coming forward, though blood was pouring from his wound. From behind him came the sound of swords slicing and thudding into the Manwolf's body. Saluiana kept the pressure on as the Manwolf lurched toward Sika, who put one more arrow in him, then he fell to one knee and slumped to the floor.

"Treachery!" Queen Saluiana fumed.

"Yes," Sika agreed. The queen went over to see the fallen wiseman. His fellow, Osala, stood looking down upon the now lifeless body tearfully. Ohtokan lay on the floor, bleeding, and gasping. Goodswift stood beside Osala, being protective but not sure what to do now. Knowing his queen had emerged to end the conflict surprised him.

"You, what is your name?" Queen Saluiana addressed Goodswift.

"Goodswift, an army squire, my queen, and a runner," he responded.

"tell King Kotutan what happened here. We will need another way to signal the Wildriders for aid. The Manwolves are against us, and we've killed their chief!" Queen Saluiana lamented.

"Yes, but they gave us no choice," Sika responded.

"Go, Goodswift," Queen Saluiana commanded. "tell King Kotutan what happened. He will have to send for aid." She turned her attention to Sika. "Sika, we struck a delicate balance here, now broken. We can light signal fires, but the Manwolves made a promise and would have made it through faster than any man—even on horseback. A human could be shot down. The Demons are unrelenting!"

Goodswift was up the stairs and onto the ramparts where King Kotutan directed his forces. Tirelessly the Long-Striders fought on as inexorably the Demons pulled their catapults closer to the fortress. Every charge against the walls caused the Long-Striders to change their focus, giving the Giants time to pull the catapults closer. Kotutan feared that if the catapults were employed, the power balance would favor the Demons.

"Joe is out there somewhere in the South," Sika told the queen. "Bladeswift is nearby. Light the beacon fires—then have the king do the unthinkable. Send Ataka out and charge the enemy, delay them. I will use the diversion to get clear of the area and find Bladeswift. If he is not encumbered, he will come!"

"It will be done," King Kotutan said after hearing Sika's plan laid out by Queen Saluiana, who had hustled up to the ramparts. "Have Ataka form up two columns of ten knights each. Make sure they have weapons loaded and spare ammo. Bows can be strapped on as well. Give each man a shotgun and a pistol." It hadn't been long since Joe had shared the shotgun with the Long-Striders and some of the Wildriders. King Kotutan knew he needed every opportunity to bolster their ability to survive. Hell was coming, and Heaven's only gifts were an Angel, more firepower, and a combat Messiah.

"Form up, form up!" Ataka screamed. Goodswift had already run to light the two beacons in the north, east, and southeast towers of the fortress.

Now the Demons would know the Long-Striders were signaling for aid. With the help of the Manwolves, securing aid would have been more secretive than the signal fires, which would outwardly underscore the desperation of the Long-Striders. The Demons would know their window of opportunity was apparent. *Would anyone come in time?* King Kotutan wondered. Now his sins against the Manwolves had come to haunt him.

Sika kissed Saluiana on the cheek. "Be safe," the queen said.

"I will," Sika answered as the queen kissed her other cheek. They embraced, and Sika went out to the forest right behind the column of twenty riding to stall the enemy. Three hundred yards out, Sika darted around the column heading north. Ataka let out a war cry, and the knights spurred their mounts into a fast gallop, forming a line charging across the field of grass. The ground had large pits the knights avoided from earlier cannon shots used to disrupt and thwart the Demon charges.

Sika was soon out of the sight. Goodswift walked with the queen to the ramparts. She trusted him after his performance in the hall of the fortress. "Now is the time," King Kotutan muttered as the queen stood beside him.

Sika's large, fast horse was before long out of sight. The Long-Striders rode almost unerringly straight. There were three catapults in view behind the line of Demons. Burly Giants ten feet tall pulled the catapults, two Giants to each one. The Demons, seeing the strategy, fired arrow after arrow at the knights, but Ataka knew this type of warfare. Before he got close enough to the Demons' archers, he fired his rifle at a Giant coming directly in front of him, now only one hundred yards away. *Boom!* Ataka was a good shot at a dead gallop; considering he was under this kind of duress—and on horseback to boot—his shot was a dream in the chaos of a nightmare.

Giants were ten feet tall and big shouldered, which may have helped Ataka's shot. The Giant reeled and fell to his knee.

Ataka's knights swerved in the direction of the other two catapults. Ataka guessed he would handle the one. Speeding his horse up and leaning down, he drove fast for the line of Demons. His charger was dressed in dragon scales, and not many arrows could pierce that density. As he approached twenty meters, he let his pistol open a hole for him leading to the catapult. *Kapow!* The shot knocked a Demon backward. Ataka squeezed down low in the saddle, riding through the opening left by the Demon he had shot. Sharp stings made him grimace as the Demons found openings with their most vicious spear and sword thrusts. Suddenly Ataka was falling forward, sliding on his chest as his horse rolled to the ground. Instantly Ataka was up on his feet, fitting an arrow to his bow. *Thwup!* He caught the remaining Giant in the lower abdomen just as he rose from ministering to his comrade. Ataka fitted another arrow. The Giant fell backward, another arrow now protruding from his chest.

The Demons realized what was happening and mustered to attack Ataka. Seeing this unfold, the knights swung into the gap created in the Demon line by Ataka. The knights followed Ataka and shot Demons, with their arrows distracting them from Ataka before they peeled left and right to shoot the remaining four Giants pushing two catapults on either side of Ataka's position. Several shots brought down the four Giants as the knights swarmed them before the Demons could respond. Carefully taking measured shots, the knights exploited their opening, killing or badly wounding the Giants. Finally, the knights wheeled around to face the Demons. Arrows now held the Demons at bay. The knights had lost several men, but the element of surprise had saved the day. One of the two knights swept into Ataka's position to aid Ataka, who flung himself onto the knight's horse riding behind him.

It seemed like a suicide mission, but no one had said the words. Ataka looked up to see the swarming Demons coming toward the knights. Sitting behind his fellow, he had time to load his weapons. He knew they had to move quickly, but where were the Demon supply lines and reinforcement? They had none, Ataka realized. What type of cavalry was this? *No backup support.* The Demons were known for scavenging the lands around them rather than creating supply lines and reinforcements.

But now Ataka saw a hopeful chance. "Ride!" he screamed. "Shoot their ammo in the carts behind the catapults, move quickly…hold your fire until we get close as the Demons protect those catapults."

The Demons were massing around the catapults, trying to get closer to them, very angry the Giants were down. Ataka could see his horse trying to come to him. It was covered in battle dress, but the Demons tried to hack at it. The armor kept it alive, and when it spied Ataka, it sped up and kicked at the Demons who sought to kill it. Ataka jumped onto his horse, and the twelve knights rode away to a small ridge, wheeling around above the catapult ammo.

"Hit that catapult ammo!" yelled Ataka. *Pop, pop, pow!* Shots rang out; then there were cracking explosions as the three ammo carts exploded.

The Giants were meant to be a deterrent to the ammo being lost, but they had been eliminated. The explosions were horrendous, though the knights were out of harm's way—the heat of the blast rushed up the ridge, raising dust and debris. The swarming Demons beside the catapults were all but decimated. Now hearing the explosions, the Demon cavalry rode back toward the ridge.

Sika heard the explosions and wondered, *what is happening?* She looked north. No sign of the Wildriders. She continued to ride north, then back east into the forest. The sun was starting to dip, and afternoon would soon be upon her. What could best aid the situation? Two beacons were lit. *What now?* she wondered. Seeing no other course, she rode back toward the forest.

Ataka rallied his remaining force. There was no way they'd fight through one hundred or so Demon cavalry to make it back to the fortress.

Sika rode fast. Her hearty mare was strong, fast, and enduring. *Now is the time*, she thought. She made sure her rifle and pistol were loaded. Picking up speed, she could see the Demon horde falling upon Ataka. One hundred arrows cut Ataka and his men down. Even the horses with their armor were pierced with arrows. Ataka was ringed by the Demons with naught but five knights. Swords drawn, shields held firmly, they knew this was their time.

"Now!" King Kotutan bellowed. "Fire on their position. Now!" he screamed in desperation. The boom of the canons echoed for miles. The distance was too far, but the Demons closest to the fortress were crushed in belching flames and a cascade of shrapnel.

Recognizing that this was it, Ataka led the charge. "Attack!" he bellowed. The Demons still ringed his position. Sika was bearing down from behind Ataka. She stopped her horse and took careful aim. She blasted the chest of one Demon directly in front of Ataka, who lost not a split second of forward motion. Now she moved to her left, attempting to flank the Demons closing in on Ataka as another of his men fell, several arrows through his neck and chest. Sika was close now. Drawing her pistol, she fired at a Demon closing in on Ataka's left. *Boom!* The Demon slumped to his knees. Ataka veered left. "Follow me," he said. "To the fortress!"

Now it was just him and his two guardshieldsmen, knights sworn to defend him, both heavily armored for the task. Both carried frontier shotguns. Seeing the threat to Ataka, both slung their swords, and they each fired one barrel in unison. *Bam! Boom!* A small path was cleared. Several arrows whistled through the air as Sika rode on the left flank. Her bow, propelling several arrows into the Demons, opened the path to the fortress even more. The Demons, always motivated by revenge, looked for signs of their distress. Suddenly their attention was upon Sika, who leaned over the left flank of her horse to avoid a volley of spears and arrows striking her mount. Though somewhat shielded by leather war dress and dragon scale, her mount crashed to its knees. Sika rolled left and clear, rolling then standing and running, her short sword in one hand, the pistol in the other. She sought to reach Ataka and his two guardshieldsmen. *Boom! Boom!* The guardshieldsmen answered the threat with the last two shots of their double-barrel shotguns.

Reloading and moving forward, Ataka picked up a spear from the corpse of a dead Demon and hurled it straight ahead into the face of a remaining Giant, panicked and attacking with the Demons. The Giant careened backward, taking down two Demons with him. Before they could scramble to their feet, the Demons were being cracked in their heads by the rifle butts of the guardshieldsmen's shotguns. Sika was finding a path to them but faced several Demons on her way.

Where are you, Joe? she thought. Dipping low, she avoided an arrow, then sprung forward, slicing the neck of a Demon half through. Rolling right, she sprang up and pierced the sword arm of another Demon, severing his bicep and piercing the chain mail. Spinning and leaping forward, she heard the crack of the rifle fire from the fortress as it blasted into the Demons surrounding her and Ataka.

A glancing arrow stunned Sika, and she sprawled down on her hands and knees. Blood ran from her temple where the arrow struck at an angle—not straight enough to penetrate but enough to cause damage and knock her unconscious.

† † †

Joe felt good. The buzz of the bee's wings became a comfort to him. He warmed to the experience. How far north would they fly before they saw Demons? If they went a lot farther, they wouldn't really be in the South anymore.

Joe munched dried mushrooms and sipped warm coffee from a canteen he had brought. Suddenly his comfort was gone. He felt a frustrating sense of dread. *Sika*, he thought. *Where are you? North. I must get them north.* Finally, he said, "I have people north of here and tools that can help this fight. Can we go…?"

The Hive leader looked at Joe with as much expression as he'd seen in a Hiver. And though there were no words, there was an answer. "We are going now, Joe. Now!"

13.

SURVIVE

Sika was barely conscious. Blood streamed down the side of her face where the arrow had glanced against her temple. She felt numb. Ataka was almost to the fortress gates when he realized Sika was on the field of battle. The Demons closed around him, now recovering from their initial surprise. Shots rang out from the fortress. Demons staggered and dropped as they came toward Ataka and his two remaining guardshieldsmen. The Demons could sense that these people were important. They drew closer to Ataka, firing their arrows and clanging sword to shield to create confusion if they could not throw a spear or shoot an arrow.

Goodswift was over the ramparts and into the field of battle. He rushed past Ataka and his two guardshieldsmen. He sought to reach Sika but fell back under an onslaught of arrows and spears. Already bleeding from a score of wounds, he formed ranks with Ataka and his two remaining men.

Now Queen Saluiana was on the gated ramparts with King Kotutan, who directed his attention toward Sika, who was crawling and soon standing. Shots were fired around her from the ramparts as several Demons gained proximity to her. There was a path leading away from the fort with less opposition. Sika thought, *I will not let them surround me. I have to move now.* Time was running out.

"*Whooo ahhh!*" Sika called for her horse. She ran away from the fort but doubted the horse would arrive. Finally, she just started running. If the horse showed, great. She shook off the cobwebs, moving away from the fort, back where the catapults had been—away from the Demons who seemed so committed to killing Ataka and his two guardshieldsmen joined by Goodswift.

✝ ✝ ✝

Joe was in view of his ship, the drone of bee wings somehow comforting to him again.

Sika was feeling less hopeful but struggled forward. A small detachment of Demons pursued her. She was starting to run a little faster.

Joe was in the ship now. He grabbed the sniper rifle and several pistols, and he picked up an assault rifle and some explosives. There were several messages from New Castle. But no time for that now.

✝ ✝ ✝

The Devil was fuming. "Get her! Get her!" he raged, his brick-red skin growing redder. The Demons now became confused. They still stormed toward Ataka and his small group, but more broke off in pursuit of Sika, who looked up to find her horse running beside her. She quickly mounted and spurred on the horse, which was bleeding from a score of wounds.

Joe was closing in on the fortress. His mind scanned for some way to explain things before his arrival. Bee wings hummed. Hivers rarely had reason to go north. Long-Striders had gone south only to be annihilated as the potential threat they were.

✝ ✝ ✝

The Devil continued to fume. "They could have had her. They became indecisive, fearing for their lives...why? They are already from Hell. I own their souls."

"My love, come back to me," the woman implored. She was brownish red, like all the Demons and the Devil himself. She was beautifully formed in the most voluptuous manner, her symmetry and tone perfect. She was nude and lounged on a tiger skin, smoking from a water pipe. Her eyes were dilated. "Come, master," she implored.

The Devil turned to face her. He was tall and muscular, and each stride had the rhythm and grace of a champion athlete. "You know," he began, "I was an Angel once upon a time. I have no more success making anyone follow me than God." At that he laughed mightily. He began smoking with the woman. He was nude as well. He began to fondle her and stroke her body.

☩ ☩ ☩

Sika kept riding toward the plateaus of the Wildriders. Her people and her homeland. The Demons continued to attack the fort but with less intensity. Ataka, the guardshieldsmen, and Goodswift were not yet inside the fortress. Queen Saluiana and King Kotutan went to greet them.

Joe could see the field of battle now. The Hivers swept low, hurling spears to keep the remaining Demons from storming the fortress. *Saluiana.* Joe's mind tried to reach her. *I am here with the Hivers as promised. Calm your people. One panicked shot and we are undone.*

Queen Saluiana spread the word to the king. "Focus on repelling the Demon ground attack. The Hivers and bees are our support."

Joe veered away. Where was Sika? He searched the ground. He looked hard using the ABS scanner. There on horseback—riding away toward the high plateaus further west. *Sika.* His mind sought to reach her. Suddenly she reined her horse to a halt. Joe glided down on the bee and leaped down beside her.

She dismounted, and tears streamed down her face. "Joe, Joe!" They hugged intensely. Joe reluctantly released her. "I have a Hiver army in the air. The field will be clear soon: wait and return. I have to see to everything to make sure it works out!"

Joe jumped up and, latching his hands on one of the bee's thoracic legs, was back in the saddle.

Joe sought out Saluiana while the Hiver Bee-Riders skewered Demons with spears and swords. At times Bee-Riders rode double. The rear rider would jump from twelve feet or so and, with sword drawn, land on a Demon from behind sword first, bringing an instant and sudden death from above. The Demons were being routed. Joe swung low. Even the Long-Striders could see the Hivers had no interest in them.

Joe saw the Long-Striders begin to relax. He jumped from his mount and, landing within the fortress, was greeted by cheers. He saluted in return and took off his visor and helmet so his face could be seen. He now had a slight growth of beard. Saluiana hailed him and embraced him momentarily. "There is much to do," Joe started.

"Yes, I can see," Saluiana replied.

"This momentary victory will not hold."

"Yes, I know," Saluiana replied. "I have had terrible dreams we are all in danger. The Demons, they are building…something to bring a final surge against us!" She finished and seemed to deflate.

Before, Joe saw her and took in only her beauty and vitality. Now he saw her as someone stressed tremendously—not like stress on a job, but stress that all the good in your way of life could come to an end.

Joe went to the ramparts. The battle was almost over. Several of the Demons were wounded. Hiver strategy was always to kill every enemy. Joe implored them to wait and let him and Queen Saluiana interrogate them.

This was a great test of faith between the Hivers and Joe, who explained himself, trying to tie the interrogation to mental images of future success. The future was circular for Hivers. Seasons changed—food was stored, fall, foraging and hunting—all in a cyclical manner. The idea of how the enemies may come again only created another *now* to be managed aggressively, as this one had been, but now Joe's pheromones were strongly connected to those of the Hivers. They seemed to sense his intent. *Then they can kill them*, Joe thought.

Three Demons were brought before Joe and the queen. They were heavily chained and shackled. One of the Demons was missing a hand. Blood gushed from his wrist. One of Ataka's knights staunched the blood flow with a dirty rag. Queen Saluiana moved forward with Joe for the interrogation.

"This one first." She directed the guards to bring forth the Demon with the missing hand. Queen Saluiana gazed into his red eyes. He seemed to be gathering sputum in his mouth, perhaps to spit on the queen.

Joe rushed toward and slammed his fist into the Demon's face. "Swallow it!"

The Demon slunk to his knees and was dragged upright again. Queen Saluiana looked at him: the forked tongue, brick-red face, the mouth, now bleeding, sharp canine teeth prominent. Hot breath smelling of fear and rotten flesh. Queen Saluiana yanked his helmet from his head, revealing spiky jet-black hair. She locked her eyes upon his. "Now I see," she uttered and was silent. "No need to have the rest..."

She turned to look at Joe, who responded, "The Hivers will want to finish them."

Joe contacted the Hivers and sent his bee back with them. Before he did, he found a bow and quiver of arrows. "Send this to your king! You have seen them being used. Ask him what benefit they may hold. I will return once again to the Hive. Let the king know the queen here." He looked toward Saluiana. There was an immediate and shared mental connection.

"Where is Sika, Joe?" Saluiana asked.

"She should be coming soon," Joe replied, suddenly alarmed. "She should be here any time!" Joe looked at Saluiana, suddenly shaken. "Ataka, can you ride with me?"

Before long, Ataka, Joe, and several knights were riding from the fortress. As they left, Sika's horse drifted riderless and bloodied toward the entrance. Joe felt a sudden pang of guilt and sadness.

There was blood in the horse's saddle. In Hell, the Devil grinned, sipped some wine, and thought about the future. Soon his mind turned to the voluptuous Demoness lying naked in his bed.

✝ ✝ ✝

Bladeswift was fighting the type of battle he hated. There were women and children in the village, and there was hardly a way to send them away and off the plateau. He wondered where Sika might be and how the Long-Striders were faring. But he could send no one to aid them now.

† † †

Joe examined Sika's horse. He scanned for evidence with the ABS. There were animal hairs in the saddle. Joe cross-referenced them. They were familiar. Manwolves. How could this be? Joe scanned ahead—nothing was clearly apparent. "Back to the fortress," Joe commanded. He could see no clear clues about what had happened to Sika.

Queen Saluiana waited at the fortress entrance. Its gates were open. A mop-up operation was in effect. The Long-Striders had set up temporary medical treatment stations—though a primitive people, they were efficient in using herbs and splints to treat wounds and set bones. They healed quickly, and their bodies overall showed remarkable resilience. Another upgrade from God in hopes of ensuring his success while creating a people "in His image."

Joe, Ataka, the king, and the queen quickly conferred. Joe recounted his success with the Hivers, and they decided they must find Sika. Joe had hated to send the Hivers back, but he knew they needed to prepare for the coming struggle in their own way. The fact that Joe had gotten them to the Long-Striders' fortress was a mark of distinct connection. An alliance had been formed, and because Joe made that connection, the bow he sent would be considered seriously. An army of Hivers with bows would be devastating. Before, the Hivers would see bows used against them, and they would wipe out the threat and ignore any implements their shared consciousness did not connect to. But now Joe had made the connection for them.

Queen Saluiana insisted she go out on the mission to find Sika. Her ability to connect and harmonize her mind to the charged psychic energy around her was great.

"No, my queen! It could be a trap!" King Kotutan protested.

"There is little time," Joe announced. "I am going. If I only use my own tracking ability, I have a chance…Of course, any aid I might receive will help, but it must be now!"

"Help!" Queen Saluiana said. "She is my sister. I am her help!"

King Kotutan looked lost. He knew how this would work. The queen was going on a search for Sika. He wasted no time as the realization hit him. "Get Goodswift here. Ataka, I need you here; the queen will show Joe the way to Sika. We will, God willing, find Sika…but we must guard against another Demon attack as well."

Joe agreed. "Who can you give me, King Kotutan, my liege?" Joe sought to prop up the king, who was at least a competent administrator. If nothing else, he knew how to hold a frontier outpost.

Goodswift arrived, and the queen acknowledged him with a warm greeting. "He is a competent warrior who has already proven his worth!"

"Let's do it then!" Joe said. King Kotutan offered three of the guard-shieldsmen, including the two who had just helped Ataka get back in the fortress. Joe, three guardshieldsmen, Queen Saluiana, and Goodswift the scout: five people. The guardshieldsmen, Joe had learned, were the commandos of this time. They were highly trained and conditioned: tremendous bowmen and marksmen. All were armed with frontier double-barrel shotguns.

Out of the fortress entrance, they rode. "How could your king, your husband, allow you to come upon such a danger for Sika, Saluiana, my queen?" said Joe. "After all, you are a queen! She is a great ally, but we are all at risk."

"Yes, I know," Saluiana replied, "but Sika, myself, and the remaining wiseman are channels to the one true God. Without Sika, the channel will be broken!"

"What the Hell!" Joe exclaimed. "Seems to me that all this time, the more I spent time with the two of you, the more I understood, without really knowing, what I had to do—why I am here."

"Yes," Saluiana said. "Joe, you are here to liberate us, but not just from the Demons—from our own greed and extremism! You see, if we kept going like we were, clash after clash, we'd drive ourselves south again; the

Hivers would dismantle our growth, or we would have clashed with our allies, like the Wildriders. All in the name of more holdings. The Demons had put that on hold, and then you came. A crisis time—a time we are forced to share and group together, noble and commoner alike, trying to preserve an uncertain future. Already we had alienated the Manwolves, who could have been useful allies. But instead, their bitterness remained from our past transgressions against them. The betrayal could easily have been expected, no? Now they are on the verge of extinction, and the betrayal will not rest lightly on my husband's brow."

14.

WHERE ARE YOU?

Sika was running now faster, faster still, ahead. She had been pursued by Demon-Riders, then wounded when a bowshot pierced her upper shoulder. She had slipped down sideways on the saddle, blood oozing onto the saddle from the wound. When she reached a thicket of small trees, she dropped from her horse to the ground. She started running into the trees, running west, away from the Demon-Riders. She was acutely aware of her condition. She ducked away and slumped down behind a tree and low brush.

She grabbed a clean wrap from her pack, and she patted and compressed it against the wound. The arrow had shot clean through. She then began packing herbal compounds onto the wound. She breathed deeply and tried to slow her racing heart, which hopefully would slow the breathing and the blood flowing from her wound. Sika was a master—slowly but surely, she took command of herself. Her heart rate began to slow. She drank from a canteen she carried. The Demons were now on foot, pursuing her into the wooded area. The low brush afforded some cover. Sika rolled to her side and began to crawl facedown. Slowly and inexorably, she made her way east again. The fortress was her most reasonable hope, she recognized. The Demons had been cleared from around the fortress. Joe had said to wait and then return. Surely, she would see friendly faces at the fort. She wondered how Joe had befriended the Hivers. She was beyond all else cold—the blood loss was not fatal, but it was significant. Sika passed out, hidden in the low brush.

☦ ☦ ☦

The Devil fumed. "Find her! Find her!" The harsh mental intonations boomed like so many drumbeats in the mind of the Demons, literally beating the brush and bushes to find Sika.

☦ ☦ ☦

Joe and his crew picked up speed. Queen Saluiana said, "The trail for Sika lies somewhere on the edge of the woods."

Joe scanned ahead with the ABS. A large throng of Demons waited at the woods' edge. Several of the Demons had set a picket for their mounts. The rest continued to search the woods and low brush.

"They are mostly beyond her, west of her," Queen Saluiana noted. "A large throng lies in front of us, and there are those that are guarding their mounts."

"We may need to split up!" Joe strategized out loud. "Queen Saluiana, please go with the guardshieldsmen so that you're protected. Locate Sika. I'll create a diversion and drive off the Demon mounts."

Joe struck off southwest and looped around, heading north, straight for the Demon picket. "Wait for my shots to be fired. Goodswift, your choice: scout ahead or hang back with the queen."

"I'll scout ahead and kill as many as I can—I hope to thin their numbers," Goodswift replied.

"Good," Joe answered. His ABS scan showed there were about thirty Demons who survived the Hivers—in part because their master sent them away from the fort to find Sika.

Joe rode north, urging his horse to a canter. He wanted to move quickly. Then he had another thought. He slipped from the side of his horse and rolled into the brush. Then, unsheathing his Vibro-Blade, he crawled silently toward one of the three Demons guarding the picket line of their mounts. Joe slipped sideways in between the trees. Soon he was a tree away from the picket line. He could almost reach around the trunk and touch the Demon just beyond it. He eased around the trunk. The Demon shifted uneasily, looking around for enemies. He was looking toward the sky as well. Joe brought his blade up and then down onto the Demon's head. The helmet split in half, and the Demon fell to the ground—dead. Joe cut the picket, and a few of the mounts wandered off.

The Demon nearby moved along the trees, following the picket line. Joe had dropped down into the brush and worked behind him. Coming up to the Demon's back, he noted the uneasiness. Was an alarm going to be sounded? Quickly he slammed a horizontal cut into the Demon's neck, and more mounts ran off.

The third Demon emerged from the trees, following along the picket line. Then came the shot—*bam!* right in the forehead. The Demon staggered backward, falling. Joe could see where Goodswift fired his shotgun. There were sounds in the woods as the Demons growled and sought to determine what was happening. The picket line mounts were all scattered now.

Joe scanned for Sika. He fired his pistol into a throng of Demons. Where was Sika? Then he saw her tied behind a Demon mount. Then he noted another mounted Demon. His firing had alerted them to his presence. The two riders—one with Sika tied to his mount—rode off. Those remaining blocked Joe's pursuit. Out of the corner of his eye and with the ABS scan, Joe could perceive Queen Saluiana and the two guardshieldsmen riding fast, blasting the right side of the Demon line with their shotguns in order to gain ground on the Demons with Sika. Joe ran as fast as possible, pulled a second pistol, and charged the Demon line. *Pop! Pop! Pop! Blam! Blam!* The din echoed between the trees as Joe fired his gun and his semiauto 10 mm pistol. By the time he started firing, he was ten feet away from the Demon line. Now he was past it.

He called for his horse. Goodswift emerged, riding at a dead gallop. The Demons and Sika broke into the northern plains. Joe looked for the horse but kept running. No one of their party wished to risk a shot, fearing a wounded horse or fallen Demon might endanger Sika. Joe's horse came to him. He leaped and mounted it to continue the pursuit. Queen Saluiana and the guardshieldsmen were in sight as well. There was scattered resistance from the Demons, and Joe was feeling hopeful. Soon they'd be in pursuit on the open plains, Sika in full view, but they'd be in full view as well. Joe tried scanning ahead. *The plains seem clear except for some meandering quadrupeds that might be herd animals*, Joe thought.

Soon Joe and his party were in pursuit as a unit. Queen Saluiana and the guardshieldsmen approached several Demons and came into the plains as well, seeming more urgent than usual. Queen Saluiana fired her pistol as several mounted Demons swung out of the forest into the plains, seeking to cut off their pursuit. Joe was trailing, hoping to get in position to use his pistols to cut down the Demon pursuit. But now he had ground to make up and two horses' energy to conserve.

Queen Saluiana took one Demon down from about fifty meters. She shot its mount, taking no chances. Sika lay ahead, tied behind a mounted Demon. The pace quickened. Joe relaxed and stopped pressuring his horse, simply letting it run at its natural, sustainable pace. He decided to trust Queen Saluiana, now riding ahead and outpacing the two guardshieldsmen.

☦ ☦ ☦

The Devil laughed between puffs of smoke that blew from his mouth and nose. "*Ummh*," he hummed to himself. He lounged on a fur rug. Several Demon women, voluptuous by any standard, lay naked in a semicircle around him. "Perhaps now...I win."

God looked to Arleosa. "Everything hangs in the balance as it always does," God intoned. "Such a meaningful cliché." God was being sarcastic now, Arleosa felt. "Things have happened. You have moved factions together, restructured a society...small steps, but your Messiah, Joe Brown, has done much!" Arleosa just waited, not wanting to speak. She was finally getting the acknowledgment she had craved. "But the Devil can still deflate all of Heaven's new stars, Arleosa!"

He rarely spoke her name, but He must be pleased, she thought. *We all depend so much on Him, but in this I followed my own feelings. I still have feelings, even in Heaven*. Arleosa drifted back. "I know, my Lord. But still, after all, it is God's plan." *Such subtlety*, she thought. *His plan, my plan,*

Joe's plan. Does it really matter unless questions are answered? What will be the true nature of this world revealed? Will it be civilization leading to its own destruction? Or will the pain and despair lead to a greater understanding?

† † †

Joe calmed himself. Drawing his 10 mm pistol, he fired from behind Queen Saluiana and the guardshieldsmen. Using the angle, he had to stop the ongoing pursuit flooding from the forest and into the open plains. West was the direction Sika's captors took. The forest to the east had been crawling with Demon pursuers. In their haste, the Demons did not take time to notify the forest pursuers that they had a captive. But some had seen the commotion spill into the plains and now took up the pursuit. Joe watched it unfold as Queen Saluiana sought to bear down on two mounted Demons, one of which carried her dearest friend and ally.

Several Demons fired arrows as Saluiana slipped sideways to the left of her horse to avoid being hit.

Her horse, lightly armored, withstood the first few arrows. Joe desperately picked off a few pursuing Demons. But more were pushing from the forest and surrounding areas. Joe could see new horned faces joining the fray. He began to grow panicked. *What now? No time to scan. Have to react.*

There was another patch of brush and woods to the left. Demons rode out and started shooting, covering the escape route of Sika's captors. Goodswift had sought to position himself to block the Demons heading west to cut off Queen Saluiana, who reloaded and fired again. This time she struck a Demon—pursuing from the second patch of wood and brush—in the chest.

Joe sought to move against this second threat. Both pistols out, he fired, momentarily hammering the Demons with added firepower. Abruptly those Demons who survived the onslaught swung behind Joe. *This is going to be a problem*, Joe thought. Even as he pursued Sika and while he supported Queen Saluiana, he, too, was being pursued. He swung to one side of his horse, as Queen Saluiana had done, reached back, and blasted the Demon closest in pursuit. His shot rang out, but he was losing ground. A

222

line of Demon cavalry converged to block him from further pursuit. He couldn't see Queen Saluiana nor Goodswift and the two guardshieldsmen.

"Get him!" Joe could hear a voice in his mind. "Get him!" Suddenly Joe's horse went down. Joe rolled forward, holding his pistols. He rolled over his shoulder and came to his feet in a crouching position, Demons circling his position. Immediately he started firing into the throng. As spears were hurled at him, he slipped sideways, firing. A few Demons fired their arrows. Joe moved sideways yet again. One of the Demons' arrows struck one of his own. When the Demons tried to circle behind Joe, his awareness kicked in—he was not just defending himself but finding ways to attack. His only concern was losing sight of Sika, Queen Saluiana, and the others. Joe had both guns that were empty—a pile of Demon bodies were nearby.

Joe kicked one Demon straight in the groin. The impact bounced the Demon back, and he lay writhing in pain. Joe danced sideways and threw a withering straight punch from the full torque of his hips after a stabbing jab that stunned the Demon. He, too, fell back in pain. No time to load. But he could release the Vibro-Blade. Once out, the sizzle of the Vibro-Blade created an odd sound. It was unusual, and it gave any creatures encountering it pause. Joe, Vibro-Blade in two hands, spun and twirled like a top, dancing away from arrows to spin back to archers and cracking them with the Vibro-Blade. He ducked and jumped and came down with hammering blows as Demons careened clumsily about, trying to strike him. A cloud of dust rose around Joe. When it cleared, he was alone, and battered Demons were dead at his feet. He scanned ahead with the ABS. Nothing but Demons pursuing the queen, and much farther, Sika was still captive. Soon she would be out of range of his ABS.

Joe looked around for a horse, any horse. There were straggling Demon mounts, but Joe didn't think they would be good mounts for a man. Instead, Joe started running. He had the ABS power support to enhance his speed. Scanning ahead, he could still sense Queen Saluiana. He started loading his pistols on the run, jamming the magazines in place then racking a round in each chamber. *Run*, Joe thought. He was able to just barely use the ABS to stay in the hunt. He cursed himself for not having secured Sika himself when the Hivers were present.

Joe kept running faster and faster. He kept his breathing even and controlled. *Just run*, he thought. The ABS helped. But somewhere in his mind, he could sense that golden glow enveloping him. He could feel his dream benefactor nearby. Her energy being absorbed by his.

✝ ✝ ✝

Satan grinned and puffed, drawing deeply from his cigar. He was on the verge of once again thwarting God. He believed he had worked hard at this. Harvesting and creating mutant mounts for his Demons and trying desperately to get them motivated to do his bidding. He had introduced more options for them as well. The Demons could rotate in and out of campaigns to refresh themselves. They had concubines and feasts worthy of the Devil himself. However, they remained as thralls to the Devil. Satan's only goal was to overthrow humanity and curse God's efforts. His generals and officers understood this. Even the ordinary Demon foot soldier experienced it. Motivation was at times uneven, hence the refresh camps where whores, concubines, and feasts were sampled in excess. But no one stayed at a refresh camp very long. The hell of combat awaited them, all in about a month's time, depending on Satan's needs.

To be sure, the troops got their fill of cheap wine and lots of sex. But this refreshment put a cramp in the Devil's resources.

Recently the Devil's captains had been less than highly motivated. The Hivers, never seen so far north, had crushed Demons pitted against the western fortress of King Kotutan. Kotutan surely would have lost all if not for the interference of this new threat, Joe Brown. "Joe fucking Brown," Satan fumed. "How did he get the Hivers into this now!" Satan must fight in the South as well. He could no longer afford to simply raid, as he had in the human settlements; he must prevent any aid from coming north, but it had. Now he had to attack and plunder the South more effectively for resources to fuel his war effort. Supply lines, possibly vulnerable from Hivers and Greenflyers, must be operational. The South, with its verdant, lush environment. All manner of beasts romanced its forests. The Devil had to have the plants and primitive beasts that could be harvested and hunted. Now, at least, the Devil had made do. He had Sika in custody and on the way to him. Joe Brown had been stalled, but the formidable Queen Saluiana was on the chase (with the guardshieldsmen and Goodswift). The young Goodswift had thwarted his ploy to have the Manwolves kill the queen. He could have averted this chase that frayed his nerves had the queen been captured or killed.

What of the ploy to stop and cripple the Wildriders? They were out of the main fight for now, having to defend their plateau strongholds.

Now with Sika on her way to him, even as a captive, Satan knew the fight might come home to Hell. He had done more with the Demons, fitting their genetic codes to make them more easily motivated to fight. He had urged on traits of acquisitiveness. When the Demon commanders conquered human outputs or settlements, they consumed everything in it. Their raids were seen as increasingly terrifying as they ate human flesh more readily.

Using all the mystic devilish influence he could muster; it would require undying motivation and a likely reward from Demons fulfilling certain goals.

The Devil was becoming a better manager.

☦ ☦ ☦

Sika was beginning to stir. When she woke up, she realized she was on the back of a Demon's mount, hands tied, lying stomach down. Her wound seemed to have stopped bleeding. She needed food and water. Her hands hung toward the ground below her head. She started working her fingers around the bindings, trying to release them.

Joe kept running. He scanned ahead with the ABS. He could barely make out the biosignatures of the queen and her group. Sika must be somewhere ahead. Mixed in were the biosignatures of Demons—seemingly disorganized remnants left from the assault of the fortress and those coming to reinforce and support the capture of Sika. A mass of random

Demons—just enough to get in the way. Joe kept running, sweat pouring out of him and being absorbed, cooling him through the moisture-wicking feature of the ABS.

Joe, Sika sent out a thought. *I am still alive. Come quickly. I think they are taking me to Hell.*

Queen Saluiana heard the thought as well, and she urged her mount faster. But they were having to shoot Demons as they progressed. The resistance mounted.

The sun began to swing low in the west. Joe knew he should stop the pursuit. He felt that Queen Saluiana could lead Goodswift, and the guardshieldsmen would keep going. But he could be sure except to see Sika himself. He had heard a whisper in his mind. It was Sika.

Joe still needed a horse. But he kept running; that whisper he had heard seemed to help him. Darkness fell.

Queen Saluiana rode at a canter. She and her small force were well armed. Goodswift used his bow effectively from horseback. The two guardshieldsmen fired their frontier shotguns with effectiveness as well, but now they had to slow down to not exhaust the horses. As the resistance came in waves, they rotated their firepower. Goodswift and Queen Saluiana would lead, at times firing pistols, bows, or carbines while the guardshieldsmen reloaded and then swung into the lead, often firing their double-barrel shotguns simultaneously at approaching Demons. This effectually sent a cascade of shots to demoralize the Demons and clear them from blocking the trail to Sika.

Sika kept working her hands free. The Demons had slowed to a canter, but they were afraid they would fail this important task before its completion, which seemed so imminent. Sika looked around, barely moving her head. The pursuit was her best ally. The Demons, thinking her unconscious, paid her no mind. They had stripped her weapons, but now they felt her languish. Dead or alive, the reward would be big, they thought. "Once we bring her to Satan, we win," Satan heard one of them comment.

"Watch her!" she heard the words that cut like a knife. They were paying attention, being careful. Now several Demons joined their party.

Two followed behind Sika to make sure they had their eyes on her. All other Demons were sent back to stymie the pursuit.

Bladeswift was leading the women and children through a narrow pass from a plateau that joined a rocky ridge. His warriors had taken defensive action when the Demons had surrounded the village. Bladeswift received a call for aid. In truth, all the villages in the whole mountain range were his responsibility. He had waited until night. Then he crawled among the Demons, silently cutting their throats, hacking their hamstrings, and otherwise bringing terror in the night against creatures that were nightmare visions of Hell's dark pits.

Eventually, Bladeswift had snuck upon the Demon chief, and in one mighty blow, cut off his head.

A chill went through the chief's followers. But before the chill could be thawed, Bladeswift punctuated it with his frontier shotgun. Stealth, then fireworks—the formula needed to strike fear and liberate his people. The morning found Bladeswift clearheaded and momentarily content. He would move the whole village to safety, burn the Demon bodies, and move to help his allies.

The mountain ridge seemed to go on forever. There were thin trees where the altitude was high. Bladeswift could see the sun rising in the east. Birds chirped; wildflowers were in bloom. A clear blue sky framed the mountains.

Sika looked west. She could see plains that seemed to stretch on endlessly. Looking east, she saw no signs of pursuit. Her heart dropped. There she also recognized the endless plains. Thick grass grew in places punctuated by small stands of trees. Carrion birds could be seen flying overhead to the east. Sika wondered whose bodies they would feast upon. *Hopefully just Demons*, she tried to assure herself.

Joe ran and ran. The sun was rising. The fact that he had run so far and long was amazing. He felt a strange elation surging through his body. He kept running. Ahead he saw a small campfire two hundred meters away easy to spot on the open plains. Four people sat in a circle by the fire, seemingly eating. There were horses tethered nearby in a small stand of trees. Joe picked up speed, scanning through the ABS. There was Queen

Saluiana. He kept running. They were gathering the horses. Slowly the queen stood up and looked his way. No words were spoken. But clear as day, he heard her voice: "Joe. You have made it to us."

Joe began to relax, still running. In the distance, either north or south, he could see scattered herds of buffalo and wild horses.

Joe finally reached the campfire and fell to his knees. Queen Saluiana, surprisingly strong, held him and lifted him into her arms. The guard-shieldsmen looked shocked seeing their queen embrace Joe—their savior, perhaps, but not their kind. Goodswift looked on sternly. Joe undid his helmet. The queen gazed lovingly into his eyes. "Stay strong, Joe. Stand… we have yet to reach Sika." With that, Joe felt stronger. His legs regained some vigor. Queen Saluiana offered him some nuts and water. A warm glow seemed to envelop him. Then frustration hit him. He had never really questioned what was going on. The warmth seemed to recede. His frustration grew. He tried to slow his breathing, which was still labored. The sun's rays became apparent as it rose higher in the sky.

Saluiana looked sternly at Joe, still clutching him. Even after eating a few bites, he looked like he might fall. "Sit, Joe, for a minute." Saluiana could sense Joe was feeling down. Joe wasn't wearing his helmet, and she could see the worry in his face. She didn't even know how old he was, but she could see the crease above his nose, just below his forehead. Joe's eyes were ringed, with creases below as well. Saluiana had not seen his face look like that earlier.

Joe sat. He needed a moment of rest. Saluiana knew he was despairing. He needed a horse as well. The odds of finding one were difficult this far west—except for the wild ones. "Joe!" Saluiana tried to get his attention; he had dozed off, it seemed. Dreams came in waves to Joe. He wasn't just asleep; he had passed out.

Saluiana despaired. They had to get going. Arleosa—where was she? Joe's eyes fluttered. Then he felt Arleosa. His heart ached for Sika. Where was the help that always came? Where, now when he needed it the most? A voice came to his consciousness. Saluiana could sense it as well and brightened immediately. Joe's despair had blocked him from his source of spiritual strength.

Arleosa had watched Joe's doubt come upon him, but she had also watched him develop the trust with the Hivers. The Hivers, whose connection with each other and now Joe was the living embodiment of practiced faith. Arleosa touched Joe, intending to shake him awake. Before she could push his shoulder, his eyes opened. He looked up into the sky, looking east. Joe was no longer blocked. Arleosa touched him. Saluiana felt it as well. A beautiful presence radiated through Joe. Arleosa rested her hand on Joe's forehead, gently stroking it. She felt a stirring of energy seeming to awaken in Joe.

"Don't stop," he said. "Don't stop connecting." The guardshieldsmen watched the odd interaction, as did Goodswift. He also looked for any threats on the horizon.

Joe stood up. He needed a horse. He looked in the distance—the wild horses were on the plains eating the grasses there.

Saluiana followed his eyes and nodded approvingly. "Yes, you need a horse. There are the horses, Joe." A large black stallion stood in the distance with a small herd of mares and a few colts. Joe's eyes rested on the stallion about one hundred meters way. The horse returned his gaze. Joe's mind reached out to the stallion, as it had with the Hivers, Saluiana, and Sika. A bandwidth was opened. In Heaven, Arleosa reached down as well, radiating her energy, connecting her and Joe to the stallion, who was cantering toward Joe and his small group.

Sika contracted her arms and yanked them apart. Her bonds were loosening. She could smell the burnt odor of the Demons and their mounts filling her nostrils. The Demons had not stopped during the night. Their mounts labored and slowed, but on they had ridden, away from the rising sun heading west, across the plains. Sika despaired—*When would they stop?*

Bladeswift urged his people on across the mountain range, where they entered a narrow pass. They were on foot and horseback. Dogs from the camp followed them. Warriors made up the rear. Bladeswift felt they'd be safe now. His body was smeared with the blood of Demons. He wore a leather and bone vest over his upper body. His blade rested easily in his right hand. He was on foot but urged his horse forward to follow his tribesmen through the pass. There in the distance stood a large-walled village. Timbers lined its boundaries. The large ten-foot doors stood open. Huts could be seen inside. An expanse of grasses and small trees surrounded the city. This was the largest single holding of the Wildriders. Several thousand tribesmen and women made their homes here, if only on a seasonal basis. Tribesmen often went from the village to hunt and forage and returned to it again.

Now Bladeswift could hold a brief counsel, raise an army, and smite the Demons. Bladeswift knew the threat would never go away unless something was done. An act of completion. An act of completion to the Wildriders meant an enemy's existence was eliminated from the land of the Wildriders.

Sika could see the land changing. The plains gave way to rolling hills. They were heading west beyond the lands of the Wildriders, which were to the north now, as Sika continued to be carried west beyond the plains. Larger hills began to be visible. A few caverns started to appear as well.

Joe reached out to the stallion. It snorted and moved toward him. Coal black and strongly built, it would be a proper warhorse. The stallion nuzzled Joe's hand. He let it know what would happen next. Joe positioned his helmet and guns. He didn't have a saddle, so everything had to be secured effectively upon his person.

In a moment they were all riding west. "Now is the moment," Joe said. Saluiana replied, "Beyond the plains, Joe. Godspeed!"

Bladeswift entered the great hall of the village city. It was called High Quarters. A central council governed the city, though they were all aligned with Bladeswift, who was considered the greatest of the Wildrider chiefs. But there were no chiefs at High Quarters. There were representatives of the tribesmen and women who organized the work and protection of and within High Quarters.

There was a great deal of tribesmen in the hall when Bladeswift arrived. High Quarters had generally been unscathed by the Demons. But many of its inhabitants had encountered them during their travels—during hunting trips or when responding to the other villages to provide help—and High Quarters tribesmen knew the threat was real. Here stood Bladeswift to confirm the threat.

"Let me make it clear," he spoke to the assembled counsel. "The path I have chosen led me to protect our people from their gravest threat. Though High Quarters is unscathed, you know what threat lies beyond. The Demons have harmed and disrupted your lives and killed your kinsmen. Now my sister, Sika, has joined the Long-Strider's to thwart this threat, which only grows daily. I ask quickly for an expedition to be formed to find the source of the Demons' lands and make plans to annihilate them."

Cosan, senior counsel member and acting chief of High Quarters, spoke directly to the point. "We have twenty seasoned volunteers ready to ride as soon as you are ready. Now if necessary. Find out what you need to know, and we will be ready with a fully provisioned army of your kinsmen. Tell us your path, and we will follow it with more aid as we prepare. Don't waste time, Bladeswift. We will follow, anticipating your request. No fire need be lit, no ravens sent. We will know the moment of your need."

Bladeswift understood saying. "Then now is the moment!"

Cosan had spoken in the spiritual knowing of Wildrider culture—the sense that support would be there, because the bond that exists will light a path to those Wildriders in need.

Living in a city wasn't wild, Bladeswift thought. But still, the city was a convenient waypoint. The old Wildrider spiritual path was still intact.

The wind caressed Joe's visor and helmet. He was rushing forward, now riding the big stallion. He was a whirlwind of momentum. He quickly outdistanced his followers. Saluiana pushed forward. The two guard-shieldsmen, with their heavy armor and big horses, fell behind. Saluiana and Goodswift followed Joe.

The horses sweated and labored. Joe could scan ahead and noticed Sika's signature immediately. He pushed on. Then as quickly as it appeared, Sika's signature was gone from the scan. He checked again. It showed momentarily, then disappeared again. Joe ran a feed back to the ACV. The signature was going down. There was space where the signature showed again, then it was gone, but the feed indicated down below the ground. Sika must be about a half mile to a mile away, Joe determined. But the scan wasn't accurate about the distance she was from him. If he could get closer, he could narrow down where her descent took her.

Joe's stallion had run fast for several miles after he mounted him and was starting to falter. Joe's pace had been unforgiving.

The resistance from the Demons had dissipated. But now groupings of Demons began to show up in twos and threes, firing arrows and charging at Joe. Joe urged his horse to a canter. He fired his pistols and kept going. A brief interlude, and the stallion was pushing forward again. Joe could mark the last signature spot before Sika's signature descended. He knew where he was.

Sika unraveled the last of her bindings. She was going downhill quickly. Lights and torches met her view. She lay limp, hands pressed together as if she was tired.

She could see the ground changing below her—rocky ground—and she smelled sulfur and brimstone.

She was going down again and came to a loop that angled downward. The Demons dismounted. They paused to check Sika for injuries. Her shoulder was examined and appraised. There were three Demons who had finished the trip. The others had ridden back to follow the trail backward and ward off pursuit.

The first Demon hoisted Sika off the mount. As quickly as a candle flicker, Sika was off the horse and grasping the Demon's arm, slamming him to the ground. The remaining two were stunned as Sika grasped the blade from the fallen Demon. She gutted the second Demon with the blade of the first. The third drew his sword and lunged toward Sika. She deflected his blade and slammed hers upward into his throat.

Then she started to move back the way she had come. She heard growls and guttural sounds above her. More Demons to block her path. She had to go down—Who knew what was above her? She slipped behind a group of boulders. Crawling on her belly, she held the blade before her. The path was opening below. Fires burned brightly, and Sika could see tunnels in the distance below. There were isolated huts as well.

15.

TRAPPED

She clamored down, avoiding the torchlight. She could hear Demons coming down above her. She found a low spot surrounded by boulders. Then what she feared must happen, did. There was yelling and growling. She figured the oncoming Demons found the bodies of those she had killed. She tried to interpret the sounds and growls. The Demons rushed out of the cave, moving up and away from Sika. They were sure the threat must be beyond the cave mouth. Somewhere in the rolling hills. It was, but Joe had not quite reached their position.

Sika decided to wait. She was relatively safe right now. The moment might pass, and her safety would be in jeopardy. But pressing the issue was foolhardy. Instead, she would wait, watch, and look at the rhythms of the Demons. She rose to one knee and searched the area. Demons rushed around and went in and out of the huts. Now and again a voluptuous female Demon would walk out of the various huts nude and take a drink from a goatskin vessel.

From below Sika could see two columns of Demons marching up from below. Sika dropped down to her stomach again. She found cover between large boulders. She crawled down into a small pocket that lay just beyond the curved road heading down. From here she could see the Demons coming and going. But she was also going deeper down into the pits.

Joe knew where Sika descended. He saw the cave pit where his scan revealed her path below ground. At once he was under attack from the surrounding area. Arrows flew. Joe signaled a retreat. Saluiana, Goodswift, and the guardshieldsmen followed. Joe found a high-rising hill above but near the cave mouth. He shouldered his sniper rifle and fired at Demons coming up from the cave. Saluiana and the rest held off the surrounding Demons who tried to rally toward their position in desperate pursuit. Saluiana was covered by the guardshieldsmen on either side of her. They had all dismounted. Saluiana was quickly firing her bow. She wasn't worried about killing; she was focused on taking down as many Demons as possible. Goodswift danced around the flanks of their attack. He moved left and right, firing his shotgun, low and steady, taking down any Demon near him.

There were so many Demons that Joe was worried. Their horses were tethered nearby but growing nervous. Joe had also dismounted to better aim his sniper rifle.

Down below, Sika's hopes were raised. She could hear the distinct report of Joe's sniper rifle. A bellowing crack that momentarily drowned all the sounds surrounding it.

Joe's worries were starting to magnify. He was close to Sika but not close enough to reach her.

The sky was darkening, and it began to rain. Bladeswift headed southwest down the mountain pass. Twenty seasoned warriors followed him. They were loaded with full quivers of arrows, lances, shields, and leather and bone vests. Some wore leather and bone helmets as well. They all rode big warhorses painted with the symbols of their villages. These included lightning bolts from the high mountain tribes. There were symbols of arrowheads from the Flint Mountain tribe. But most of the twenty were from Cosah, and their symbol was a cloud-covered hammer. Cosah was considered the greatest unifying entity of Wildrider culture. "The hammer builds and defends, allowing the city of Cosah to exist undisturbed in the clouds," Bladeswift explained to a young warrior riding beside him. His name was Heavy Blow. He had been on several sorties and shown himself to be more than adequate in combat. He carried a long, double-edged broadsword slung across his back. His arms were hugely built, and the muscle groups stood out in bold relief. Bladeswift smiled to himself. He could see where the "heavy blow" would emanate from.

Joe stared down from the knobby hill. The Demons continued to pour forth from the cave mouth. He was running out of ammo. So were the rest, arrows and shots both running low. Joe made a decision. He unsheathed the Vibro-Blade, turned it on, and tuned it to its highest frequency. It would be hard to control, but each blow would be a finisher, he hoped.

He ran down the hill. "Wait, don't come after me," Joe said to the others. "Hold your ground, 'cause there's no place to go." Joe fired a few rounds at the cave mouth. He could hear the howl of Demons hit by his shots. Once near the cave mouth, he leaped to one side, waiting. It wasn't long before Demons started coming out of the cave. Only three could pass at a time, but they came in a rush. Joe stepped in the middle of their path. To his right, the first blow cracked the middle Demon in the face. Pivoting left, Joe swung his sword in a flat, horizontal arc, catching the Demon across the kidney, if Demons had kidneys. Both Demons dropped, and the last turned to swipe his sword at Joe, who parried the blow and spun as the Demon's guard dropped with the force of Joe's block. *Bam!* The blow crashed into the Demon's helmet, sending him flying as the Demon collapsed.

A second wave of Demons appeared. Joe pivoted briefly into the cave, sword cutting the air in diagonal blows. His last stroke brought him spinning out of the cave, hiding once again to the right of its opening. It was a game of cat and mouse. Joe rolled to the center of the cave opening, popped up, and slammed the tip of his blade into the oncoming Demon's chest. Though it was designed to send vibratory disruption into a foe's body, it was not meant to penetrate. But it did ever so much, and the Demon's body was sent reeling backward, gushing forth a great stream of blood. Joe kicked hard and knocked the Demon down to his left. He spun right, dipping low underneath a blow and slamming his sword into the ribs of another Demon, who simply crumpled into a heap. Joe shuffled left, and as the Demon arose from the ground, he rammed his sword point into the nose. Blood spewed back into the cave. There was a pause, and Joe moved back from the cave mouth. "Get the horses!" he bellowed. "The scan revealed Sika's position." But the Demons were swarming past her, toward Joe.

For a moment Joe was taken aback. He remembered his first experiences as a martial arts trainee. A white belt. He had learned to fight with rhythm and precision. Now he was the master that small boy always hoped to be. "Ride!" he yelled to Saluiana. "I will follow. Don't hesitate, believe, and I will be at your back...before long!"

The tunnel entrance was starting to fill with Demons. Some came out with only spears and swords and no armor. Others had no horns and seemed smaller or weaker looking than those previously seen on the frontier or even by Joe in New Castle.

Joe tuned the Vibro-Blade again. This time its blows hit with a flattening effect like a fly swatter. Every blow knocked Demons back into the tunnel. Joe looked like a spinning top. On the outer orbit of his trajectory was the tip of the Vibro-Blade. The Demons continued to surge from the tunnel. Joe blasted into the tunnel mouth and swung at anything that moved. Sika was still somewhere in the darkness, perhaps making her way to him.

Joe's ammo was about spent—he needed more to make a better assault into the tunnel. Now he was feeling indecisive. "Sika! Where are you?" He could sense her signature below the cave mouth behind a hundred Demons.

Then Joe did what he had to—he ran and jumped on the stallion waiting on a hill above the cave mouth. In a short time, he could see Saluiana, Goodswift, and the guardshieldsmen ahead.

"I knew you would have to wait, Joe." Saluiana looked at Joe reassuringly. Her reassurance seemed strained. Joe knew he had to think of everyone. The queen must return to the fortress. A major loss like Saluiana would hurt the Long-Striders' morale.

"I hate this, Saluiana," Joe said, "but let's get you back and straighten out everything. I could see Sika's image through the scanner in my suit. She was alive. Hiding, I believe, somewhere below."

Sika reached into a small pouch on her belt. She opened it and sucked from a vial. The bitter paste melted in her mouth, immediately making her feel more alert, even vibrant. The gunshots had died. *Did Joe leave me?* She thought. *Where is he?* Tears momentarily filled her eyes. So far from the mountain passes of home, she was in the very opposite environment.

A Hell pit. She could hear the Demons milling around above her. Some were beginning to go past her hiding place.

She waited for a gap and crept out onto the main path. Quick as a panther, she angled her blade into the throat of a slow-moving Demon who looked to be wounded slightly. She dragged his body backward behind a boulder, checking the path above and below. He had a wineskin. Not what she wanted, but anything was better than nothing. Sika flattened and rolled over on her back. She tasted the liquid after briefly sniffing it. It wasn't wine. It was coffee. Better than wine right now. She took a few gulps and closed the skin with its cork. She dragged the Demon's body farther into the shadows. That would have to do. Then she found a small area between two boulders and curled up to sleep for the night.

Joe, Saluiana, and the rest arrived at the fortress in the darkness of the night. It was late. Joe checked his suit. It was midnight.

The king greeted them excitedly. Saluiana gave him a less than enthusiastic embrace. "We're yet to find Sika," Saluiana mournfully and exasperatedly told her husband.

Joe was back in his familiar room in the fortress. It had been a long time. He unfastened his helmet and lay down. He was asleep in seconds. But he tossed and turned. Then Arleosa came to him like a golden ghost, more radiant than ever. She seemed to take on a human form, her face perfectly oval, her lips round and succulent. She was beautifully formed—a goddess, not too different from Samantha. Joe stopped tossing and was still. His mind went to Sika. He felt the sense of guilt he had felt when he realized his mercenary work for the oil companies was wrong. But this was different. He had let himself down then. This time, he decided, it was Sika who would suffer, die, or worse. That he could not abide.

He awoke before sunrise. Saluiana had let herself into his room. She looked refreshed and was dressed in fresh combat leather armor. There was a glint of polish to her garments. The leather vest was inlaid with steel bands. She leaned over and kissed Joe fully upon his lips. Then she withdrew as Joe, disoriented by just waking up, found himself lusting for the queen more powerfully than ever.

Saluiana handed Joe a cup of steaming coffee. Joe was still in his battle suit. He had paused to take his helmet off before falling asleep. "Come, hurry, and get into the king's bath. Refresh yourself," Saluiana urged. Joe followed Saluiana to the bath. He had the ABS recede into a belt that compressed it into a small compartment. Joe was still troubled as he took in the warm water of the bath. He soaked his head. He thought he needed a haircut. The tight curls of his Afro was beginning to billow over onto his forehead. Joe mused. No one here had an Afro. He'd have to cut his own hair eventually.

Rising up and getting out of the bath, Joe could hear a commotion down the hall.

Joe dried himself and walked to the main dining hall. Breakfast was being served by serving girls. Joe sat down next to the main table, where King Kotutan was joined by Saluiana. Several guardshieldsmen were present. All wore heavy leather armor like the queen, although appreciably thicker.

From the far entrance, Bladeswift entered followed by twenty Wildrider warriors. He looked tense. His gaze turned to Joe. "Sika was a great servant to us all. We must find her. Hopefully alive. Queen Saluiana has explained where she is and the grave risk. Any help given will be welcome. But I have only a moment to wait!"

Joe rose. "Bladeswift, I feel as though I am to blame. I left Sika in what I thought was a position of safety. I was careless and wrong. Let me go first into the cave. I will have weapons on my ship that allow me to enter decisively before the Demons are fully roused. But our escape will need to be covered."

"Then I will enter the cave with you, if needed" Bladeswift said. "The rest of our forces can cover the escape. But before we leave, a mighty blow must be struck."

With that Joe headed to the stables. He grabbed a few strips of bacon and stuffed them between two slices of bread. He consumed it just slowly enough to enjoy the bacon and the memories from home it ignited.

His stallion was still there but had bolted out of the corral, jumping out and wandering around the stable area. When it saw Joe, it paused and went directly to him.

Soon he was riding with a contingent of guardshieldsmen, the queen, and the twenty warriors who came with Bladeswift.

Joe stopped at the ACV. He gathered ammo and several grenades. He looked for the mobile claymores. He knew he would need those to hold off pursuit once he found Sika. Joe scrambled around and was able to find a silencer in the ship's gun compartment. He fitted it onto his 9 mm pistol. Stowing the sniper rifle, he picked up an assault rifle. No silencer could be found for it. This would have to do.

16.

DEEPER

In moments he was back on the stallion, riding hard toward the western caves. *To Hell*, he thought, but there was only one goal. Rescue Sika.

Bladeswift rode up beside Joe, who was fearing a confrontation with the Wildrider chieftain. "Sika always did as she was motivated," said Bladeswift. "By our custom she was always a force of her own. If she chose to help you, it was in her heart." Joe started to speak, but Bladeswift stopped him. "No, Joe. Do not allow fear to crowd your thoughts. Fear and guilt are enemies, just as the Demons." With that he rode on. "Consider any wrong forgiven," he said.

Joe rode with a formidable force. He was eager to get into the cave mouth. The journey involved very little resistance. Joe and Bladeswift scouted ahead, at times working in tandem. They would need to be sure of each other's style when they entered the cave mouth.

There were a few hornless Demons moving about ahead of the main force. Some were merely camping, waiting for any provocation, Joe guessed. He and Bladeswift dropped from their horses and crawled on their bellies to within easy range of the Demons. Joe quickly rose once within fifteen feet and, springing, slammed his Vibro-Blade into the back of one Demon while Bladeswift cut the throat of another. Suddenly a Demon on watch stumbled into the area. Seeing Joe, he charged at him. Bladeswift shot an arrow into his back. Joe stepped up and hammered the Demon's head with the Vibro-Blade before he could scream. Joe waited for a moment to see if any other Demons lurked around. Then he and Bladeswift mounted and rode back to the main force.

Sika rested between the boulders. She had been napping off and on into the night. The cave was cold, and she often found herself shivering.

She had stumbled upon an isolated hornless Demon walking past her hiding place at dawn. She snuck behind him, covering his mouth with one hand, then cutting deep across his jugular vein with a knife. She quickly cut his dirty garments off, dragged him away, and then did her best to mop up the blood and push dust over it. In any event, she hoped Joe's earlier shooting into the tunnel would be an answer for any blood seen. She was still lucky, having killed the Demons who brought her, that none realized she was right here in their midst.

She was careful, feeling it was only a matter of time before she was discovered. A sense of evil resonated into her consciousness as she hid. Perhaps this was the hub of all the Demons. Even more she felt a great presence waiting to break out. *Where is Joe?* she thought.

Joe was feeling angry now. He hated the delay. The next party of Demons on patrol wasn't dispatched in stealth. Joe just rode in ahead of the group. His assault scope allowed him to knock down three of them before they could wheel around to meet him. Almost miraculously, Saluiana fired a bow that protruded through the neck of one Demon, while the speedy Bladeswift drove his arrow into the throat of the last at full gallop, his warhorse running smoothly with nary a ripple of up and down movement to throw off his aim.

On Joe went. "Good shooting," he complimented Bladeswift and the queen. *Where have I come to meet such people?* he thought. *Truly the Angel who guided me knows so much.*

"Indeed, there is so much to understand about all of this, Joe," Saluiana spoke, as if answering a query that she had heard aloud. Joe nodded his agreement and pushed harder, his horse running effortlessly across the plains.

Suddenly Sika saw what she feared would happen in time. She had been stuck here in the cave mouth tunnel, trapped between Demons below and those feverishly coming in and out of the tunnel mouth above. There was no chance for escape—not enough cover for a stealthy departure. She had only a blade, whereas a bow and a quiver of arrows might suffice.

Perhaps one of Joe's guns might have been the answer, but those things were not available to her.

Coming up the tunnel with a throng of horned Demons flanking him was a seven-foot, thickly muscled Demon Goliath. Joe was finally close to the cave mouth—perhaps less than a half mile away. The Demons seemed to be concentrated at the cave mouth, none seeing the party arriving. Joe scanned ahead. There were figures swarming around one big Demon: Deathmet 2.0, Joe guessed. Quickly he dismounted. "This is going to have to be quick and quiet. Wait for us but move up once we get to the cave mouth and enter it. Bladeswift and I will get Sika! Cover the exit."

Joe and Bladeswift furtively ran and scrambled, sometimes crawling on their bellies, until they reached the knoll above the cave mouth, where one lone Demon guard waited, holding a horn. Joe fitted his silencer on his gun. He signaled Bladeswift to wait. The lone Demon was intrigued by all the commotion. He turned to peek. Joe moved up just as he saw the Demon's head turn completely away from him. He crept closer, hoping to cut the Demon's throat, but as he did, the Demon must have sensed him. Turning, he faced Joe squarely. *Phit!* The silenced round caught the Demon just below the forehead. He dropped to his knees, as if having found something peculiar on the ground. Joe dragged him a small distance and broke the horn in pieces with the butt of his pistol.

Sika was wondering what would happen next. The Demons were flowing behind this Demon Goliath as though he were their Messiah.

Joe watched as Bladeswift crept up beside him. "Too many!" Joe whispered.

Sika scrambled closer to the tunnel wall. The Demons were starting to crowd the area, seemingly in expectation of something big about to happen. She didn't want to do it but felt safer heading deeper down the tunnel, away from its mouth, hoping the Demons would reduce in number when the commotion was over.

Joe was feeling uneasy. "Bladeswift, I can pick up Sika's signature on my scan. It's moving further away from us! She must be trying to get clear of them. My scan says there are about fifty or sixty at the cave mouth. The big guy out front looks just like Deathmet, but it's not him as far as I can tell. Never scanned him, but he looked to be different and very similar as well."

Bladeswift nodded. "You cut off Deathmet's head—so I've been told!" he added.

"Deathmet 2.0." Joe sighed.

"What is a 2.0?" Bladeswift asked.

"An update." Joe smirked.

"Update for us is another warrior trained and similar as the one before." Bladeswift said.

Sika crawled farther down the tunnel. There were scores of Demons lining the wall she had just left. She rose to a crouch and kept heading downward. She knew this wasn't good, but as long as she remained undiscovered, she had a chance.

Joe gritted his teeth. "We need a diversion. Call up the rest, if you will, Bladeswift. Get them in position behind this hill. When you get there, I'll start shouting—they'll pour out like flies off of day-old shit. When they come for me, let 'em have it; then I'm going down to get Sika."

Joe crept to the edge of the hill and looked over the edge. He could see the Demons milling around behind Deathmet 2.0. Bladeswift was already down the knoll, running toward their comrades.

Bladeswift gestured to his tribesmen to move up. The rest followed. As the first warrior approached, Bladeswift explained the plan. They would get a few warriors on the knoll and wait to see what Joe would do. The rest moved toward the flanks of the knoll.

Joe rose and let out a burst from the assault rifle. *Blipblipblip!* Joe aimed through the sight, then pulled out a mobile claymore and sent it skittering toward the cave mouth. The Demons, including Deathmet 2.0, started toward him. The cave mouth was about fifty meters away. The mobile claymore was moving toward it at top speed. The Demons hardly cared—they were fixated on the knoll where Joe fired, taking down several Demons and landing a shot on Deathmet 2.0 to no avail. The horde of Demons came. Joe ducked as a rain of arrows started to be fired on his position. Then Joe peeked up. The Demons were streaming toward him and would have to separate and come up the hill behind him to climb it. Just as they realized this, *kablam!* The claymore exploded.

The explosion left a big hole in the surging Demon forces. They went down in a heap of smoke and dust. Joe swung over the edge of the knoll and dropped down. Now he had his pistols out, arms outstretched, firing into the Demons on the peripheral edge of the explosion. *Pop-pop-pop-pop!* Demons fell before they could recover from the claymore explosion. Joe holstered his pistols and ran like hell for the cave mouth. Deathmet 2.0 was right in his path. Joe had no time to reach for a weapon. He launched himself in the air and shot out his heel in a brutal front kick that slammed into Deathmet's chin. Deathmet went down, falling backward. Joe stepped over his body after landing on his chest. Bounding toward the cave mouth, he had twenty meters to go, and Demon resistance was closing in around his flanks. The sound of arrows flitting through the air was apparent on either side of Joe. The middle of the cave mouth was still guarded. Joe pulled the Vibro-Blade, rolled forward, tripping two Demons, and rose, slamming his blade into each of their backs. Then quickly he dashed to the side of the cave and ducked behind a group of boulders, scanning down the tunnel to find Sika's signature.

17.

FAMILIAR FACES

Joe kept moving down. The Demons pursued, but they had a hard time locating him. As Joe moved, he targeted the Demons, now using the silenced pistol. He peeked from behind boulders and fired at whatever Demon was nearby. If he was close to more, he kept moving. When possible, he dragged the bodies behind the boulders. The Demons kept streaming up from the deeper recesses of the cave as Joe kept going down. He kept to the side of the cave opposite Sika's signature, hoping to avoid bringing Demons near her position. Then he dropped to his belly and started to crawl, looking out behind a boulder in both directions: the cave mouth and down below. A score of Demons were running past him to the cave mouth. Joe leaped out behind the last one and crossed the cave tunnel floor in a crouch. They never saw him. Now he could determine Sika was nearby.

Sika waited in her hiding place. There was too much commotion to dare leave it. She sensed Joe must be trying to rescue her. She froze, holding her knife, waiting.

Joe crept downward toward another boulder. Sika should be here. "Joe!" she exclaimed. Joe, hearing his name spoken so tenderly, almost forgot he was in the Demon cave.

"Back up to the cave mouth!" Joe exclaimed. Moving along the boulders, he grasped Sika's free hand.

"Joe, it will be okay—let me have my hand! We will need all our hands...Joe, there will be time to take my hand in yours but not now!"

Joe released her hand and kept moving. He knelt into a crouch. Sika followed his lead. Though much smaller, she recognized the advantage of keying on Joe's movement. They were getting close to the cave mouth. A throng of Demons surrounded the opening. Joe was flustered. He couldn't pass to let Bladeswift know he needed help. He put a fresh clip into the assault rifle and looked through the scope. Deathmet 2.0 was surrounded by Demons. They were jeering and chanting, shaking their bows, spears, and swords in the air. That was it, Joe realized. They were ready to face an invading force. Not so concerned that Joe had invaded their perimeter.

Sudden sounds of footsteps echoed in the cave behind Joe and Sika. "What? Stay close," Joe whispered to Sika. He set a mobile claymore, sending it skittering toward the footsteps. Almost half a minute passed. *Boom!* The claymore went off. The footsteps were silent after the explosion. "Let's move," Joe said. He crept toward the cave mouth. A few seconds passed, and the Demons came streaming toward them and the sound of the explosion. A few even moved along the cave walls. "Stay close," Joe whispered to Sika. He handed Sika a pistol and cocked it. "Point and shoot," he said. "Press easy."

Joe set his eye to the scope of the assault rifle. *Bobbobboomboompop!*" He fired heavily into the cave mouth. Several Demons went down. Deathmet 2.0 took several shots to the legs and went down on his knees. Joe aimed at his chest and fired. *Poppoppow!* Deathmet 2.0 staggered. Joe fired around him. More Demons went down.

Joe aimed all around Deathmet 2.0, taking down the nearby Demons who might support him. "Let's go!" Joe urged Sika, who needed no urging. They pushed their legs out of a low crouch after about ten meters. They were in full sprint, flying on foot to the cave mouth. Sika tried the pistol. *Kapow!* She handled the recoil and laid down suppression fire.

Joe had the Vibro-Blade out set on high recoil. *Vooom!* He was spinning away from Sika, making a hole to his right, slamming the Vibro-Blade into a contingent of three Demons. Each in turn was thrust backward. Sika aimed the pistol at Deathmet 2.0, who lurched forward aiming a crossbow directly at Joe. *Bam! Bam!* Two shots hit Deathmet 2.0 square, slamming him backward, his reeling arms swinging away from his body and dropping the crossbow. *Pow!* She let out another round that glanced off his forehead, knocking off his dragon-scale helmet.

He bellowed his rage. "Argh." Blood poured down his forehead into his eyes.

Joe looked up. Sika was right in the path of Deathmet 2.0, who lurched uncertainly toward her. Joe had no time. *Pop pop pop!* He just kept firing the assault rifle at Deathmet 2.0's head and torso. Deathmet 2.0 staggered and slumped to one knee. Sika, seeing the opportunity, tucked the pistol into her belt and leaped onto Deathmet 2.0, her legs wrapped around his neck and shoulders. She drove her blade hard into his left eye, piercing his brain. He fell in a cacophony of spasms as Sika rolled clear.

Before she could stand, Joe was lifting her to her feet. "Go! Go!" he yelled. They were running toward the knoll. Joe could see through his scan a throng of Demons running out over the cave mouth to pursue them. He pulled Sika in front of him to shield her. As he did, a rush of arrows launched by guardshieldsmen whistled over his head, followed by the *thump* of arrow tips hitting armor and penetrating flesh.

Joe spun and fired from a crouched position. *Pop pop pop!* Demons fell back from the withering fire.

Joe had one more mobile claymore. He urged Sika toward the right side of the knoll, where Bladeswift and Saluiana quickly greeted her and rushed her to a horse behind the knoll.

A small group of guardshieldsmen mustered around Sika on horseback. "Are you good to ride?" Bladeswift asked, noting the wounded shoulder still covered by the herbal poultice. "Yes," Sika said, voice heavy with weariness.

Joe remained below the top of the knoll. He let the last claymore go skittering toward the cave mouth. The Demons started toward Joe, Bladeswift, and the remaining Wildriders, several of whom had ridden away with the guardshieldsmen to take Sika and Saluiana back to the fortress.

Joe waited for the explosion. The cave mouth went up in a plume of smoke. But some of the Demons had run past the claymore toward the knoll. Joe activated the Vibro-Blade. Running toward them, he rolled under a volley of arrows from the Demons. Bladeswift and ten Wildriders joined him. Joe darted between the Demons, who were heavily armored with swords and plate mail. The Wildriders used long swords and short swords to defend and attack simultaneously. Joe spun and hammered his sword with horizontal strikes. He ducked under a sword stroke from a heavily armored Demon and slammed his shoulder into the Demon's chest, sending him flying backward into a group of Demons still coming. In Joe's mind he needed to give Sika time to get away.

Joe fought like a wildfire, his blows landing powerfully as he fought a multitude of Demon combatants.

Bladeswift yelled out at Joe in the throng of Demons: "Pull back, let's go!"

Joe was out of ammo for the assault rifle and had only a few more clips for his pistols. He pulled back. Several Wildriders were already back to the horses. Joe started running and dodged past the remaining Demons. He slammed his blade in an arc, knocking Demons out of his path. The Vibro-Blade was set on high, sending wicked armor-bending blows into each Demon who got hit with it.

Joe ran around the knoll and jumped on his horse. Several Wildriders were bleeding from Demon-inflicted wounds, and their tribesmen helped them get from the battlefield and on horseback.

Joe covered their retreat with the remaining clips of ammo. His armor was covered with grooves from a multitude of sword blows. Pressing his knees into the stallion's sides, he wheeled around toward his now east-bound companion. *Phwil!* An arrow flew past Joe to land in the forehead of a Demon, who a second before was on one knee but had risen and was lurching toward Joe. Bladeswift winced and released several more arrows.

Now they were riding east in a hurry. More Demons had flooded out of the cave. "This must be the main camp," Joe spoke tensely to Bladeswift, who nodded agreement.

"My world will never rest as long as they are here," he intoned.

"My world either. Back home I fear they still must be stopped. They are a sign—an embodiment of our worst intentions."

"There may be pursuit," Bladeswift said.

Pushing the pace. Joe scanned backward. Indeed, there would be a pursuit.

Joe scanned ahead to pick up the signature of the queen and Sika, who were riding hard east about a mild ahead.

Demons started flowing out of the cave mouth on horseback, or whatever their mounts were.

The race was on. Joe's stallion lurched forward, bounding wildly.

Joe, Bladeswift, and the other Wildriders were making up the distance to the queen and Sika's party. Joe desperately wanted them all back at the fortress without taking any more risk. He felt he had kicked the hornet's nest.

Joe was out of ammo. He needed more, and there would be nothing left at the ACV if he kept having to fight the way he had. There was no way the Long-Striders could produce the sophisticated ammo his weapons required. Only the fission pistol's ammo could be easily reproduced. Joe would need numbers, and the Hivers were his only option.

Joe could see the Demon-Riders trying to catch up to his group. The Demons had spread out behind them in a line. "They're going to flank us!" Joe bellowed. With that, he wheeled to the right. "I'll take one edge of the flank down."

Pushing southeast, Joe intercepted two the southernmost Demon-Riders heading east to cut off his escape. He struck the first with his sword and slashed downward on the mount, sending rider and mount into the dust of the plain. A second Demon rider broke stride to face Joe. No surprise was possible this time. The Demon raised his sword and managed a strong swing toward Joe, who parried with the Vibro-Blade and cut hard, slamming it into the Demon's head in a horizontal cut. The Demon fell back in the saddle and slid to the ground. Joe hustled his horse toward his group as more Demons fired arrows at him and responded to his flank-breaking attack.

Bladeswift had himself and two Wildriders launch a similar attack just northeast of Joe. Intuitively they knew that the pursuit must be narrowed down to one group of Demons that they could manage; however, the pursuit would be ongoing.

Joe moved back to the main group, driving a line toward Sika and the queen.

Bladeswift, too, resumed pursuit of the queen's party. They were catching up to the queen. As they did, they could see banners in the distance where a great force of Long-Striders came riding directly toward them. Several new guardshieldsmen rode out as well. The queen was rushed toward the fortress and Sika as well. They rode toward the fortress with the guardshieldsmen, who wielded frontier shotguns along with their traditional weapons.

"Go to the fortress!" Joe bellowed. "I have to get to my ship. I will see you soon."

Joe fought a few Demons who had pursued him. He reversed position and used the Vibro-Blade to knock their horses down. Joe dismounted and hacked them down as they rose to meet him—one then the other. Suddenly Joe was overtaken by feelings of great anger. One of the Demons tried to rise, Joe slammed the Vibro-Blade so hard into his chest that his breastplate crumpled, and he slumped to his knees. The other Demon was groveling on the ground. He did not move but put his head down in surrender, releasing his weapons. Joe stopped. He walked to his horse and rode away.

"Master," the Demon gurgled out.

Looking back Joe said, "Get away from this place. Seeking death will kill you!" He rode off, wondering if every Demon should just be killed. If Joe's allies won the war that was sure to continue, *what then?*

Joe was in deep thought but reached the ACV without further combat.

Joe entered the ACV and locked it down behind him. He scanned toward the location of the Demon cave. As he expected, there was lots of activity. He went to his ammo supplies and checked them—not nearly as much as he had hoped for. There had been several bags full of ammo clips. The sniper rifle, two semiauto pistols, and an assault rifle. He reached into another nearby compartment below the cockpit and took out the fission revolver. He found six cylinders that could be loaded.

Joe went back to the cockpit and looked at the scan of Demons hustling about the cave mouth. There'd be a battle to remember soon at the fortress. He would have to make sure it still stood. Sika and Saluiana—he owed them that much.

Joe felt hunger and started to reach into the ACV's survivor portal for a packaged meal, but he thought better of it. "Um, sure would be good to have a meal at the fortress."

When Joe came out of the ACV, he found his stallion foraging for grass and leaves. He carried his sniper rifle and one semiauto pistol and ammo for both. One man, two weapons. He wondered if Saluiana or Sika might benefit from using one of his additional weapons but thought better of it. Sika already had the one semiauto, and Joe made sure he had ammo for it—that should do for now.

Saddleless, he rode on with all his supplies strung onto his ABS with its magnetized surfaces, so no sounds were made. The stallion lurched forward with vigor toward the fortress. It was dark now; the sun had set while Joe worked on preparations in the ACV. He rode into the gathering darkness using his senses to link with the stallion. The two of them rode as if it were daylight.

When Joe reached the fortress gates, he could see the signal lights burning. Banners waved from the ramparts. The guardshieldsmen opened the gate, and a detachment led by Ataka rode out to meet him.

"Quickly now, Joe," Ataka urged. "We've been fighting mounted Demons all night. The king waits. We've brought the animals back from the pastures—but not before the Demons made off with a few. We saw them slaughtered in the pasture. Demons had built a fire; they were going to have a feast before we drove them off. Frontier shotguns are being passed to the guards. We're preparing for the worst."

Joe was ushered into the main hall after quickly dropping off his weapons and ammo.

Joe sat before King Kotutan and Queen Saluiana, and Sika stood to the left of the queen.

A large platter of venison was placed before Joe. Bread, wine, and cheese were all set before him as well.

Joe looked around. The only remaining wiseman was also present; Osala sat off to the side. No one talked to him. All eyes turned to Joe, who took of his helmet, sipped some wine, and rose to speak. "A lot is about to happen. The Demons will come, but we cannot wait for them. We have to meet them head-on while still making preparations for the inevitable siege. I would say send your women and young ones east, but there is likely no time! The Wildriders will aid you."

"Bladeswift has already gone to signal his clan and allied tribes for aid," Ataka, sitting with a few of the guardshieldsmen, spoke out.

Joe continued. "I will have to reach out to the Hivers again, the southern insect men who came to aid us before. There is no way we can be totally victorious without them. Be clear in your mind. The Demons must be contained. Remember your religious stories. The Devil and his minions. These are not myths."

With that, Osala stood before Joe. He raised his hand to speak. "The old myths tell of an Angel cast out from paradise…In his anger, he builds an army to smite all of God's creations. I believe we are those creations. The power of the Devil lies with him once being an Angel. He has the power to create…just enough to dash the hope of God!"

Joe looked around. "Your priests are right, but now the Demons are becoming more human, adapting to fight you. But with that adaption comes flexibility. Flexibility that breeds a thought process—choice and change in tactics, hence their cavalry. They will begin to think about options, choices. If that is their evolution, we must make them doubt the very choice to wage war, which their sire, the Devil, must not want but cannot easily dispel. If he gives them a choice in the way they wage war, it will affect other thoughts as well." Joe kept to himself about the Demon who had surrendered, as it was too much to hope for. "Make the Devil himself doubt the outcome, and his minions will use their choice to turn back."

With that, Joe sat down. He gulped his wine and ate ravenously. Saluiana and Sika came to his side.

"Strategic planning in the morning then," King Kotutan bellowed. "First light!"

Joe greeted Bladeswift, Saluiana, and Sika warmly. To Sika he whispered, "Forgive me, I almost lost you." Sika and Saluiana joined Joe in his room for a cup of wine.

Saluiana wanted to know his plan as much as she wanted to linger near him, at times caressing his shoulder or arm absently as they talked. Sika leaned against Joe and seemed to melt into his lap. Saluiana stiffened and straightened as they were all on Joe's bed.

She sat up. "Joe, tell me how we can bring your plan to fruition."

Joe wondered if Saluiana was becoming jealous of Sika. Sika was drowsy after her ordeal and leaning heavily on Joe. "I need to think about getting the Hivers back to our aid. I need to sleep on it too. It's my dreams that once seemed to have answers for everything, but lately I haven't had the connection to my dreams I've needed."

Saluiana looked at Joe appraisingly. "Yes, dream, Joe. All prophets need to dream." With that, Saluiana stood up to leave. "I must go to the king...I'll leave you to your dreams. Perhaps Sika's presence will be reassuring to you and bring the dreams we all hope will help us." She briefly caressed Joe's forehead and left the room.

Sika remained, half dozing. Joe covered her and went to the king's bathing chamber. The king was there, bathing alone. "Joe, tell me truthfully—can you save us from the Demon onslaught?"

"Fear not, King Kotutan, I will know in the morning. Dreams will help me see the path I need." Joe bathed quickly. There were no serving girls in the bath—just King Kotutan, who seemed to be brooding.

"You know, Joe, my wife believes you will deliver us, but I don't know. This or that—she often says you are the chosen one...I see how she looks at you...so...so lovingly. You've helped a lot, but perhaps we are beyond help. I carved a frontier civilization out of this wilderness. My wife, Saluiana, criticized me when I was so aggressive against the Manwolves. That almost cost us dearly. Saluiana could have been killed by Ohtokan. This happened while you were away seeking the Hivers."

"I had heard that," Joe commented. Joe toweled off and walked out.

In his room, Sika was sound asleep. Joe had nothing on but the belt that carried his ABS, which was retracted.

He slept. Sika remained. He looked for the aid he needed in his dreams. Suddenly he awoke, panicked. "Where are you?" he said, wondering where the entity had gone that had guided him this far. Instead, he felt concern and doubt.

A voice came to Joe's mind. "I am here. I had thought leading you would be easy, but the carnage, the blood spilled—even the hapless Demons become more conscious. I revel in your relationship with Saluiana and Sika—there is much love there. But the battles have hardened all of us...You must end all of this, Joe, and bring peace. But peace comes at a price. Where do Demon souls go? Only God knows. Maybe the Devil keeps them in Hell to foment more unrest."

Joe slept soundly. No more words entered his mind, but the reassuring warmth returned to him as on previous nights. A deep sense of security pervaded his mind.

Answers would flow from the dreams, Joe knew now. As he slept, his mind flowered and flickered like a light. He was a part of everything but beyond it as well, dreaming securely. He saw the lands of the South: The Hivers, the Greenflyers, the teeming jungle, its vines and cliffs. Large flowering plants, abundant wildlife, giant bees, and cavemen. Jungle cats and mastodons were there as well, but Joe had yet to see them. Joe saw a Hiver shooting a bow. A Hiver with a bow. Joe had sent a bow back to the Hiver king.

His dreams continued, and Joe recognized another thing only hinted at. Arleosa was horrified by the violence Joe wrought. But she was enthralled by the joy of victory and the loves of his life. Be it Saluiana the queen, Sika the Wildrider scout, or should he ever get back home, Samantha—one of these women would send a wave of pleasurable emotion through Joe to Arleosa—to Heaven and perhaps the Almighty as well.

The morning came, and Joe awoke rejuvenated and feeling somehow joyous. He snapped the ABS on and noted how new it looked. Particles of an Angel must resonate in this suit, he thought. Sika still slept. Joe bent down and kissed her cheek. She stirred, smiled momentarily, and slept soundly again.

Joe left his helmet off and wandered to the main hall, where breakfast was being served. Joe quickly found a mug and poured himself hot coffee. "*Aah*," he intoned. The whole hall seemed drawn to him. He looked around and smiled. Serving girls were gathering food—bacon, buttered bread, fried eggs—and then settling it in a plate where Joe normally sat. Obliging, Joe sat down. *Man*, he thought. *This is good.* He ate ravenously. *Was this like Heaven?* He thought.

Soon Queen Saluiana and King Kotutan arrived. Everyone rose, as did Joe, to bow deeply to the king and queen. Joe wondered if most would rather be bowing to Saluiana alone. She was wise as well as beautiful, always seeking a path of understanding, staying the hand of violence toward the Manwolves, though too late to avoid a final treachery from them that was perhaps more like revenge. Sika soon joined Joe at the table. She was dressed in a gossamer gown with overlays that masked her torso and hips, but the suggestion of feral beauty still remained.

Joe drained a second cup of coffee and couldn't help smacking his lips as he tasted a warm slice of buttered honey cinnamon roll. *Just like back home*, he mused.

Sika rested a hand on his knee. "Joe," she said. "What now?"

"A good question." He nodded. "We both got a glimpse of the Demon structure. How they're being made is anybody's guess. But I came upon a strange thing going back to my ship. A Demon surrendered—begged for mercy. I let him go."

Sika interjected. "How can any creature so humanlike not be affected over time by this war? It's asking too much. The horror is ever in my mind. Even death would be a mercy to a life like this!"

King Kotutan rose from his chair at the front of the table. His armor glittered of polished silver with golden trim. His resolute bearing masked what Joe considered flawed leadership—too aggressive for his own and his people's good. Manwolves would be good allies now, but oh well! "Joe!" King Kotutan boomed. "Our Messiah tells us what our path must be!"

Joe rose and looked around to take in the whole room. "If not for your adoption of a shared life, this conversation would not even be an afterthought. I have given you the means of protection, and you have grasped that means. The frontier shotgun is such an example. No less important are the shared pasturing and rotation of cattle. The rotation of crops—again, shared—to make more for many instead of abundance for a few. All of this has made you strong as a group and enabled you to sustain yourselves during these dangerous times. Now you must hold on while I go to the South and find the Hivers, bring them to our aid."

A hush fell over the gathering of nobles, frontiersmen, and various tradesmen, blacksmiths, and laborers.

"That's right!" Joe added for emphasis. "You are all you have right now. Small raids of Demons are already being seen. Soon throngs will hit at a very hard time. You can prepare for the onslaught about to happen. Defenses can be set up—hopefully they will hold the Demons until I return."

Joe laid out a plan. Where the siege engines of the last Demon incursion were likely to be mounted, he set bombs with fuses, all developed by the Long-Striders. The development of bullets had gone well. Now a simple scope could be mounted on the rifles, making the Long-Striders effective snipers. They could also use the long-range rifled barrels to send several hundred-meter rounds into the oncoming Demons. They could even use these to detonate the Demons' own explosive catapult ammo. But Joe warned that sitting behind walls firing long range was just a tool. Scouts and teams of fighters must be gathered to harry the Demons before they arrived. Knowledge of the arriving force must be secured, the state of the countryside understood.

"Even as I speak, Bladeswift is scouting the area," said Joe. "Work with him, find the enemy's location, harass and kill them. But doubt not…a siege is going to happen. The Demons' numbers are great. They grow now like well-fed cattle or rotated crops."

Joe stood up and looked around. King Kotutan promised to support all efforts of the plan.

Sika rose and stood near Joe. "I want to go south with you, Joe. You may need me."

"I always need you," Joe responded. And he gently pulled her to his side "Come, then. I have to get going, and quickly." Joe walked to his quarters, and Sika met him there in a few moments. She was clad in her leather armor. A bow, two swords, and a frontier shotgun were strapped to her back; knives were at her waist.

Joe had donned his full ABS. He had punched few dials and set some camouflage coloring that would best mirror the jungles of the South. This took a few minutes: Joe had to work with the dials of the suit and work through a few protocols before it could happen. Joe took some time to arm himself. He started working the sniper rifle and made sure it was cleaned and functioning smoothly. He packed a 10 mm handgun to the holster on his left hip and a 9 mm pistol with a silencer on his right hip. A fission revolver was packed at the small of his back. The suit had semiopen holsters with a magnetic component that released the weapon to Joe when he grasped it.

Joe even checked the tread of his suit's boot bottoms. Still looking new. A semiaggressive lug tread was unworn. Joe checked the Vibro-Blade. It was charged and ready. Joe's suit stored kinetic energy, which in turn charged the Vibro-Blade.

Joe was ready. Sika asked about the route he was going to take. "No time," Joe answered. "I'll use my ship. Will land in the South by the Hive and return hopefully on bees."

"Yes, I remember you used the ship to heal me." Sika said.

"Will ride out and on the way see how things are looking," Joe said. He handed Sika a sniper rifle with a bag of ammo. He gave her a hasty explanation of how to use the sniper rifle. "Just temporary," Joe said. "When we get to the South, stay close. Your smell and mine must inter-mingle—that is part of how they know each other. The Hivers, I mean. How they will know us as friends."

Joe took a deep breath. He reached out to Arleosa, hoping for a reply. He received one.

"Joe." Arleosa's voice came into Joe's head like a flute—soft but with unmistakable tones. "Now is the time to bring peace. Peace through the sword. Then there can be peace. Even the Devil longs for it. He just doesn't understand it yet. His bitter resentment clouds his judgment. Even as his servants grow more human, doubt the path of their liege. They long for peace and pleasures. The same pleasures you still can have, Joe…because you are truly alive."

As quickly as she came, she was gone. Sika looked at Joe. "I felt it too," she said. "Fully human." She looked at Joe. "The way we feel about each other…is fully human, Joe!"

Joe hugged her tightly. "Something of us must still exist in Heaven, or else the Angel would not have sought me out. And with me came you and Saluiana."

She pulled back. "You know she wants you, Joe. Saluiana has never been in love with King Kotutan, and his cruelty settling the land has been a constant pain for her. Hence the conflict with the Manwolves."

"Wait, wait…" Joe said. "That's part of it. Mistakes are human. Jealousy is too." He pulled Sika close again. She relented. They held each other for a short while. Each of them wanted more from the other. But they knew a mission of grand design counted on their equanimity. Being human, after all, could mean good judgment—at times.

Sika looked up at Joe, her brown eyes reading him. "I love you, Joe! So does Saluiana the queen. I feel it."

Joe looked her in the eyes. "I know, Sika, I love you too. More than anything! But now the time grows short. My love makes me want to save this world and all its people. But I would do anything to save you above all."

Sika's eyes teared up. She grasped Joe tightly. He kissed her deeply. Their tongues entwined in each other's mouths.

They were both totally absorbed with one another. Joe paused.

"I want all of you," Sika said. They held each other for only moments, but they felt like they were transported from the stress of the journey.

Joe stared into Sika's eyes. He felt sad and relieved at the same time.

Joe strapped on his weapons after donning the ABS. Sika again donned her battle gear. Joe hugged Sika tightly. "Now to my ship. I have just enough fuel to get us there with some left over to get me home."

"Joe, this is your home…You have to stay!" Sika said.

"Okay…maybe we…my home will be with you!" Joe said.

† † †

Arleosa visited with God. "He is not a puritan." God said. "Now does love make one fight harder or dull the resolve for fear of losing those you love? Or if you don't fight...you lose them anyway!"

Arleosa had been thrilled by Joe. She had longed to be in Sika's place. Oh, to be human again—if only God knew how she felt. If only she could be by Joe's side. But at least she could aid him and support his actions—heal him, repair his equipment by will. Give him the essence to continue.

God focused on Arleosa. "You know one never truly leaves their humanity behind!" With that, God was somewhere else. Arleosa shone down on Joe. *Now is the time*, she thought.

✝ ✝ ✝

In the ship, Joe powered up the controls. He scanned the area quickly for Demon patrols or other contingents. There was a scouting force moving ahead of a large force.

Joe wondered if his advice would be acted upon. The Demons knew where the fortress outpost was, and they would get there soon. The surrounding settlers would begin to arrive at the fortress, hopefully ahead of them. What Joe advocated for was a hit-and-run technique to give Long-Striders an opportunity to reduce their casualties when the siege finally began. Then Joe hoped to bring in the Hivers and decimate the Demon threat. But first the Demons must be given something to think about before the siege started and bombs exploded. The Long-Striders would be once again gathering food from surrounding orchards, hay for cattle and horses. Perhaps a last hunt to briefly secure game before the walls were closed.

Joe would help with this first stalling move to rally the Long-Striders. King Kotutan would be slow to ride out of the gates. He would rather stay within, hold all his resources for a big defense. He was slow to act in some ways and overly aggressive when he sought an easy advantage. No wonder Saluiana despaired of his leadership.

"Come, Sika, show me a way." Joe outlined on the control panel where the Demons had started to encroach.

"I know the place; it is just west of the fortress by a few miles," Sika said.

"Does it have any hills that overlook it? Or cover, such as woods?" Joe asked.

Sika responded, "Just a tree line where a small grove stands."

"Then that will have to do," Joe said. In moments they were on foot, racing to the grove.

Joe and Sika reached the trees on the east side of the grove where they were shielded from the Demons' view. Slowly they moved to the west end of the grove—an expanse of trees about forty meters in depth. Joe set up his sniper rifle between two small trees. He had activated a camouflage pattern on the ABS. Sika was in black just behind Joe, looking over his shoulder. Joe produced a pair of binoculars from his suit. Peering ahead, he guessed the Demons were less than half a mile away.

"I want you to use these to spot for me…Tell me where to shoot." Joe's request had Sika looking through the binoculars, then putting them down.

"I can see them, Joe," she said. "Almost as well without your glasses."

"Pick one for me to kill then."

Sika looked again, then put the binoculars down. "There to the right is their commander."

Joe peered through the riflescope. *Kapow!* The Demon with wider shoulders than the rest slumped back in his saddle. Those on foot looked up to see the heavily armored Demon commander fall back over his mount's rump to the ground. The rest started to scatter. About twelve of them, from what Joe could tell. They started to spread out and move toward the grove, using tall grass and bushes for cover. Joe could easily spot them, and Sika easier still. Joe waited, then Sika nodded in the direction of a small bush one hundred meters away. Joe could see a shiny helmet just behind the bush. *Bam!* The helmet flew off, and a spray of blood hit the air.

Joe had seen what he needed to see. The Demons were approaching. Suddenly there were no signs of the Demons. Joe scanned. They were there hunkered down in the tall grass and whatever scrub brush was available.

Joe took aim at a clump of brush he had scanned. A Demon rested behind it. *Boom!* The Demon lurched back away from the brush, lying sprawled out on his back.

"Joe, what are you doing? Is this the plan?" Sika shook his shoulder.

"No, this is not. I'm waiting to see what happens…waiting for King Kotutan to get out here with an expeditionary force to put the brakes on their advance."

"What, a brake like on a cart or wagon?" she said.

"Yes," Joe said, "like a cart or wagon." Joe looked Sika in the eyes through his helmet visor. "King Kotutan will wait for the Demons to approach the fortress where the mines and bombs, coupled with long-range snipers, will give him an illusory advantage."

"Yes," Sika said. "He is slow to see what really needs to happen, but Saluiana will prod him."

Almost on cue, Joe scanned to pick up a force of about thirty Wildriders and thirty guardshieldsmen riding toward the brush where the remaining Demons hid.

Joe waited. "This looks good," he said. "Let's go!"

Back to the eastern edge of the tree line, they started toward the ACV. Sika and Joe were running hard flowing around and over brush to the ACV.

Ataka rode into the tall grass and brush, swinging his sword into the neck of a Demon who was trying to run away. Bladeswift fired his frontier shotgun, riding full speed into the small trees covering Demons. The Demons fell back out of his path—one for each barrel. Ataka motioned ahead; the larger force of Demons was moving toward them. A force of roughly five hundred Demons.

"Quickly now," Bladeswift urged. "Get to their flanks." Ataka led his contingent left to the south and Bladeswift headed north. Between them they could see the dust of the five hundred Demons, some on mounts and the rest marching with pikes and shields. Several Giants pulled siege engines in the rear.

Almost simultaneously Bladeswift and Ataka led their forces to the rear of the Demons' formation. Shotgun fire raked the sides of the Demons marching on the north and south edges of the formation.

The Demons started to react, firing arrows and sending mounted riders to intercept the flanking guardshieldsmen and Wildriders.

Three Demons pulled their outriders to give chase. The formation slowed. Bladeswift and his Wildriders swept to the rear of the formation.

The guardshieldsmen suddenly turned toward the main body of Demons. Shotguns echoed on the plains. A throng of Demons fell. As quickly as the guardshieldsmen shot, they turned, then circled to the rear of the Demon formation. Bladeswift sped to the formation's rear as well. He rode swiftly, ducking under his horse's neck and firing his shotgun at a Giant pulling a catapult. The shot from one barrel crippled the Giant's right knee, which was closest to Bladeswift. The second barrel exploded into the Giant's torso. He slumped to one knee, struggling to pick a club out of his belt.

At once Ataka and his men surged to the rear of the formation. The Demons turned to face them. Then Ataka faced them, and arrows flew. Several of the oncoming Demons fell, but many kept firing arrows and running toward Ataka and his crew, now down in number after taking a few casualties.

Bladeswift fired arrows at the next Giant—no time to reload the shotgun. Time and surprise were moving away from the initial attack. Another Giant fell. A shotgun blast struck the catapult ammo. *Boom!* Another Giant fell.

"Withdraw!" Ataka bellowed.

"Speed out!" Bladeswift bellowed. Before the dust could clear, the Wildriders and guardshieldsmen were headed west.

Deathmet 2.0 surveyed the damage. They must do as the Devil commanded, regardless of the loss of equipment. The siege would have to happen. He was frustrated by the attack, by the "at all costs" attitude Satan demanded. Deathmet 2.0 would have liked a more flexible strategy.

Joe and Sika were airborne over the battlefield in the ACV. "They did it," Joe stated.

"Yes," Sika acknowledged.

"Wish this thing had been armed." Joe said. "I could have fired a few shots from the ACV cannons. But they were never armed." He said, mostly to himself, not sure if Sika fully recognized his thoughts. "Yes, I get it!" Sika said. "You want to fire from this ship like you fire from your guns."

Joe set the ACV autopilot south, toward the Hiver-controlled canyon.

King Kotutan waited for information about his stalling tactic. He had recognized Joe's plan and knew they could not wait for a full-on Demon assault. Even Queen Saluiana wanted him to take aggressive action. Ever the cautioning influence, she had become much more involved since the coming of their "Messiah," Joe Brown.

In the distance King Kotutan could see a banner. Minus a few casualties, the expeditionary force was returning. He looked through his spyglass. There were a few Long-Striders slumped on their horses. *Dead or severely wounded*, Kotutan thought. The guardshieldsmen headed straight back to the fortress. Bladeswift headed back toward the northern plateaus. He had the protection of villages and a defense to organize.

Joe checked his equipment: the Vibro-Blade and his rifles and pistols. He was ready. Not many explosives left though.

"Joe," Sika began. "You are one of the few to go south and tell of it. You even allied with the Hivers. Can they stop the Demons?"

"Yes," Joe said. "Perhaps they are the natural antidotes for the Demons. Existing here, just waiting to bring your world into realignment."

The high canyon's walls were coming into view. Joe could see vines peeking up over the walls. The giant bees swung low to feed from the blossoms on the vines. Sika had to catch her breath as she observed the multiplicity of giant blossoms: red, purple, yellow, and blue. Two dragons could be seen in the distance, high over the canyon walls. Greenflyers darted through the sky and into the dense foliage.

There were large dragonflies riding soft warm currents of air. Joe scanned. There were Hiver-Riders on those dragonflies.

Joe turned back to land the ship. In the canyon below, the Hiver mound stood in bold relief. An elevated anthill amid a jungle surrounded by canyon walls and paths of egress as well. East and west, the canyon opened to grasslands beyond the jungle.

"Ah! Let's land!" Joe said. Sika looked out the ship's cockpit, sitting with her hand resting on his shoulder. "When we land, stay close to me. Our pheromones must comingle. The Hivers already recognize me; when they recognize me, they'll know you as well."

The ship started down, and Joe wondered how much of a disturbance it would cause. Joe looked for signs of Hiver activity. The watch guard areas at the top of the Hive were vacant. Joe felt a certain worry creep into his consciousness. Then a head popped up at the top of the Hive. Joe scanned closer. A heavily built warrior-caste Hiver stood up. He had a bow and quiver of arrows. Joe's spirits rose. "Look at the scan," Joe implored Sika. "Look, he's carrying a bow. I sent a bow back when they rescued us. It was a suggestion—now they have it." Joe now saw four columns of Hivers marching back to the Hive. The two middle columns were bowmen. The two flanking columns were heavy warrior-caste Hivers. Their exoskeletons, inherent armor, shone.

The ship landed on a canyon wall edge. Joe passed a semiauto handgun to Sika. "Use this if things get tough as we make our way to the Hive, but don't worry about the Hivers. Stay close and they'll know you're with me."

Joe and Sika locked the ship down and began climbing down some large vines. Sika was adept at climbing, which came naturally to her despite so much time on horseback. Joe kept a close eye on Sika. He had nearly lost her before, and though she was very capable, he felt responsible for her. The romantic connection between them flowered within their friendship. Joe looked down. An hour of careful climbing had brought them close to the canyon floor. Here mosses and ferns grew plentifully. The canyon walls made moisture more prevalent, as the canyon walls shielded the canyon floor from the heat of the sun.

18.
A GATHERING OF ALLIES

Once at the floor, Joe looked at the Hiver mound. The lookout carried a bow. Joe scanned in close. He was pleased. The columns of Hivers had long since entered the Hive mound.

Joe was getting hungry. He hoped to be in the Hiver mound by nightfall, reunited with his old comrades. He wanted to see the Hivers before they saw him and Sika—make sure the pheromone memory was in place and could be easily transferred to Sika as well.

Joe crept silently out of the brush and started to climb the Hive mound. He kept a close eye on the top lookout point. Suddenly, as if on cue, the heavily built Hiver at the top turned to face Joe, who was about fifty meters up the mound. Joe tensed. The Hiver communicated happiness, and Joe heard *Joe* as if it were carved into his inner consciousness. *Aah*, it seemed to say. *A mated pair.* Joe relaxed and ran up the mound toward the Hiver. Sika followed quickly behind him, her steps light and effortless.

It was like a celebration. The honey wine flowed. The Hivers gathered around Joe and Sika. Joe's past two Hiver lovers came to join the party, each in her own way seeking to make both Joe and Sika comfortable.

After a while, the king and queen joined the celebration. The king came straight over to Joe, holding a large compound bow made of the materials that the Hivers used to make their limited equipment. Joe had only seen them with rigid weapons like swords and spears. They had all the components of any bow he'd seen, but it was heavy, and its string, when tested, lively and strong. The king handed Joe a quiver of arrows.

What a fine bow, Joe thought. Sika looked at it, admiring its design and apparent craftsmanship.

Sika was in awe of everything. The Hivers were finely articulated humanoids with exoskeletons that could be partially retracted to reveal a more human figure. She thought of them as nimble little warriors who could have a great time drinking honey wine. But soon she began to pick up their thoughts. After all, she was awash in Joe's pheromones. She reacted at first as though there were living dreams inside her head. Joe, noting her strange expression, commented using words, something he really didn't need to do when among the Hivers.

Sika began to catch on, and a flood of information poured into her mind. The honey wine made her feel giddy. She had wondered why Joe received a bow from the Hiver king. She had never seen him use one. Now she knew. He would have intimate knowledge of the bow. Just as the thoughts, images, and feelings of the Hivers were transmitted, so were skills and knowledge. Joe would know how to use the bow because the Hivers knew. He was a part of the Hive, so to speak. And now that Sika was here, she shared in the pheromone-triggered telepathic highway that the Hivers enabled with their existence. Sika knew the Hivers had a powerful force making the South virtually impenetrable. But now she understood.

Joe sat with the king and queen of the Hivers. Each was about a head taller than their subordinates.

✝ ✝ ✝

King Kotutan received Ataka and Bladeswift eagerly. The expeditionary force had managed to hamper and destroy some of the Demon siege engines. "They are a formidable force," Ataka said as they stood in the parade ground behind the ramparts.

Queen Saluiana joined the king, her shapely, muscular form still recognizable inside her leather armor. "I will be leaving soon," Bladeswift reminded them. "But if things go well, I might return to help. Joe has left you a good plan. The snipers can do a good deal of damage from the ramparts. But another foray to slow the Demon ranks is advised."

"Agreed," Ataka said. "We need to slow them down and do more damage. Taking a chance that they could get close with their catapults will likely finish us!"

19.
THE COST OF LOYALTY

Samantha covered her mouth. Tears ran down her cheeks. Captain Johnson and several federal investigators were interviewing her for the tenth time in several months. They had gleaned evidence of Joe and Samantha's relationship. The investigation was ongoing.

"Is there anything else you can remember, Samantha—I mean Ms. Jameson?" Captain Johnson asked.

Dick Swan, the chief investigator, was a little more direct. "We're going to start bringing charges if you're not a bit more forthcoming."

"That's enough!" Joel Small, her attorney interjected as he stood. This time they had called her into the police station.

There was a buzz outside the investigation room. "Jameson—man, she is hot," one of the cops was saying to the other as they strode through the station.

Samantha sat patiently. Her feelings drifted between anger and ignorance. How could Joe disappear and leave her holding the bag, so to speak? Didn't he care about her? She was crying quietly and trembled slightly, though she held herself with dignity. She was wearing a conservative business suit.

"Do you or did you ever know Sam Thames or Tim Jacks, Ms. Jameson?"

"I did not," Samantha said.

"Did Joe ever mention them to you?" the investigator grilled in a heated tone.

"I believe Joe mentioned his foreign mercenary service was somehow connected to Jacks..." she responded.

"Anything else he might have said that stood out to you?" the investigator asked.

"No, except he had a sonic or vibro sword. Just like Joe," she offered. After a few more minutes of explaining and offering little, the interview ended.

"One last thing," the investigator said. "Do you know what happened to them after they came out of that tunnel with Joe?"

"No, I don't," she responded.

"Well," the investigator said. "Thames disappeared, and Jacks became a storefront minister. To be clear, we have no charges to bring against you. We thought you might know something that could help. I'm sure you're wondering what happened to Joe. After all, you had a relationship with him."

"Yes, I—"

"Hold on," the attorney said.

"It's okay. I mean just a relationship, like we're having here now—you know, we know each other!" the investigator said, chuckling.

The attorney said, "Okay, is that it? You're done with her?"

"Well, one last thing. We did get some transmissions from Joe, but they don't explain too much." The investigator trailed off.

Samantha perked up.

"Nothing much to help," continued the investigator. "Just like the phone message he left you. Whatever he had on his mind consumed him. He went to take care of it. Jacks a minister and Thames just gone. So, one big mystery," the investigator said.

"Joe's out there somewhere," Samantha said. "I can feel it."

"Okay, okay," the attorney Small said. "That's it, right?"

"Yes," the investigator agreed. Samantha and Small exited the police station to a waiting limo. Reporters stood by, taking pictures, and trying to get an interview. Then Small and Samantha drove off.

Sam Thames stood on a tall skyscraper just below its peak. He was hunched on bended knees. He looked and scanned the city. The tunnel's closure after the terrorist attack had left everything calm. But still things happened in ways they never used to. Deaths in the city had become more prevalent. People described odd creatures in the night. Thames was looking for these creatures. He'd seen a few, but more lurked in the darkness.

The restaurant area near the intersection of Clown and Wine Street had been quiet for a while. Now, like the center of a spoked wheel, it came to life. Young up-and-comers from all over came to dine under lavish if not festive circumstances. Friday night, and the discos were buzzing. Beautiful women and handsome men cavorted about like locusts. Intellectuals filled the coffee houses, philosophizing about end times and what the appearance of Demons meant for them, their city, and humankind altogether.

Thames leaped into the void beneath the skyscraper, gliding on currents of air with transparent wings that sprouted as if by magic from his back. He wore a golden suit of armor.

Just then a couple was walking away from the restaurant area into the park. They seemed a bit tipsy, to say the least. A green expanse of grass and willow trees lined the cobblestone walkway.

Thames circled low to follow their path. The scent of curry and barbecue floated in the air behind them. Thames's nostril was filled with the smell. *Must be one of those new fusion restaurants*, he mused, gliding along above.

Beyond the smell of food and of course, wine, was another odor. The smell of dead flesh and wet fur. Thames soared high, not wanting to alert them to what would soon be obvious.

To the untrained eye, what appeared to be a hairy naked man furtively made his way toward the couple. The hairy man's teeth glittered in the moonlight. *Twenty-five meters out now!* Thames thought. The hairy man made a mad dash toward the couple, lunging at the woman, who was wearing a black minidress and carrying high heels.

Um. Thames thought. He came down hard at a diagonal angle, slamming the Vibro-Blade down hard on the hairy man's head and neck. The hairy man fell on his ass. The woman screamed and fainted. The man, overcome by shock, barely caught her. "Get her out of here!" Thames yelled. The hairy man rose, teeth barred. Clawed hands pushed him up onto two feet. He lurched forward as Thames slammed a horizontal blow into his rib cage. The hairy man fell to his knees. Wings fluttering like a hummingbird, Thames rose a few meters in the air and then slammed the blade down on the crown of the hairy man's head. The hairy man went limp. Thames landed and kneeled by the hairy man's body. He took out a steel hunting knife and carved off the beast's head. A fine trophy. *A Wolfman after all*, Thames thought. Trophy in hand, he flew off at great speed.

The headlines the next day were unmistakable, as ridiculous as they were. "Wolfman's head found in front of city hall!"

Samantha found comfort in prayer these days—prayer and meditation. Why were things going so poorly? No job, no Joe. She had always thought she might have to make a choice. But now her job was gone and so was Joe.

Her job had always been in jeopardy when she dated Joe while he still played football. When he stopped, she relaxed a bit but knew they had to keep it quiet. Now he was gone with little explanation and a whole heap of trouble left on her doorstep. She made some coffee and turned on the TV. "Today a couple will tell us about the golden Angel who saved them from a werewolf."

Samantha turned the volume up. "Yes, a man in gold flew down and saved us..." the man spoke excitedly. "My girlfriend fainted—then we got outta there."

"A body was found in the park by the restaurant area near Clown and Wine!" said the television newscaster.

Thames was squatting in an old building near the tunnel. He had rigged some electricity, and the plumbing still worked. No one seemed to pay much attention. The area had been condemned by the city.

Now he had a headquarters of a sort. He used a police scanner and watched the local news incessantly. He was getting disability from the police department in the form of a check that came to a post office box. He figured the checks would run out eventually. He wasn't hurt physically, and the emotional toil of the tunnel experience was growing old to the psychologist assigned to review his PTSD symptoms. Every now and then, he'd go by and see Jacks at his storefront ministry. It was growing, and after a while, Jacks had given him his Vibro-Blade.

"Don't need it anymore." Jacks had said. "I think my *awakening* was a little different than yours. Been fighting too long. You take the fight to the Devil; I'll spread the word!"

Thames remembered Jacks had been a mercenary with Joe for quite a while. He guessed Jacks was tired of fighting. But each man came out of that tunnel changed. Jacks's storefront ministry was a growing success. He had been able to start some city gardens after the tunnel closed. Real estate was cheap for a minute. He put together some church cooperatives from growing gardens to raising goats in the local parks. He was making the city near the pit come alive. The poor and disenfranchised were a big part of his ministry. But it was still a dangerous place. Human crime dropped but malevolent crime did not. A wolf's head shaped something like a man's at city hall was testimony to that. Werewolf—no one wanted to say it, but it looked true enough.

Thames sat back and sipped some coffee. He was watching the news, which was highlighting his handiwork. The TV blared on, and the announcer said, "A werewolf head found on the steps of city hall is being examined by a police forensic specialist and matched potentially to a headless corpse—human but covered in similar fur." Job done, Thames was waiting, hoping to wake up the city. Things had become quiet after the tunnel was sealed. People tried to get back to normal. But Thames had dreams that were not normal but prophetic, he believed, telling a desperate story of horrific threats and ancient myths coming to life. Thames sipped his coffee. He looked across at his suit. Golden battle armor he had stolen from the mercenary Corporation within the oil company he had worked for. It had been camo colored before, but one night he woke up to find it gold. Battle suits were being developed all over the country with the hope of giving police a technical advantage. The military also worked on them, but as usual, corporate ingenuity pushed the process faster. Oil money drove the mercenary development of battle suits.

Dreams came often to Thames. He always remembered them as secure feelings of childhood happiness and contentment. Somehow the dreams assured him that he was doing the right thing. If he needed reminding, he walked to the one mirror in his borrowed apartment.

He could stand shirtless in that mirror, look at his shoulders, and see transparent wings sprout from behind him. He'd flutter them gently. Dust would fly around; papers would blow. If he became too excited, he might lift up off the floor momentarily. *This was different*, he thought. *I'm a Black Angel. Damn it, I really am.*

✝ ✝ ✝

Joe awoke with a start. Sika was coiled around him, their arms entwined, his battle suit retracted. He sat up, and Sika rested quietly after adjusting her head. He had been here at the Hive for three days, sharing memories and pheromones. Some of the memories were horrific: filled with Demons assaulting both the Hive and the Long-Striders' fortress. He had dreamed as well. Dreamed of home and Samantha. He had a sense that Thames and Jacks were still involved, as he was, in the fight against the Demons.

Gold flooded the pod where he and Sika rested on a bed of furs. The gold cleared like a swirling vapor, parting as if the sun was shining through and melting it. Soon Joe could hear the Hivers milling about. He reached out to touch the vapor as it melted into nothing. In a moment Sika was awake, kissing Joe lightly on the lips. She dressed quickly and armed herself as Joe snapped on the body of the ABS, leaving only his head clear of protection. He and Sika rushed down a ramp to where he saw the Hiver king and queen gesturing vigorously. Images sprang into his mind as he drank the warm chocolate. Joe had put the compound bow across his back. The king was holding a bow as well. They were identical.

Joe knew he was now very familiar with the bow. The very air in the Hive triggered memories. He saw the king take down a large boar with his bow and a feast honoring the kill. Then the memories became darker, filled with horrific emotion: he witnessed an assault by Demons upon the Hive. The fighting was grim. Both Joe and Sika recoiled from the memories that came flooding into their minds. Many Hivers died, but then those armed with bows turned the tide, driving back the Demons with concentrated volley after volley of arrows. This was the king's point. The old way cost too much. Now pikemen and swordsmen would make an initial retreat to open targets for the bowmen. A new class of Hivers in their first generation of life. Some of the most agile genetically designed swordsmen and women as well, their vision enhanced by the vision of need from the queen and king. They developed a quick-moving, agile, far-seeing Hiver with a lighter-armored body. They moved quickly from position to position and fired volley after volley at an oncoming enemy. Mounted on the giant bees and sometimes dragonflies, they could devastate a foe by shooting down from the sky.

Joe looked at Sika. They understood what happened here. The Hivers had quickly adapted and even produced offspring to fight and destroy the Demon threat through the use of the bow. Biological adaptation was their strength. But Joe, introducing the bow, had caused them to adapt physically to use the technology more effectively to survive this new biological threat—the Demons.

Joe understood the main question plainly. Would helping destroy the Demons' onslaught against the Long-Striders help the Hivers? The king looked at Joe. A message came through from the king's mind directly to Joe.

† † †

Samantha was reading ads about missing persons—she did this at least once or even twice a week after the investigation had started. *Joe where are you?* she thought. Not only did she miss Joe but having investigators and the press sneaking around her affairs made things unbearable. She had lost her job and thus was living a very socially constrained life. Girlfriends gave her unheeded advice. They castigated Joe for leaving her; some colleagues had stayed in touch. But she could feel their judgmental tone. She was a jilted woman. She had disregarded professional boundaries with Joe and paid a hefty price. No love, no job, no man. She was also living off unemployment. She had been urged to write a book exposé about the whole thing. But no, she couldn't bear to do that. She might be able to move back to her parents' if she had to. Her loyalty to Joe was like a straitjacket. She could just write something, cash in, and condemn Joe and herself. But she still had faith in both herself and Joe. She looked in the bathroom mirror. She had a cute, even beautiful, face and a body to die for, but she looked up, waiting for who knew. "Joe, where are you?"

✝ ✝ ✝

Joe was feeling a little tired. He'd been sneezing lately. He coughed at times. Sika advised him to rest. He wanted to get back to his goal. Still, he was very tired—a few days to rest wouldn't hurt. Ironically, he hadn't been sick in a long while. Probably since childhood. He'd been healthy as a young man—until now.

The previous night, the dreams had become more vivid. They had immersed Joe in a world previously unknown to him. Arleosa swathed him in golden light, caressed him with rays of metaphysical light. The sun shone brighter in his dreams than it ever could in real life. Gold and light blended into a talisman on Joe's suit belt and was partially absorbed by his body. He awoke with a start. Sweat poured over his whole body. He lay back.

Sika offered him a hot beverage, which he drank greedily. The chocolate of the Hivers. She watched him intently. He pulled her to him, embraced her, and they made love for hours. Writhing in ecstasy, Sika's legs locked around Joe's thighs. He plunged deeply into her loving acceptance—an invitation to share her life. She moaned. He exulted in the pleasure coursing through his body after each tremulous orgasm.

Morning passed. Joe woke healed and energized. He was no longer sneezing or coughing. He had some more chocolate, some nuts, and dried jerky. Staples of the Hivers' food stores.

The king's message to Joe had been profound: all humanoid life was at risk and the bow had been a game changer. The Hivers could overwhelm enemies with less loss, less sacrifice. The time for Demon annihilation was now.

The Hive was buzzing with activity. Joe sipped more chocolate. Sika hydrated and sipped chocolate as well. Her olive-brown face had a mild flush of red color in it. She smiled easily at Joe, who kissed her on the lips.

The two of them armed themselves: compound bows and blades and Joe with his guns and Vibro-Blade. Sika loaded the frontier shotgun and slung it over her shoulder. Joe cleaned the sniper rifle and oiled it lightly. He and Sika had quivers full of arrows, the resin tips of each arrow made by the Hiver craftsmen. Light, strong steel that could drive through armor and bones.

A cloud hovered over the Hive; the sound of wings buzzed above. The bees had arrived. Joe was beckoned to the top exit of the Hive. He could sense the pheromones mixing in the Hive. One message came with the pungent odor, not mixing back and forth: *Bring the end to the Demons. If there is a place called Hell, complete a cycle of its life. End it.*

† † †

Thames flew high above the city. He danced in the air on transparent wings. He was on patrol. He wanted to wake the city up. He felt urgently that he had to get things done now!

Samantha woke up the next morning. She'd made a decision. There'd be no turning back. She'd found out where Joe went. She had a plan.

† † †

Joe was high above the jungle canyon, part of an armada of giant bees carrying Hivers. Joe thought of great battles in history. What an expedition this would be. Joe loaded the sniper rifle. He was headed north to the rear of the flight column. A large dragonfly carried the Hiver command. The king would never leave the general vicinity of the Hive. He would remain with a contingent of defenders, as would the queen. But the dragonfly carried a trusted Hive commander. Thickly muscled, he would direct the attack from above, then as requirements commenced, land and fight with the rest.

The battle would reach into the cave of the Demons and destroy everything there; Joe had held onto the remaining explosives in his arsenal. He would end the Demon reign here and then return home to end it there as well, if needed. He would fight for his way of life, for hope.

The sky was crowded with giant bees as Joe neared the fortress of King Kotutan.

There were large pits in the ground from explosives Joe had set up on the plains west of the fortress. Joe could see the Demons plodding forward with a few remaining siege engines. Explosive blasts came close to the fortress ramparts. But not close enough. Bee-riding Hiver archers fired arrows that cut down the Demons and Giants manning the catapults. Joe wielded the sniper rifle from above. He blasted one Giant in the back. He stumbled and lay face down, dead, a bullet through his back and heart. The battle ended quickly. The Hivers, unified in attack behind their bows, were deadly and decisive.

The Hivers wheeled away from the fortress. Snipers on the ramparts had set the stage for the end of the remaining Demons. The blasts of snipers echoed from the ramparts. *Boom! Boom!* The concussive shots struck down Demons and any remaining Giants who were manning siege engines.

The wave of giant bees moved west at Joe's insistence. The final onslaught must begin. Joe slung the sniper rifle over his shoulder. Sika, riding nearby, slung her bow next to a frontier shotgun and readied her two short swords. Joe was ready. He brought out the Vibro-Blade. The battle would be a ramp into Demon territory. Hivers descended from the back of the still-flying bees using ropes. Arrows from the cave mouth flew forward, striking them. A few bees went down, but a mass of Hivers descended. The bees flew south as about two hundred Hiver warriors, the best of the Hive prepared to assault the Demons. Joe and Sika crept to the knoll above the Demon cave mouth. He unslung his sniper rifle and fired into the cave mouth. Demons fell and growled in pain.

Joe set a few mobile claymores toward the cave mouth. He waited. The claymores entered, and time passed. Blasts were heard within the cave.

Joe moved forward. Sika was near; she seemed like his shadow. Joe fired into the cave mouth as he approached. Sika shadowed Joe's right shoulder. She fired the frontier shotgun repeatedly, reloading and pushing forward. Demons swarmed from the depths of the cave. Hivers flanked left and right of Sika and Joe. Arrows flew from their bows like clockwork. Demons surging from the depths of the cave were met with sharp-tipped arrows that ripped through armor and Demon flesh. Sika had Joe's pistol and fired rapidly. Joe had switched from the sniper rifle to his assault weapon, firing short bursts, taking down Demon after Demon.

Then, as dust cleared, Joe saw what he knew would be there to meet him: Deathmet in another incarnation. The Goliath strode forth, crossbow in hand. His horned helmet sat squarely on his head. Deathmet, or Deathmet 2.0, it did not matter. Sika steadied the frontier shotgun and fired it. Deathmet stumbled backward. Joe unsheathed the Vibro-Blade. He ran forward. Hivers flanked him in a mobile phalanx. Joe shot his last rounds from the assault rifle. He danced into the oncoming Demons as Deathmet moved toward him. Sika emptied her remaining clip. Joe slammed into Deathmet with his Vibro-Blade, slamming it hard across Deathmet's helmet. The helmet cracked and rolled off of Deathmet's head. Deathmet reeled and staggered but righted himself and used an armored forearm as a shield. Joe, feeling his advantage, cut under the forearm and hammered toward Deathmet's waist. As he did, Deathmet stepped back, leveled the crossbow, and fired it point-blank into Joe's chest, just above the heart. Joe staggered back. He felt the sharp pain of the bolt. But his eyes were fixed on Deathmet. There was great pain, but he knew death could easily follow if combat discipline was not maintained. Deathmet pushed forward and was almost on top of Joe. He wielded two large steel clubs, each topped with a sharp blade. Joe rolled right and jumped up. Deathmet turned to adjust his attack and desperately attempted to poke Joe with the sharp blade point of the club. Joe stepped to Deathmet's rear side, inching further away from being an easily reached target. Joe crashed into Deathmet's lower back and left side, using his shoulder. In the small space of separation between them, Deathmet was pushed back. Joe swung the Vibro-Blade in a two-fisted horizontal arc. Joe landed the blow squarely into Deathmet's lower back. The Goliath staggered and stumbled to his knees.

There was a hush of activity as the Demon legions paused momentarily and perhaps fearfully as they saw their war leader go down. Deathmet twisted as he rose, trying to locate Joe, who, though exposed more to Demon arrows, sought to remain completely behind Deathmet. Sika and the Hivers recognized his plan and fired everything they had at the nearby Demons to keep them at bay. Joe swung again with the Vibro-Blade, bringing it hard against Deathmet's vulnerable bare head. It was like the sound of a nut cracking. Deathmet fell sideways and lay dead. Joe touched his chest where the bolt had landed. There was a hole in the suit, and blood had spilled from the wound. The pain was great, but soon it seemed as if the hole was disappearing; Joe was feeling stronger, his pain subsiding.

The cave opened to more expansive proportions as the Hivers pushed forward. Joe tried to get in gear, moving forward at a slow jog but feeling more comfortable by the second, Sika's arm slipped around Joe's waist. She squeezed him tightly. Joe's pace picked up. Now the tunnel widened, and even more Demons fired upon them from above, hidden in a series of connected paths above the cave floor but just below its ceiling. Joe found cover and set aim with the sniper rifle; its lethal thunderbolt sound cracked and echoed. At various times, following Joe's shot, a Demon archer would tumble down to the cave floor below.

Another surge of Demons came running into what was now a combat arena. The Hivers took cover behind boulders and unleashed a torrent of arrows.

Joe signaled to hold. He set out a mobile claymore and watched it skitter to the mouth of another tunnel from which Demons surged forward. *Boom!* A concussive blast set off a vibration. Joe waited for the dust to clear. The Hivers moved forward to position themselves. As they did, they retrieved arrows from bodies of Demons, wiped them off, and requivered them.

Joe paused to reflect on the progress he and the Hivers had made. He felt the battle with Deathmet, though potentially a great risk, was too easy. Yes, he'd been hurt, but he sensed something he'd not felt before. Had Deathmet been afraid?

Joe shrugged inwardly. Sika, seeing him lost in thought, got his attention. "Joe, we must keep going!"

The Demons were falling back. Now they seemed more hesitant. Sika urged Joe on: "We have them, Joe. We have them!" Joe strode forward at a trot. The Hivers flanked him as they crowded into the next tunnel. There was a sound of clawed feet as beyond the tunnel lay an expanse barely seen illumined by torchlight.

The lights grew dim as Joe and his large army of Hivers began to file into the cave expanse. Then the lights blazed bright torches seemed to burst into flame. One hundred Demons surged forward, swinging swords, throwing spears, and engulfing the Hivers along with Joe and Sika.

The battle was a last-ditch effort, it seemed. The Demons wanted to end the threat Joe and the Hivers posed. The sense of fear Joe had detected was gone. The Demons threw themselves headlong into the attack. Joe signaled the Hivers to fall back as he fired his assault rifle. Sika emptied a clip from her pistol and drew her sword and a large knife that was more like a short sword.

Joe and Sika had cleared some space between the Hivers and the Demons. The Hivers replaced their swords with bows and fired repeatedly into the Demons. Joe was out of ammo for the assault rifle. He had a fission pistol attached to his suit at the small of his back. Something told him to hold on. He reached for his bow and started firing arrows. His shots traveled farther and more accurately than those of the Hivers or Demons.

The battle seemed to be at a standstill. Sika urged Joe to press forward. She was a veteran of many battles. The Wildriders often used a strategy of overwhelming, violent speed. But Joe said, "No, Sika. Get low, hold on."

Down the tunnel to their rear came the sound of angry buzzing. A large dragonfly came flying through the tunnel, its wings barely fitting the mouth of the expanse where the battle had stalled. The smell of rotted flesh could be recognized. Several more dragonflies followed. They all carried nets that were quickly released. The nets held Greenflyers who were caught using the carrion as bait. The Greenflyers tumbled out of the nets and became airborne. They panicked in the cave and immediately attacked the nearby Demons. They hacked with their claws and darted to the rear of the Demons, creating mayhem wherever they landed, slashing briefly, then rising back in the air, then falling upon more Demons. Joe's pheromones mingled with those of the Hivers. His communication was to wait and let the mayhem of the Greenflyers strike fear into the Demons. "Be still. Don't attract them to us." There were about fifteen Greenflyers—now down to five. Joe waited. He could see splashes of dark blood fly in the air wherever a Greenflyer landed on a Demon. Finally, at great cost, the Greenflyers were all skewered by either arrows, spears, or swords. The Demons seemed to collectively sigh in relief.

Joe emerged from the cover and pushed forward his message. Pheromones floating in the air between Joe and the Hivers carried the message forward. They moved as one body. The Demons reeled as the shock of arrows hit them. Some plummeted from the cave walls high above. Joe pushed forward, quickly closing in on the Demons who tried to defend the next tunnel opening. Joe had one modern weapon left with ammunition: the fission revolver. He checked it briefly. Then he went back to firing arrows toward the tunnel. His bow shot arrows with velocity unseen heretofore. One of his arrows skewered two Demons at once. What started as a hundred Demons defending the cave was dwindling in numbers.

Joe knew they were close to the next cave expanse. A few more meters, and they were in the expanse. A tall ceiling greeted Joe. Its arches were as wide as they were tall. There was a throne of red rocks on which sat a handsome, brick-red man, perfectly formed and magnificently muscular. The man was naked except for a loincloth. He sat glaring at Joe. "So you have come now. To lose everything after gaining so much." Voluptuous female Demons surrounded him. They, like him, had no horns. They were beautiful to behold. "I am the Archangel Satan. You have come here to find me!"

Joe sneered and loosed an arrow from his bow. It soared toward him who called himself Satan. The creature rose and with a simple flick of his wrist knocked the arrow aside. The women surrounded him and fitted on his armor. It was like iron, but iron that had rusted to a red hue. It seemed to glow. Satan reached beside his throne chair and picked up his great broadsword. It was six feet long. Satan stood seven feet tall. At least as tall as Deathmet. His shoulders were broad and his chest deep. His legs were like supple pillars of muscle. He wore heavy boots that looked to have been made from dragon scales. Satan descended the throne dais. He hefted his sword, and it moved through the air effortlessly.

Joe watched his approach and readied his bow. He urged Sika back toward the protection of the Hivers, who fired a volley of arrows at Satan. He swung his sword and deflected most of the arrows. One glanced off his boots; another glanced off his headgear. Gathering his resolve, Joe shot one more arrow that lodged in Satan's helmet. Joe could not see how deep it penetrated, but Satan screamed "argh."

So, Joe thought, *he is not invincible*. Many of the Demons seemed fearful. They began to fall away from the battle and started pouring out into nearby tunnels. The Demon women were soon gone as well. A wave of Demon cavalry was soon upon Joe and the Hivers who fired arrow after arrow. The cavalry was gone, decimated. Joe turned on his Vibro-Blade. He ran toward Satan. Satan slowed his own advance, sword at the ready.

Joe ducked the first cut that came blindingly fast, almost decapitating Joe, who dropped low in the nick of time. Joe's suit started to glow. Gold seemed to ground and hit Satan's legs. Joe swung the Vibro-Blade up into Satan's groin. Joe rolled away and danced to his feet. He didn't know what would come next. Satan crouched and sprung toward Joe.

A second wave of Demon cavalry swarmed into the cavern expanse, empty save for the two combatants and Satan's throne. Waves of Demon cavalry came charging into the expanse, and Hiver archers cut them down almost before Joe could notice they had entered.

Satan rammed into Joe, knocking him into the air and five feet back. Now he brought his sword up for a killing blow. *Bam! Bam! Bam!* The fission revolver cracked the air like thunderbolts. Satan, taken by surprise, stumbled backward. Joe swung and ran forward, hammering down with the Vibro-Blade. *Whack-whack-whack!* Joe felt a surge of energy rising within him. Satan rolled away from Joe's attack. He glowed a hot red. Satan stood up, then crouching low, circled Joe, sword held defensibly—he looked unsure of himself. Joe's gaze met Satan's. Satan surged forward, swinging his sword. Joe brought the Vibro-Blade up in defense, but Satan beat him back. Joe stepped sideways out of range of the oncoming onslaught.

All around Demons poured in, gaining strength from Satan. Joe sensed this would be the difference. Motivation versus the fear of defeat. Joe danced backward and to the side. He set the Vibro-Blade down on the cave floor. He pulled the fission pistol. Satan, anticipating the move, dived forward and was upon Joe, who quickly picked up his Vibro-Blade and rolled aside. Satan's sword smote the rock on the cave floor, sparks flew, and Satan growled. "*Ugggh.*" In a moment Joe was on his feet. *Boom! Boom! Boom!* The fission pistol erupted, hitting Satan in each arm, then the chest. Joe followed and bound into the air. He twisted sideways and jumped high, landing a sidekick on Satan's chin. Satan fell in a clanging heap of red armor. A cascade of arrows pummeled Joe as the Demons sought to rescue their savior. Hivers were low on arrows but answered with a volley of anything they could fit into their bows: demon arrows plucked from their Hive mates' corpses or arrows plucked from dead Demons.

Joe rolled away from the cascade of arrows that served as a flying barrier guarding him from Satan. Satan frowned. He looked groggy and spent. Joe fired the fission pistol, its energy close to being spent. It still had a concussive effect as it slammed a round into Satan's body. "Science over ancient evil," Joe mocked Satan. Satan scrambled to his feet, turned, and ran very fast, considering all that armor. Joe gave chase. Sika remained in cover, firing arrows into any Demon visible.

Joe dodged arrows and rolled to the cave floor only to jump up again and pursue Satan, who ran from the expanse into an adjoining tunnel. Joe, in pursuit, was gaining. It was just him and Satan, both running. Joe could see ahead. Satan was running toward a hole, black and unfathomable. Joe stopped and fit an arrow in his bow. He fired. It struck Satan in the back, driving him to his knees. Armor protected a possible entry, but Joe couldn't be sure. Satan was fifty meters away, still crawling to the black hole, which was twenty meters away from him. Joe was closing in fast. Satan rose to his feet, half staggered, half jogged, and disappeared into the hole. Joe picked up speed and lunged hard. He hit top speed in time to pass right behind Satan into the unfathomable darkness of the hole. His last thoughts were of Sika—he did not want to leave her. He could feel her thoughts, smell her, and he prayed he'd come back to her one day. Then all was a mass of darkness, and he was breathing hard; but then the golden glow enveloped him, and he could breathe easier. He looked ahead. He could see a dim figure that had to be Satan. The black hole seemed to be narrowing, closing, tightening. Joe landed on concrete.

20.
HOME AGAIN

Satan got up, still staggering but gaining momentum. He ran down the sidewalk. It was night; few people were on the sidewalk. They recoiled at his presence. A large man, magnificently built, was staggering under heavy armor, trying to evade a man in golden armor, wielding a Vibro-Blade. The humming of the VB made alarming sounds resonate into the night.

Joe's anger was spiking. Arleosa fed off of his emotions. How sweet was the taste of adrenaline, the bitter urging of resentment! Arleosa loved it all, remembering her humanity. She urged Joe on in the symbiotic embrace that made his hormones light up like a fire. With that, Joe renewed his pursuit. Satan stepped forward. Recognizing his mistake late, Satan hammered his broadsword toward Joe's head as Joe raised the Vibro-Blade, barely deflecting Satan's blow. Joe fell back, dazed. Satan lunged forward; broadsword ready for a killing blow. Joe turned sideways, stepping away at the same time. From the corner of his eyes, Joe saw the silhouette of wings. Thames drove downward from the sky. A Vibro-Blade slammed into Satan's shoulder. Satan crumpled to his knees. Joe swung his sword heavily at Satan's shoulder, then quickly at Satan's torso. A tremendous crack could be heard. Satan gasped. His armor fragmented under the blow. He rolled away and started running toward a wooded area—a nearby park, Joe realized.

Sam Thames soared above and made a flying surge toward Satan. Too late—Satan disappeared under a canopy of trees.

Sam rose in the air again. He couldn't locate Satan. Joe stood up and looked ahead. Nothing. Scanned. Still nothing.

Thames landed right in front of Joe. "Old friend!" he began. "I've missed you. Waited for your return." The two friends embraced. "Where have you been?"

Joe raised his head, shrugged momentarily, and said, "I had to go and find a way to save another world. Now what I wanted to save it from has landed here. I have to find a way to save us, or we will all be enslaved in a hell of our own selfishness." Joe and Sam walked in the park down a path toward Sam's borrowed accommodations.

Entering, Sam turned on his light switch. "Still got electricity," he murmured.

Thames opened a can of Steak 'n' Beans. "Hungry?" he asked Joe. Joe nodded. Thames opened a bottle of wine. "Here." He proffered the wine to Joe in a plastic cup. Joe doffed his helmet. "It's almost over, Joe!"

"What do you mean, Thames?"

"I mean, the end of the world is coming, and we're stuck playing out the drama!"

"I don't get it," Joe said.

"Well, where'd you come from just now, Joe? They been looking for you quite a long time now."

"I can guess, Thames. I didn't expect to come back this soon. I left some people I was helping. I was going to save them from the same Demons we fought here. I don't have time to answer questions from the police. I've gotta get going. Find Samantha. I owe her an explanation."

"Not so fast," Sam warned. "She's being watched. They know about you and Samantha. She was investigated. Here's the paper." Sam handed Joe a paper. It had a picture of him and Samantha with different captions. The line over the top saying "Football, Mercenary, Police Hero Disappears. Secret Girlfriend Hasn't Seen Him Either." Sam said, "You can't just go on with finding your girl. We gotta find that guy too."

"Yes!" Joe said. "That guy is Satan himself. Now he's here, this is gonna get crazy. Perhaps I did help those people where I came from. I got Satan out of there."

"Get some rest," Thames implored. "In about four hours, it's gonna be daylight."

Joe's dreams were a kaleidoscope of nightmares and visions. In one dream Joe ascended into Heaven and embraced Arleosa. Sika was there, smiling and happy. In a nightmare Satan shot an arrow through Joe's heart. Joe fell but rose again. When he awoke, it was daylight. He knew where he could find Satan. But first he was going to steal some weapons and ammo while finding a way to see Samantha.

Sam handed Joe a cup of coffee. "Drink up, my friend." Joe had slept in his suit, helmet off. He sipped the hot coffee as he sat up.

"How can I get some weapons, ammo, and see my girl, Thames?"

"Well, Joe, I've been watching everything. I've been using scanners and completed police reports from hacked files. There's surveillance all over, but they don't think you'll show up. So surprise is gonna help."

"Let's go," Joe said. "Broad daylight, walk right in—how's that for surprise?"

"Okay," Sam said. "We've both been touched, Joe. Use your senses to find the best path. I'll monitor from above. Samantha's condo is on the third floor of a five-story building. Once you get in the building, you should be fine. This should help."

"A trench coat?" Joe looked at Thames, who was holding a pale-gray trench coat. Joe put on the coat. "Let's go!" he said. "By the way, how'd you get those wings?"

Thames unfolded the wings, and Joe gazed at their luminous quality. They were compact and clear to the eye, but on Thames they made him look like a hummingbird. He sighed. "I woke up one morning after a dream. A dream about an Angel. Recurring dreams have been going on for me ever since we were in the tunnel. I was taken by surprise. But soon my dreams helped me realize I could fly with my wings. Really fly."

"Okay then," Joe said. "Let's move on and see my girl. Then I can go after Satan with a clearer conscience. I know I'm supposed to find Satan, but I just need a little time to reconcile with Samantha."

"Okay. I'll get you in, but then I'm going to check around for him too."

Joe put the trench coat on over his armored battle suit. His helmet was under it, hidden. They walked out into the early morning light. Sam also wore a trench coat. His armored suit was hidden as well.

They headed uptown. Joe looked around—these were largely abandoned slums where Thames squatted. The odors of rotting food and something dead were in the air.

The weather was warm—even in the morning. Joe noticed a small group of five men in ragged clothing bunched together. "You got something for us?" they called out to Joe and Thames.

"Nope, don't even bother," Sam called out. One of the men laughed maliciously, but they stayed put. The men laughed. They looked like tough men who lived any way they could. "Mostly homeless. Criminal minded."

Thames led Joe uptown through alleys and backstreets.

Before long Joe looked up and saw good-looking buildings and middle-class gardens. "Start getting small," Thames said. Joe recognized Samantha's building. They were about a block away. "Let's climb," Sam said.

Soon they were up one side of a building, avoiding windows, until they reached the roof. Joe scanned around, trench coat off, helmet on. He could see a black sedan parked below Samantha's complex across the street. "They probably have surveillance cameras set up in the parking lot on the other side," Sam reported. "Probably your best bet is to walk in the front, buzz her door, and hope she lets you in!"

"Really kind of risky, don't you think?" Joe responded. "How about the basement? Or roof?"

"Look," Sam finally said. "You get ready. I'll distract them or something. Get on the other side of the building. Get that helmet off. Hope she's glad to see you or just not too angry." With that Sam swooped into the air and swung low behind the sedan.

Joe watched Sam shake the vehicle while kneeling low, near its trunk. Suddenly the doors swung open as two men in black suits emerged from the sedan. Sam was gone in an instant. Joe was already down the building to the street and into the lobby of Samantha's building. Joe scanned quickly, revealing a code in the lobby interior door. He relaxed for a moment, then punched the code, and yanked the door open. He was up to the third floor in a heartbeat.

There was a man in the hallway in a black suit. He turned to face Joe, hand going to his shoulder-harnessed pistol. Joe was on him in a heartbeat, slamming the pistol back in its holster by pushing forcefully down on the man's wrist. The man seemed flummoxed: How could anyone be so quick? Joe wheeled around behind him, grasping his neck, squeezing hard until the man slumped down, unconscious. Joe took the gun and extra ammo as well as the badge. Might come in handy. He pushed the unconscious body into a corner near the stairs coming up from the lobby. He thought for a while and pulled the man's handcuffs off and locked them around his wrists.

Joe knocked on Samantha's door. "Who is it?" The response came from inside after a few moments.

"Joe!" he said. He had taken off his helmet. His hair was long, but he had been shaving while among the Long-Striders.

Samantha was looking through the peephole, unbelieving but recognizing all the same. The door swung open. "J—Joe!" She stammered. "What? Where have you been?"

"Let me in, and I'll tell you, but you will doubt me even more than you do now!" Joe said.

"Okay, okay," she whispered. "Come in, Joe—I want to tell you how upset I have been." Joe made a tentative attempt to hug her. She seemed hesitant, and he did not want to assume anything. He slammed the door behind him. He turned back to Samantha, who had folded her body into his. Then she looked into his eyes and kissed him deeply.

"Tell me if you had strange dreams while I was gone!" Joe said and she had. She never lost faith in him. They hugged and kissed.

"You stink, Joe," she said. They hugged tightly. Then almost reflexively she pushed him away. All the times they had been together flooded back into her mind. Joe tentatively reached to embrace her again. She threw off her doubts and embraced him. The doubt and sense of betrayal started to melt as her joy at seeing Joe overwhelmed her. They both suddenly erupted in a fit of happy laughter. Arleosa beamed, experiencing their love as though God was with her in the same way. She, too, felt the sense of completion that Joe and Samantha were experiencing.

Joe and Samantha held each other longingly. "We don't have long," he said. The story unfolded. Joe transmitted his experience in a flood of pheromones and expansive mental output reminiscent of how he communicated with the Hivers.

"One more thing Samantha," Joe said, "I've never been with you the way I should have. You always supported me, and I know my leaving suddenly must have caused you pain. You received my power of attorney?"

"Yes, I received it," Samantha replied.

"Well, these are my account numbers. I'll write them down with the passwords and you transfer the money to your account now; I want you to be taken care of because you have always taken care of me." Joe paused and Samantha could see tears streaming down his face as he validated for her who she'd been in his life.

Overjoyed Samantha took in the moment. She hugged Joe tightly, then asked him, "What will you do now? I'm not sure I understand what you're doing."

"I made a choice to follow a path I was invited onto. That path is connected to what's happening here, and it could help stop the chaos too. Don't venture out; stay inside. Something is going to break one way or another. Oh, and transfer that money."

Joe looked around and out the window of Samantha's bedroom window, blinds down and narrowly cracked. The street was alive with activity. More officers in uniforms were arriving. He expected them to come knocking on Samantha's door any minute.

"Ms. Jameson. Are you in there? Are you okay?" Joe exited through the window and using the Magni Grip of his ABS, climbed quickly to the roof.

"Yes, I'm okay," Samantha spoke through the door.

"Can we come in, see for ourselves? Just want to keep you safe."

"No, I'm okay," was her response.

On the roof, Joe could see Sam flying down and dragging officers away and compressing their necks as Joe had done to the plainclothesman outside Samantha's door. He was furtive and explosive all at once.

The officers were left unconscious one by one. Joe was amazed by Sam's stealth and efficiency.

Joe crawled down to street level.

The pit erupted with an explosion and the smell of brimstone. Joe and Sam heard a rumbling from miles away.

† † †

Bladeswift swept through the tunnel with as many horses and warriors as could fill the cavern area. He wanted to bring aid to Joe but had to make sure his own village and people were safe first. But now his nimble horses and Wildriders came like a scouring surge, creating a wave of destruction for the Demons.

The Hivers and Sika were shocked by Joe's departure. But as arrows soared and horses galloped, they were relieved by a victory over the Demons, whose remaining captains surged forward only to be cut down by the arrows and swords of the mounted Wildriders. Bladeswift, first among them, fired his frontier shotgun in the face of the last remaining Demon captain. "Ha!" Bladeswift chortled. "Ha!" was the response of a dozen Wildriders nearby.

The Wildriders and Hivers regarded each other suspiciously, but they were unified by common pheromones. Joe had been a catalyst to bring them together in recognition of each other.

Deep in the cavern, the Demons had constructed a breeding mechanism. There were female Demons who picked up swords to fight with. They were soon killed, and some even surrendered before they could be killed.

"Spare all those who surrender." Bladeswift gave the order. The Hivers seemed to understand his intent and relaxed their onslaught against the retreating Demon women.

Demon utensils, plates, cups, and other forms of pottery were strewed about. Blankets and bedding could be seen. But beyond lay another pit. The Hivers and Wildriders were drawn to it.

Sika peered into the abyss. "This is their link," she said. "The portal of their true origin."

Arleosa had exhausted herself. She had brought Joe through the portal back to the city. She needed him there to track Satan. Sadly, but with some joy, she thought he had abandoned the mission to see his lover. He still had time to find Satan. Sam would help him.

Joe and Sam headed toward the precinct station of Caption Johnson. Joe was wanted, but that was incidental in his mind. It was now twelve noon. The city was fully alive. People milled about and got into cars, all moving away from the rumbling, which was followed by concussive sounds.

"Joe, maybe our problems have an answer—the precinct will be all but abandoned. We need weapons and ammo, judging from the sounds I'm hearing. Let me scout from above—keep that trench coat on." Joe still wore the trench coat, having retrieved it before leaving Samantha's condo. "That's a necessity in our work," Sam noted. He, too, wore a trench coat when on the ground. He stuffed it into a small compartment in his suit and soared high above the street. Sam had a great vantage point and could see the precinct building. Officers were getting into police vehicles. A SWAT truck was being equipped with weapons, and black-suited officers milled about in various stages of preparation. Some wore urban camouflage.

The building was empty except for dispatchers and administrators. Joe ran a scan using the ABS memory chip. His scan revealed the combinations to the gun lockers and munition stores. He quietly made his way to the upper floor where the armory was. Joe scanned again. He used the ABS memory chip to try a password. There were several that popped up for various stations around the city. This was the station nearest the pit. Joe entered the password on the console of the locking mechanism. The gate swung open. Ammo boxes and automatic rifles were stored on shelves.

Joe loaded up, and Sam came down from the roof. Joe attached several pistols to his suit holsters, and ammo packs were bulging from the suit's harness.

Joe came out of the armory packed. He went to the roof and looked toward the pit, still about a mile away. He could scan and see the beehive of activity he anticipated. The pit had erupted, and every manner of Demon, werewolf, monster, and beast only the imagination could conjure came running out of it. Some of the creatures were winged and flew into the afternoon sky.

Joe recoiled at what he was seeing. Devils, Demons, winged Demons, and werewolves, growling and slobbering.

The police at the pit started firing their weapons. Some Demons and other creatures were weaponless but came at the men and women officers with fangs and claws. Joe could see the guns made a difference, but the monsters just kept coming out of the pit. Joe looked on from the roof. Sam flew above. It looked hopeless, for Demons, werewolves, and winged dragons took to the air. Guns didn't matter. The officers were outnumbered. Not just outnumbered but overwhelmed by monstrous numbers.

What now? Joe thought. *What now!* For the first time in his quest, he didn't know what to do. There was no divine inspiration. He felt whipped. He was frozen in time. *Join the fight*, he thought. But what could be achieved?

The monsters were breaking through the police line or flying over it. Soon they'd be spread across the city. The populace would be victimized. Then Joe realized what he must do—but he couldn't have done it earlier. Satan had opened the pit. Joe's time with Samantha after failing to stop him had given Satan the time to break back into the pit, activate its devilish power somehow, and summon his forces. Suddenly it all fit together. Could he have stopped this? Pangs of guilt swept through Joe. Had Arleosa abandoned him because of his poor judgment? *Well maybe I made a bad choice, but I have a choice to make now.*

"The Devil is in the pit," he yelled to Sam.

"Why didn't you say so?" Sam responded.

"This is going to be bad," Joe said. Sam darted toward a dragon high above the pit and dodged as its mouth erupted in flames, and he slammed it across the neck with his sword. It fell to earth in a pile of scales and leathery wings.

Joe was on foot, running toward the pit. He was approaching top speed. He fired his pistols, one in each hand, taking down any monster in his path. He was precise and reunited with his purpose. Now he and Sam would finish this—finish Satan as well.

Joe reached the edge of the pit. Sam flew down. "Don't come with me," Joe said. "Stay above ground. Help control the monsters. The city will need you. I'll find Satan. If I don't make it back, well, you know what to do. Just clean up this city like you've been doing."

"That's hard for me, to let you go alone." Sam sounded dejected.

"Don't worry for me—worry for all the rest in this city. I've seen what life needs to be. I'll be okay. Stand firm, fly high. See you later."

With that, Joe was running into the pit at a fifty-mile-per-hour speed that surprised even him. A steep descent was immediately apparent. Joe kept running fast. He was lugging a full complement of ammo; he had picked up flash-bang grenades and tear gas canisters. Nothing more deadly could be found in the precinct station.

Monsters came out of the pit, lurching toward him. He threw the flash-bangs forward, igniting a full belt of them. He needed an advantage now. He ducked behind a large portion of debris consisting of concrete and mangled steel beams. Joe sprang up firing an assault rifle with quick snapping bursts that cut down wolfmen, Demons, and trolls. Joe had never seen such a variety of horrors. The trolls carried hammer and shields, sometimes swords. Joe moved past many as he sought to find Satan. Weretigers saw him and leaped out to rake him with their claws. They were bipedal and formed like men with tiger stripes. Joe dodged behind debris rather than engage the turmoil and naked aggression swirling around him. If he took out Satan, somehow it would work out for the best.

Arleosa reached out to Joe, and he felt her presence. He pushed forward, shooting, and throwing tear gas bombs ahead of him. The tear gas seemed to stymie the Demons and monsters. They would writhe about, choking and slobbering. Joe's suit protected him, so he had an advantage. "Run, Joe!" he heard the words in his head. It was like football again. Joe weaved and sprinted. He fired until his assault rifle had nothing left. He was running faster, but the monsters seemed to slow down. *Boom! Boom!* Run and fire. A weretiger went down, and trolls cowered behind their shields, afraid to move forward. Joe was growing in confidence but was running low on ammo. He drew the Vibro-Blade, darting left, right, and then forward. Joe was well down the tunnel now.

There were dark lights shining. Red lights flickered, and some torches seemed to emanate from shadows and darkness.

Joe pushed forward, rolling down and rising to strike heavily with the Vibro-Blade. The pit began to flatten out. A debris-filled expanse was apparent. An area of about two hundred meters in diameter. In the distance, Joe could see a Giant. More monsters were drawn to his position. On the throne he saw a figure—Satan. He threw himself sideways as a spear from a stocky troll whistled past him. The sight of the throne doubled Joe's determination.

A black hole opened behind the throne. Out of it poured Bladeswift and Sika on Wildrider horses. A cavalry of Wildriders followed them. Bladeswift fired his frontier shotgun. Satan leaped away and came running directly toward Joe. Werewolves, trolls, and Demons rallied to their master.

Joe wet his lips under the ABS helmet. *Now he is coming to me*, Joe thought. Then came aid from above; Winged Hivers hovered in the air. *I have never seen winged Hivers, but there they are.* They released arrows down upon the pit floor creating chaos from above. The Demons and monsters ran to attack Joe, but the arrow fire from Bladeswift, Sika, the accompanying Wildriders, and the flying Hivers was withering. A were-tiger collapsed in a puddle of blood, pinned by about ten arrows.

In spite of the added support, Joe was being overwhelmed by strong numbers. The cave floor of the pit was filling, and Joe needed to pull his pistol and fire a few rounds to get some space. Then he started running, dodging Demons, sometimes engaging them, and at other times moving away from opposition. Satan was in front of him, about four meters ahead. Dressed in blood-red armor, he looked like a Goliath. *He looks like Deathmet*, Joe thought. *There is a lineage here*, Joe realized. Satan carried a large, two-handed blade—a broadsword he carried easily in just one hand. Joe fired a shot from the pistol; a glancing blow struck Satan's helmet.

Satan staggered but came forward. Sika, seeing Joe's dilemma, came riding up on Satan from behind and fired an arrow that hit Satan square in the back of his head and rested in his helmet. Satan stumbled forward.

Joe fired again, this time lower, into the chest. Satan grinned and came forward. Bladeswift fired his frontier shotgun low to make sure he stopped Satan's advance. *Bam!* The shot hit Satan in the back of one knee. He stumbled again and dropped to his knees. Joe was running full speed. He swung the Vibro-Blade in a horizontal arc that Satan narrowly blocked with his broadsword. Joe swung it again; this time Satan was not so fast, and Joe caught him on the opposite side of his torso.

A large troll jumped in front of Satan, who scrambled to his feet. Joe stepped back and blasted the troll in the face. The pace of Satan's protectors increased. As soon as an arrow took one, another sought to block Joe's path. Joe reduced himself to firing his remaining shots. Bladeswift and the flying Hivers made sure to stay out of each other's way. But Bladeswift wouldn't wait while Joe's attack was ongoing. The flying Hivers, with their powerful fly-like wings, swung low in the air. A barrage of arrows followed. Satan staggered forward, then fell to his knees again.

Arleosa came like a phantom into Joe's mind. Joe stopped for a moment, perhaps less than half a second, then he bounded forward, Vibro-Blade humming in the air, making a swift horizontal cut at Satan's head. Arrows were flying toward Satan's back. Joe lowered the swing of his arc, hitting Satan's arms.

Satan dropped to a prone position, chest down, face hitting the pit floor.

There was silence—stillness in the pit. Joe looked around. Arleosa became visible as an orb of golden light.

The light hovered over Satan. Joe could feel the warmth of Arleosa. She was sharing in the pheromones of the Hivers and Wildriders. The brimstone odor of Satan also spread throughout the cave. Satan rolled over to face Joe. Slowly he got to his knees. He took off his helmet. His face was clear and handsome. He did not look to be the beast of legend. Joe looked at Satan, and they held each other's gaze.

Joe sheathed the Vibro-Blade. The trolls and monsters chittered about aimlessly. Joe gave a sign, and a hundred arrows slammed into the remaining trolls, Demons, and monsters.

End it, came the message from every corner of the pit now filled with Joe's allies. Sika urged her mount toward Joe. She dismounted and stood near him. She patted Joe on the shoulder.

God looked upon the scene. He hemmed and hawed. His fallen Angel, Satan, was at risk. He was at risk and might be killed by one hundred arrows launched by Wildriders and Hivers.

Satan stood and took off his armor, stripping to his loincloth. He looked above. God made an entreaty. "Come here, son. Come home." Satan turned his eyes above; a tear rolled down his cheek. "Okay," he said.

A whole lot of light opened above Satan and received him. The Hivers and Wildriders seemed to disappear into the darkness of the pit.

Joe watched Satan disappear. "Is that it?" Joe asked Sika, who stood closely by his side.

"Maybe," she said.

A golden glow emanated from within the cavern. Joe knew it was Arleosa. "Now, my warrior. You have done it. You have stopped Satan and returned him to God. He went willingly, as he must!"

Sika looked around—it was just her, Joe, and a few remaining Demons who seemed aimless.

They dropped to their knees almost in unison. Joe sighed. Sika slung her bow.

Arleosa glowed brighter. "Now go home, Joe, whichever home you choose here in the city of your birth or back to the place you just came from."

"I'm probably still wanted around here." Joe sighed in weary resignation. "I can't stay here." Sika looked at Joe expectantly. "I'd have to stand trial. Don't want to do that. After all I've been through. I owe Samantha an explanation."

Sika's jaw tightened. Arleosa sought to reassure him. "I think she will know enough, Joe, though not everything. She was touched and shared your consciousness. She will go on with her life now as never before."

"Let's go then, Sika, if you would still be with me. We probably could do some celebrating." The Demons were all dead or gone. Some ran up the tunnel to the surface. Sam will get them, Joe realized. "Let's go, Sika." Then, they disappeared into a golden light.

Joe and Sika could both see the outline of the fortress. Demons' bodies still littered the surrounding area. They made their way to the fortress doors. They walked hand in hand. Ataka looked over the ramparts, squinted, then yelled with glee. The fortress doors spilled open. Joe and Sika jogged forward. It was finally over. Joe felt a sense of relief.

It was dinnertime. The great hall was prepared for a feast. Joe realized he had done all that to bring the fallen Angel back to God. He had humbled a devil but also a fallen Angel. Now that Angel had found a way home. Was he duped? Did he gain a new understanding? Or both? Sika, sitting next to him, looked into his eyes. He had discarded his helmet a while ago.

The evening melted away into food, revelry, and wine. There were testimonials to Joe and Sika. Bladeswift joined the feast briefly before heading back to his villages on the high plateaus of the western frontier.

The next morning Joe went out to survey the grounds, pastures, orchards, and crops to the east of the fortress. To the west lay a war-torn field of burnt-out devastation.

Joe averted his eyes and walked to the east. He put on his helmet and scanned the distance. The orchards, fields, and pastures lay virtually untouched. Demons wanted flesh. The herds of cattle and horses were sheltered near the fortress for safety.

Joe surveyed the lands, more bountiful than he remembered when he first arrived. This despite the Demon threat.

Sika, King Kotutan, and Queen Saluiana approached from the fortress. "It was possible because we learned to share, Joe!" Saluiana said. "The fields, crops, orchards, everything…shared. That helped us survive!"

Joe could feel Arleosa's presence. He smiled. Sika laughed.

Epilogue

"No more world building," God whispered, which was heard throughout Heaven. "Nothing within us is beyond the people below us. Our celestial conflicts are often played out by the humans we wish to instruct."

Arleosa smiled. "There could be no better world," Arleosa mused to God. "The world should not be as it has always been—a struggle between God and his rival, the Devil."

When we bring our devils home, we can stop fighting them. Even the Devil ceases to compete. It can happen—and maybe that was the solution God overlooked. His competition with the Devil had been mirrored in His creations. God's unrest had opened the door to the very thing He wanted to change. The very ceasing of God's competition with the Devil could bring harmony to Him and His creations. If the humans were truly built in His image, they'd find a way to establish harmony if they didn't have to spend time fighting the Devil, Arleosa pondered to herself.

Appendix

ABS or Armored Battle Suit: protective, flexible formfitting armor with automatic camouflage capability

ACV or Air Command Vehicle: flying vehicle that hovers and moves like a flying saucer, can scan with radar-like capacity and send communication from data transmissions

Arleosa, the Jewel of Heaven: identifies Joe as the Messiah and promotes his development through angelic intervention

ATTITUDE: an acronym for Advanced Training Techniques Investigation Technical Undertaking Development Enhancement. A facility devoted to military and police investigative support research with practical working prototypes being developed and then tested

Beastmen: short, squat, hairy primitive men with muscular bodies and canine-like jaws. Aligned with the demons against the men of Hellrun

Destrier: large horse used for war by knights most often a stallion

Hellrun: a primitive planet with medieval development

Fission pistol or revolver: a pistol or revolver that uses atom-splitting technology in batteries that shoot powerful blasts as long as the battery lasts

Giants: large, muscular beast men evolved into giants for survival who become aligned with the demons for mutual convenience

Greenflyers: primitive, insect-like carnivorous men who fly and attack anything that bleeds or has meat. They stand four feet tall and have great flying speed and maneuverability. They live in packs joined together by the smell of blood and hunger meat. They have exoskeletons with forearm claws that shear like long razors

Hivers: manlike insect creatures living in hives connected through phero-mones that bind them to shared experiences and allow them to read each other's minds and act in unity. Primitive weapon capability. Four feet tall, very strong like an ant re body weight to strength, exoskeletons provide natural armor

Kotutan: king of the western settlements

Long-Striders: medieval settlers on Hellrun who seek to colonize the land

Magni Grip: adhesive climbing grips in the shoes and gloves of the ABS, allowing the wearer to climb like an insect when activated

Manwolves: a dwindling group of wolflike men living in caves but being pressed out of existence by the settlers of King Kotutan

Osala: priest of the Long-Striders

Terra: an earthlike planet where technology has taken root and God starts a new existence for Humans in hopes of drawing them to his purpose

Saluiana: queen of the Long-Strider western outpost

Tribesmen: any group of primitive men in the same species

Shield wall: a group of warriors huddled together in a line using shields to defend themselves

Wildriders: a group of indigenous horsemen who live in a tribal setting on high plateaus and have developed a culture and way of life revolving around horses and nature. Five feet tall with muscular build, adroit at fighting from horseback with sword, lance, and bow. Green skin pigment allows them to blend with the forest and plains of dirt

Vibro-Blade: a weapon three to four feet in length that when turned on emits a solid wave of energy akin to sound waves that repel and potentially damage anything it makes contact with, depending on the force of its strikes. It can be tuned to various frequencies causing sharper injuries like a sword or blunt blows that injure internally

CPSIA information can be obtained
at www.ICGtesting.com
Printed in the USA
BVHW040841140222
628966BV00006B/43